CHRISTMAS (M); 2024

THE
ISLAND
OF
COFFINS

THE ISLAND OF COFFINS

*and Other Mysteries from
the Casebook of Cabin B-13*

John Dickson Carr

Edited by
Tony Medawar and Douglas Greene

Crippen & Landru Publishers
Cincinnati, Ohio
USA
2020

Copyright © 1948, 1949 by John Dickson Carr

All other materials copyright © 2020 by the estate of John Dickson Carr.

All characters in this publication are fictitious and any resemblance to real persons, living or dead, is purely coincidental.

All rights reserved.

No part of this publication may be reproduced, stored in a retrieval system, or transmitted, in any form or by any means, without the prior permission in writing of the publisher, nor be otherwise circulated in any form of binding or cover other than that in which it is published and without a similar condition including this condition being imposed on the subsequent purchaser.

For information contact:
Crippen & Landru Publishers
PO Box 532057
Cincinnati, OH 45253

Web: www.crippenLandru.com
E-mail: Info@crippenlandru.com

ISBN (softcover): 978-1-936363-51-3
ISBN (clothbound): 978-1-936363-50-6

First Edition: December 2020

10 9 8 7 6 5 4 3 2 1

The editors and publisher would like to thank Mike Nevins, Geoff Bradley, James Keirans, author of *The John Dickson Carr Companion* (Ramble House, 2015) and Sam Brylawski of the Library of Congress.

CONTENTS

Introduction: Suspense at Sea   3

Series 1

A Razor in Fleet Street	9
The Man Who Couldn't Be Photographed	24
Death Has Four Faces	38
The Blind-Folded Knife Thrower	52
No Useless Coffin	67
The Nine Black Reasons	81
The Count of Monte Carlo	95
Below Suspicion	109
The Power of Darkness	122
The Footprint in the Sky	135
The Man with the Iron Chest	148

Series 2

The Street of the Seven Daggers	163
The Dancer from Stamboul	177
Death in the Desert	191
The Island of Coffins	205
The Most Respectable Murder	219
The Curse of the Bronze Lamp	233
Lair of the Devil-Fish	248
The Dead Man's Knock	261
The Man with Two Heads	275
The Bride Vanishes	288
Till Death Do Us Part	301
The Sleep of Death	316

Cabin B-13 Air Dates on CBS   331

Suspense at Sea

"CBS brings you John Dickson Carr's famous Dr. Fabian, ship's surgeon, world traveler and host in Cabin B-13 for strange and incredible tales of mystery and murder."

For many years, little was known about John Dickson Carr's last major radio program, *Cabin B-13*, beyond the facts that it could have been heard on the Columbia Broadcasting System in the late 1940s and that it took its name from a radio play by Carr first broadcast in 1943 on CBS's long-running radio program *Suspense*. Frustratingly, the titles of some of the plays in *Cabin B-13* were known because they had been given in contemporary press reports and, as well as recordings of three of the plays[1], the edited script of one of these had been published in an obscure British magazine. Professor Mike Nevins therefore spoke for many when, in 1978, he lamented, *"that I have heard none of these plays and that no radio buff of my acquaintance has a tape recording of any in his collection are matters I deeply regret. From the titles alone they sound fascinating"*.

Full details of *Cabin B-13* —and even the exact number of plays —remained unknown until the early 1990s when the scripts—23 in total— were discovered in the largest library in the world, the Library of Congress. The discovery was reported in a 1991 article in the much-missed magazine for crime and mystery connoisseurs, *The Armchair Detective*, and the authors concluded by expressing the hope that, one day, the scripts would be published, a hope that Crippen and Landru has fulfilled, a little over seventy years since the original, all too fleeting appearance of *Cabin B-13*.

During the Second World War, John Dickson Carr produced countless radio scripts for the British Broadcasting Corporation, including "Speak of the Devil" (1941), a thrilling mystery serial, and "The Man in the Iron Mask" (1942), sub-titled a historical detective story. There were also many propaganda plays and five series of the immensely popular "horror" program *Appointment with Fear*, an anglicized version of CBS's *Suspense* in which, like Carr's contributions to the American original, each episode was introduced by the sinister voice of "The Man in Black". It is therefore not surprising that, on leaving the BBC and returning to America, Carr expressed relief at being freed from having to grind out scripts. Nevertheless, he remained very keen on radio as a medium for mystery and, in the spring of 1948, he reached an agreement with CBS for a new program, which CBS announced

---

[1] "A Razor in Fleet Street", "The Bride Vanishes" and "The Sleep of Death". The recordings are widely available online.

in a press release dated 23 June 1948.

> "Cabin B-13 *unfolds tales of mystery, romance and adventure as told by Dr. Fabian, ship's doctor of a world-cruising luxury liner, the* Maurevania. *The liner sails form Southampton to Cherbourg then down the French coast into the Mediterranean and the Near East. Each Monday night, Dr. Fabian will relate a mysterious adventure experienced at some port of call or nearby inland areas.*"

Two series of *Cabin B-13* were broadcast, between 5 July 1948 and 2 January 1949. All of the episodes were directed by *Suspense* veteran John Dietz with Charles S Monroe acting as editor. Incidental music was provided by Merle Kendrick for the first series and for the second by the prolific radio, film and television composer Alfredo Antonini.

While *Cabin B-13* was no relation to the *"original show"*, they did have one thing in common, at least initially. The radio play "Cabin B-13" had been set almost entirely on an ocean liner, the steam ship *Maurevania*, and the ship's Austrian surgeon, Dr Paul Heinrich plays an important role in unravelling the mystery. The cabin and the SS *Maurevania* also feature in the two series of *Cabin B-13* but the surgeon is now *"the sagacious and widely-travelled"* Dr John Fabian, played by Arnold Moss in all but four plays. Moss had begun life as a stage actor, and in the film *Reign of Terror* (1949) he played the duplicitous Joseph Fouché, Napoleon's Minister of Police—admirers of Carr's "Carter Dickson" novels will not need reminding that a portrait of Fouché had hung over the white marble fireplace in the office of Sir Henry Merrivale. However, Moss's immortality is guaranteed not by his many film appearances or his work for CBS radio but by his portrayal of a Shakespearean actor—who happens also to be a former genocidal dictator—in an episode of the evergreen television series *Star Trek*. The other actor to play Fabian was Alan Hewitt who took over while Moss was fulfilling a film commitment in Hollywood. Like Moss, Hewitt never became a major star but his long career encompassed roles in many of America's most successful television programs of the 1950s and '60s including *Alfred Hitchcock Presents*, *Dr Kildare*, *Ironside* and *Perry Mason*, in three episodes of which he portrayed the murderer.

Each broadcast of *Cabin B-13* began with a ship's horn sounding four times, followed by a burst of suitably atmospheric music. Over this, the announcer intoned the series' title and introduced Fabian, usually speaking from his surgery on the *Maurevania*'s A deck.

> *"From his notebooks of the strange and sinister, Dr. Fabian brings you tonight's tale ... another great tale of mystery and murder written by the world-famous bestseller mystery author John Dickson Carr."*

This was followed by another musical flourish and then the play itself commenced. Although the substance of the stories in *Cabin B-13* had much in common with those Carr had written for *Suspense*, the format of the program was to be quite different. Instead of *Suspense*'s "Man in Black", recounting stories without his having any personal connection to them, Carr intended that Dr. Fabian should narrate stories of which he had direct knowledge. The character of Fabian is possibly named for Robert Fabian, an English police officer who rose to the rank of Detective Superintendent in the Metropolitan Police and was treated as a minor celebrity by the British media in the 1940s and 50s, not least for his heroism in dismantling a terrorist bomb in 1939. After retiring in 1949, Robert Fabian wrote crime fiction and curiously, he was once replaced by Carr for an appearance on the BBC television program *Guilty Party* in 1957, in which Carr was challenged to solve a mystery, "Murder in Train", written by the radio scriptwriter Edward J Mason.

It was also the original intention that the *Maurevania* should follow a logical course but this was only ever loosely the case. The structure of the first series, more or less, is a plausible route from England around Portugal into the Mediterranean and on to the Middle East but by the second series this device had largely been abandoned and Fabian is for the most part "The Man in Black" in all but name, simply a narrator of strange stories. And what strange stories they are. Murderers that can enter or leave a locked room without leaving a trace and others that can kill from a distance without leaving a mark on their victim. Places where time stands still and others where time does anything *but* stand still. Unusual weapons. Baffling clues. Pure Carr.

The coda of the early *Cabin B-13* shows was a brief statement that *"these Dr. Fabian stories are all newly written for you by Mr. Carr and have not appeared before on the air or in printed form"*. Indeed, all but two of the eleven plays in the first series were original and their plots so effective that Carr would go on to build novels around three of them and use the device of another for a short story. When it came to the second series, CBS would also promote it as comprising *"baffling originals"*. However, only three of the dozen scripts Carr produced were genuinely new; the rest were re-worked from scripts he had written previously for *Suspense* or *Appointment with Fear*.

Quite simply, the strain of being tied to a regular commitment had become too much, as Carr later explained to his friend Val Gielgud, the BBC's Director of Features and Drama, who had produced several of Carr's BBC radio plays and collaborated with him on two stage plays[2]:

> "What happened was what always happens. I overestimated my stamina in keeping going indefinitely ... and I did pretty well, keeping up a new story a week for well over six months (sic), squarely down to the two week ahead deadline. But I was down for the count. This did not particularly please CBS who had a sponsor on the book. There were a number of "conferences", which means that people tear their hair and bang the table. I pointed out that I was willing to go on, but the story quality would drop, the ratings follow it, and the sponsor follow that."

Reluctantly, CBS accepted Carr's decision and on 2 January 1949, *Cabin B-13* concluded with another repeat broadcast. At the end of the show, an announcer stated "*Next week at this time, over many of these same CBS stations, you will hear the program, It Pays to Be Ignorant*".

And, as it disappeared from the airwaves, *Cabin B-13* passed into radio legend.

However, Carr was not finished with the concept behind *Cabin B-13*. In 1949, he approached his old friend, the BBC's Val Gielgud, with a proposal that would see him revising some of the scripts for a new series of *Appointment with Fear* with Dr. Fabian identified as "The Man in Black" from *Suspense* – in Carr's words "*he's got to have some kind of background and that may be as good as any*".

Gielgud was very optimistic and prompted Carr to send some of the *Cabin B-13* scripts to his BBC colleague Martyn C. Webster who had produced the war-time *Appointment with Fear* series. Encouraged, Carr submitted 12 of the first 13 plays, omitting only "The Footprint in the Sky" because a version of this story had already appeared in *Appointment with Fear*. Disappointingly, Webster was far from impressed. He scathingly dismissed the scripts as "*crude and ... well below standard*" although, on reading them and in light of the producer's *next* encounter with Carr, these remarks are hard to understand.

Five years passed and in December 1954, Carr contacted the BBC and

---

[2] Collected in *Thirteen to the Gallows*. Crippen & Landru, 2008.

again suggested a revival of *Appointment with Fear*. He had a meeting with Gielgud and they discussed several plot outlines, which—unknown to the BBC man—were those of several *Cabin B-13* plays. Two were discounted almost immediately: "Death in the Desert", which Carr accepted *"didn't fit the pattern"*; and a revised version of "No Useless Coffin", which puzzlingly Gielgud felt would be *"just a little too much on the gruesome side even for* Appointment with Fear*"*.

Carr duly produced some draft scripts and called in at the BBC with the intention of leaving them with Gielgud. Unexpectedly, he encountered Martyn C. Webster again. The *Appointment with Fear* producer was, in Carr's words, *"as doubtful as at times I myself have been [and] agreed that it couldn't be done unless the new shows were knockouts"*. Carr accepted Webster's challenge and finalized new versions of several of the *Cabin B-13* plays, which he then submitted along with a few entirely new scripts. The BBC were delighted and, in the summer of 1955, they were broadcast as what would prove to be the final series of *Appointment with Fear*.

Nonetheless, *Cabin B-13* remained at the back of Carr's mind and ten years later, in November 1964, his agents submitted to the BBC a proposal for a new program, *MV Suspense*, along with a brief outline:

> "The actual name of the liner is MV (Motor Vessel) Illyria, *probably a Cunarder, very much like the actual Sylvania in which I so often travel. She is on a cruise (round the world?) whose details I must work out with the Cunard line so as not to set her on course which would be illogical or plain crazy ... The principal character, who can also act as narrator, shall be the ship's purser ... Let's call him Adam Benson – a man in his late forties or early fifties: suave, highly educated, with much good nature and a sense of humour ... As the liner enters a given port, Benson tells a story which has occurred either in that port or a large city associated with the country ... Each will be a suspense story, usually a mystery, always with a surprise twist-ending but with every clue given so that the alert listener can solve the mystery for himself ... Such a show should be good fun for the listener; assuredly so, it will be so for the writer."

On this occasion, the proposal was reviewed by Richard Imison, the Sound Script Editor at the BBC. Disappointingly, he was not taken with the idea and, as Carr had returned to America shortly after providing his agents with the outline, the *MV Suspense* sank before it had even sailed.

More than 70 years after the series was first broadcast, it is possible to see *Cabin B-13* as the final flowering of the truly great days of radio. As well as ingenious and satisfying plots, the plays integrate music in a way that is more filmic than sonic and the atmospheric settings and tightly defined characters are conjured with interesting and unusual sound effects. Monsieur Bo's fly swatter in "The Nine Black Reasons". The roulette wheel of the Grand Casino in "The Count of Monte Carlo". The zitherist of "The Street of the Seven Daggers" and the mournful howling of a jackal in "Death in the Desert". The shuffleboard game in "Below Suspicion" and the gentle spinning of a globe in "The Most Respectable Murder". All carefully incorporated to build atmosphere and, of course, suspense. And in *some* of the plays—it would be unwise to say which—the sound provides a crucial clue—sometimes *the* clue—to the mystery.

Now it is almost the time you have been waiting for.

Find a comfortable chair; preferably by an open log fire.

Pour a modest libation; preferably a Scotch.

Tune in your radio; preferably to *Cabin B-13*.

… and *open* your eyes.

Tony Medawar
Wimbledon, London

A Razor in Fleet Street

(*Sound: a ship's whistle*)
ANNOUNCER: *Cabin B-13.*
(*Music: in and behind*)
FABIAN: My name is Fabian...ship's surgeon of the luxury-liner, *Maurevania*. Tonight, as we lie alongside the docks at the great port of Southampton, the ship is ghostly, deserted. Our passengers on this world cruise have gone to London. And as I sit here in my Cabin, B-Thirteen, I am reminded how the tides and storms of a thousand voyages have wrought nothing more strange, more sinister than man's desire for adventure in the strange ports and lands we touch. I remember Bill and Brenda Leslie—it was years ago, before the war—and the effect on their characters of the mortal terror that overtook them in London.
(*Music: fades out*)
FABIAN: London—and Hampden's Hotel, in Norfolk Street, off the Strand. A quiet little street sloping down to the river, a quiet little hotel: so dingy, with its stuffiness of old carpets and yesterday's tea-trays, that you'd never suspect how fashionable it is; or how expensive. Can't you hear the lift whining...
(*Sound: the elevator can be heard from the word "tea-trays"*)
FABIAN: as its two latest arrivals—the husband American, the wife English—go swaying up to a bumpy stop.

(*Sound: follows to stop; wire gate creaks open — then steps along a dingy passage, into a room ...*)
PORTER: (*old man, short of breath*) this way, sir?
BILL: Come on, Brenda.
PORTER: (*old man, short of breath*) Will there be anything else, sir?
BILL: That's all, thanks. Oh! Wait a minute! Here!
PORTER: Thank *you*, sir.
(*Sound: door closes*)
BRENDA: (*amused*) Bill, darling, please don't look so bewildered!
BILL: *Was* I looking bewildered, Brenda?
BRENDA: I *know* the furniture's red plush and dates back to the 1860s! I *know* we can't get a private bathroom!
BILL: By George, the waiters look as old as the furniture!
BRENDA: But if only we'd gone to Claridge's, or the Savoy, or any one of a dozen places I suggested ...
BILL: Brenda, you don't understand.
BRENDA: No?

BILL: Who the devil *wants* to go to Claridge's or the Savoy? This is London!
BRENDA: Bill, I'm afraid I still don't understand.
BILL: I've been in the Diplomatic Service for seven years. I've been stationed in three capitals. But I've never been here.
BRENDA: (*carried away*) It's a lovely old town. It's home.
BILL: It's home to me too, In a way. It's put a spell on my imagination ever since I was a boy so-high. Sherlock Holmes! Doctor Fu Manchu! Hansom-cabs rattling through the fog ...
BRENDA: (*concern*) Darling, you don't think we still ride about in hansoms?
BILL: No, but it's the spirit of the thing! Here! Look out of this window!
BRENDA: Yes?
BILL: Grey-and-black buildings. Twilight coming down. And—yes! Look down there!
BRENDA: Where? I don't see anything.
BILL: It's one of your famous barrel-organs. Here; let's have the window up!
(*Sound: window raised, not easily*)
BILL: It's under our windows, Brenda.
(*Sound: we hear the barrel-organ grinding, off. it plays a music-hall song of the 'nineties:* A Lassie from Lancashire. *It registers before playing under*)
BILL: What's the tune, dear? Do you know it?
BRENDA: Something about, "She was a lassie from Lancashire." It's a very old one.
BILL: But it's *right*, don't you see? Everything's right. And if I crane out of the window—sideways, like this—I can see down to the river. That's where the bodies fall off wharfs, and the police launches...
BRENDA: Bill! Please listen to me!
BILL: Yes?
BRENDA: Put your arms round me. Look down at me. There! (*she laughs again*)
BILL: (*with dignity*) I have a funny face. I *admit* I have a funny face.
BRENDA: I love you terribly, Bill. I don't mean any words like "very much", or "a lot;" just silly and terribly. But of all the romantic Americans I've ever met, you have the most absurd and fantastic ideas about England. You don't really expect to find Scotland Yard men, in bowler hats, trailing you every step; now do you?
(*Sound: the barrel-organ has begun to fade at the beginning of the preceding speech; it has faded by the end*)
BILL: That wasn't the point. Brenda! I only said ...
BRENDA: When you think about it, just remember the barrel-organ. Safe. Stodgy. Comfortable. That's London, Bill. Will you remember?
(*Sound: the telephone rings; a double-ringing tone*)
BILL: Well, at least they've got telephones in this place.
(*Sound: the receiver is lifted from hook*)
BILL: Hello!?

MAN: Mr. William Leslie?
BILL: Yes. Speaking.
MAN: (*filter*) This is the reception-desk, Mr. Leslie. There is a man here who insists on seeing you. In fact— (*Sound: slight pause, as of head turned away*) —the man is on his way upstairs. He is a police-officer.
BILL: A ... what did you say?
MAN: A police-officer, sir.
BILL: A police-officer, eh? I see, (*struck by a wild thought*) He isn't by any chance from Scotland Yard?
MAN: Yes, sir. (*coldly*) I thought you might like to know.
(*Sound: the phone connections severed, receiver replaced.*)
BILL: Did you hear that, Brenda?
BRENDA: Yes! I heard it! But surely ...?
BILL: About six hours in England, and ...
BRENDA: Oh, this is ridiculous! There must be some mistake!
BILL: There probably is. All the same, come to think of it, I don't feel very keen about facing one of these bowler-hats in real life.
BRENDA: But why do they come to *us*? We haven't done anything!
BILL: Nothing I can think of. That's what worries me.
(*Sound: the rapping at door; not too loud, but insistent*)
BILL: (*under his breath*) Get ready for the hat and the raincoat, and the cropped moustache.
(*Sound: the door opens*)
BILL: Yes.
RADFORD: (*off*) Mr. Leslie? Mrs. Leslie?
BILL: That's right. Won't you come in?
(*Sound: door closes*)
RADFORD: (*fading in*) Sorry to have to trouble you, sir. I'm a police-officer. Metropolitan C.I.D. Here's my warrant-card.
BILL: I see. "Chief Inspector..."
RADFORD: Radford, sir. And I'm bound to tell you I'm here about a pretty serious matter.
BRENDA: (*bursting out*) But *we* haven't done anything to —
BILL: (*under his breath*) Easy, Brenda. (*up*) Sit down, Inspector.
RADFORD: Thank you, sir. — Now ... don't mind my notebook, It's a mere formality ... You and your wife arrived this morning by the *Maurevania*. Your wife is British, and carries her own passport. Correct?
BILL: Yes. That's correct —
RADFORD: A week from today you leave, by the same ship, for Lisbon. At Lisbon you take up a new diplomatic assignment at the American Embassy. Correct?
BILL: Yes! But ...
BRENDA: How does that concern you?

RADFORD: Just one moment! I'd like you to look at this snapshot I have here... Who is it?
BRENDA: But—it's Bill! (*hesitates*) I mean: except for that awful shirt and tie; well, it *is* Bill!
BILL: So help me, I never had that picture taken!
RADFORD: (*grimly*) I know you didn't, Mr. Leslie. That's Flash Morgan. Ever hear of him?
BILL: Never. Is he—wanted for something?
RADFORD: He's wanted for several murders; we won't mention bank-robbery. Also he's a ripper, if you know what that means. Uses a razor; and—likes it.
BILL: *Me*? The image of a famous murderer?
RADFORD: (*drily*) They don't look so different from the rest of us. —Do you realize, sir, you can't leave this hotel without being nabbed, as Morgan, by the first copper you meet?
BILL: But I can prove who I am! I've got my papers!
RADFORD: You've got your papers. Right! (*slight pause*) Suppose Morgan gets 'em?
BILL: Morgan?
RADFORD: The *Maurevania* sails a week from today. Somebody called William Leslie, carrying diplomatic immunity, sails with her, What's to prove it's really you?
BILL: You mean he might...?
RADFORD: I do.
BILL: That's impossible! He couldn't get away with it!
RADFORD: (*coolly*) No, I don't think he could. But I'll give you ten to one he *tries* it. This is too small a country to hide in, and he can't get away. He's desperate. This is his last hope.
BILL: What about—Brenda here?
RADFORD: There are several things that might happen to Mrs. Leslie. All unpleasant. (*slight pause*) There's Just one more matter I'm bound to warn you of.
BRENDA: (*weakly sarcastic*) You've warned us, Inspector Radford. We—we appreciate it most awfully. What else could there be?
RADFORD: Morgan may try to get into this hotel.
(*Sound: the barrel-organ, off but approaching, with* A Lassie from Lancashire.)
BILL: (*hold for cue*) "Safe." "Stodgy." "Comfortable". I see what you mean, Brenda.
RADFORD: I beg your pardon, sir?
BILL: Just a little joke between my wife and myself. It's getting chilly; (*turns off*) better close the window.
(*Sound: the window closes and the barrel-organ stops*)

BILL: (*fighting the situation*) Look here, Inspector! This ripper, or whatever he is, couldn't possibly know there's a man who looks just like him!
RADFORD: He couldn't, eh? Have you seen *any* evening paper?
BILL: No.
RADFORD: (*bitterly*) Some fool took a picture of you getting off the boat-train. It's been published, with comments on the resemblance. You'll find Morgan's story, also with pictures, on the front page. (*temper rising*) Here's the *Standard*. Read it!
(*Sound: the newspaper is viciously folded up and flutters as though thrown.*)
BRENDA: But haven't you got *any* idea where this man is?
RADFORD: No, madam; we haven't. He used to have a hangout at 96 Fleet Street, up over a barber's shop. But he won't go there now. He's loaded with money from the Whitehall bank-job. He's got a razor, and he's ready to use it. (*abruptly*) And now, if you'll excuse me..
BILL: Inspector, wait! What do you want us to do?
RADFORD: I want you to stay in this hotel, both of you, until that boat sails.
BILL: Cooped up here for a week? Just on a *theory* of yours?
RADFORD: Yes, Mr. Leslie. Just on a theory.
BILL: Suppose I do go out?
RADFORD: I can't stop you, sir. The guard I'm leaving here can't stop you, But I might send you some photographs of people with their throats cut. Sorry to have upset you. Good day.

(*Music: in and behind.*)
FABIAN: Hardly any change, yet, in the purplish-white tinge of early evening. No street-lamps alight. But a thin mist, white with late October chill, creeping up from the river as Bill and Brenda Leslie still sit in the red-plush room, staring at nothingness...
(*Music: fades out*)

BILL: Brenda!
BRENDA: Yes, dear?
BILL: (*slowly*) What was the number of that address Radford gave us? Where Morgan used to hang out?
BRENDA: (*deliberately*) I don't remember.
BILL: Ninety-six, wasn't it? 96 Fleet Street?
BRENDA: Why do you want to know?
BILL: Because I'm going there. And I'm going now.
BRENDA: Yes. I thought that was it. (*bursting out*) Bill, you can't! You mustn't! You can't do anything there!
BILL: I know.
BRENDA: Then why go at all?
BILL: Sweetheart, you know what our life is.

BRENDA: It's a wonderful life.
BILL: With you, yes. Every minute of it! But the Diplomatic Service? (*mimicking himself*) "Vous allez bien, Madame la Comtesse?" "I am sure, *signore*, that the Rio Alta Bridge will be a great success." Who precedes whom at dinner? Does the Envoy's wife eat artichokes? (*abruptly*) Look, Brenda. Suppose I captured Morgan before the police do?
BRENDA: (*slight pause*) Bill, are you absolutely mad?
BILL: Oh, no. Once or twice, in every man's life, something taps him on the shoulder and says, "Come on; I dare you!" Mostly we turn away and pretend we don't notice. But not this time. I'm taking the dare.
BRENDA: Bill, come back here! You're not to go!
BILL: (*slightly off*) Where's my overcoat? I've got it! Now, this address...
BRENDA: If you go, I'm going with you.
BILL: Oh, no. This isn't a woman's kind of dare; and you know it.
BRENDA: It's as much my dare as it is yours!
BILL: 96 Fleet Street. Up over a barber-shop. How do I get there?
BRENDA: I...
BILL: If you don't tell me, Brenda. I can easily find out. (*Throughout this Brenda has been hesitating, in despair of his lunacy but secretly rather admiring it*)
BRENDA: As a matter of fact, it's — it's not very far from here. You could walk it in ten minutes.
BILL: That's better! That's much better!
BRENDA: What about your identification papers?
BILL: I'm throwing them out here on the bed. Morgan won't get *those*.
BRENDA: But, if you haven't got those papers, you won't be able to prove who you are!
BILL: I'll have to risk it, Brenda. (*fade*) See you later!
BRENDA: Bill, come back! (*voice rising*) If you had any reason for going there, I wouldn't mind! But it's idiotic! Don't leave me! Please come back! *Please...*
(*Sound: the door slams. slight pause*)
BRENDA: I'll be with you, Bill. I'll be with you. If Morgan doesn't see me first.

(*Music: in strongly, and behind*)
FABIAN: Footsteps.
(*Sound: steps on asphalt, a man walking slowly*)
FABIAN: Slow-moving footsteps. Footsteps on gritty pavement: where, beyond Temple Bar, Fleet Street curves down into dimness. A dead street, hushed and shadowy, with St. Paul's like a grey cloud far ahead. Too late for office-workers; too early for newspaper offices. That's Bill Leslie on the left-hand pavement. I can tell you, believe me, every half-thought that tumbles through his brain as he walks.

(*Music: fades out*)

BILL: Can't see the numbers. That's the trouble. Fool stunt. I wish I hadn't tried it. Can't turn back now. Seem afraid. What if something *jumped* out of one of these doorways?
RADFORD: (*on filter*) He's a ripper, if you know what that means.
BRENDA: (*on filter*) Are you absolutely mad?
BILL: Mustn't remember things like that. Fleet Street; Doctor Johnson; 18th century. No people around. No street-lamps lighted. Good thing. Might walk a little faster. No harm in walking a little faster.
(*Sound: footsteps, under, quicken in tempo*).
BILL: There! Number thirty-four. Even-number side of the street, too. Can't be far off now. Mist rising, and cold as ... Is that a policeman's helmet? Behind me? Up against the sky? Doesn't matter. Police mean safety.
BRENDA: (*on filter*) If you haven't got those papers, you won't be able to prove who you are!
BILL: Still doesn't matter. Nobody can see my face. Another policeman's helmet! Swear to it! Over in that alley. A little faster... take it easy, now; don't run. They can't possibly...
MAN'S VOICE: (*bellowing, off*) You, there! Stop! Wait a minute!
BILL: Mustn't get panicky. How do you stop panic? Got to find that address; got to justify myself; got to ...
(*Sound: a police whistle: several long blasts*)

BILL: Run, Run!
(*Sound: heavily running footsteps, which suddenly stop*)
BILL: Ninety-six! Little entry. No door. Flight of steps. Easy on the jump, now! Quiet as you can run up! Door with glass panel. "Henry M. Jenkins, Barber." Door open, and ...

FABIAN: A large room, perhaps not too clean, with a cork floor giving back no sound. Facing you, a window. On your left, another door. On your right, a wall of mirrors with two white barber chairs. That was what Bill Leslie sees, amid a gleam of mirrors and a thick odor of hair-tonic. On a white stool sits a little old man with yellow-white hair and a reddish nose, peering up from a paper with cockney friendliness...

BILL: (*getting his breath*) I ... I beg your pardon. I didn't mean to crash in like this.
JENKINS: (*heartily, off*) Not a bit of it, sir! Nobody 'ere, sir! Glad to 'ave you come up any way you like!
BILL: I've... come about something important. I want —
(*Sound: distantly, more blasts on a police-whistle*)

BILL: (*hastily*) I want a shave, please. And I'll just close this door.
(*Sound: the door closes*)
JENKINS: (*nearer*) Shave, sir? *Very* good, sir! If you'll just come over 'ere ... that's it ... your overcoat, sir; allow me ... and in *this* chair, please. Now we'll just whip out the cloth...
(*Sound: the thrum of a neck-cloth shaken out*)
JENKINS: And round your neck it goes!
BILL: Wait a minute! Don't tilt me backwards yet! Are *you* Mr. Jenkins?
JENKINS: (*hugely delighted*) Now that, sir, is wot I'd call a real honor!
BILL: What's so funny about it?
JENKINS: Sorry, sir. Only a joke. Me name *is* Jenkins, and that's a fact. But mostly the gentlemen call me Old Scratch.
BILL: Old Scratch?
JENKINS: Oh, not in any religious way! Lummy, I should 'ope not! With me a chapel-goer for forty year, and a teetotaler so's me 'and wouldn't shake? Excuse me, sir. Mix the lather.
(*Sound: the water runs, and lather being mixed in a china mug, under the next speech*)
JENKINS: (*heartily*) No, sir, it's only their joke. If they call me Old Scratch, or as it might be Old Nick, it's 'cos they know I *won't* nick, 'em. Never miss with a razor, *I* don't. There now! We'll just tip the chair back...
(*Sound: the grind of a chair.*)
JENKINS: And I'll bet this lather I'm putting on is as comfortable as — well, as going 'ome to tea and kippers on a night like this. It's remarkable, sir 'ow comforting.. (*suddenly alarmed*) 'Ere! Sir! (*slight pause*) What is it? What's wrong?
BILL: (*fiercely muttering*) I was trying to signal you, that's all.
JENKINS: Eh?
BILL: (*muttering close*) Keep on lathering, and don't speak any louder than I do.
JENKINS: (*in the same tone*) Wot is it, sir? Wot's up?
BILL: Flash Morgan has just come in.
JENKINS: (*bewildered*) 'Oo? BILL: Flash ... Morgan.
JENKINS: (*in a normal tone*) But there's ...
BILL: Quiet!
JENKINS: But there's nobody 'ere but you and me. Lift your 'ead up and look!
BILL: You didn't see him. You were looking at the shaving-mug. I saw him come in by the door from the stairs when you moved the chair. You're *sure* you don't know who Morgan is?
JENKINS: (*fervently*) Swelpmearry I don't!
BILL: He's a killer. Wanted by the police.
JENKINS: The police, 'ere now, are you—
BILL: Finished with the lather? Then start shaving, but make it quick. Get a

razor! That's it.
(*Sound: through the next part, intermittently, the scratching sound of a razor through lather.*)
JENKINS: (*growing alarm*) But where *is* the bloke? Is 'e a ruddy ghost?
BILL: He didn't look at either of us. He didn't make a sound. I saw him in the mirror. He bolted the glass paneled door on the inside. Look over and see if it isn't bolted.
JENKINS: Oh, ah, yessir. It's bolted!
BILL: He walked to a door at the back of this room. Behind me. Can you see it?
JENKINS: Yes sir. 'Course I can see it!
BILL: Where does that door lead? Upstairs?
JENKINS: No, sir. There's no upstairs on this side of the 'ouse.
BILL: But there's got to be! Morgan lived, or had some friends!
JENKINS: Don't move your chin like that! Keep your 'ead where I put it! — if you was looking for ninety-six proper, you must 'a seen the numbers in a bad light.
BILL: Oh?
JENKINS: That's under the arch and round the back, like a lot of these old 'ouses. This is ninety-six-B.
BILL: Then where *does* the door lead?
JENKINS: Only to a cupboard, sir. A big cupboard. (*suddenly galvanized*) And somebody's 'iding there now.
BILL: That's right. Morgan's there with his razor.
JENKINS: (*bursting out, loud voice*) That's the end of the shave, sir. I trust it's satisfactory. 'Ot towel?
BILL: (*also loud voice*) Yes thanks. Hot and steaming. (*low voice*) Hang on to your nerve. Old Scratch, and we'll get him in two minutes!
JENKINS: (*loud voice*) Towel satisfactory, sir? (*low voice*) I'm a peaceful man, guv'nor. I don't want no trouble.
BILL: (*low voice*) Now listen. When you take the towel off, go to the shelf under the mirrors and mess around with the bottles. Ask if I'd like some kind of lotion, and edge towards the glass door. When you get near it, run like blazes and yell for the police. The whole neighborhood is full of cops. Morgan will come out fighting when he hears you run. I'll pick up that high stool and try to hold him off. The cops didn't find me, because they went to the wrong ninety-six, but...
JENKINS: (*urgently*) Sir! That door behind you!
BILL: Well?
JENKINS: The knob's moving.
BILL: Then we'll have to do it when I count three.
JENKINS: (*crumpling*) I *can't*, sir. I just ain't up to it.
BILL: You can run, can't you? One! ... Two! ... Thr—
(*Sound: a bursting crash of glass, as of some weapon through the glazed panel*

 of a door.)
RADFORD: (*off: casual*) Better stay where you are. Both of you.
BILL: (*dizzy with relief*) Well, well! Do I hear Chief Inspector Radford?
RADFORD: You do. Sorry to break the glass door, Old Scratch; but it seemed to be bolted on the inside. Yes. It is.
(*Sound: the door opens, though we need not hear sound of bolt*)
RADFORD: (*over his shoulder*) In you go, boys. We may need several men here.
BILL: Inspector, don't you recognize me? I'm Bill Leslie!
RADFORD: (*fading on*) Yes. You probably are. Where's Morgan?
BILL: He's in that cupboard over there. *I* don't want to handle him. Have your men got guns?
RADFORD: We don't carry guns. Sergeant!
SERGEANT: Yes, sir?
RADFORD: Go over and guard that window. Davis, you stay here. I'll take the wasp out of his nest. (*fading a little off*) Coming out Morgan? No? All right. Have it your own way. I'm turning the knob, and ...
(*Sound: the door opens, flat, heavy thud as of body falling forward on floor*).
RADFORD: (*jarred*) Lord Almighty!
SERGEANT: Mind that blood, sir!
RADFORD: It's Morgan, all right. But he won't give any trouble now. His throat's been cut.
BILL: His throat's cut? But who—?
RADFORD: Curse it, Mr. Leslie, why did you have to go and kill him?

(*Music: in and behind*)
FABIAN: There is a famous building on the Thames Embankment: once red brick with white trimming; now smoke-darkened, redolent of old stone. Inside it looks rather like a hospital, does New Scotland Yard. Not far away down the misty river there is a great clock, as three persons sit in a small official room ...
(*Music: fades out*)

(*Sound: Big Ben, muted; strikes three*)
RADFORD: Mr. Leslie, why don't you tell us the truth?
BILL: (*wearily*) Inspector, I *have* told you the truth. So has Old Scratch here.
JENKINS: Aye! Every word of it.
RADFORD: Let's face it, Mr. Leslie. You killed Morgan, and you don't seem to understand the law here.
BILL: How do you mean?
RADFORD: To kill a wanted man, even a murderer, is just as serious an offence as killing the Prime Minister. I can't help you if you say you didn't kill him! But I can get you off scot-free if you admit you did it in self-

defense.

BILL: (*patiently*) Look, Inspector. I never set eyes on Morgan except when he walked through that shop. Scratch never saw him at all. I never stirred out of the chair for one second. Scratch never left me for a second. Neither of *us* did it.

RADFORD: Then who killed Morgan?

BILL: I don't know!

RADFORD: The door was bolted on the inside. The window was locked. How could anybody get *in*?

BILL: I... just don't know.

RADFORD: You don't think a ghost got in and killed him?

BILL: Well, what do *you* think happened?

RADFORD: (*comfortably*) I *know* what happened.

BILL: Oh?

RADFORD: Oh, yes. We rather thought you and Morgan would try to corner each other. You were both in Fleet Street, within twenty yards of each other, when those police-whistles blew.

BILL: (*hitting back*) And you lost both of us. What happened in the meantime?

RADFORD: You and Morgan met at the barber's. There was a fight, and you killed him unintentionally.

BILL: I killed him with what?

RADFORD: With his own razor. We found it in the cupboard, Then you bribed Old Scratch to keep his mouth shut.

JENKINS: 'Ere now, Inspector. I—

BILL: Easy, Scratch! Stop rocking back and forth!

JENKINS: (*not loudly*) I'd like to tangle up me 'air and Pull it out by the roots. I'd like to stand on the track wiv an engine coming. I'd like to ... (*almost in tears*) ... Lummy, ain't there *any* justice?

RADFORD: Morgan was loaded with money. Carried a thousand quid in an oil-skin tobacco-pouch. It wasn't on his body. If you gave it to Scratch, and Scratch hid it in the confusion after we broke in ...

BILL: (*abruptly*) You know, Inspector, I've been wrong about this whole thing.

RADFORD: (*quickly*) Oh? That's better!

BILL: Not in the way you mean! — *I* thought my big trouble would be to prove my identity. But you don't doubt my identity. (*suddenly wondering*) Or *do* you?

RADFORD: *I* don't, no. (*uneasily*) But officially, until your wife identifies you...

BILL: That's what I've been asking all night; and you won't answer! Where *is* Brenda?

RADFORD: (*uneasy but grimly official*) Well, sir. The fact is...

BILL: You haven't got her looked up somewhere?

RADFORD: No, of course not! The fact is — we can't find her.

BILL: Isn't she at the hotel?

RADFORD: No. Your wife left the hotel just after you did.
BILL: Brenda left the ... (*alarm growing*) Where did she go?
RADFORD: To 96 Fleet Street.
BILL: She... how do you know that?
RADFORD: The real entrance to 96 is at the back, up a flight of stairs past the barber's window. One of my men saw her there... then lost her.
BILL: You mean Morgan may have seen her before he came in to the shop... and attacked her.
JENKINS: Mr. Leslie, you're the one who's got to take it easy. Now just sit down, gentle-like.
RADFORD: Do you see now why you've got to give up this crazy story that you didn't kill Morgan and that you and Old Scratch were never out of each other's sight.
BILL: But it's true!
RADFORD: Don't you see what I want to know—did Morgan kill your wife? I want to know whether there was any blood on the razor before you fought Morgan?
BILL: This, as they say in the nursery books, is an office. That's a filing cabinet. You are smoking a pipe. Better hold onto things because they're getting blurred. Blast you! I never fought Morgan!
RADFORD: Want to... think it over for a while...
BILL: Brenda's dead? That's what you're saying? Don't start to object. That's what you're intimating. And if Brenda's dead I'm the cause of it.
SERGEANT: (*entering*) Chief Inspector.
RADFORD: Sergeant, keep out of here, I told you not to.
SERGEANT: Yes sir but I couldn't help it. She's here. She's been in the anteroom listening to every word you've said.
RADFORD: Who's here?
SERGEANT: Mrs. Leslie. She say she wants to give herself up.
BRENDA: (*imploring*) Bill, Bill!
RADFORD: Please stay where you are, Mrs. Leslie... you want to give yourself up?
BRENDA: No, not for murder. I'm so horribly frightened and mixed up I don't know what I did say but I had to talk to you... because I saw the murder committed.
RADFORD: You saw it? From where?
BRENDA: From outside the window. On the back stairs. Bill, darling, I got there before you did – you had to ask directions at the beginning. I, I saw you come in...
BILL: Into the barber's shop?
BRENDA: Yes, but I think I'd have known what happened even if I hadn't seen it.
RADFORD: Are you one of our women detectives, Mrs. Leslie?

BRENDA: Please, Mr. Radford. It's because I am a woman that I'd have noticed —you're too used to it. Bill thinks that that man you call Old Scratch was never out of his sight for a moment, but he's forgotten something.
BILL: Forgotten what?
BRENDA: You've forgotten there were thirty seconds when you had a hot towel over your face and eyes.
RADFORD: Sergeant, better grab our friend Scratch's arms, quick!
BRENDA: Keep away from me!
(*Sound: a scuffle as the Sergeant takes hold of Jenkins*)
RADFORD: Go on, Mrs. Leslie.
BRENDA: He went to the cupboard. He opened the door, only partly, and slashed inside. He dropped the razor inside and came back with an oilskin pouch of money. He put the money under a trap in the cork floor. It took less than thirty seconds if you timed it.
(*Sound: a scuffle as Jenkins is taken away*)
JENKINS: It's a pity I ain't got another razor! Old Scratch *never* misses with a razor!
RADFORD: Better put cuffs on him, sergeant.
BRENDA: You see, I'd already guessed he was an accomplice of Morgan.
RADFORD: You what!
BRENDA: Bill, you're so adventurous you won't use common sense. He was reading an evening paper with pictures of Morgan and you too but he said he'd never heard of Morgan. You spoke first so he knew you were the American and he saw a way of killing his partner Morgan for the money. If he'd just dropped that razor in the cupboard the police would think it belonged to Morgan. Wouldn't they?
RADFORD: I'm afraid they would.
BRENDA: Only I'm an awful coward and so paralyzed I couldn't even scream. Somebody chased me, maybe it was the police, and I fainted in some old woman's room. I... Inspector, may I go to my husband now.
RADFORD: You may, Mrs. Leslie... with the apologies of the C.I.D.
BRENDA: Bill, please take me away from London before your sense of adventure starts again. I don't understand these detective stories!
(*Music: in and behind*)
(*Sound: ship's whistles*)
(*Music: fades out*)

Notes for the Curious

For the opening play of *Cabin B-13*, John Dickson Carr wrote an entirely new story. It was, however, based on an idea that, three years earlier, he had planned to use in a short story for *Ellery Queen's Mystery Magazine*. Furthermore, although the story is original, a crucial aspect of the plot is strongly reminiscent of "The Vanishing of Vaudrey", a Father Brown short story by John Dickson Carr's great literary hero, GK Chesterton. One other *Cabin B-13* script has its roots in the Father Brown stories and, like "A Razor in Fleet Street," another play in the series also has a minor element in common with "Harem-Scarem," a short story published in the (*London*) *Daily Mail* in 1939.

For Carr, a passionate anglophile, pre-war London was "Baghdad on the Thames", a place with excitement around every corner. When Bill Leslie describes how the city had cast a spell on his imagination since he was a boy, the young diplomat is surely voicing Carr's own feelings—"*Sherlock Holmes! Doctor Fu Manchu! Hansom cabs rattling through the fog ...*". And it was in London that, in 1927, Carr had met a young woman who became the inspiration for the character of Dorothy Starberth, the heroine of the first Doctor Fell mystery, *Hags' Nook* (1933), and it is not too fanciful to conclude that Bill and Brenda Leslie—"*the husband American, the wife English*"— owe something to John and this woman.

As Carr may well have known, there wasn't a barber's shop at 96b Fleet Street before the Second World War. On the contrary, since at least the 1830s, 95-96 Fleet Street has been the address of *The Old Bell*, a public house that survives to this day as does the newspaper referenced in the story, the *London Evening Standard*. However, as Carr would certainly have known there was a barber's shop at *152* Fleet Street, albeit in fiction. It belonged to Sweeney Todd, the murderous "Demon Barber" who first appeared in *A String of Pearls* (1846) by James M. Rymer; with this in mind, it should be noted that in the revised version of the script published in *London Mystery Magazine*, Carr—or the magazine's editor—changed the name of the barber from "Henry M Jenkins" to "Henry S Todd". Moreover, in creating Hampden's Hotel for this story, Carr almost certainly had in mind London's famous Howard Hotel, which was located in Norfolk Street until it was demolished and, with an unknowing nod to the kind of mystery constructed by Carr, the hotel–indeed the entire street–disappeared ...

Like a later play in the first series, "A Razor in Fleet Street" has a minor element in common with "Harem-Scarem", a short story published in the

(*London*) *Daily Mail* in 1939.

An edited version of the script of "A Razor in Fleet Street" was published in the *London Mystery Magazine* for February/March 1952 under the entirely inappropriate title "Flight from Fleet Street", a title that seems unlikely to have been selected by Carr.

The Man Who Couldn't Be Photographed

(*Sound: a ship's whistle*)
(*Music: in and behind*)
>ANNOUNCER: CBS brings you John Dickson Carr's famous Doctor Fabian, ship's surgeon, world traveler, and collector of strange and incredible tales of mystery and murder, directed by John Dietz.

(*Music: fades out*)
>FABIAN: Don't you remember Bruce Ransom? He was the greatest romantic film-star in the first decade of talking pictures. Don't you recall the boiling crowd-scenes, the magnified voice from the screen, of Bruce Ransom in...

(*Sound: a heavy whip-crack*)
>BRUCE: (*the grand manner*) You need not call me Arrius the Younger. I am Judah Ben Hur. Shall I not take the chariot-reins against mine enemy?

(*Sound: whip-crack*)
>FABIAN: Or Bruce Ransom, in chain-mail, with a Crusader's Cross on his robe, as...

>BRUCE: Richard of England, called Lion-heart. (*tone changes*) Yet I have known compassion, my lady. I have known pity. And since you entered the camp, my lady, I have known love.

>FABIAN: (*ironically amused*) Real life, of course, can't be quite so magnified. Nor can people. But, when Ransom crossed with us on the *Maurevania*—it was summer, '33—people said he was modest and unaffected, I saw little of the light-haired film-star, with his affable smile. But I saw something of Miss Nita Ross, his (*slight pause*) social secretary.

(*Sound: faintly, a crowd-murmur has come up during this speech*)
>FABIAN: And, as the passengers crowded towards the gangway to get off at Cherbourg...

>NITA: (*above crowd murmur*) Good-bye, Doctor Fabian.
>FABIAN: Not goodbye—yet, Miss Ross. I am travelling to Paris myself.
>NITA: Then perhaps Bruce and I will see you there. It's been a wonderful crossing, hasn't it?
>FABIAN: (*quietly*) Are you sure of that?
>NITA: Sure of it? (*trying to laugh*) Of course I am! Why shouldn't I be?
>FABIAN: You're not looking particularly well. And you've recently been crying.
>NITA: But that's only—! (*she stops*)
>FABIAN: Yes?
>NITA: Only the excitement, that's all! I've never been in Europe before. (*trying lightness again*) And don't let my name deceive you. My forbears were Spanish, Bruce always says—

FABIAN: By the way. I believe Mr. Ransom and I have a mutual friend in Paris.
NITA: Oh? Who's that?
FABIAN: His name is Sherwood. Tom Sherwood.
NITA: (*sincerely*) Of course! Tom Sherwood! Bruce used to talk a lot about him. (*suddenly*) Anyway, Doctor Fabian, if I *am* upset, it's partly your fault.
FABIAN: My fault?
NITA: Yes. Those frightened stories you told in your cabin. The one set in Barcelona, for instance!
FABIAN: (*sharply*) About the murder?
NITA: (*bursting out*) No. About the suicide.

(*Music: in and behind*)
FABIAN: Evening in Paris, red-grey evening. Bruce Ransom's newly rented house: whose long and elaborate drawing-room, upstairs, overlooks the lamps and the motor-cars of the Champs-Élysées. Study Bruce and Nita in that drawing-room now! Watch the turn of their eyes as...
(*Music: fades out*)

BRUCE: (*ironically*) Thanks, Nita. Thanks very much.
NITA: (*unheeding*) Oh, dear! These Paris telephones are dreadful, but I cleaned up most of your engagements and... (*waking up*) I beg your pardon, Bruce What did you say?
BRUCE: In case your hearing is deficient, my dear, I said, 'thanks very much.'
NITA: (*surprised; attempting humor*) Well, thank *you*, Bruce. But what for?
BRUCE: (*suppressing wrath*) For getting me out of that filthy crowd at the Gare du Nord. In another minute I'd have hit somebody.
NITA: I'm sorry, Bruce.
BRUCE: (*magnanimously*) Mind, I don't say it was altogether your fault. Klein should have taken care of it. That's his job.
NITA: Bruce! Darling! Listen!
BRUCE: Yes, my angel?
NITA: I know you hate being mobbed. Anybody *would* hate it. But—
BRUCE: But what?
NITA: Those people idolize you! They think... well...
BRUCE: They think I'm more than I really am. Is that what you mean?
NITA: I didn't say that! I didn't even *think* it! That is: not exactly.
BRUCE: I see. (*breaking off, viciously*) Hamley! Where the devil's that servant of mine? Hamley!
HAMLEY: (*coughs*) If you'll pardon me, sir. I've been here all the time.
BRUCE: Oh! Yes, Sorry. — Did you get the dart-board?
HAMLEY: Yes, sir. It's here in this box.
BRUCE: An *English* dart-board?
HAMLEY: (*very faint humor*) *I* can testify to that, sir.
BRUCE: Good! Give me the darts. That's it! Now hang the board on the wall...

let's see...
NITA: Bruce, what on earth are you doing?
BRUCE: In less than a month, Nita, I'm due in England to make a picture for this new fellow what's-his-name. Have you read the script?
NITA: No, I'm afraid not. But, Bruce—!
BRUCE: That's too bad. *I* play a young lord of the manor; democratic sort of fellow; just suits me. I'm popular with everybody; I'm a champion darts-player at the local pub... (*breaking off*) There, Hamley. That's the place for the board!
HAMLEY: (*a little off microphone*) Here, sir?
BRUCE: Under that wall-bracket with the glass prisms. Hook the wire round it!
HAMLEY: Very good, sir.
BRUCE: I don't fake my sword-fights, Nita. And I won't even fake a tiddlely-winks game like this. Does that make me so very small?
NITA: Darling, I was only trying to tell you about your engagement-book!
BRUCE: (*controlling himself*) Engagement-book! Even in Paris!
NITA: There's one here I don't understand. It's tomorrow and says 'photographer.' More publicity stills?
BRUCE: No, my dear. This is on my own. The best photographer in Paris, (*Incensed*) Anyway, why are you bothering about tomorrow?
NITA: I'm not! But tonight, in about fifteen minutes, you're supposed to have dinner with Mr. and Mrs. Lawrence.
BRUCE: Who's Lawrence? Is he important?
NITA: N-no. Not in the way you mean.
BRUCE: Then cancel the engagement. (*slight pause, then pleasantly*) Did you hear what I said, Nita? Cancel the engagement.
(*Sound: the telephone rings*)
NITA: (*shaken, glad of a diversion*) I'll answer it, Hamley.
(*Sound: the phone lifted*)
NITA: Allo?
Tom Sherwood: (*filter*) Allo? C'est Élysées cinquante-cinq—quatre vingt-sept?
NITA: Yes! I mean — (*correcting herself*) Je veux dire: oui! C'est—
TOM: (*pleased*) It's all right. We're both Americans. I wonder if I could speak to Mr. Ransom?
NITA: Who's calling please?
Sherwood: Well — it's an old friend of his. Name's Sherwood; Tom Sherwood.
NITA: Mr. Sherwood! Of course! (*turning around*) Didn't you hear that, Bruce?
BRUCE: (*deliberately ignoring*) Have you got the board ready yet, Hamley?
NITA: (*holding her fury*) At college, Bruce, Tom Sherwood was your best friend. In the old days you never stopped talking about him. Don't you want to speak to him now?
BRUCE: No. Tell him I'm out.
NITA: I'm sorry, Mr. Sherwood. He *is* at home, but I'm afraid he's just too busy

to speak to you.

TOM: (*embarrassed*) Oh. I see. Well, I... I didn't mean to butt in, or anything like that. Just thought I'd call; *you* know how it is; old times, Thanks. Good-bye.

(*Phone replaced.*)

NITA: (*dangerously quiet*) Bruce, do you know how much you've changed in the last two years?

BRUCE: I've grown up, that's all. Let's try the darts!

(*Sound: thud of dart in board*)

BRUCE: Middle ring first time! Now I can start to score. (*coolly*) I've got along in this world, Nita...

(*Sound: thud of dart*)

BRUCE: Sixteen! Not bad. I've got along in the world, Nita; and I can't be bothered with nobodies.

(*Sound: thud of dart*)

BRUCE: Forty! I'm getting good!

NITA: So you — can't be bothered with nobodies. Is that it?

BRUCE: That's about it.

NITA: Bruce, you *swine*!

BRUCE: (*pause*) Hamley!

HAMLEY: (*a little off, uncertain*) Yes, sir?

BRUCE: Bring me the darts, and stop looking so embarrassed. (*sharply*) Bring me the... There. That's it. Thanks. (*abruptly, almost pleading*) Look, Nita. I wish I could make you understand things!

NITA: I wish you could too. Dear heaven, how I wish you could!

BRUCE: These people were all right once, yes.

NITA: You're very gracious, Mr. Ransom.

BRUCE: But what's the use being sentimental about it? I've outgrown them, that's all. Or, if you don't like that, say I've grown away from them.

NITA: (*tensely*) Will you answer one question, Bruce?

BRUCE: Certainly.

NITA: These people you've 'grown away from'. Am I one of them? (*pause*) Am I, Bruce?

BRUCE: (*coolly*) Since *you* mention the subject, Nita...

(*Sound: thud of dart*)

BRUCE: Six! That's bad. — since *you* mention it, Nita, I'd better be just as frank.

(*Sound: thud of dart*)

BRUCE: Forty again! — (*angrily*) And I've got to tell you, Nita, I'm completely sick and—

NITA: (*a half sob*) No! Please! Wait!

BRUCE: (*uncomfortable*) I don't *like* telling you that, you know.

NITA: Bruce, look at me. Give me your hands. Put that dart on the table; there! Now look at me.

BRUCE: All right, all right!
NITA: I worshipped you. More than those crowds, more than anybody, even though I *knew* you. I wasn't jealous of other women. I couldn't be, any longer; you'd humiliated me too much. But I had one hope, Bruce. Just one. I knew it wasn't real, but I hoped. That was when you asked me to go to Europe. Why did you do it, Bruce? Haven't you any pity? Or was it because you thought... it'd be easier to get rid of me?
BRUCE: Yes. It was.
NITA: (*enraged*) Bruce, you—!
BRUCE: (*gives a wince and a half-stifled exclamation of pain*) So you'd jab me in the shoulder with a dart, eh? (*alarmed*) I can't see it! Pull it out! Pull it ... (*releases his breath*) Now drop it!
(*Sound: a faint wooden clatter and roll, as of the dart on a wooden table-top*)
NITA: I'd like to jab your eyes out. I'd like to make your face so horrible that even lepers would turn away.
BRUCE: I believe you, all right! — Look at her, Hamley!
NITA: Yes! Look at me!
BRUCE: Quite a beauty, if you like 'em dark-haired. All soft, and silky. You wouldn't think she could have claws. But these Southern Europeans...
NITA: (*cutting in*) You're right about that, Bruce. Do you believe in the devil?
BRUCE: Oh, stop it!
NITA: The devil could put his mark on your face. Oh, yes, he could! If I bargained with him.
BRUCE: (*uneasy*) Stop it! You're hysterical!
NITA: (*as though in religious vow*) I offer my life, I offer my soul, if that man never faces a camera again. And this I swear by the reversed cross of Satan.
BRUCE: Nita! Come back here! Nita!
(*Sound: a door opens and closes.*)
HAMLEY: (*pause: now on mike: almost sardonically*) I've gathered up the darts, sir. They're quite clean. Do you wish to continue playing?
BRUCE: Yes, Hamley. I do!
HAMLEY: Very good, sir. (*human now*) Sir, will you let *me* offer an opinion about this?
BRUCE: I pay you to serve me, Hamley. Not to offer opinions.
HAMLEY: (*stolidly*) Yes, sir.
BRUCE: We'll just imagine, you see, the center of that board is the head of somebody I don't like. *Then* I can score a bull's-eye. Watch!
(*Sound: thud of dart*)
BRUCE: Missed it. But close!
(*Sound: thud of dart*)
BRUCE: Missed again. Getting nearer, though!
(*Sound: thud of dart*)
BRUCE: Got it! Straight through the head!

(*Sound: off but clearly, the sound of a pistol-shot*)
BRUCE: (*pause; shaken*) Hamley!
HAMLEY: (*also shaken*) Yes, sir?
BRUCE: That fool woman couldn't possibly have ... No! It's crazy!
HAMLEY: (*with an effort*) The young lady was carrying her handbag, sir. And her maid spoke of—a small revolver.
BRUCE: You're lying!
HAMLEY: (*stolidly*) No, sir.
BRUCE: Then what are you waiting for? Don't stand there shaking like a—like a bowl of jelly in a white wig! Go and see!
HAMLEY: Yes, sir.
BRUCE: (*muttering, incredulously*) Nita wouldn't do a thing like that. Nita loves me. She's always loved me.
(*Sound: the door opens and closes as Hamley leaves*)
BRUCE: All this talk about praying to the devil to... Nothing wrong with *my* face! See it in a mirror. She's kidding me, that's what. Fired a shot just to scare me. A scandal would ruin me. Nita knows that. She wouldn't ...
(*Sound: the door opens and closes*)
BRUCE: Don't stumble over the furniture, Hamley! Anybody'd think you were drunk. Here! Come over here and tell me! Well?
HAMLEY: (*on mike*) Through the head, sir. With a small revolver.
BRUCE: (*dazed*) I see. (*pulling himself together*) Now listen, Hamley! I'm going out.
HAMLEY: But you can't sir, with the young lady dead in —
BRUCE: Shut up and don't argue! Just listen!
HAMLEY: Yes, sir.
BRUCE: As soon as I've gone, you 'phone Mr. Henderson at our office here. Mammoth Pictures; it's in the book. He'll fix everything; don't worry. I want some fresh air. Maybe a bottle of champagne. (*virtuously*) After all, I've got to look my best tomorrow morning. I'm going to the photographer!

(*Music: in and behind*)
FABIAN: The gay city. The city of dark-eyed ladies. *La Ville Lumiere.* Why shouldn't Bruce Ransom feel gay and confident, less than two days afterwards? When one has influence, when a girl's death really *is* suicide. Life can *flow* as smoothly as the sleek cars in the Rue de la Paix. Bruce Ransom had sat for close-up photographs in the studio of Dulac and Son, Rue de la Paix; and received only obsequious attention. Shouldn't he smile, shouldn't he be happy?—when next morning he again opened the door of the soft-carpeted, dim-lit reception-room of Dulac and Son ...
(*Music: fades out*)

(*Sound: the faint characteristic Paris traffic-noise, which we hear only briefly before a very light wood-and glass-door is closed*).
BRUCE: Good morning, mademoiselle!
FRANCINE: (*off; cheerfully*) Good morning, monsieur! And 'ow may I serve you?
BRUCE: (*as though smiling*) I was in here yesterday, remember? Monsieur Dulac said I could see the first prints if I dropped in this morning, and...
FRANCINE: (*on; in sudden horror*) *Dieu me garde! Non!*
BRUCE: What's the matter with you?
FRANCINE: It is—dark in here. When you come in I do not recognize you. I ...
BRUCE: Yes; but what's wrong? Why are you backing away?
FRANCINE: *Pardon, monsieur. Il faut chercher le patron.* (*cry of relief*) Ah! *Voici Monsieur Dulac!* (*appealing*) *Monsieur Dulac! Je vous en priec*—!
DULAC: *Va-t'en, ma petite! Va-t'en!* (*formally*) Mr. Ransom!
BRUCE: Yes? What's all the fuss?
DULAC: I have some news for you. It is about the photographs. They were all—failures.
BRUCE: You mean they didn't come out? The whole bunch of 'em?
DULAC: Not one. I regret! (*hesitation*) It was some flaw in the camera, no doubt.
BRUCE: (*on his dignity*) This is a nuisance, you know. You've put me to a lot of inconvenience. We'll just have to try again.
DULAC: (*formally*) Mr. Ransom. I would not photograph you for a million francs.
BRUCE: Are you crazy?
DULAC: No. And I have tried to deal with you in all courtesy. Now please be kind enough to leave my shop.
BRUCE: Just a moment, Mr. Dulac! I don't think you know who I am!
DULAC: I know who you are. I would not *be* who you are. In the name of *le Bon Dieu*, go!
MADAME: (*biting, sardonic*) Young man, I am Madame Vernet. Our photographic sign, Vernet, has hung in the rue de la Paix since the time of the third Napoleon. And I say: *get out.*
BRUCE: (*unnerved, now*) Give me one minute, madame! Just one little minute!.
MADAME: Very well. I count it by the watch.
BRUCE: Yesterday, after I left Dulac's, I went to three different photographers and had my picture taken.
MADAME: And this morning, I make a guess, two of them telephoned you. (*sardonically prodding*) Ye-es?
BRUCE: Yes! They said —
MADAME: Go on!
BRUCE: They said the pictures hadn't come out. They were lying! They saw something on those prints that terrified them as though they'd seen.

MADAME: What, for instance.
BRUCE: Madame Vernet, you're my last hope. You were the third photographer. Now *you* won't tell me. All right: here's my cheque-book. Name any amount you like. But tell me what you saw on those prints!
MADAME: In Paris, young man, nearly all things are for sale. (*very grimly*) But not this.
BRUCE: *Why* won't you tell me?
MADAME: Because I think you are accursed. And also because it is not wise.
BRUCE: Not wise?
MADAME: You see me sitting here, an old eccentric woman in an old studio, with the skylight pale as death and the tawdry canvas all around. But all the fashion in Paris still comes here, because Vernet is Vernet. (*venomously*). Take that answer; and *get out.*
BRUCE: (*losing his head*) We're all alone here. Suppose I choked it out of you?
MADAME: *Tiens*, these are fine *manners*! And if *I* press this button to the burglar-alarm?
BRUCE: Wait! Stop! I didn't mean that!
MADAME: *Merci bien!*
BRUCE: I didn't mean it, I tell you! I'm confused. I can't think straight. Will you... shake hands?
MADAME: I would rather shake hands with the devil.

(*Music: in and fades out behind.*
FABIAN: Once more, at evening, the long drawing-room above the Champs Elysees. The drawing-room with the crystal chandelier, the brackets with the prisms, the dart-board still on the wall. Long windows now stand wide open. But the window curtains stir uneasily; the breeze stirs; the sky is darkening with a distant approach of...
(*Sound: the long roll of thunder*)
BRUCE: (*calling*) Hamley! (*pause to himself*) They look at me in horror. Why? There's nothing in the looking-glass; nothing at all. (*shouting*) Hamley!
HAMLEY: (*fading on*) Sorry I was detained, sir. You required something?
BRUCE: I want company, that's all. Just a little company.
HAMLEY: Yes, sir. I... thought I heard thunder as I came upstairs. Shall I close the windows?
BRUCE: No. I like the cool air. (*suddenly dropping his defenses*) Hamley, what's wrong with me?
HAMLEY: *Is* anything wrong, sir?
BRUCE: Don't evade. You know what I mean!
HAMLEY: In that case, sir: I can't say.
BRUCE: What do you *think* is wrong?
HAMLEY: I am paid to serve you, sir. Not to offer opinions.
BRUCE: Hamley, I'm in trouble! I need help!
HAMLEY: If you're in trouble, sir, why not ring up the film company? They

seem able to manage—most things.

BRUCE: But that's just what I *can't* do! Don't you see? If there *should* be anything wrong...

HAMLEY: (*filter*) I offer my life, I offer my soul, if that man never faces a camera again.

BRUCE: (*involuntarily*) You can't get away with it, Nita!

HAMLEY: (*startled*) *What's that,* sir?

BRUCE: Never mind, Hamley. I'm not really hearing Nita's voice. It's in my own head; and I know it.

HAMLEY: Speaking of the young lady, sir—I'm afraid I forgot. The Inspector from the *Sûreté* was here, and asked me to return *this.*

BRUCE: Return what?

HAMLEY: This, sir. The revolver.

BRUCE: You mean it's —?

HAMLEY: Yes, sir. The young lady's revolver. This Surete Inspector said there was no doubt about suicide. But he added... they'd better not hear of any *more* trouble from this house.

BRUCE: What does he think *I'm* going to do? Kill myself too? No, thanks, Hamley! I've got along in this world. Life's much too sweet for me.

NITA: (*on filter*) Is it, Bruce? If you never faced a camera again?

(*Sound: the roll of thunder.*)

HAMLEY: Is anything wrong now, sir? You're as white as..

BRUCE: Never mind. Give me that gun. Thanks. I'll just drop it in ray pocket for safe-keeping. Anyway, I may need it tomorrow.

HAMLEY: I don't quite follow you, sir.

BRUCE: There must be a hundred photographers, a thousand even, who'd tell me if I paid 'em well enough! All that money, and I can't find out ... it's grotesque!

HAMLEY: You realize, sir, that it *may* ... be all in your imagination?

BRUCE: It wasn't imagination that four different people took that picture and then destroyed everything. (*feverishly*) But again—suppose somebody *does* find out? The publicity. Or I might be blackmailed for years. Lots of people recognized me today. Raised their glasses at sidewalk tables, *Vive Monsieur Ransom!* And vet I never felt so much *alone.*

HAMLEY: (*dryly*) Most unfortunate, sir. With all your popularity.

BRUCE: Stop torturing me! Haven't you any pity?

NITA: (*on filter*) Bruce, haven't you any pity?

BRUCE: If only I could have pictures taken here. In private! Where nobody'd know! If only I had some friend I could trust, who ... (*suddenly realizing*) Hamley!

HAMLEY: Yes, sir?

BRUCE: *Tom Sherwood!* He used to mess around with photography!

HAMLEY: If you remember, sir, you weren't very cordial to Mr. Sherwood three nights ago.

BRUCE: Never mind! He'll do. Get him on the 'phone.
HAMLEY: As you wish, sir.
BRUCE: Then I'll know! Then I'll *know*!

(*Music: in and fades out behind*)
FABIAN: And so, against the windows, Bruce Ransom posed for his most important picture. Tom Sherwood, large and red-headed, used only the crudest materials, which any amateur could better today: an ordinary camera with portrait attachment, and two photoflood bulbs. But, as the bulbs glared against a storm-darkened sky.

(*Sound: the roll of thunder.*)
BRUCE: Is that all, Tom?
TOM: That's all. (*easy and sympathetic*) Now relax, old horse; and I *mean* relax. You know, you scared the ears off me over the 'phone.
Bruce; Hadn't I a reason to?
Tom; Easy, now! Easy!
BRUCE: How long will it take you to develop the prints?
TOM: Fifteen minutes, maybe twenty. Maybe a little longer. I'll do the best I can.
BRUCE: (*hesitant*) There's one other thing, Tom. About that night. When you called up. I want to explain —
TOM: Look, Bruce; forget it!
BRUCE: Yes; but I want to explain —
TOM: Remember when I scored the touchdown and we beat Cornell six-nothing? I had a swelled head like a pumpkin.
BRUCE: Have you got the blasted nerve to say I'm conceited?
TOM: (*humoring him*) No, Bruce. No! Let's drop the subject. No — Now what can I use for a dark-room?
BRUCE: Ah! Yes! Dark-room! You see that door over there?
TOM: Yes, but—! Your butler said ...
BRUCE: Said what?
TOM: Well! (*uncomfortably*) Isn't that the library where this girl killed her-self!
BRUCE: The door leads to the library, yes. But in between there's a big place like a washroom. Won't that do?
TOM: Yes. I guess so. (*hesitates*) Listen, Bruce! About this girl Nita Ross. It's none of my business, but you got in touch with her relatives, of course?
BRUCE: How do I know who her relatives are? *I* met her in New York. Years ago. Working for a doctor on the East Side. Probably came from a slum. That's where she belonged.
TOM: (*under his breath*) You used to be a good guy, once.
BRUCE: *What did you say*?
TOM: Nothing, Bruce! You're in a jam; that's all *I* know.

BRUCE: (*suspicious*) You wouldn't fool, me, Tom?
TOM: About what?
BRUCE: Whatever's on that picture, you'll show me? Just as soon as you develop it?
TOM: Yes. Word of honor.
BRUCE: If you double-cross me, Tom, I'll kill you. And I'm not joking.
TOM: (*wearily*) You'll kill me with what? You're not in a film now, Bruce. Your nerves are all ragged. Just leave everything to me.
BRUCE: You'll hurry, now?! Twenty minutes!?
TOM: Let me get my developing-stuff out of the hall. Then—twenty minutes!

(*Music: in and behind*)–
FABIAN: 18 minutes. No; 18 and a half. Quiet as the tomb. Thunder prowling. No sound out of that dark-room... No sound at all. What if Tom Sherwood slipped out of there? What if he got away without showing the pictures? Hamley's in the hall, over beyond the arch. Hamley will know.
(*Music: fades out*)
BRUCE: Hamley! Hamley!
HAMLEY: (*off*) Yes, sir?
BRUCE: Do you happen to know where Mr. Sherwood is?
HAMLEY: I ... I believe he's using the extension phone in the library.
BRUCE: *Extension—phone! Library!*
HAMLEY: Yes, sir. If you'll excuse me, there's someone at the back door.
BRUCE: Where's the phone here? Listen in! Where's the ... Got it!
(*Sound: phone picked up*)
TOM: (on *filter*)—and that's the whole thing. Come over here as quickly as you can! Ransom's not in a mood to take it, and we may have to use a straight-jacket. Understand? Right! See you later!
(*Sound: on filter—the -phone replaced*)
BRUCE: Very interesting!
(*Sound: the phone replaced*)
BRUCE: So you're a traitor too, Mr. Tom Sherwood. And you *don't* think I've got a gun. Let's just imagine you crossing the library; easy steps; no hurry; into the dark-room. In a second or two that door will open, and (*Sound: the door opens*)
TOM: (*subdued but cheerful, fading in*) Well, Bruce! I've got the results for you!
BRUCE: *Have you, now?*
TOM: This big enamel tray thing—I've got to carry it carefully—is called a mustard bath. You can look down through the solution; it's like water; and see yourself. I've got to carry it carefully, and...Bruce! What are you doing with that gun?
BRUCE: You didn't think I meant what I said. Did you, Tom?
(*Sound: three pistol-shots*)

Tom: Bruce—Bruce—I—I— (*gasps*)
(*Sound: we hear the water pouring down on the floor. then the bang of the enamel dish as it falls, a thud as of someone collapsing face forward.*)
Hamley: (*fading on*) Mr. Ransom! Mr. Ransom! What in the name of—(*he stops suddenly*).
Bruce: I've finished him, Hamley. It's a relief to see *you* looking human.
Hamley: (*slowly*) Oh, I'm human!
Bruce: Glad to hear it!
Hamley: I'm 'uman. As you'll find out. (*bursting out*) You bloody *fool*!
Bruce: (*astounded*) *What did you say?*
Hamley: Mr. Sherwood was trying to save you. And you shot him. Do you know what's *really* wrong with you?
Bruce: No! Do you?
Hamley: I didn't, till I heard Mr. Sherwood on the 'phone. But I guessed the first part. And I tried to warn you.
Bruce: (*contemptuously*) *You*? Warn *me*?
Hamley: You were jabbed in the shoulder, weren't you? And you thought it was a dart!
Bruce: Yes! That's what it was!
Hamley: Oh, no. Not one of those darts had blood on it. I told you so! — It was a hypodermic needle.
Bruce: What are you trying to tell me?
Hamley: The young lady carried a handbag for the hypodermic. And she'd worked for a doctor in New York. And she went back there, her maid says, and stole something. The truth is—you've got smallpox.
(*Sound: thud of metallic object fallen*)
Hamley: That's right! Drop the gun!
Bruce: But I *couldn't* have—what you say! I —
Hamley: The spots show up on a photographic plate four days before the eye can see 'em. Those people were scared of a panic among their swell clients. They couldn't tell *you the truth,* because you'd have had to tell the Sûreté how you *learned* you'd had smallpox.
Bruce: (*horrified*) But this is worse than anything! Never ... face ... a camera...
Hamley: Never face a camera, my eye! You could have been cured easy! Not a mark on your 'andsome face. Mr. Sherwood was only phoning Doctor Fabian, to arrange for treatment. But you didn't trust anybody! Not a soul in the world! And you've killed your only friend.
(*Sound: the police-whistles off*)
Bruce: Hamley! Those whistles! Do they mean—?
Hamley: (*returning to his old sedate manner*) Yes, sir. I should say police-whistles. But then, Mr. Ransom, I am not paid to offer opinions.
(*Music: in and behind*)
(*Sound: ship's whistles*)
(*Music: fades out*)

Notes for the Curious

The second play in the first series of *Cabin B-13* is again original. It also features a ploy that John Dickson Carr had once planned to use in a short story. As well as presenting the impossibility of the title, the play also includes the only occasion on which we learn of an untold *Cabin B-13* mystery, or rather two, both are set in Barcelona with one involving suicide and the other murder.

"The Man Who Couldn't Be Photographed" is set largely in Paris, which Carr had first visited in 1927. Five years prior to that, he had recorded his dreams of traveling to Europe to see *"all the thousand scenes that bring with them the faint, musty breath of the past"*. Why Carr went specifically to France is unclear though family legend has it that Carr had been due to take up a place at the University of Paris (the Sorbonne). An article in the local newspaper, published on his return, said only that Carr's purpose was to perfect his French. On that level, the trip was certainly successful on that level for he became proficient in the language.

Douglas G. Greene, Carr's biographer and the foremost authority on his work, has observed that the months that the young writer spent in France greatly influenced his writing, transitioning his settings away from melancholic Poe-esque darkness and into more vivid portraits of real places, grounded in what he himself had seen.

As Carr makes clear in the script, the inspiration for the mystery was the following reference in *Criminal Investigation: A Practical Textbook for Magistrates, Police Officers and Lawyers* (1934), adapted by John Adam and J Collyer Adam from *System Der Kriminalistik* by Doctor Hans Gross:

> "A woman, apparently in the best of health, had her photograph taken, and when the photographer developed the negative he noticed that the face and the neck were spotted over with a multitude of dark marks; yet the photographer did not remember having seen such marks upon the skin of the woman; his astonishment increased when he learned that the woman had become ill some days later and that her illness was small-pox. This fact is only explicable on the assumption that the marks of the illness were already existent when she posed for her photograph, but that they were as yet slightly red and that the sensitised plate had registered them when the human eye was unable to perceive them."

This curious phenomenon also inspired the Irish playwright George Bernard

Shaw to write his only detective story, "The Brand of Cain", which was written—and lost—in the 1880s.

Madame Vernet *may* be a relative of the celebrated Vernet family, three generations of which achieved some fame for their painting: Carle Vernet (1758-1836); Claude Joseph Vernet (1714-1789); and Antoine Vernet (1689-1753). Carr will have been mindful that, in Arthur Conan Doyle's story "*The Adventure of the Greek Interpreter*", Sherlock Holmes states that "*My ancestors were country squires... my grandmother... was the sister of Vernet, the French artist*", without specifying which of the three Vernets he regarded as his great uncle. On the other hand, Bruce Ransom *might* be related to the character of the same name who appears in the 'Carter Dickson' novel *My Late Wives* (1946).

John Dickson Carr revised 'The Man Who Couldn't Be Photographed" for a play of the same title first broadcast on 23 July 1955 as the opening play in the ninth and final series of the BBC program *Appointment with Fear*.

Death Has Four Faces

(*Sound: a ship's whistle*)
ANNOUNCER: *Cabin B-13.*
(*Music: in and behind*)
FABIAN: This city in the Midlands; let's call it Birchespool. Soot from the factories drifts down into grey air. Its rain is less a rain than a sort of greasy mist. At night, off the main dingy thoroughfares, gas-lamps sparkle on wet cobblestones. It's a network of railways; and always, in Birchespool...
(*Sound: a train at high speed with a very thin, piercing whistle-blast...*)
FABIAN: Let's look at the North Station: at a slow train clanking towards it one autumn evening only a year ago. Let's look at three men in a compartment of that train. One of them, young and dark-haired, in an old raincoat, sits near the corridor-side and stares at nothing.
(*Sound: the click of train-wheels has begun to come up.*)
FABIAN: On the other side, near the compartment-door, a little businessman bends towards the broad, burly figure of Superintendent Bellman, City Police. And Superintendent Bellman holds up—watch them gleam, now!—a pair of handcuffs.
BUSINESSMAN: So those are handcuffs! Eh, Superintendent?
BELLMAN: Yes, sir. Those are the darbies.
(*Sound: The handcuff-chain jingles as though shaken like a toy*)
BUSINESSMAN: To tell you the truth, Superintendent, I never saw real handcuffs before. Only in films.
BELLMAN: To tell *you* the truth, sir, I don't see 'em much myself. But I had to take Joe Felton up for trial at Lancaster. (*amused but tolerant*) And Joe can be pretty tough, sometimes, when he don't like company. (*As though turning*) Would *you* like to look at 'em, young fellow?
STEVE (*Canadian; about 35*) (*starting*): What's that? (*rousing out of day-dream*) Oh! Sorry! I was thinking about something else.
BELLMAN: You didn't seem to like your day-dream. I only asked if you wanted to look at these.
STEVE (*pretending amusement*): Handcuffs, eh?
BUSINESSMAN: What Superintendent Bellman calls the darbies. All ready to snap!
STEVE: No, thanks, Superintendent. You keep 'em for the criminals. (*hesitates*) But—I wonder if you gentlemen would give me some information?
BUSINESSMAN: Easy to tell *you're* a stranger. American, I take it?
STEVE: No. Canadian. But I've lived In London for years.—We're getting in at the North Station, aren't we?

BELLMAN: That's right, son.
BUSINESSMAN: In... let's see...about half a minute now.
(*Sound: train is now gliding slowly*)
STEVE: And that's where I get the London train, isn't it?
BELLMAN: London train? No, lad! You want the South Station.
STEVE: South Station? Is that far away?
BELLMAN: 'Bout the middle of town. Chamberlain Square.
STEVE: I can get a taxi, can't I?
BELLMAN: Shouldn't like to bank on a taxi these days. Specially in this weather. Have you got much luggage?
STEVE: No. Only that bag up on the rack. But that's not the point! It's—(*he stops*)
BUSINESSMAN: Come, now! A husky young chap like you! You can walk it in fifteen minutes!
STEVE: (*ignoring this*) Tell me, Superintendent. There'll be a hotel at *this* station, won't there?
BELLMAN: Not *at* the station, no. But pretty close.
BUSINESSMAN: (*pleased*) And here *we* are. I'd better get the window down...
(*Sound: thud as window in compartment-door falls down into its slot*)
BUSINESSMAN: *And* the door open.
(*Sound: the compartment door-handle opened. Train has now stopped. In the background we hear mingling hollow sound of many people's footsteps on station platform under train-shed. It continues under.*)
BUSINESSMAN: (*fading off*) My wife'll be waiting, gentlemen! Good luck!
STEVE: (*sharply*) Superintendent!
BELLMAN: Yes, lad?
STEVE: *Put those handcuffs on me.*
BELLMAN: (*slight pause*) What in lum's name are you talking about?
STEVE: (*controlled*) I want you to put the handcuffs on me. Superintendent, can you sit down again for just a moment? And listen?
BELLMAN: 'Course I can, lad! That's part of a copper's job. What's up?
STEVE: My name's West. Stephen—Steve West. Wait! Inside-coat-pocket... Passport. Identity-card. And *this* letter.
(*Sound: a sheet of stiff paper. Like a large letter, is unfolded.*)
STEVE: Read it. I'll be eternally grateful if you read it!
(*Sound: station noises up and down*)
BELLMAN: (*uneasily*) Lord! Then you're—?
STEVE: Yes. *Now* do you see?
BELLMAN: (*even more uneasily*) I see a good bit. Ah! But—what do you want me to do?
STEVE: Snap the cuffs round my wrists until they lock. Will you do that?
BELLMAN: I don't like this, Mr. West. But—
(*Sound: the double click of handcuffs.*)

STEVE: Thanks, Now get a good grip on me. March me to that hotel as though you were taking me to prison. *Prison!* If I try to get away, or if... anything happens...
BELLMAN: Yes, lad?
STEVE: Don't let go, do you understand? *Don't let go!*

(*Music: in and behind*)
FABIAN: Cotton-Exchange Street, Birchespool. Even here I fell, its clamminess, the soot of the Midlands. Part of Cotton Exchange Street is a viaduct; and under it, ceaselessly...Just beyond, the huge grey-stone bulk of the Metropole Hotel. Built in the 'nineties, once garish with gilt and gas-lamps. Half-lighted now, for fuel economy in this year '47; its big marble foyer, with the palms and the arabesque-work, unchanged except for decay. Near the revolving doors, unseen by newcomers, posters which atmosphere of this foyer makes people read in whispers...
(*Music: fades out*)

FIRST VOICE: (*softly*) Giant Air Display, Commemorating Battle of Britain, September 12th!
SECOND VOICE: Lyric Theatre. Miss Diana Borden, famous Canadian actress, in *The Merchant of Venice.*
(*Sound: two pairs footsteps fading in behind.*)
FABIAN: Half-lighted. Half-deserted! And, as two newcomers approach the marble reception-desk...
BELLMAN: (*under his breath*) The handcuffs are off, Mr. West. Nobody saw 'em.
STEVE: Thanks, Superintendent. Now! (*Aloud*) Good evening.
RECEPTION CLERK: (*not affably*) Good evening, sir.
STEVE: I'd like a single room, please.
RECEPTION CLERK: Have you a reservation, sir?
STEVE: No. I didn't even know I was going to be here!
RECEPTION CLERK: Then I'm sorry, sir. I'm afraid we... (*stops; hesitation*) Of course it—it *might* be arranged.
STEVE: Thanks again, Superintendent.
BELLMAN: Thanks again? What for, Mr. West?
STEVE: Too many mirrors here, I saw you signal 'yes'.
RECEPTION CLERK: (*more human*) I wasn't trying to put you off, sir. We've got a hundred empty rooms. It's the linen, the furniture, the staff: we can't get 'em! (*Hinting*) Even the accommodations we do have...
STEVE: Put me anywhere. I don't care. But for the love of mike get me a room!
RECEPTION CLERK: You see, sir, it's what we call the Imperial Suite. On the top floor. And it's rather expensive.
STEVE: That doesn't matter. Here: do you want payment in advance?
BELLMAN: Easy, lad! There's a mort o' brass in that wallet! Put it away!

RECEPTION CLERK: We shouldn't *dream* of payment in advance, sir. Very well then. If you'll just fill out this form? A pen? Here you are!
STEVE: Thanks.
(*Sound: the writing under next speeches*)
BELLMAN: What's more, young fellow, I think you're going to get a surprise when you turn 'round.
STEVE: (*engrossed*) Oh?
BELLMAN: Ye-es. I think you've got a friend at this hotel.
STEVE: *I* have? Here?
BELLMAN: Yes. A young lady; *and* a stunner. Red hair piled up on 'er head; frock like—I dunno. Paris, maybe. Look as though she couldn't believe her eyes.
RECEPTION CLERK: That's Miss Borden, sir. At the Lyric Theatre.
(*Sound: at the word 'Borden,' the writing stops abruptly*)
STEVE: *Diana* Borden?
RECEPTION CLERK: Yes, sir. The young lady with her, beyond the palm, is Miss Kent.
STEVE: (*desperately*) If you don't mind, I'll finish this form later. Can't you have me taken up to my room *now*?
RECEPTION CLERK: Certainly, sir! Immediately! (*Calling*) Porter! One suitcase. (*Less loudly*) Here's the key: ten-o-one.
STEVE: Come on, Superintendent! Go as far as the lift, anyway!
BELLMAN: But look here, Mr. West, The young lady's...
DIANA: (*off, calling*) Steve! Steve West!
STEVE: Don't turn around, now! Follow the porter. That's it!
BELLMAN: I hope you know what you're doing. What's Diana Borden to *you*?
STEVE: (*Bitterly*) Only the girl I'm engaged to, that's all!
DIANA: Please! Isn't there anyone at this reception-desk?
RECEPTION CLERK: (*fading on: a deep admirer*) Sorry, Miss Borden! Only took a step away!
DIANA: (*casually*) That man who just registered. The one in the disreputable raincoat. He *is* Mr. Stephen West?
RECEPTION CLERK: Yes, Miss Borden! He's gone up to ten-o-one. Shall I wait a moment, and ring him?
DIANA: No, thank you. That won't be necessary.—Jenny!
JENNY: Yes, Diana?
DIANA: Steve heard me, all right. (*controlling fury*) He heard me!
JENNY: Yes. I think he did. But, Diana! There's something—
DIANA: There are a lot of things I don't mind, Jenny. But I don't like being humiliated: I'm-funny that way. He comes rushing through here, dressed like a tramp and looking as though the devil were after him...
JENNY: Yes! That's what I mean!
DIANA: What you mean?

JENNY: Diana, there's something horribly wrong. Maybe he's in trouble. Maybe he's in—danger, even.
DIANA: Jenny... dear! (*represses mirth*) Now what danger *could* Steve be in?
JENNY: I don't know. Aren't you at least going to see him and find out?
DIANA: No, dear. No. I don't think I shall have time.—Oh... you there!
RECEPTION CLERK: Yes, Miss Borden?
DIANA: Would you have them put through a trunk-call to London, please.
RECEPTION CLERK: Certainly, Miss Borden! Try to get you a line as soon as we can!
DIANA: It's a personal call to Mr. Hubert Lodge. L-o-d-g-e. The number is Langham double-o-two-four.
RECEPTION CLERK: Anything *you* want, Miss Borden!
DIANA: Thank you *so* much. (*alerting tone*) As I say, Jenny, I don't think I shall have time, to see Steve. *What* a relief this is Sunday night and no show! I'm taking the ten-fifteen back to London!
JENNY: But, Diana! You can't!
DIANA: Listen, Jenny, I'm tired. I've had a long tour; I hate the road; and I'm tired. Anyway, in three weeks I start rehearsals for a West End opening. If this play here closes a week early, it doesn't matter. I'm going back. You'd better go with me.
JENNY: Diana. I.... if you really mean that, I—I think I'll stay here.
DIANA: Stay *here*? Even if the play closes?
JENNY: Yes. Just for a day or two.
DIANA: Jenny... darling! It's Steve! Of course! It's Steve!
JENNY: What are you talking about?
DIANA: The terrific passion! It's Steve!
JENNY: Don't be absurd! I've never even met him!
DIANA: No, but you've heard...I'm just putting the evidence together.
JENNY: Evidence?
DIANA: Shall I give you a note of introduction to him, Jenny? I can tell you exactly what I shall say..."Dearest Steve. This is to introduce Miss Jennifer Kent."
JENNY: Diana, please! People can hear us!
DIANA: *I* don't care. It's my business to be heard 'Miss Kent is the daughter of Colonel and Mrs. Something Kent, of Something-Something Old Hall, in Devon. She doesn't really need to earn her living.' (*changing tone*) Sometimes this infuriates me! (*back to dictating*) 'In The *Merchant of Venice*, she plays the innocent and lovely Jessica. And, heaven help her, she's really *like* that. She has conceived a violent passion—you should see the color of her face now—for Mr. Stephen West, well-known playwright and former R.A.F. fighter-pilot, who...'
JENNY: (*pleading*) Diana, wait! Please!
DIANA: (*biting now*) Yes, dear?

JENNY: I don't know what you're thinking, I don't believe you've ever bothered to notice what I think. But—are *you* in love with him?
DIANA: I *was*, yes.
JENNY: And not now?
DIANA: For one thing, dear, Steve is too easy-going. He never looks at his contracts; anybody can cheat him. That's not *my* kind of husband. On the other hand, he's temperamental and he's not very gallant. Anyway, what's the good of finishing my note? You'd never have the nerve to deliver it.
JENNY: Diana, listen! I don't want to quarrel...
DIANA: And who's quarreling, please?
JENNY: But are you daring me to go up there and find out what's wrong?
DIANA: I hadn't thought of it, dear. Still! It's an idea.
JENNY: Because that's where I *am* going, Diana. *Now*!

(*Music: in and fades out behind*)
FABIAN: You'd better hurry, Jenny Kent. There *is* danger, though not the kind you expect. Up in one of the gilt-and-bronze lifts, with more posters of the giant air-display for tomorrow. Hurry along the corridors of the bleak hotel: half-deserted, like a haunted house, except for the trains below. Hurry towards the Imperial Suite just under the roof. For in the drawing-room of the Imperial Suite, Steve West stands by the writing-table, and...

(*Sound: the key rattling and knob starting to turn, a little off*)
STEVE: (*tensely*) If that's the maid at the door, keep out! I don't need anything. I'm all right! I...
(*Sound: the door opens. And closes off*)
JENNY: (*off, frightened, but fairly steady*) Hello, Mr. West.
STEVE: Who are *you*? I thought—
JENNY: (*nearer*) I don't know anything about guns. Even what looks like— an Army revolver. Except that they're dangerous.
STEVE: Yes. I think I've heard that, somewhere.
JENNY: Especially when you put them...up to your head.
STEVE: Was I doing that? (*tries to laugh*) Yes! I guess I was. Funny. Hadn't meant to.
JENNY: No. Of course not.
(*Sound: not too loudly, as though heard from below, a train goes past with a thin scream from the whistle*)
STEVE: I'd better put the gun down. On the table.
(*Sound: the gun down*)
STEVE: There, (*sharply*) Excuse me; but *who*—?
JENNY: I'm nobody important. Truly! Just someone who's your friend. Or

wants to be. May I sit down?

STEVE: (*trying to recover*) Yes, of course, I'm not—very presentable. I've been on the Yorkshire Moors for a couple of weeks. (*dropping all pretense, fiercely*) You know why I had that gun at my head, don't you?

JENNY: Yes.

STEVE: You don't sound—very shocked.

JENNY: I'm scared, yes. I'm terrified to death for fear you'll pick it up again. But—all of us want to kill ourselves, at one time or another.

STEVE: Oh. (*pouncing*) Why? For what reason?

JENNY: Mostly for reasons that seem foolish, in a year or so.

STEVE: Then that's no good! It won't apply.

JENNY: Why won't it apply? (*appealing*) Tell me!

STEVE: I don't know how it is with women. But there's one thing no man can ever stand, if it's to go on for years and years.

JENNY: What is it that you can't stand?

STEVE: It's being laughed at. All your friends, all your enemies, up there like people in a theatre. Laughing till they can't stop.

JENNY: (*startled*) Laughing at *you*? Whoever laughed at *you*?

STEVE: Nobody has, yet. That's because I've gritted my teeth. But the funny part is—

JENNY: Go on!

STEVE: The funny part is: it's a comic story. I mean that! It honestly is!

JENNY: Why is it comic? Tell me!

STEVE: (*blankly*) Well... can you imagine something?

JENNY: Of course I can!

STEVE: (*far away*) Imagine you're on an island. Just a little handkerchief of an island. You're lying face up; both legs broken; you think it's your back that's broken. Plane smashed, but no fire. Just lying there. Looking up at the sky. Alone. A night, then a day. Then—

JENNY: Go on!

STEVE: First some Jap fighter-planes went over. On a mission. They weren't trying to kill me, they knew I'd die anyway. They were just having some fun; not even using much ammunition. They dived; and dived; and kept on diving.

JENNY: Go on!

STEVE: They must have passed the word to their friends. By the second day, it was quite an amusement-center. I could hear the bullets everywhere except on *me*. Diving. Diving out of all that open sky, straight down in your face. By the third day...

JENNY: That's enough! I think I understand.

STEVE: Oh, no! You don't, There's one particular noise a plane makes when it dives. It's...

(*Sound: a train, as though underneath, comes up under this speech. Its whistle*

becomes the scream and whine of a diving plane.)
STEVE: I can't go outdoors. Unless it's in a taxi or something enclosed. If an attack comes on, I'm apt to run berserk.
JENNY: And you had one of these attacks tonight?
STEVE: Yes! At the station. If it hadn't been for that police-superintendent and his handcuffs... Look here, who *are* you? Why am I telling you all this?
JENNY: It's because you know I sympathize. With every nerve of me! You don't know *why* you know it; but you do! Isn't that true.
STEVE: (*surprised*) Yes! Yes, it *is* true!
JENNY: Come and sit beside me. On the sofa.—That's it!
STEVE: What's your name? Tell me your first name, anyway!
JENNY: It's Jenny.
STEVE: (*testing it*) Jenny! (*moved*) I apologize for all this, Jenny. You see, I can't help it.
JENNY: Do you think I don't know that?
STEVE: If I ever heard *real* planes diving again, I think I'd... What's the matter?
JENNY: (*horrified*) Then you didn't see the posters—
STEVE: What posters?
JENNY: (*hurriedly*) None! None at all.—Steve, couldn't the R.A.F. doctors help you?
STEVE: Yes. They cured me completely.
JENNY: Cured you completely?
STEVE: Yes. I was discharged from one of those convalescent places, mentally fit and well, over 18 months ago. At least, I thought I was cured.
JENNY: (quickly) What did you do then?
STEVE: But afterwards I wanted to make doubly sure. I went to a first-rate psychologist in Harley Street. Fine fellow; old friend of mine. Hubert Lodge.
JENNY: *Hubert... Lodge*? Is he a qualified medical man?
STEVE: I don't think so, but why?
JENNY: Listen! A while ago Dia—a friend of ours asked for a trunk-call to Hubert Lodge.

(*Music: sneak for transition*)
JENNY: They must be speaking now. I wonder what they're saying?
DIANA: (*in difficulties*) Hubert! This is Diana. *Diana.* I said I'm in a telephone-box at the Metropole Ho... Can you hear me?
(*Sound: the buzzing and dimming of a bad telephone-line, heard on filter, die away.*)
LODGE: (*filter through*) Hear you perfectly, my dear.
DIANA: Ah, that's better!—Hubert. This is going to be awfully sudden. But...

do you still want me to marry you as much as you did two years ago?
LODGE: (*slight pause*) More than I did then, Diana. More than I did then.
DIANA: Then... oh, I can't talk over the 'phone! But—All right Hubert.
LODGE: (*faint triumph*) Life is very good to me, Diana. (*pause*) What about—Stephen West?
DIANA: Hubert, if you could only *see* him! He... (*remembering*)... Wait! Don't you two know each other? Weren't you friends, once?
LODGE: Ye-es! Yes, indeed! I was very fond of Steve. Haven't seen him for years, though. (*casually*) How is he, by the way?
DIANA: Oh, let's forget Steve! He's *here*! At this hotel!
LODGE: Is he, now? Very interesting!
DIANA: Anyway, Hubert, I'm taking the ten-fifteen train. Could you be *terribly* sweet and meet the train at Euston in the morning?
LODGE: Stay where you are, my dear. I shall come up there and fetch you back in triumph.
DIANA: Hubert darling, that's what I *call* being gallant!
LODGE: We-ell! It's partly business, I have a patient in Birchespool now.
DIANA: Hubert, you're not going to spoil everything by seeing one of those tiresome patients?
LODGE: It will be brief, my dear. The patient's condition is quite satisfactory. But just one more treatment, I think! Just one more treatment!

(*Music: transition in and fades out behind*)
(*Sound: rattle and whistle of a train*)
STEVE: Jenny, what's the use asking me about Lodge's methods? They were different from the R.A.F. doctor's. More up-to-date, probably. He's a *friend* of mine.
JENNY: I wonder... Did you ever tell any of this to Diana?
STEVE: No, of course not! (*suddenly*) What do *you* know about Diana?
JENNY: Never mind! *Why* didn't you tell her?
STEVE: Diana's not the sort of girl you can bother with idiocy like this!
JENNY: And that's why you've got to think it's funny! And that's what's killing you!
STEVE: There's nothing killing me, Jenny. Except... look around! Four walls. Four walls, always there. If you go out, you think you hear planes diving. That's why the walls are unbreakable. They'll never fall down.
JENNY: Isn't there something in the Bible about the walls of a whole city falling down?
STEVE: Yes. (*laughs*) Funny! Did I ever tell you... no, of course I didn't! But my father was a Presbyterian minister. I could recite hundreds of pages from the King James's version.
JENNY: Then you *do* remember the story?
STEVE: Joshua and the walls of Jericho? Naturally! But you can't get help from

a legend out of somebody's imagination.
JENNY: *This* is in your imagination.
STEVE: (*taken aback; then recovering*) It's not the same thing. (*bitterly*) The Powers That Be won't even give *me* a shock.
JENNY: A 'shock?' What do you mean?
STEVE: Colonel Williams—that was the R.A.F. doctor—said *his* cure took some time. But he said if I ever got a terrific emotional shock, something that wiped the fear-business out of my mind even for two minutes, I'd never fear it again. (*grimly*) That's funny too.
JENNY: Steve! Don't go near that table! Please don't go near that table!
STEVE: The gun, you mean? I was only picking it up, that's all! No harm in that!
JENNY: Won't you come back and sit down? *Won't you*?
STEVE: (*quoting*) 'And Joshua said unto the people—' What's next? Can't remember. Anyway, no walls of Jericho here. Four walls. After a few years, the walls look like faces; four faces. That's madness. Then death.
JENNY: Did your friend Lodge tell you that?
STEVE: Excuse me, Jenny. I'm going into the other room and lie down.
JENNY: Before you do, will you give me that revolver?
STEVE: No.
JENNY: I thought you might, Steve, if I asked it for a—for a purely selfish reason.
STEVE: Selfish reason?
JENNY: Yes. I love you. (*quickly*) That doesn't matter! That's not important. (*in tears*) But I thought you *might*: if I were selfish enough.
(*Sound: long pause. Revolver rattles on table.*)
STEVE: There's the gun, Jenny. Good night…
JENNY: Steve! Wait! Steve!
(*Sound: the door opens and closes, off.*)
JENNY: I forgot to warn you…
BELLMAN: (*moving on*) To warn him about the air-pageant? *I* shouldn't.
JENNY: (*crying out*) Who are *you*?
BELLMAN: Superintendent Bellman, miss. City police, I expect you didn't hear me come in by the corridor door?
JENNY: No! No, I didn't!
BELLMAN: *You* got in with the maid's key, they tell me. Never mind! I've listened at the switchboard to a very rum 'phone call. I've also listened to you and Mr. West. You're a fine lass, miss. Would you risk that fellow's life in a try at helping him?
JENNY: *Can* you help Steve?
BELLMAN: (*heavily*) I don't know. It might kill him.
JENNY: If you've got any hope for Steve, tell him so!
BELLMAN: I can't tell him, Miss! That's a part of the trick!

JENNY: (*tensely*) Maybe I can guess, a little, what this trick is. When would you try it?
BELLMAN: Tomorrow morning!

(*Music: in and fades out behind*)
FABIAN: Monday morning. Eleven a.m. "Spitfires and Hurricanes will dive as low over our city as municipal safety permits." Outside the Imperial Suite, a red-carpeted corridor leading towards carpeted stairs to the roof. Inside the suite, in the drawing-room by one of the three wide-open windows, stand two conspirators…

JENNY: Superintendent, where is Steve?
BELLMAN: In the bedroom, Miss. He won't come out 'till I tell him *Or until*…
JENNY: Listen!
(*Sound: very faintly, the throb of massed aircraft a long distance away and travelling at comparatively slow speed. Very slowly this noise grows a little louder as the scene continues*)
JENNY: (*cue*) It's the first wave of planes. You can barely hear them!
BELLMAN: They're coming up from Plymouth, Miss.
JENNY: And you *haven't* told Steve! And…what if this trick doesn't work?
BELLMAN: Then we're *for* it, Miss. But I'm waiting, I'm just waiting, for a knock on that corridor-door…
(*Sound: rapping on door, light but authoritative.*)
JENNY: Yes? Come in!
(*Sound: the door opens and remains open.*)
LODGE: (*off, cheerfully*) Good morning!
BELLMAN: (*restraining himself*) Morning, sir.
LODGE: (*approaching*) Er—I do hope I'm not in the wrong suite. My name is Lodge, Hubert Lodge. I'm looking for a patient of mine: Mr. West.
BELLMAN: You can't see Mr. West. Not yet.
LODGE: Indeed, sir? And by whose authority?
BELLMAN: *My* authority. I'm a police-officer.
LODGE: Come! Has the poor devil got himself into trouble? That's *most* unfortunate!
JENNY: Yes. *Isn't* it unfortunate?
LODGE: One moment! Don't I hear planes getting nearer. (*Pleased*) Yes! Yes, I do. Mr. West may need me soon. If he does, I shall be up on the roof. Hotel guests, I believe, are forbidden to go on the roof because of blitz-damage. Still! I think I shall…
BELLMAN: (*sharply*) Better stay where you are—Doctor, Didn't you *say* 'Doctor?'
LODGE: My good man! No! (*condescending*) In some ways, of course, I have the greatest respect for the medical profession. But…

JENNY: *But they don't deliberately kill people? As you do?*
LODGE: (*slight pause*) Young lady, are you out of your mind?
JENNY: No! But Steve nearly is. That's what *you* did.
BELLMAN: Easy, Miss! Better let *me* handle this!
JENNY: (*unheeding*) You took everything they'd taught Steve, and reversed it. You taught him fear, fear, fear. Always and always. Over, and over. Month after month. Then you sent him up to the Yorkshire Moors, to all the open spaces. That was murder.
LODGE: Do you know, young lady, you're talking slander?
BELLMAN: Is she, Mr. Lodge? Did you ever hear of a man named Colonel Williams? In the R.A.F.?
LODGE: There's a distinguished analyst named *Doctor* Williams. Why?
BELLMAN: Colonel Williams is in that room—over there!—telling young West what we're telling you. And why did you do it, Mr. Lodge? Just to get West's girl away from him!
LODGE: That's a lie!
JENNY: Diana! Come in from the corridor! Diana!
DIANA: (*fading on, badly frightened*) Don't blame *me*. I don't know what's been happening!
BELLMAN: We know that, Miss Borden, Do *you* think this is true?
DIANA: I *did* promise to marry Hubert, yes. But...
BELLMAN: Anybody can cheat young West, Mr. Lodge. Anybody he thinks is his friend. What was the blasted rubbish you told him?
JENNY: 'The walls look like faces, four faces. Then madness. Then death."
BELLMAN: He could break you in three pieces, Mr. Lodge, It's a good thing he can't hear what I'm saying!
(*Sound: the door opens, off*)
STEVE: (*slow, heavy, as though half-drugged*) Don't worry, Superintendent, I could hear what you said.
JENNY: (*crying out*) Steve!
LODGE: (*heartily*) West, my dear fellow! It's a pleasure to see... (*tone changing*)...to see...
BELLMAN: There he is, Mr. West. Walk towards him. Easy; slow steps, that's it!
LODGE: You! The police-officer!—This man's insane! Look at his eyes! He's insane!
BELLMAN: Oh, no! Just what they call 'emotional shock.'
LODGE: (*pulling himself together*) I'm not afraid of you, West. Don't you hear the planes overhead? Don't you hear? (*suddenly*) Why don't you look where I'm pointing?
BELLMAN: Sudden... emotional... shock.
LODGE: (*voice fading backwards*) There's one place you won't follow me, West. Up on the roof. You don't dare. Listen! You can't face it. You...
BELLMAN: (*fiercely*) (*close to mike*) They're out in the corridor, Miss Jenny!

Come on! Follow!
JENNY: (*fiercely*) What if Steve kills him?
BELLMAN: It's not that! The test comes when those fighter planes start to dive. Come on... softly, now!.... over to the door. There!
JENNY: (*hypnotized*) Along the red carpet—look at them! towards the stairs to the roof...
LODGE: (*calling, off*) You can't stick it, West. That's why I'm backing away and keeping my eyes on you. You'll crumple up. You'll scream. You'll cry for help.
(*Sound: against a not-too-loud background of throbbing bombers, a fighter-plane dives steeply and sheers off. Then another*)
BELLMAN: Go on, lad! You were muttering all night about the walls of Jericho! Go on!
LODGE: (*nerve breaking*) I'm climbing up these stairs, mind! It's worse up there. They'll dive in your face. They'll... why don't you speak? Why don't you *stop*!
BELLMAN: Up to the roof, Miss! Follow 'em! Come on!
(*Sound: the plane-throb grows louder, as though microphone is moving up on roof. More fighters dive and sheer off*)
BELLMAN: Mind the step, Miss, This is the top!
JENNY: I can't *see!* The sun's in my eyes!
BELLMAN: (*grimly*) He hasn't touched Lodge, Miss. He's just—looking up. Dazed-like. There!
JENNY: (*terrified*) Does that mean he—?
BELLMAN: It's worked! *He's waving to the planes.*
JENNY: (*calling out*) Steve!
BELLMAN: Mind your step on the roof, now!
JENNY: Steve, you're free! You needn't be afraid any longer!
(*Sound: the plane rises and shears off*)
JENNY: What are you thinking? What is it?
STEVE: (*pause*) (*slowly*) 'And Joshua said unto the people, Shout!—for the Lord hath given you the city.'
(*Sound: the fighter plane dives and shears off*)
(*Music: in and behind*)
(*Sound: ship's whistles*)
(*Music: fades out*)

Notes for the Curious

It is likely that "Death Has Four Faces", John Dickson Carr's third *Cabin B-13* play, was inspired at least in part by his experience fire-watching during the second world war.

On several occasions Carr took part in the fire-watch in Bristol and London, including on the roof of Broadcasting House, the headquarters of the BBC, where the fire-watchers' role was to extinguish any fires started by German incendiary bombs.

It is also likely that Steve West, a Canadian playwright R.A.F. who has "*lived in London for years*" is based in part on Carr. While West is an R.A.F. fighter pilot, Carr's main contribution to the war effort was the many propaganda plays he wrote for the BBC. These were so effective that they led the BBC, unsuccessfully, to urge the American authorities to allow Carr to remain in the United Kingdom for the duration of the war.

Curiously, "Death Has Four Faces" is not related to Carr's earlier play of this title—broadcast in the fourth series of the BBC program *Appointment with Fear*—However, the *Cabin B-13* play does have a minor element in common with *Appointment with Fear*. This is "I Never Suspected", first broadcast on 5 October, 1944. Carr clearly liked the title, a quote from Islamic theology, and he had planned to use a variant of it for a novel in 1935.

The street names and other references in this play appear to suggest that Carr saw "Birchespool" as an amalgam of three of the largest cities outside London, Birmingham, Manchester and Liverpool. However, he *may* also have had in mind that, in Sir Arthur Conan Doyle's epistolary novel *The Stark Munro Letters* (1895), several of the letters are addressed from Birchespool, which Conan Doyle describes as a spa town in the North of England with a population of a hundred and thirty thousand, noted for its "*lamp-posts and curb-stones*" as well as its main newspaper, *The Birchespool Post*.

Bellman's curious phrase "*a mort o' brass*" is seventeenth century British slang for a large amount of money.

The Blind-Folded Knife Thrower

(*Sound: a ship's whistle*)
(*Sound: thud of a knife*)
(*Music: in and behind*)
ANNOUNCER: *Cabin B-13.* Tonight: "The Blindfolded Knife-Thrower".
FABIAN: Yes, the *Maurevania's* engines churn slowly now. Up the broad Tagus River at last; that's Lisbon close at hand. From a distance it looked white, didn't it? Terraced up on all its hills, against waxy green foliage? Now the morning sun catches a sparkle from all those little colored house-tiles.
(*Sound: a voice calling for someone*)
FABIAN: It was only some passenger in the corridor, calling her mother to go on deck and watch the colored sails of the fishing boats. But to me, Doctor Fabian of Cabin B-13, it brought back a grim and evil memory of what befell Madeline Lane on a previous voyage. It was many years ago, before the air-clippers landed at Cabo Ruivo. Lisbon—clean as washed tiles luxuriant as its own gardens—was quieter then. The *Maurevania* had docked, the passengers gone ashore. I was following them when… I went back, and the door opened.
(*Music: fades out*)

MADELINE: (*guilty, as though caught*) Doctor Fabian!
FABIAN: Good morning, Miss Lane.
(*Sound: tug whistle*)
MADELINE: (*trying a light tone*) Couldn't you call me Madeline, Doctor? After all, we've been sitting at your table in the dining room for the whole voyage.
FABIAN: That glass cabinet, Madeline…
MADELINE: (*pretending*) This one?
FABIAN: (*lightly*) Yes. It contains bottles of drugs, many of them dangerous. Will you let me have the small bottle there, Madeline?....Thank you. Now open your *right* hand, please.
MADELINE: Don't be angry with me, Doctor Fabian! It's…
FABIAN: Two quarter-grain tablets, I see.
MADELINE: I didn't mean any harm! That's not enough to *hurt* anybody, is it?
FABIAN: No, Madeline. But you're not addicted to this—medicine, why do you want it?
MADELINE: I want it…for my mother.
FABIAN: Your mother?
MADELINE: Yes! It's true! If only you understood!
FABIAN: You're—joining your mother here in Portugal?

MADELINE: Yes! That's true too! But *they* don't understand, either!
FABIAN: You mean: the other people in your party?
MADELINE: Yes! I mean my father, and Doris Leighton, and even Phil. They don't know and I can't tell them! (*trying to be humorous*) Now *you're* going to preach a sermon, I suppose?
FABIAN: I never preach sermons, Madeline; or I should have to begin with myself. How did you get in here? Was the door unlocked?
MADELINE: Yes! I didn't...break in!
FABIAN: Then we'll just drop these tablets back into the bottle, like this; put the bottle back on the shelf...
(*Sound: Clink of bottle on glass shelf*)
FABIAN: ...close the cabinet door; and say no more about it. But you're staying in Lisbon for some time, I understand. If you *should* need help...
MADELINE: What makes you think I'd need help?
FABIAN: I'm not being gallant, Madeline, when I say you're something more than attractive. That combination of fair hair and dark eyes...
MADELINE: They say I look like my mother. Only... (*she stops*) Go on!
FABIAN: You have a delicacy, a fastidiousness!... it sounds intangible in words. This fiancé of yours...Philip... what is it?
MADELINE: Stanley. Philip Stanley. I—love him very much.
FABIAN: And he's a thoroughly good fellow! But he's a painter; imaginative; just as unworldly as you are.
LANE: (*calling off*) Madeline! Madeline!
FABIAN: Isn't that your father calling?
MADELINE: Yes! (*calling:*) I'm here, Dad! (*low voice*) What were you telling me, Doctor Fabian?
FABIAN: (*not loudly*) Nothing to alarm you. But I wish you'd go and meet a friend of mine. His name is Colonel Da Silva, at the Hall of Justice in the Rossio. He...
LANE: (*fading on*) Madeline! My dear! (*amused but chiding*) What kind of game is *this*, now? I've been looking all over the ship for you.
MADELINE: I'm terribly sorry, Dad! I was only saying good-bye to Doctor Fabian!
LANE: Then run along, my dear! Phil and Doris are down on the quay. Go along, now; and I'll follow.
MADELINE: Of course, Dad! (*moving off*) Good-bye, Doctor Fabian!
FABIAN: Good-bye, Miss Lane.
LANE: (*wryly*) Ah.... did Madeline come too?
FABIAN: Consult me, Mr. Lane? No, No, I shouldn't say that.
LANE: That's good; that's very good! What did you talk about?
FABIAN: Not a great deal, actually. She spoke of her mother; and joining her mother here in Lisbon, and...
LANE: (*appalled*) *Joining her mother? Here in Lisbon?*

FABIAN: Yes. Why not? What's wrong?
LANE: Her mother has been dead for ten years.

> (*Music: in and behind*)

FABIAN: Lisbon, towards dusk. Up and beyond the great square called the Rossio, beyond even the glittering *Avenida da Liberdade*, lies the residential section. There, at nightfall, it is quiet. In a little garden, hemmed in by eucalyptus trees and heavy with the scent of roses...
(*Music: fades out*)

MADELINE: Do you understand now, Phil? *Do you?*
PHIL: (*groping*) I understand a good deal, Madeline. It's just that... I don't know what to say!
MADELINE: He thinks I'm out of my mind. (*quietly*) Do *you* think so, Phil?
PHIL: No, of course not! But... Your mother! All these years! I never guessed you felt—
MADELINE: (*calmly vehement*) I hated her. I've always hated her. Just as she hated me!
PHIL: Madeline! Easy!
MADELINE: (*pleading*) Does that shock you, Phil? Do you think I'm hateful, and without any feeling? But I can't help it!
PHIL: Of course you can't!
MADELINE: (*shaken*) She was—"the gay Mrs. Lane." She didn't want children. She wanted to be the gay Mrs. Lane; blonde and beautiful; always and always. When I was a child she only disliked me. Later ... I didn't understand. (*pleading*) I was only thirteen or fourteen. How could I understand?
PHIL: (*wretched*) Don't go over it again! You'll only upset yourself.
MADELINE: Later she started taking drugs to keep up her gaiety. At the least thing, even if you only knocked a spoon off the dinner-table, she'd fly into a rage. Finally she killed herself.
(*Sound: off, an old-fashioned street-car, with clanging bell, is heard and lumbers past.*)
MADELINE: (*tensely*) Shall I tell you *exactly* what happened the day mother died? Mother was in her dressing-room that day. Sitting in front of a mirror, trying to put on lipstick so the lipstick wouldn't show. Mr. Leighton...
PHIL: Any relation to Doris Leighton in our party?
MADELINE: Yes! Doris's father. They lived next door.
PHIL: This was when— 1919?
MADELINE: Yes, Mr. Leighton brought back a revolver from overseas. Mother was terrified of noises. She made him promise not to fire it near the house. He must have forgotten. Anyway—next door, while mother was sitting in front of that mirror—he fired two shots.

PHIL: And then?
MADELINE: Mother shivered: just once. Her eyes, in the mirror, went—blank. As though the soul had gone. She said … very casually, it was… "I can't stand this." She got up and went into the bedroom. *I* didn't realize anything, and her maid didn't, until we heard her scream.
PHIL: You heard her … (*stops*) What had she done?
MADELINE: She swallowed a bottle of something with acid in it. She might have lived for a while, in agony. But the shock of pain killed her. She was lying beside the bureau, with the red acid-burns round her mouth.
PHIL: (*low-voiced*) I never knew she killed herself.
MADELINE: We're big people in a little city. Dad got it all hushed up as a heart attack.
PHIL: And…afterwards?
MADELINE: After she died, Phil, I cried all night. I was frantic.
PHIL: Then that proves you're wrong, doesn't it? You must have had *some* affection for her!
MADELINE: I don't know.—Anyway, about two weeks later I woke up in the middle of the night. And I thought I saw her standing at the foot of the bed. Looking at me. With hate.
PHIL: Madeline, It was your imagination!
MADELINE: Yes. I think it was. At that time.
PHIL: But not—now?
MADELINE: No. Not now. I told you a while ago: she's getting closer. She writes notes in the dark, and whispers to me when I'm half asleep. She's coming to take me with her.
PHIL: Have you ever…*seen* her?
MADELINE: No, Not yet. When I do see her, that will be the end.
PHIL: Listen! How long has this…let's say persecution… been going on?
MADELINE: Just under a year.
PHIL: *And you've never said a word to anybody*?
MADELINE: Only in my diary. But *she* reads that.
PHIL: Madeline, stop talking about her as though she were alive!
MADELINE: She is alive. To me. (*changing tone*)
PHIL: Look, Madeline! There's an obvious explanation; someone's playing tricks. Hadn't that occurred to you?
MADELINE: Of course. It's my only hope. But don't you see?
PHIL: If it's a trick, I'll prove it is! So help me, I will.
MADELINE: (*almost in tears*) We *could* be happy, couldn't we?
PHIL: We *will* be happy!
MADELINE: I can't reason; I can only feel. Sometimes I think Doris Leighton is…(*breaking off*) Listen!
PHIL: What's wrong?
MADELINE: Somebody's getting into the garden. Can you see who it is?
PHIL: *I* never saw the fellow before! Portuguese; very—distinguished-look-

ing.

MADELINE: Phil! Speak to him!

PHIL: (*breaking down, querulously*) How the devil do you say, "Is there anything you want?" in Portugese?

DA SILVA: (*agreeably, moving on*) Merely say, "Is there anything you want?" That will suffice.

MADELINE: (*surprised*) You speak English?

DA SILVA: Alas for pride! When I took my degree at Cambridge, Miss Lane, I believed myself almost fluent. (*changing tone: gravely*) Stop! I ask your pardon.

MADELINE: Pardon? Of course. But for what?

DA SILVA: That was a dig at your complacence. And I don't wish our acquaintance to begin with insults.

PHIL: (*half-amused*) *Are* we getting acquainted, then?

DA SILVA: May-I-join-your-party-I-thank you. If I call myself C*o*ronel Da Silva, please pronounce it as Colonel Da Silva.

MADELINE: Colonel Da Silva! I've heard that name!

DA SILVA: From Doctor Fabian of the *Maurevania*, no doubt?

MADELINE: Yes! That was it!

DA SILVA: If I add that I am *Chefe da Policia Secreta*, please don't think it means "secret police" In Portugal it means only—Chief of Detectives.

PHIL: Chief of Detectives!

DA SILVA: Yes. This young man in the white suit, I take it, is Mr. Philip Stanley? The painter?

PHIL: (*bitterly*) Painter! That's a good one!

MADELINE: Phil, don't *talk* that way!

PHIL: I'm bad at oils and worse at watercolor. Ask any critic. (*as though seeing relationship*) A bad watercolor! That's me.

MADELINE: Colonel Da Silva, excuse me: but—what do you want?

DA SILVA: I want the answer to one question.

MADELINE: Then ask it, please! I'm afraid we've got to go!

DA SILVA: Ah, yes! Your father has rented a villa. Of great elegance, and Moorish design. But I fear you will have a noisy neighbor.

PHIL: A noisy neighbor?

DA SILVA: (*sardonically amused*) We-el! He is a fat man with a pretty wife. They call him the Great Gaspar; at the Grand Theatre they idolize him. He is a knife-thrower.

PHIL: (*not Amused*) Only professionally, I hope?

DA SILVA: (*unheeding: acting it*) His wife, in costume or lack of it, stands against a wooden target. The drums roll. The knives thud. The ladies scream. And he throws—blindfolded.

MADELINE: (*slowly*) The blindfolded knife-thrower.

DA SILVA: Yes, I could draw a parable from that. But let me ask my question, Miss Madeline.—How long have you been hoarding drug tablets?

PHIL: (*pause: crying out*) Hoarding drug-tablets?
MADELINE: It's true, Phil. I didn't tell you; but it's true. I suppose, Colonel Da Silva, you've seen Doctor Fabian?
DA SILVA: Doctor Fabian, like my humble self, is one who wishes only to help you. You were *hoarding the tablets.*
PHIL: Wait a minute! Hoarding them for what?
DA SILVA: When she comes face to face with an evil spirit, when she *knows* it exists, she will poison herself. Yes?
MADELINE: Yes. How did you know that?
DA SILVA: A simple deduction. And, of course, in listening to your conversation a few minutes ago, I...
MADELINE: You listened to what...?
PHIL: Haven't you got a devil of a nerve to—
DA SILVA: Be silent! You are children! (*pause: kindly*) I can show my teeth, you see. But also I can smile. Let me persuade you to be sensible, Miss Lane. These drug tablets. You must have too many of them now...give then into *my* keeping.
MADELINE: No! And you can't find it, either! I'm sorry, Phil!
DA SILVA: When you meet this evil spirit, what do you expect to see?
MADELINE: She will look real and solid, as she did in life. But the face chalk-white. The eye sockets blackened with death; And the acid burns round her mouth.
DA SILVA: When do you expect to see her?
MADELINE: A note from her aboard ship. Scrawled in lipstick. It said...
DA SILVA: *When* do you expect to see her?
MADELINE: I expect to see her...tonight!

(*Music: hits hard, and continues in a low sinister note.*)
FABIAN: The blindfolded knife-thrower.
(*Sound: through music, the thud of a heavy knife into wood*)
FABIAN: Centuries ago, the Moors left Portugal. Yet their influences remain. White houses, with barred windows and wrought-iron balconies. Cool courtyards, murmurous with fountains. In one such house tonight *Senor* Gaspar, like fate or *destiny,* practices his skill.
(*Sound: thud of knife, still through music*)
FABIAN: In the house next door, separated from it only by a paved alleyway, look into the back bedroom on the ground floor. Note the old-fashioned full-length pier-glass on castors, the one electric light on a table beside the bed. The one light burns, Madeline Lane.
(*Music: fades out*)

(*Sound: off, clash-clang notes of clock very slow, in time to speech.*)
MADELINE: Nine... ten... eleven.

(*Sound: off, knocking on door*)
MADELINE: Yes? Who is it?
PHIL: (*muffled*) It's me! Phil! Can I come in?
MADELINE: Yes, of course!
(*Sound: door opens and closes*)
MADELINE: Phil, I don't like your look. All grim and—come over here...that's it. Sit down on the edge of the bed.
PHIL: (*suppressed emotion*) Look, Madeline.
MADELINE: Yes?
PHIL: I—don't know whether you meant everything you said in that garden.
MADELINE: (*unable to face him*) I don't know myself.
PHIL: But we're going to *prove*, tonight, that somebody's playing tricks on you.
MADELINE: Prove it? How?
PHIL: Look 'round the room. Solid walls. Solid floor and ceiling. No fireplace. Two windows, so closely barred that you couldn't even get your hand through. You see that?
MADELINE: Yes! But...
PHIL: Now look at the door: (*forestalling objection*) I know you can't lock it! There's only the bronze handle. José and I are going to sit outside that door until morning. Now do you understand?
MADELINE: Yes. I understand.
PHIL: This room will be sealed up like a bank vault. Windows barred; door watched. No living person can possibly get in!
MADELINE: *That* part of it is true, anyway!
PHIL: So if *nothing* happens in the night, if *no* acid-burned corpse comes to grab you and—
(*Sound: off but loud, thud of knife in wood*)
PHIL: There's that knife-thrower next door!
(*Sound: thud of knife*)
PHIL: Madeline-angel, does that rumpus bother you?
MADELINE: (*trying to laugh*) No. Not really. But I wish he'd throw knives in a series. So you don't wait and wait for the next one. Like... *this* waiting.
PHIL: We'll settle it! José and I ...
MADELINE: Who *is* José? One of the servants?
PHIL: No. Colonel Da Silva sent him.
MADELINE: Colonel Da Silva?
PHIL: Yes. José is a five-foot Hercules who hasn't had a haircut for six months. But he's all right, Da Silva says. We can trust him.
MADELINE: Suppose... something *does* happen?
PHIL: It won't, I tell you!
MADELINE: Listen, Phil, About those tablets. (*pause*) I did mean to take them, yes. But I won't, whatever happens, if *you* believe in me. Or try to. Just try to! If you ever turn away from... no; let's forget that! I get all sorts of silly

notions. (*suddenly*) You're not in love with Doris Leighton, are you?
PHIL: In love with ... *Doris Leighton*?
MADELINE: I tried to mention it in the garden tonight; but I couldn't. You're not, are you?
PHIL: Lord Almighty, No!
MADELINE: She's in love with you. (*silencing him*) Oh, Phil! Any woman can tell that. Doris is so—vivacious! Just as my mother was, only Doris is a brunette. Doris—
(*Sound: off, door opens*)
DORIS: (*off*) Did somebody mention my name?
PHIL: Oh. Hello, Doris. Come on in.
DORIS: Thanks. I will.
(*Sound: door closes.*)
DORIS: (*off*) But—darlings! Really, now! I mean to say!
PHIL: (*rather snappishly*) What's the matter, Doris?
DORIS: (*fading on*) Your late-night-visiting is very unusual I'd say. (off handedly) But then I would. (*ecstatic*) Isn't this house absolutely *marvelous*?
PHIL: It has its advantages. Yes.
DORIS: I love it! Even if there is only one light to each room! And... do you know why the Moors put fancy bars on these windows? It was to keep the men out and the women in. I mean: their lack of control must have been absolutely *thrilling*. Look at the window on each side of Madeline's bed!
PHIL: (*grimly*) I've looked at 'em, thanks.
DORIS: Gorgeous moonlight, too! If anybody got in there...
PHIL: (*very sharply*) Nobody can, Doris! Nobody can!
DORIS: Look, you two. What's wrong?
MADELINE: (*drowsy now*) There's nothing wrong, Doris! Really there isn't!
DORIS: Oh, yes, there is. It's panic. It catches somebody. Then it's contagious. Madeline's father is sitting upstairs like a—like an old ghost in eyeglasses. (*sympathetically*) Madeline, dear! You worry too much. You take after your father.
MADELINE: (*laughs, drowsily*) I'm all right! It's only that—I'm getting terribly sleepy.
PHIL: Wait a minute! You didn't—*take* anything except the sedative.
MADELINE: No! I only laughed because... you see, Dad isn't my real father.
DORIS: (*astonished*) Not your real father?
MADELINE: No. Step-father. Not that it matters. Nobody in the world could be kinder than Dad's been.
DORIS: (*on edge*) He's kind enough! But he's a rotten bad host!
MADELINE: It's my fault, Doris.
DORIS: I put on this new evening-gown...where's-the-big mirror? Over in the corner; never-mind; who cares?... I put it on to go and see the sights tonight. Now—panic. It catches you. And you don't know why!

(*Sound: three knife thuds*)
PHIL: Curse that infernal knife thrower!
DORIS: (*chiding*) Now! Darling!... You aren't going to blame our poor Gaspar, are you?
PHIL: Our poor... do you *know* him?
DORIS: Well! I like to get acquainted. (*rattling on*) He's a fat man who spikka da English and proud of it. Tomorrow he says, he'll give us a *real* show. In the passage between the houses. He'll throw a knife fifty feet. He'll...
PHIL: (*to quiet her*) Doris!
DORIS: (*pause; slowly*) I see. You don't... need me. Is that it?
PHIL: Thanks, Doris. No; I don't... need you. (*pause; then bedevilled*) Doris! Wait! I didn't mean...
(*Sound: door closes*)
PHIL: Madeline, I'm going to switch off this lamp. There's a bowl of water and a face cloth on the table. If it's warm in here...
MADELINE: (*faintly*) It's not warm. There's a breeze. (*sudden horror*) But if—
PHIL: José and I will be outside the door. *Nothing gets into this room*!

(*Music: hits hard; then sinks into eerie backing*)
FABIAN: (*thoughtfully*) "Nothing". A strong word.
(*Sound: knife-thud*)
FABIAN: Now, from eleven-thirty until nearly four in the morning, that bedroom door remains closed. Inside, Madeline Lane is restlessly sleeping. Outside, with a table drawn up in front of the door, Phil Stanley and José sit playing cards in a Moorish drawing-room with only one dim lamp hanging far from the table. Through the long hours, while the church-clocks clang and black depression clouds the mind...
(*Music: fades out*)

PHIL: (*tired*) José!
JOSÉ: Okay, *Senhor*?
PHIL: I still don't understand this game. Except that you always win. Isn't it *my* deal now?
JOSÉ: Okay! Dill!
PHIL: Thanks.
(*Sound: card pack rattles as it is straightened and shaped together on wood; then riffle of cards.*)
PHIL: Not a sound from in that room! Nothing at all. In another half-hour it'll be daylight. Then...
LANE: (*calling, off*) Phil! Phil Stanley!
PHIL: Easy, José! Don't reach for a knife! It's only Madeline's father!
LANE: (*fading on, near anger*) Phil, what's the meaning of this? What are you doing at this time in the morning?

PHIL: We're guarding Madeline, sir.

LANE: (*wary*) Guarding Madeline?

PHIL: Yes. At half past eleven she was just about asleep. I sent José next door, and he persuaded the knife-thrower to stop practicing. We've been here ever since. With ...

(*Sound: riffle of card pack*)

PHIL: These cards...

LANE: Phil, let me ask a straight question. We haven't dealt much with straight questions in our family. How much has Madeline told you?

PHIL: About your wife's insanity and suicide?

LANE: Yes.

PHIL: She's told me everything.

LANE: (*perturbed*) *I* should have told you. I intended to. But—the madness wasn't hereditary! Or so I thought. I'm not sure, *now*.

PHIL: Couldn't you have helped your wife, sir? Cured her? Even—put her under restraint?

LANE: (*quietly*) No. You see... I loved her.

(*Sound: riffle of card-pack.*)

PHIL: Yes. Sorry. I understand.

LANE: That's an old-fashioned view, I know. (*voice rising*) But if Madeline is insane, and let's face the fact she may be, would *you* have her put—under restraint?

PHIL: No. I wouldn't.

LANE: (*groping*) Why do these things happen, anyway? My wife killed herself because of a trifle. Poor old Bob Leighton, in the back yard next door, fired two revolver-shots at a tin-can in a sand-heap. And her brain snapped. Two revolver shots! A mere coincidence that couldn't happen again in a million...

(*Sound: off, a revolver shot. Pause; then another*)

PHIL: (*off balance*) Did those shots come from...?

LANE: (*blandly*) Yes. From the bedroom.

MADELINE: (*screaming, off*) Phil! Phil! *She's... here!*

PHIL: (*wildly*) Get that table away from the door!

(*Sound: rattle and bump of heavy table moved sideways.*)

JOSÉ: (*loudly; alert*) Okay, *senor*!

PHIL: Now listen, José. I've got the door-handle. When I open it, you stand in the doorway and don't let anybody out!

(*Sound: door opens*)

PHIL: Madeline! (*his voice slowly moves off, but is always audible*) There's still some moonlight. But I've got to grope across... round here... (*exclamation of pain*) bumping into furniture! Wait a minute!... round to the other side of the bed, where the lamp is...

LANE: (*calling*) What is it?

PHIL: The lamp won't work!—*Madeline*!
LANE: Let *me* go in there!
JOSÉ: You—stay—out.
PHIL: She's not hurt! She's fainted.—Mr. Lane, will you watch the door? José! Come forward and search the room!
JOSÉ : Okay, *Senor*! I look! I look good! I come over like dees...
(*Microphone follows José, so that we now hear Phil on*)
PHIL: Water! Face cloth! Here!
(*Sound: faint splashing of water*)
PHIL: Bathe her face. Gently! Don't miss any hiding-place, José! She's stirring a little... more water... It's all right, Madeline! Nothing can hurt you!
MADELINE: Phil! She was here! I saw her!
PHIL: Sit up... Put your arms round me... *Where* did you see her?
MADELINE: At the foot of the bed. With her face all—(*stops, shuddering*) And the acid-burns. She moved. She started to...
PHIL: JOSÉ! Is there anybody hidden in this room?
JOSÉ : No, *senor*! There ees—nobody!
PHIL: Mr. Lane! Did anybody get out the door?
LANE: No! (*he begins to fade on*) Madeline dear, this was all your imagination! You know that!
MADELINE: (*hysterical*) *She was here! In—dead—flesh! I saw her*!
LANE: (*low-voice but tensely*) The girl... *is* mad!

(*Music: up strongly and behind*)
FABIAN: Look now, as the morning sunlight illuminates fully the drawing-room where Phil and José last night sat on guard. A long room, tiled but carpeted, with three Moorish arches opening on a passage between this house and the next. A room filled now with emotion, with pleading, overshadowed by certain words spoken last night.
LANE: (*on filter*) The girl... *is* mad!
(*Music: out with a sting*)
MADELINE: I'm not, I tell you! (*pleading*) Doris! Don't you believe me?
DORIS: (*uneasy*) Well, dear! After all! I wasn't here, you know. *I* was upstairs asleep.
MADELINE: Yes. But don't you...(*flatly*) No. I can see by your face you don't. Dad! Don't *you*?
LANE: (*upset*) Madeline, listen! You know how fond I am of you...
MADELINE: That means you don't believe. and you said... Nevermind! (*alarmed*) Where's Phil?
LANE: He's only getting dressed, my dear. He'll be downstairs in a moment.
MADELINE: Phil Believes me! I know he does. If he didn't it would be... well, it would be the end.
DORIS: (*under her breath*) He'll have a lot to believe.

LANE: Yes, Madeline! That's true!

MADELINE: The windows are on either side of the bed. The upper part of the bed was shadowed, but you could see the lower part by moonlight. She was there. Glaring! Drawing back her burned lips and... No. You look away; you're uncomfortable; you pity me. And that means —I'm alone.

DA SILVA: (*fading on*) Not alone, Miss Lane. Not *altogether* alone!

MADELINE: Colonel Da Silva!

LANE: (*off ended*) Who are you, sir? What do you want here?

DA SILVA: Merely justice. Forgive my dramatic entrance—aren't all Latins like that?—through the front of the house. Forgive also the fact that your house is surrounded with police.

(*Sound: off, heavy knife-thud*)

DA SILVA: (*interested*) Come, now! Is the Great Gaspar at practice?

DORIS: Yes! And for heaven's sake, you people, don't walk out through those open arches!

LANE: (*fussed*) He's throwing knives in the passage, Doris?

DORIS: Yes; just outside. You can *see* the knife flash past when—

(*Sound: knife-thud.*)

DA SILVA: (*pleased*) And destiny, like a blindfolded knife-thrower, is as blind as we. Destiny would not hurt us; but the knife slips at times. And who knows whether the knife strikes the guilty or the innocent?

LANE: You believe in a world governed mainly by chance?

DA SILVA: Good as well as bad! Yes!—I don't, for instance, believe in an evil spirit who fires revolver-shots. No, no! Thank you! That is too much! (*slight pause*) *Someone*, yesterday, hired a wharf side thug to fire two shots *outside* Miss Lane's windows, at an arranged hour. It was to wake her, of course! To make her see... what she did see.

MADELINE: (*hope dawning*) Colonel Da Silva! Tell them! I'm not insane! I did see her!

DA SILVA: Oh, yes. You saw her.

(*Sound: knife-thud.*)

DA SILVA: I will solve your small problem. On evidence reported by José. You need only answer—*true* or *false.*

LANE: Ask your questions, then, Colonel.

DA SILVA: Miss Madeline Lane greatly resembles her mother as a young woman. (*sharply*) True or false?

MADELINE: True! I... told Doctor Fabian so.

DA SILVA: In that bedroom, over there, is a full-length looking-glass movable on castors. True or false?

DORIS: True! *I* noticed it!

DA SILVA: Mr. Philip Stanley, groping his way across a half-dark room, blundered into a misplaced piece of furniture at the foot of the bed. True or false?

LANE: *I'll* answer for Phil! True. But are you saying... it was the mirror? And

Madeline—saw her own face?
MADELINE: That couldn't be! That face...was horrible. Its colors...
DA SILVA: (*snapping it*) Will you hear my next question then?
LANE: Go on!
DA SILVA: Mr. Philip Stanley is a watercolor painter. *True or false?*
  (*Sound: heavy knife-thud.*)
DA SILVA: Center of the target!
MADELINE: Phil! You're there at the door! He says *you* did this! Come in and answer him!
DA SILVA: Yes, Mr. Stanley. Don't look so white. Answer true or false.
PHIL: I'll answer, all right.
DA SILVA: At eleven-thirty you sent José next door to see the knife-thrower. True or false?
PHIL: True! But...
DA SILVA: Miss Lane was in a drugged sleep. You made her face into a devil's mask, with child's water-colors. You carried the mirror to the foot of the bed. You disconnected the lamp. Then you closed the door before José returned. True or false?
PHIL: False! Every word of it!
DA SILVA: When your confederate fired the shots outside, you entered that bed room alone. True or false?
LANE: *I'll* tell you; true! (*realizing*) He carried that looking-glass back to the corner; we couldn't see him! Then he went to the head of the bed, in deep shadow...
DA SILVA: —and washed off the watercolor...oh, admirably! before witnesses who could hear, but couldn't see.
DORIS: I don't believe all this! Why should Phil do it?
DA SILVA: Can't *you* guess, Miss Doris Leighton?
DORIS: No! How could I?
DA SILVA: He built this whole cruel hoax—persecution, notes, whisperings—from family history and entries in her diary. If *he* ever ceased to believe in her, she would take poison and die. He would marry her for money. Then—'cease to believe,' Presently he would have money; and you too.
MADELINE: (*hysterical*) Stop it! Stop it! Stop it!
DA SILVA: (*badly shaken*) It is cruel hearing, Miss Lane. But the truth will set you free.
PHIL: You can't make any charge against me!
DA SILVA: As a personal matter, sir, I will shoot you dead if I can't! You see this police-whistle?
DORIS: Don't run, Phil! *Not towards the arches!* Gaspar is—
(*Sound: off, a knife thud which is not in wood.*)
PHIL: *screams, ending in a gurgle*
(*Sound: fall of body on flags*)

LANE: (*hypnotized*) Under the left shoulder blade. He doesn't even...move!
DORIS: It's horrible.
LANE: It's a judgment on him!
MADELINE: (*in tears*) No! It's only...
DA SILVA: Destiny. The blindfolded knife-thrower!
(*Music: up to curtain: then behind.*)

FABIAN: I was wrong, you see. I, Doctor Fabian, viewpoint as ship's surgeon of the Maurevania, thought Phil Stanley a fine young fellow. But it reminds me that there was a case, at Gibraltar, where I had the good fortune to solve a very ugly mystery. And so, next week when the Maurevania is at Gibraltar and I tell you the story of *No Useless Coffin,* will you join me in *Cabin B-13*?
(*Music: in and behind*)
(*Sound: ship's whistles*)
(*Music: fades out*)

Notes for the Curious

The fourth play is another original mystery though some elements of the plot hark back to *He Who Whispers* (1946). A few years later, Carr re-used the ploy by which Madeline's stepmother appears and disappears from within a locked room in the twentieth Sir Henry Merrivale novel *Night at the Mocking Widow* (1950).

The play's central device may well have been inspired by Carr's observations of the British actress June Whitfield and other members of the cast of the various theatre plays he wrote during the Second World War. The first of Carr's stage plays, initially called *Murder Takes the Air*, had been planned with Val Gielgud, then the BBC's director of drama. It featured Inspector Silence, a character created by Gielgud but which Carr had used in a short radio play "Inspector Silence Takes the Underground", first broadcast on 25 March 1942. In April 1942, the stage play, under its new title "Inspector Silence takes the Air", opened as a touring production but a planned transfer to London did not take place. Nonetheless, Carr enjoyed the experience and he and Gielgud wrote a second thriller, *Thirteen to the Gallows*; this also toured but again closed without transferring to the West End. Carr's final work for the theatre were two plays, which with a third by another playwright—were presented under the banner of Carr's great radio success for the BBC, *Appointment with Fear*.

Forgotten for many years, Carr's stage plays were eventually rediscovered, and the scripts have been collected in *Thirteen to the Gallows* (Crippen & Landru Publishers, 2008).

No Useless Coffin

(*Sound: a ship's whistle*)
(*Music: in and behind*)
FABIAN: Turn your field-glasses *there*. That's the Rock of Gibraltar, dawning grey on the port bow. If you remember: my name is Fabian, ship's surgeon, from Cabin B-13. Last night, in the *Maurevania's* lounge, I heard some passenger on our world-cruise say that Gib is dull. (*amused*) Dull! (*changing tone*) On that rock, with its naval base and its army-post and its racetrack, I once was present when a girl, Vicky Fraser, disappeared like a soap-bubble under the eyes of witnesses.
ANNOUNCER: CBS presents John Dickson Carr's famous Doctor Fabian, ship's surgeon, world traveler, and teller of strange and incredible tales of mystery and murder, directed by John Dietz.
(*Music: changes and suggests the theme of "Rule Britannia". Behind:*)
FABIAN: Gibraltar, 1938. (*slight pause*) As you got into a rattling motor-car, and they drive you up and up the paved winding road to the cliffs, the whole light-stung sea is spread out below. In the harbor, dull-grey except for the Union Jack painted on her hull, lies the British battle-ship *Frobisher*. If you tuned in to the far-off Italian radio, In this September of '38....
(*Music: fades out*)
(*Sound: on radio, heavy chanting of men's voices in a two-syllable word roared over and over, becoming in a second or too distinguishable as "Duce! Duce! Duce!"*)
FABIAN: The drive along those cliffs, towards Europa Bay. Somewhere, amid dwarf scrubs, is a white house whose rear balcony overlooks cliffs and sea. On that balcony, at mid-morning, we see a woman in a flowered summer dress, and a man in the uniform of the Royal Army Medical Corps.

BARTLETT: (*worried*) The question is, Cynthia.... will your friend agree to it?
CYNTHIA: (*on edge*) Jim, he's *got* to agree! After all, it's a simple request. And I—worded it strongly.
BARTLETT: Yes, Cynthia. Maybe too strongly.
CYNTHIA: (*more worried*) Jim, look over the ledge of the balcony! Far down to the right: that *is* the *Maurevania*?
BARTLETT: Three red-and-black funnels. White decks. Black hull. That's the *Maurevania*, right enough.
CYNTHIA: She's been in harbor for two hours!

BARTLETT: Take it easy, now! Your friend may have been delayed, you know!
CYNTHIA: (*attention distracted*) Jim.... look! Out at sea! Moving towards the breakwater!
BARTLETT: So! A battle-cruiser and two destroyers!
CYNTHIA: To join the *Frobisher* down there? (*significantly*) And bring—? (*she stops*)
BARTLETT: Must be. But.... Cynthia!
CYNTHIA: Yes, dear?
BARTLETT: (*lightly*) That battle-cruiser: The forward gun turrets are moving. Don't jump if they fire a broadside out to sea. They're only testing the guns.
CYNTHIA: (*Amused*) As though I didn't know! (*serious again*) But at the time of the Munich conference! (*quietly*) Jim, what's going to happen at Munich?
BARTLETT: Just what you think. If not at Munich, then next day. Or next week. Or next year. But sooner or later, Cynthia....
(*Sound: off, at sea, a full broadside of guns from the battle-cruiser*)
BARTLETT: Like that broadside.
CYNTHIA: (*as though she had hoped to be contradicted*) Yes. *I* know. I've been trying to get the Berlin radio all morning, but.... (*breaking off*).... Yes, Luigi? What is it?
LUIGI: (*fade in*) Gentleman to see you, Mess Drew. In a—white dress-uniform. He's call himself Doctor Fabian.
CYNTHIA: Doctor Fabian? Why didn't you let him in at once?
FABIAN: (*fading on*) I took the *liberty* of coming in, Cynthia. It's good to see an old friend again.
CYNTHIA: It's good to see *you*, Doctor Fabian. May I present my fiancé, Captain Bartlett?
FABIAN: Fiancé? Many congratulations, Captain Bartlett!—You're medical corps, I see.
BARTLETT: Yes; I'm a poor-devil Army surgeon. But I know how lucky I am, with Cynthia.
FABIAN: Was that why you summoned *me* in such a hurry, Cynthia? To tell the good news?
CYNTHIA: (*bursting out*) No, of course not! That is—I mean—
FABIAN: Is anything wrong?
CYNTHIA: No! Not really! Won't you sit down?
FABIAN: (*still puzzled*) Thank you.
CYNTHIA: Doctor Fabian, I want to ask you a question that may seem absurd and even childish. (*slight pause*) Do you believe in supernatural disappearances?
FABIAN: In... supernatural disappearances?
CYNTHIA: Yes!
BARTLETT: Do you believe, for instance, that a person could vanish like a puff

of smoke before the eyes of witnesses?

FABIAN: (*tolerantly*) Frankly, Captain Bartlett, I can only say that I should like to *see* it done.

CYNTHIA: We *want* you to see it done. If possible.

BARTLETT: (*grimly*) This isn't a joke. Doctor Fabian. Oh, no!

CYNTHIA: Let me help your memory a little. Does the name "Fraser". associated with the South Atlantic, mean anything to you?

FABIAN: (*reflecting*) Fraser! Fraser!

CYNTHIA: Yes! Think!

FABIAN: I've heard of *Admiral* Fraser, naturally. The Battle of Cape Laos. His statue in Kensington Gardens…

CYNTHIA: He was a great man. There's no name more honored in our…. well! our old-fashioned little colony. (*changing tone*) His grand-daughter is a girl named Victoria Fraser. We call her Vicky.

FABIAN: Vicky Fraser! Of course!

BARTLETT: *Now* do you remember? It happened—years ago.

FABIAN: (*fascinated*) Yes. A little girl of twelve or thirteen, Vicky Fraser, disappeared one night out of a cottage with all the doors and windows locked on the inside. Two or three nights later, when her parents were nearly frantic, the child appeared again: through the locks and bolts, tucked up in bed as usual.

BARTLETT: (*grimly*) Right! Anything else you remember?

FABIAN: Yes. It was the rainy season, with high winds. They were *certain* every lock was fastened: against rattling. And yet all the child would ever say, when they asked her where she'd been was, "*I don't know.*" (*pause*) Is that true?

CYNTHIA: Every word of it!

BARTLETT: What's more, the cottage itself is only a mile from here.

FABIAN: You mean Vicky Fraser still lives there?

CYNTHIA: No. But she's on a visit from England. At the Governor's house. We're … going on a picnic this afternoon, Vicky Fraser too. That is, if *you'll* go?

FABIAN: Of course I'll go! Besides, this girl interests me.

BARTLETT: (*as though challenging*) She's an infernally *attractive* girl, anyway.

CYNTHIA: (*sharply*) Yes. *Jim* thinks so.

BARTLETT: (*flaring*) Stop it, Cynthia.

CYNTHIA: (*sweetly satiric*) Vicky's eyes are "honey-colored." Isn't that the term you used, Jim?

BARTLETT: Now look here! If you're going to remember every casual word I ever said….!

CYNTHIA: Honey-colored. Yes. Vicky's supposed to have a spiritual nature, Doctor Fabian. And yet so *terribly* obvious: except to a man. She … (*breaking off*) … I'm sorry! It's—the weather, or these international crises. Please come over here! Both of you! To the table by the radio. That's

it.—Jim!
BARTLETT: I'm sorry, too! I didn't mean....
CYNTHIA: It was my fault, Jim. Turn on the radio, will you? It's set to Berlin.
BARTLETT: Right. (*a click*) It'll warm up in a second or two.
CYNTHIA: (*forced gaiety*) And here on the table. Doctor Fabian, we have three picnic-hampers. Wickerwork; their lids absolutely bulging with food. We shall go on our picnic; we shall rest and be happy; even though the Berlin radio ...
(*Sound: under the last four words of her speech music—as though from a radio—registers and grows louder with wind-instruments. The tune is* Deutschland über Alles. *It registers for some seconds before anyone speaks*)
FABIAN: (*thoughtfully*) Deutschland über Alles!
BARTLETT: (*same tone*) Germany over all!
CYNTHIA: Have *we* an answer?
(*Sound: off, at sea, full broadside of guns from battle-cruiser*)
(*Sound: music stops as though radio switched off*)
CYNTHIA: (*mood changing*) Jim! Please turn off the radio!
BARTLETT: I've just done it.
VICKY: (*fading on*) Yes, Jim. Thanks for stopping that dreadful music.
CYNTHIA: (*startled*) Vicky!
VICKY: (*sweetly affectionate*) Hel-*lo*, you dear people!
CYNTHIA: How on earth did *you* get in?
VICKY: (*hurt*) Darling, I only walked in through the front door. I thought you wouldn't mind. Especially since I haven't seen Jim in years. Well!—months. (*stops*) Oh! I didn't know you had a visitor!
BARTLETT: It's an old friend of Cynthia's, Vicky. Doctor Fabian! Miss Vicky Fraser.
VICKY: I don't think it's very complimentary of him to stand there and grin at me.
FABIAN: Forgive me, Miss Fraser. I saw your reflection in the window-glass—a charming reflection!—when the radio was playing. (*amused*) and I could have sworn I saw you give the Nazi salute. Foolish, wasn't it?
VICKY: (*tenderly*) Very foolish, dear doctor! And how terribly amusing! (*she begins to laugh sweetly*)
FABIAN: (*joins her*)

(*Music: hits hard with the beginning of* Deutschland über Alles; *then sinister music behind*)
FABIAN: Danger. Danger! I knew, as you who listen must know, that there was some undertone to this harmless picnic: that nothing was quite what it seemed on the surface. Yet—what *was* it? In Captain Bartlett's old car the four of us drove north along the road which slopes up to the

Spanish frontier.
(*Music: fades*)
(*Sound: faint noise of car, under narration*)
FABIAN: Cynthia and Jim Bartlett were in the front seat, Vicky and I in the back. At our feet, symbolic of all harmless things, three good-sized picnic-hampers rattling with crockery...
(*Sound: momentary rattle of dishes as car moves*)
VICKY: (*as though continuing*)—My elder brother. At the Admiralty. He died a year ago; and—*I* didn't want to go on living. (*changing tone*) Oh, can't we talk of something more cheerful? Won't *you* help, Doctor Fabian?
FABIAN: (*amiably*) Just as you like, Vicky. Where are we *going* for this picnic?
VICKY: We're going to the cottage where I once disapp... where I had such a dreadful experience when I was a child.
CYNTHIA: *Was* it a dreadful experience, Vicky?
VICKY: (*seriously*) I don't remember, really. It was too long ago. I didn't understand. I hadn't developed the occult power for myself.
FABIAN: What occult power?
VICKY: (*almost naively*) To de-materialize. Of course. To vanish when I like, and where I like.
(*Sounds: sudden rattle of crockery*)
BARTLETT: (*loudly*) Sorry if the car swerved! We ran over a rut or something!
VICKY: (*pleading*) Oh, you *are* such Philistines! Such unbelievers! All of you!.... Shall I prove it, Jim?
CYNTHIA: *I* challenge you, Vicky.
VICKY: (*attention distracted*) Wait! Slow down....this is where we turn!
BARTLETT: Turn right or left? There's no road here.
VICKY: Turn left, please. That's it. I'm afraid it'll be a bit bumpy to drive over the grass....
(*Sound: the car bumps on uneven turf. Behind*)
VICKY: ....but it's only ten yards or so. There; where you see the opening in the trees. That leads to the clearing. And the house is at the back of the clearing. Against pine-trees and wild-olive trees....Now! Stop the car. That's the clearing.
(*Sound: car stops. Handbrake grinds back*)
FABIAN: Do you live here when you're at Gibraltar, Miss Fraser?
VICKY: Sometimes, yes. Not as often as I'd like to, though.
FABIAN: But isn't it—rather lonely?
VICKY: (*eagerly*) Oh, yes! That was why *they* were able to take me away. When I was a child.
FABIAN: (*sharply*) *They*? Who?
BARTLETT: (*suddenly*) Look here! Hadn't we better gather our traps together and get out of the car?
(*Sound: car door opens*)

VICKY: I'm sorry, Jim darling.
(*Sound: car door opens*)
VICKY: I mustn't talk like that, must I?—what have you got in the black case there?
BARTLETT: Thermos-flasks, my little one; and there's bottled beer in the hampers. (*grimly*) We're sensible people. And we're going to be sensible if it kills us.
CYNTHIA: Yes. If it kills us!
VICKY: I must apologize, I know, for the seedy state of the house. It hasn't been opened for months. There's a modern kitchen and bathroom. But only paraffin oil lamps.
CYNTHIA: (*faint alarm*) We're not going to stay here after dark, are we?
VICKY: (*amused*) No, dear, I forgot... You won't need lamps. Unless, of course...
BARTLETT: You mean: unless you disappear again? Is that it?
VICKY: Yes, Jim. And promise me you won't be frightened when I do.—Promise! Promise! Promise!

(*Music: in and behind*)
FABIAN: Not a word more of disappearance. Not a word: until the sun was sinking in red fire behind the black pines and wild-olive, and the evil-looking white cottage. We load our picnic on the so-called lawn. Afterwards, with the cloth cleared and the hampers pushed indoors, Vicky brought out some old deck-chairs. I was sitting facing the door of the cottage, not ten feet from it, and Cynthia Drew... how well I remember her brown hair and blue eyes and nervous hands!.... was sitting opposite me.
(*Music: fades out*)

CYNTHIA: (*on edge*) Don't look round, please. You'll only encourage Vicky if you look round. I think she's telling Jim the romantic history of the cottage.
FABIAN: About....her own disappearance?
CYNTHIA: Oh, it goes farther back than that! The cottage once was owned by a Spanish bank-robber. He made some spectacular escapes before they shot him at Cadiz. Before that, it was owned by an English colonel who...
VICKY: (*fading on*) Cynthia, dear! *Do* I intrude?
CYNTHIA: (*controlled*) Not at all, dear. What is it?
VICKY: I've just remembered, you know, that I haven't shown Jim Bartlett over the cottage. You don't mind if I steal him away from you for a *little* while?
CYNTHIA: No, dear. Of course not.

BARTLETT: You know, Cynthia, I never heard there were so many interesting stories attached to Gibraltar! And this cottage....
VICKY: It's a small cottage, Jim. When I open the front door....
(*Sound: heavy door open: slight creak of hinges.*)
VICKY: You see? Only a hall straight through to the back door. Three rooms on one side; three rooms on the other. (*archly*) Will you cross the threshold. Captain Bartlett?
BARTLETT: (*fade a bit*) With pleasure, madam!
VICKY: (*off slightly*) There! See you later, dear people!
(*Sound: door closes*)
CYNTHIA: (*fury gathering*) She closed the door. You noticed that, Doctor Fabian?
FABIAN: I couldn't fail to notice, Cynthia. But....
CYNTHIA: (*bursting out*) I won't give him up to her! I won't! I won't!

(*Music: in softly and fades out behind*)
FABIAN: And so, while the red sunset faded, and shadows gathered in the trees that hemmed us in, our talk ran endlessly on the same repetition.

CYNTHIA: I won't give him up to her! I won't! I won't!
FABIAN: All day, Cynthia, you've been wearing a mask of some kind.
CYNTHIA: What do you mean?
FABIAN: Just that. I felt I didn't know you any longer.
CYNTHIA: If it comes to that, John Fabian, what do I know about *you*?
FABIAN: (*wryly*) There's very little to know, I'm afraid.
CYNTHIA: What are you *like*? What's your ambition?
FABIAN: I have no ambition. Or I shouldn't be a ship's doctor.
CYNTHIA: What do you *want* from life?
FABIAN: Only to observe, that's all. To study man, never to condemn; to laugh that I may not....swear. (*breaking off, amused*) Here: I'm becoming pompous!
CYNTHIA: Don't apologize. When we feel any emotion, deeply and strongly, we're supposed to laugh and pretend it doesn't matter.
FABIAN: That's true enough.
CYNTHIA: Jim and I are two of a kind. His family were Army. Mine were Navy. All gone now. But they're in my blood: patriotism, Empire, all the things people sneer at today. They'll be in my blood as long as the fleet guard's the sea.
(*Sound: off, some distance, a concerted salute of heavy guns.*)
FABIAN: Hold on! That didn't sound like ship's guns!
CYNTHIA: No. It's our own guns on the Rock. Saluting the warships. Some *very* important people are arriving today.
FABIAN: For a war-conference?
CYNTHIA: Yes. And Vicky's staying.

FABIAN: Vicky is the last of *her* line, isn't she? She said something about—her brother.
CYNTHIA: Her brother shot himself, a year ago, in his office at the Admiralty. He... (*pause: change of mood: jealously flaring*)... Jim and Vicky have been in that house a long time. Haven't they?
FABIAN: Cynthia! Wait! Don't get up!
CYNTHIA: And why not?
FABIAN: I ask you not to make a scene.
CYNTHIA: I don't propose to make a scene. I'll open the door....
(*Sound: heavy door opens*)
CYNTHIA: There! I shall walk to the end of the hall, and back again. No more.
FABIAN: Cynthia!
(*Sound: briefly, high heels tap on wood, going away; they fade, and immediately return. Door bangs.*)
CYNTHIA: (*in a high voice*) The doors of all the rooms are closed. I really don't think I ought to trouble anyone.
FABIAN: Bartlett hasn't fallen for the small charmer with the eyes. If anything, he's afraid of her. Yes! I'll take my oath that....
BARTLETT: (*calling, off*) Hello, you two! Hey!
CYNTHIA: (*starting*) Isn't that Jim's voice?
FABIAN: Yes. And he's tearing his way out of that olive-tree woodland over on the left. Uniform torn; looks furious...
CYNTHIA: Jim!
BARTLETT: (*fading on, grim, shaken*) I hereby announce to both of you, that my days of chivalry are ended. Finished!
CYNTHIA: Chivalry?
BARTLETT: That's it. For half an hour I've been stumbling through that blasted wood. Looking for—yes, so help me!—wild strawberries. I told Vicky they didn't grow here. But, oh, no! She *knew*.
CYNTHIA: Then you haven't been at the cottage all this time?
BARTLETT: (*taken aback*) At the cottage?
CYNTHIA: Yes! Here!
BARTLETT: (*grimly*) I was in that house, Cynthia, for about five minutes. Then our elfin sprite, meaning Vicky, had a....(*bitterly*)...."woman's whim." She wanted wild strawberries out of what she called the "forest".
FABIAN: Just a moment! You didn't come out by the front door. Nobody did! We were sitting here.
BARTLETT: No! I went out by the back door. It opens straight on the wood.
FABIAN: (*concentrated*) I see. And don't mind if I sound like a police-officer—what happened then?
BARTLETT: Well! I went to look for those blasted...
FABIAN: No, no! What did *she* do?
BARTLETT: Vicky, you mean?
FABIAN: Yes!

BARTLETT: She locked and bolted the back door on the inside. As the door closed she said something about "keeping her promise." She... (*as though with slow realization*)....keeping her....(*abruptly*) Have you seen Vicky since then?
CYNTHIA: No! We haven't!
FABIAN: She did promise to vanish, you know.
BARTLETT: That's impossible.
FABIAN: I wonder! Suppose the back door is *still* locked and bolted on the inside?
CYNTHIA: It's getting dark. I don't like it. (*voice rising*) She's playing a trick on us! She's hiding in there!
FABIAN: That may be. We're going to find out. Ready?
BARTLETT: Yes! But this is inconceivable. It's—scientific lunacy. She couldn't have vanished!

FABIAN: (*pause: cold*) She couldn't have vanished. But she had.
(*Music: hits hard: then down behind*)
FABIAN: Nearly an hour later, when we stood again in the hall of that cottage, we were all as grimy as my white uniform. A paraffin lamp, with a white glass shade, burned dull and unsteady on the hall-table. That little limestone shell even had a faint echo. We stood near the kitchen; and it was so quiet that I could hear from the bathroom a bath-tap dropping monotonously, slowly, like drops in water-torture.
(*Music: fades out*)

(*Sound: through the next scene, which is done on echo, a drop of water splashes on enamel or metal every ten seconds or so.*)
FABIAN: I'll state what we know; *you* find a flaw in it.
CYNTHIA: There *is* a flaw in it! Somewhere!
FABIAN: When we came in here, we bolted the front door so that nobody could slip out without disturbing it. We three have been together all the time. The back door was locked and bolted. Vicky Fraser didn't get out by either of the two doors. Agreed?
BARTLETT: All right. Agreed.
FABIAN: She didn't get out by any window. The windows are all locked and dust-coated.
BARTLETT: (*bitterly*) Go on! She couldn't have disappeared. Finish stating the facts.
FABIAN: I will. The chimney-flues are too narrow to admit a cat. There's no attic, no cellar, and no secret exit. Yet we've searched every inch of this house; and she isn't here.
CYNTHIA: (*crying out*) Vicky! Vicky! Where are you?
BARTLETT: (*uneasily*) Steady, Cynthia! You don't think she's going to answer you?

CYNTHIA: No. I suppose not.—Jim!
BARTLETT: Well?
CYNTHIA: That lamp on the table! It's getting… all shadowy.
BARTLETT: I'm sorry, dear! Most of the lamps had *no* oil. That one's got very little.
CYNTHIA: There's only a kind of blue crawl round the wick. How long will it burn?
BARTLETT: A minute. Maybe two
CYNTHIA: Then we'll be in the dark. With Jim, we've *got* to solve this! I de-pended on Doctor Fabian!
FABIAN: You depended on me?
CYNTHIA: Vicky's a faker! I've always known it!
FABIAN: Yes. I agree with you. But…
CYNTHIA: There was some trick way out of here. She used it when she was a child. Just to devil her parents, and be—"mysterious". I thought she might try it today, from sheer vanity. And *you* know about such tricks. You'd expose her.
FABIAN: (*badgered*) I don't know *this* trick, Cynthia. There's not a single clue to…hold on!
CYNTHIA: (*quickly*) What is it?
FABIAN: Under the table. I hadn't noticed it before.
CYNTHIA: (*more insistently*) What *is* it?
FABIAN: (*musing*) Three feet square, when you unfold it. A large sheet of oilskin waterproof, jagged at one corner. As though a needle had….
CYNTHIA: Jim, the lamp's going out! Get the steamer-rugs and the hampers! Let's get out of here! Let's—(*she stops*)
FABIAN: The lamp's out *now*, anyway.
BARTLETT: (*soothing*) The dark won't hurt you, Cynthia. Use your reason!
CYNTHIA: Can *you* reason when you're frightened?
BARTLETT: Vicky's only playing a trick. Even if she *has* vanished, she's got to come back. We won't hear from her tonight, but….
VICKY: (*in a clear whisper—speaks close to microphone*) Oh, yes, you will.
FABIAN: (*exclaiming*) Who spoke then?
CYNTHIA: It was Vicky! I heard her!
FABIAN: Bartlett! Strike a match!
BARTLETT: All right. Steady. There!
(*Sound: match struck*)
CYNTHIA: But there's… there's nobody here!

(*Music: in and behind*)
FABIAN: And blind terror struck at us through the woods. How we scrambled out to the car, gathering up belongings as best we could, I would rather not remember. I spent that night aboard the *Maurevania* here; we were held in port during the Munich crisis. And, even though I took a sleep-

ing-draught, my mind churned on. How had this thing been done? *How?* Again I saw the inside of that cottage: its dusty furniture, its (*very slight pause*) windows in the back bedroom, its dishes on the kitchen shelves. Next morning a steward passed my cabin carrying a laden breakfast-tray.
(*Sound: crash as of laden tray falling*)
FABIAN: And I sat up in bed, stung awake. And the blindness was gone. And I knew.
(*Music: out with a sting*)
(*Sound: door-knocker rapping; then opening of door*)
LUIGI: (*servant*) Ah, good morning, Doctor Fabian! You wisha to see Miss Cynthia Drew, eh?
FABIAN: Yes, Luigi. Is she at home?
LUIGI: *Si, signore*! She is out on the balcony with Captain Bartlett! You know where eesa the balcony, eh, that look down on the sea? Straight through!
FABIAN: Thank you. I'll go on out.
(*Sound: footsteps on wood. The balcony is floored with matting so no steps there.*)
BARTLETT: (fading in as Fabian's steps carry with mike) Hul-*lo*, Fabian! Good morning!
CYNTHIA: (*fade in*) Come here to the ledge! Look down and to the right!
FABIAN: (*very grave*) Is there—anything interesting?
CYNTHIA: They're holding some kind of reception aboard the *Frobisher*. The band's playing on the foredeck.
(*Sound: The band can be heard with a few bars of the sea shanty* "Blow the Man Down" *fading away*)
CYNTHIA: (*suddenly*) John Fabian! What's wrong? I've never seen you look so—black.
FABIAN: (*bitter*) I have reason to look black, Cynthia. I know how Vicky Fraser disappeared.
CYNTHIA: (*hesitating*) You—think you know?
FABIAN: I swear I know. Will you answer a question?
FABIAN: Last night you told me the cottage was once owned by a Spanish bank robber. A man who made spectacular escapes. What that kind of a—hint?
CYNTHIA: Yes! It was!
FABIAN: I thought so. You meant there was trick-escape in that house. And Vicky, as a child, used it to fool her parents.
FABIAN: A trick window, in the back bedroom; its whole frame slid down into the wall.
CYNTHIA: Then that's how Vicky got out last night?
FABIAN: No. It won't work now. Someone, probably her father, has recently nailed up that window with heavy nails; and painted them over.
BARTLETT: Then how did Vicky disappear? And where? (*half ridiculing*) Into some... strange country?
FABIAN: In a sense, yes. She's dead. You two killed her.

(*Sound: off, band music comes up and holds for a moment with the sea-shanty; then fades*)

FABIAN: (*bitter contempt*) *I* was your witness. *I* was your scapegoat, as arranged. Shall I prove it?

BARTLETT: (*grim; no sign of guilt*) If you can, Fabian.

FABIAN: You knew Vicky Fraser would never resist a challenge to disappear. She believed she could get out by the trick window. But you two had a plan to kill her.

BARTLETT: Go on! Say what you think!

FABIAN: You, Bartlett, are an Army surgeon, I saw you take your black case of instruments out of the car. You and Vicky went into the house alone. And... why should a bath-trap drip in a closed-up house?

BARTLETT: Answer your own question!

FABIAN: Because in there, my friend, you stabbed Vicky Fraser through the heart. Then you dismembered her body. After *other* preparations, you went out by the back door.

BARTLETT: Then who locked and bolted the back door?

FABIAN: Cynthia did. Under my own eyes.

CYNTHIA: I hated that! I hated the deception. But...

FABIAN: She walked to the end of the hall, and back again. That was all. I heard her; but the hall was dark; I couldn't see her.

BARTLETT: If Vicky's body was still in the house, who took it out?

FABIAN: (*bitterly*) We all did.

BARTLETT: We.... all.... did?

FABIAN: Yes. It was in three good-sized picnic hampers, with wicker lids. *I* carried one to the car.

CYNTHIA: (*bursting out*) Do you hate us so very much, then?

FABIAN: (*quietly*) I don't hate you, no. (*cutting loose*) But ... you're honest and honorable people! Why did you do it?

BARTLETT: Sir, that's *our* secret! (*politely*) You can 'phone the police from the next room.

CYNTHIA: Jim, we've got to tell him! *He'll* understand!

FABIAN: Tell me—what?

CYNTHIA: *You* saw Vicky salute to *Deutschland über Alles*!

FABIAN: (*taken aback*) You mean her sympathies were....

BARTLETT: Sympathies! That's a fine word!

CYNTHIA: Vicky Fraser killed her own brother, at the Admiralty, because he found out *she* was the spy who hated England. Oh, I can't prove that; but it's true. And she was staying at the Governor's house, remember? With the high-placed officials for the war-conversation? Every word would have been in Berlin tomorrow.

FABIAN: But this cold-blooded mummery of a "disappearance"—! You, imitating her voice in a whisper! You, pretending jealousy—!

CYNTHIA: Did you say cold-blooded? Don't you see it was the only way to save

her name?
FABIAN: Save her name?
CYNTHIA: She'd disappeared before. Many people thought it was supernatural. Now, with you as a witness, they'd never find her. Never guess where to look. Never know that the last of the Frasers would sell her country... (*contemptuously*) For an "ideology."
BARTLETT: Do you want to telephone *now*, Doctor Fabian?
FABIAN: I...I... (*hesitates*)
LUIGI: (*fading on*) Doctor Fabian does not need to phone for the police, *signore*. I have done it already.
CYNTHIA: Luigi!
LUIGI: You forget the servant in this house, *signorina*, I regret! But I serve my *Duce* as you serve yours.
BARTLETT: Then you're an honest man!
LUIGI: (*amazed*) *Signore*, you are mad! They will hang you.
CYNTHIA: (*contemptuously*) Do you think we're afraid of that?
(*Music: band, off, in with "Rule Brittania"*)
BARTLETT: The foreign Spy, Luigi —if you are one — runs a fair risk. But the traitor and the spy among our own people, like Vicky Fraser, must be destroyed or we all die. The rope ends my life; but it will save others. Wait and see! Wait and see!

FABIAN: "To study man; never to condemn." And I thank my philosophy that I was not compelled to make that decision! (*changing tone*) But next week, when we have passed the Straits of Gibraltar, I shall tell you a happier tale, with a far happier ending, even though it deals with murder at Marseilles; and I call it "The Nine Black Reasons".
(*Music: in and behind*)
(*Sound: ship's whistles*)
(*Music: fades out*)

Notes for the Curious

For "No Useless Coffin", Carr used the central ploy of the short story "The House in Goblin Wood", first published in *Ellery Queen's Mystery Magazine* and the *Strand Magazine* in November 1947.

The title of the play is quoted from Charles Wolfe's famous poem "The Burial of Sir John Moore after Corunna", which Carr also referenced in the "Carter Dickson" novel *The Punch and Judy Murders* (1937). As a teenager, Carr wrote poetry. Examples include "Richard to the Crusaders before Jerusalem" and "Valley Forge, 1777", where around a sixth of George Washington's Continental Army died of malnutrition; these and other poems by Carr and several of his schoolmates were published in the rare collection *A Book of Hill School Verse* (1927).

Carr's verse is characterized by a strong rhythm, romantic and often with a historical theme. At Haverford College Carr won the Hibberd Garrett Prize for Poetry and, as detailed in James E Keirans' invaluable encyclopaedia of Carriana, *The John Dickson Carr Companion* (2015), Carr's crime fiction includes many references to poetry and poets. Keirans has observed that Carr particularly admired the works of Algernon Charles Swinburne, whose poem "Dolores" is referenced heavily in one of the later plays in *Cabin B-13*, as well as the Reverend R. H. Barham whose *Ingoldsby Legends* gave Carr the title of another *Cabin B-13* play.

Admiral Fraser did not exist nor did any famous naval battle take place at Cape Laos, which does not exist either. There are, however, several statues in Kensington Gardens, the best known being a bronze sculpture of J. M. Barrie's character Peter Pan commissioned by Barrie and erected in 1912.

Another Cynthia Drew is one of the main characters in *Till Death Do Us Part* (1944) in which still more curiously, there is also a Goblin Wood.

The Nine Black Reasons

(*Sound: a ship's whistle*)
(*Music: in and behind*)
ANNOUNCER: CBS presents John Dickson Carr's famous Doctor Fabian, ship's surgeon, world traveler and teller of strange and incredible tales of mystery and murder, directed by John Dietz.
FABIAN: Marseilles, on its amphitheater of hills, is not all grey-white houses or tango-tunes on the waterfront. Up on the hill lies the *Promenade des Americans*. There, stood the white and fashionable hotel, shaded by palm-trees: called the Hotel of the Grand Monarch. Attached to it were the Royal Turkish Baths. And the worst endurance-test of those Turkish Baths was the steam-room.
(*Music: fades out*)
(*Sound: very faint noise of hissing steam creeps in under*)
FABIAN: A clammy steam-cloud, faintly moving, made almost invisible the white marble walls, and tiers of marble benches along one wall. So it appeared to a young man who entered, one afternoon in the year '36...
(*Sound: steam up and down, hold faintly under scene*)
FRANK: (*uncertainly, to himself*) When the French build a steam-room, they *build* a steam room! This place is...
UNKNOWN: (*middle-aged, southern*) (*calling, a little off*) Hoy! Anybody there?
FRANK: Yes! (rather dizzy) Where are you? I can't see you.
UNKNOWN: Young man, I can hardly *hear* you. I think I'm dyin' on m'feet.
FRANK: Have you been on a bat, sir? Like me?
UNKNOWN: (*deeply affronted*) I never go on a bat, sir. I resent that suggestion!
FRANK: Sorry! No offence.
UNKNOWN: (*on microphone*) I take a little drink now and then, maybe; but I oughtn't to suffer like *this*. Where-you-from?
FRANK: New York. My name's Bentley, Frank Bentley.
UNKNOWN: (*as though explaining all*) Savannah, Georgia here. (*suddenly*) Wait a minute! Are you goin' to sit down on that marble bench?
FRANK: I've got to! You can't get your breath in here!
UNKNOWN: Then keep the cloth round your waist; and careful when you sit down. That marble's just as hot as the hinges of ...
FRANK: (*winces*) Yes. I see what you mean. (*deep breath*) They said at the hotel this was France's finest cure for what ailed you.
UNKNOWN: (*with dignity*) In my opinion, Mr. Bentley, any hangover-remedy ever invented is far worse'n the hangover. Only two fool Americans would...
FRANK: Hold on! There's somebody else here!

UNKNOWN: (*surprised*) You sure? *I* didn't see anybody!
FRANK: He's sitting on this bench. Over to the left of me. Propped up against the back. (*slight pause*) Looks as though he's fainted.
UNKNOWN: Then he's better off than we are. Let him alone!
FRANK: Let him alone? In a hundred and twenty degrees of heat? Looks like a Frenchman. Short black beard; thick-set... (*coughs*) Confound this steam!—Monsieur! (*pause*) Vous n'avez pas mal? (*pause*) I'll just shake him by the shoulder, and...
(*Sound: a dead weight noise of someone rolling off bench to floor.*)
UNKNOWN: (*startled*) Rolled off the bench! Flat on his back!
FRANK: (*jittering, bursting out*) This *would* happen to me when I feel like a skeleton on wires!
UNKNOWN: Easy, son! He's only fainted!
FRANK: No. Bend down and look. Over the heart! Little red puncture; not much blood; but a pink smear that...
UNKNOWN: (*jumping*) He ain't *dead*?
FRANK: He's dead, all right.
UNKNOWN: (*alarmed*) Listen here, son. You and I don't want to get mixed up with these French *police*?
FRANK: I know! But.. look at his left wrist! There's a wrist-chain attached to a little leather pouch that's been cut open.. (*breathing heavily*) Where are you? Mr... Savannah! *Where are you?*

(*Music: in and fades out behind*)
FABIAN: Then, three nights later, look into that broad and famous thoroughfare of Marseilles known to every English-speaking seaman as the Can of Beer. A paved version of Atlantic City's boardwalk, except that there are shops and cafes on both sides under the tall white lamps. At a table of one pavement cafe, under the lighted awning, Frank Bentley sits moodily. And out of the soft Midi dusk...

(*Sound: murmur of voices at sidewalk café rising up and down*)
HELEN: Excuse me for speaking to you; but—aren't you Frank Bentley?
FRANK: Yes! I am!
(*Sound: scrape as of metal chair pushed back*)
FRANK: And *your* face is familiar too!
HELEN: Shall I remind you?
FRANK: No! You're too attractive to forget!
HELEN: The *Maurevania's* South American cruise. Two years ago. I'm...
FRANK: Helen Parker! Of course! (*warmly*) Won't you sit down?
HELEN: Thank you.
(*Sound: scraping of metal chairs*)
FRANK: What'll you drink?

HELEN: (*nervous*) Nothing, thanks. Not now. (*hesitates*) Frank. What do you remember best about that cruise?
FRANK: I remember *you*, in a noble bathing-suit, as Queen of the Waves when we crossed the Equator. I remember you singing at the amateur concerts. I've got a Whole album full of snapshots!
HELEN: And I remember you.. (*trying to laugh*)... as the well-known writer of detective-stories. I read every book of yours in the ship's library. Now you've become something more than just well-known.
FRANK: I've had a lot of luck. You need it.
HELEN: Listen, Frank. I—I don't want to talk to you under false pretenses. I saw you sitting here. And I've been walking up and down for ten minutes, trying to get the courage to speak to you.
FRANK: But why, for the love of Mike?
HELEN: I need help. I'm in—difficulties. (*quickly*) Oh, not money difficulties! That's what people usually mean. But I'm in a trouble that... that ...
FRANK: Yes, Helen? The trouble?
HELEN: It's so crazy that nobody but you will understand it!
FRANK: You—er—overwhelm me. Thanks.
HELEN: No, I didn't mean it like that! I mean: your stories always begin with some mad situation that turns out to be quite logical. You see... I've been mixed up in a murder.
FRANK: (*jumping*) You've been mixed up in a murder?
HELEN: You sound as though *you'd* been, too!
FRANK: I have! (*uncertainly*) Crime in Marseilles is picking up. Or is it the same case?
HELEN: What happened to you?
FRANK: A middle-aged Frenchman named Jacques Morel, a jewel-merchant, was stabbed with some weapon like a stiletto. I found him, or two of us found him, in the Turkish Baths at my hotel. The police can't find a missing Southerner; he's a witness; and I've kept out of jail only by a miracle.
HELEN: Then it's not ...*my* case.
FRANK: What happened to you? Wait! How long have you been in Marseilles?
HELEN: Oh, I've been here for months. I'm—singing in a night-club. (*pause*) That startles you, doesn't it?
FRANK: (*meaning, "yes, it does"*) No! Of course not! Why shouldn't you do what you like?
HELEN: But you were thinking about the old days. And that my Uncle Fred was very well-off. Aren't you?
FRANK: Ye-es. Partly.
HELEN: Well! He still is. Or was. But...My handbag; where's my handbag! And the compact. Here! I..
(*Sound: rattle of rounded compact on metal table*)
HELEN: I'm so nervous I can't even hold a compact. And this babble of voices!

And the... (*bitterly*)... romantic Mediterranean moon. What happened this morning was crazy!

FRANK: Helen! Listen!

HELEN: Y-yes? I'm sorry!

FRANK: We're going to sit at a table inside, where it's quiet. You're going to have a drink whether you like it or not. A vermouth-cassis is mild enough. And, when you hear the soda-siphon over that drink.

(*Music: bridge into*)
(*Sound: Hiss of soda-siphon, through*)

FRANK: *Doucement, mon gars! Assez de l'eau.*

(*Sound: Siphon stops*)

WAITER: *Bien, monsieur. Un vermouth-cassis, Un fine de la maison.*

(*Sound: saucers pushed across table. Waiter's footsteps move away*)

FRANK: Now, Helen! We're all alone with the tables and mirrors. Tell me!

HELEN: I came over to Paris, nearly six months ago, to study singing. (*tries to laugh*) On the very first evening, I went out with a boy from home. We were both hit over the head and robbed. I lost all my money, including my letter of credit. And I didn't dare cable home to Uncle Fred and Aunt Hester. They'd have thought that I might be killed every day.

FRANK: Hence the night-club?

HELEN: Yes. I wasn't good enough for Paris, of course. But I landed this... this job in Marseilles.

HELEN: Anyway, three weeks ago Uncle Fred cabled me. He said he was taking the *Maurevania*, our old ship, and coming to visit me.

FRANK: *Did* he come?

HELEN: Yes. He got here this morning. Then the craziness started.

FRANK: Let's hear it.

HELEN: I've got lodgings in the Old Port. They're not very... presentable.

FRANK: Helen, why the devil didn't *I* know you were here!

HELEN: Anyway, I rushed up to the Grand Monarch Hotel. The big white place with the palm-trees, and the swimming-pool in the back. I'd cabled Uncle Fred he could find me there. Frank, what time is it now?

FRANK: It's about... let's see... twenty to nine.

HELEN: At half-past eleven this morning, Uncle Fred phoned up from the desk downstairs. He said he'd go along with his luggage to *his* room, and then come around to my room. Frank, I was scared to death. What was I going to *tell* him? I paced the floor, and paced the floor... and he didn't show up.

FRANK: You don't mean your uncle—disappeared?

HELEN: No, of course not! Why do you ask that?

FRANK: Because my Southerner, from Savannah, has disappeared like a steam-cloud. (Abruptly) Sorry! Forget that! What about your uncle?

HELEN: I wasn't exactly—worried. But he's always been near-sighted. So...
FRANK: You went out to look for him?
HELEN: Yes. I turned the corner into a short corridor, with a grey carpet leading to a cage-elevator at the end.
HELEN: Uncle Fred was standing at one of the room-doors. Sideways to me, facing in. The door was open. He was talking to someone in the room.
FRANK: Talking to someone he knew?
FRANK: No! That's just the trouble! The man in that hotel-room was an American business-man of just the same type as Uncle Fred. Middle-aged; solid; dependable. His name's Johnson. He...
FRANK: (*bewildered*) But what's so very *crazy* about all this?
HELEN: Frank, listen! I was close. I could hear them both distinctly. I couldn't see in; but I could hear. What they said, what happened then, goes round and round in my head like an echo—over and over!—and won't go out.
(*Sound: next speeches on echo: clear, but as hollow and ghostly as possible*)

PARKER: (*rather nervously*) Sorry I had to knock on your door, sir.
JOHNSON: (*amused, a little off*) That's all right! What can I do for you?
PARKER: (*fussed*) I'm trying to find my niece. She worries me. She... What I mean is, I'm looking for room number three-sixteen.
JOHNSON: (*considering*) Three-sixteen!
PARKER: Yes! They wrote it down for me.
JOHNSON: I *think* you go straight down the hall and turn to the left.
PARKER: Much obliged to you!
JOHNSON: Not at all. Glad to—
(*Sound: off, three revolver shots. A woman screams*)
(*Sound: off echo*)

FRANK: (*incredulous*) Helen, are you telling me...?
HELEN: Yes! There were three revolver-shots!
FRANK: Fired from where?
HELEN: Fired from that room where Mr. Johnson was giving directions. (*shakily*) Uncle Fred is dead. Two of the bullets lodged in his head.
FRANK: Do you mean this fellow Johnson, in the midst of saying, "Glad to help you," just pulled out a gun and shot a total stranger?
HELEN: Yes. That's about it.
FRANK: But *why*?
HELEN: I don't Know. Nobody knows.
FRANK: Is Johnson out of his mind?
HELEN: No. The police-psychiatrists say there's never been a saner man. He'd never known Uncle Fred; never even heard of him. Yet he *must* have shot my uncle, because the evidence proves it. (*voice rising*) Why. Why? *Why*?

(*Music: in and behind*)

FABIAN: The office of the *juge d'instruction*, or examining magistrate, high up at the Hotel de Ville. A dingy room, full of dyspeptic-looking law-books.
(*Music: soften for —*)
(*Sound: whack of fly-swatter on desk*)
(*Music: continues and fades behind*)
FABIAN: Yes, that's the noise of a fly-swatter on the desk. Monsieur Bo, the examining magistrate, always holds a fly-swatter in warm weather. Monsieur Bo is short and stout. He suffers from indigestion; observe the bottle of soda-mint tablets on his desk. But perhaps he has good reason to look purple-faced that evening.

BO: (*gritting politeness*) Mademoiselle Parker! Monsieur Bentley!
HELEN: Frank and I are old friends, Mr. Bo. We thought you wouldn't mind if we both came here together.
BO: (*satirically*) So! You make my day 'appy. Yes?
(*Sound: whack of fly-swatter*)
HELEN: Mr. Bo, why do you keep on using that fly-swatter when there aren't any flies here?
BO: It is not enough that I have *two* murder cases. It is not enough that I have *two* crazy witnesses. But both must visit me together.— One week more, and you will drive me to the foolish-house.
FRANK: (*has argued with him before*) You don't say "foolish-house," Mr. Bo! That's the wrong term. You say...
BO: (*immense dignity*) Monsieur!
(*Sound: whack of fly-swatter.*)
BO: I am Papa Bo. So many Americans I have thrown into the violin, which *you* call the 'oosegow or jug, that you will please not correct me in my English spikking.
(*Sound: whack of fly-swatter.*)
BO: Do *you*, perhaps, want to spend a night in the violin?
FRANK: For three days, Papa Bo, you've been threatening to stick me in that jail! (*pleading; he likes Bo*) I know your bark's worse than your bite...
BO: You think so—hein?
FRANK: ... But *you* know I didn't kill that man at the Turkish Bath.
BO: (*coolly*) Then where, please, is Mr. Savannah?
HELEN: Wait! Frank's told me *something* about that. This—this Mr. Savannah didn't just disappear in the steam-room, did he?
BO: Oh, no! No! He is seen to take his clothes from the locker; his money from the deposit box. *But!* No man answering his description is seen or registered at Marseilles.

FRANK: Suppose he's left Marseilles?
BO: No, no! Because of certain robberies, all who leave are searched and their passports must be stamped by *us*. Yet he is not here!
(*Sound: whack of fly-swatter.*)
BO: And now, *voyons*, we have another murder. The respectable Mr. Herbert Johnson kills the respectable Mr. Fredric Parker!
HELEN: Have you found out anything more? About the motive?
BO: (*desperate calm*) Mademoiselle, I tell you. There was *no* motive!
FRANK: But there must have been!
BO: (*tragically*) I am papa Bo. I have indigestion. I suffer like Job. (*as though looking round*) My soda-mint tablets!.. No, wait! I show you!
FRANK: Show us what?
BO: Sit down, both of you, at the left of my desk. Good! I press this switch—
(*Sound: a click*)
BO: —and all the lights go out. I press *this* switch—
(*Sound: a click*)
BO: —and over the witness-chair, on my right, shines down a bright beam. You will be silent, please; and not move. Now the buzzer.
(*Sound: off, faintly, buzzer sounds. Door opens, off*)
BO: (*calling*) Yes! *Bring in Mr. Johnson!* (*suavely*) I watch you, Mr. Johnson, under a light like a white pillar in darkness. You are sleek. You are prosperous. Not *too* much grey in the hair. The ladles might call you "handsome."
JOHNSON: (*bitterly*) Thanks a lot. What do you want *now*?
BO: (*changing tone; not too loud*) You killed Fredric Parker.
(*Sound: whack of fly-swatter.*)
JOHNSON: For the last time. I didn't!
BO: You killed Fredric Parker.
(*Sound: whack of fly-swatter.*)
JOHNSON: (*controlling himself*) No, Captain. Not guilty.
BO: When those shots were fired, Miss Helen Parker ran up and looked in your room. So did a number of hotel-people.
JOHNSON: All right. I don't deny it!
BO: In your room, on the floor, was the gun that killed Mr. Parker. *Yes*?
JOHNSON: Do you want to hear it *again*, Captain?
BO: *If* you please.
JOHNSON: The window behind me was open! You saw that. It leads to a back fire-escape. Somebody at the window shot Parker and threw the gun into the room. (*quickly*) No, and I didn't see who it was!
BO: Behind the hotel, Mr. Johnson, there is a swimming-pool.
JOHNSON: Maybe there is. What about it?
BO: Three witnesses, at this pool, say there was no person on the fire-escape.
JOHNSON: (*coolly sneering*) Can they *swear* to that? With a good cross-examiner? *I* doubt it.

Bo: Today, Mr. Johnson, I had many talks on the transatlantic 'phone. He came to France only because he was worried about his niece.
JOHNSON: That's the same "Miss Parker", eh? (*contemptuously*) Shabby character who sings in a waterfront dive called the *Boule Noire. He* had some fine relations!
HELEN: (*gives a half-stifled cry*)
FRANK: Steady, Helen!
JOHNSON: *Who spoke then? Who's with you?*
Bo: Only my—assistants.
(*Sound: whack of fly-swatter*)
JOHNSON: I'm blinded. You've got me pinned under this light like a torturer. Every time I move, your cops pull me back. (*starting to lose his head*) Listen, my fat friend. Do you want to know something?
Bo: (*calmly savage*) I should be delighted.
JOHNSON: There's a lawyer coming down from Paris tonight. But *I'll* tell you now.
Bo: Ye-es?
JOHNSON: *You* can't convict me of murder. *I* have no reason to kill Parker.
Bo: In France, as in England, it is not necessary to show motive.
JOHNSON: Maybe not. (*distinctly*) But no jury on earth will convict without motive. How do you like *that*?
(*Sound: heavy whack of fly swatter.*)
JOHNSON: You *don't* like it, eh?
(*Sound: whack of fly-swatter.*)
Bo: (*controlled*) I don't like *you*, Monsieur. Your nice veneer; it wear off.
JOHNSON: (*triumphant*) I didn't know Parker from Adam! Never even heard of him! But even if *I* had killed him, which I didn't. There's not a blasted thing you can do about it.

(*Music: bridge, beginning sharply and fading.*)
Bo: (*in despair*) Miss Parker, I don' know. (*changing tone*) Johnson, he is gone. The lights are on again. We sit in a room of law-books; and I don' know.
HELEN: Was the rest of it true? About the phone-calls? They must have cost...
Bo: (*satirically amused*) Ho! The French Republic; she would not pay for shoe-polish. No, no. It is your uncle's motor-car company, which give us *carte blanche.* Also your aunt.
HELEN: You've talked to Aunt Hester?
Bo: (*embarrassed*) Yes. She is—distressed. Your uncle's body is to be flown back tomorrow. For you, at the Credit Lyonnais Bank, there is a cheque for fifty thousand francs.
HELEN: (*breaking down*) He's dead. And it's my fault! It's my fault!
FRANK: It's not your fault! Don't talk like that!
HELEN: You heard what Johnson said. "A shabby character who"—That's not

true. But I couldn't have stayed there much longer. When I saw you at that cafe, I could have cried. And you didn't even remember me.

FRANK: I did remember you! I've never forgotten! But I was thinking about Morel's murder..

HELEN: (*taken aback*) Murder. Yes. Anyway, I had to come to you for help about the mystery.

BO: For help about—the mystery? (*begins to laugh. less amused than sarcastic*)

HELEN: Stop it! What's so funny?

BO: (*sobering*) Forgive me. Already I have make much fun with Mr. Bentley. (*grandly*) So the writer of the detective story will teach us our business, eh? Just like a book. *Pardon*. I give him the strawberry.

FRANK: Will it sound so funny, Papa Bo, when I tell you I've *solved* the mystery?

BO: You have... WHAT?

FRANK: In ninety-nine cases out of a hundred, you'd be right. No amateur can beat police-work. But this is the hundredth case, the fantastic case.— Johnson killed Mr. Parker. *And I know why*.

BO: (*agitated*) My soda-mint tablets! Where are... Ah! Here!

HELEN: If this is true, Frank, tell me! *Did* Johnson know my uncle? Or have a grudge against him?

FRANK: In answer to both questions: no.

HELEN: When Uncle Fred opened that room-door, did he see something he shouldn't have seen?

FRANK: No. There was nothing to see.

HELEN: Did Johnson mistake him for somebody else?

FRANK: No.

HELEN: Then there wasn't *any* reason?

FRANK: Oh, yes! There was a very logical reason. And the clue is right in front of my eyes now!

(*Sound: three furious whacks of fly-swatter.*)

BO: Will you pay attention to *me*, please?

FRANK: Easy, Papa! You're purple in the face!

BO: If this is a joke, young man, there is always the violin!

FRANK: I know that! But help me prove it! And... you can stop looking for "Mr. Savannah."

BO: You say it? Why?

FRANK: Because "Mr. Savannah" and Herbert Johnson are the same man!

(*Music: hits hard, then sinks under*)

FABIAN: It was quite by accident that I, Doctor Fabian of the *Maurevania*, strolled next evening into the nightclub called *La Boule Noire* and saw the wild ending of this business. *La Boule Noire*, the Black Ball, is an under-

ground room with whitewashed walls and only dim green lights fogged by tobacco-smoke. No platform for the band, none for the entertainers.
(*Music: fades out*)
(*Sound: crowd chatter begins to come up under narration. The sound of an accordion, faintly with the tango beginning* Je Ne Suis Pas Curieux)
FABIAN: As I walked down into the hot, smoky dimness of green light, the bare tables and dingy chairs were pretty well filled.

(*Sound: crowd noise, accordion up, and then down*)
HELEN: (*recognizing*) Doctor Fabian! South American cruise! Two years ago!
FABIAN: Yes!—Helen Parker!
FRANK: (*wrought up*) Doctor Fabian, can you persuade Helen to get out of here? Now?
FABIAN: Is it as bad as all that? Why?
FRANK: Because trouble is going to break loose in about three minutes. And there's... something I don't want Helen to see.
HELEN: But you *planned* it, Frank!
FRANK: I didn't plan *this!* Papa Bo did. It's his... (*bitterly*) ... sense of the dramatic. And now I can't find him; he's deserted me!—Doctor Fabian, will you help?
FABIAN: Yes, if I can! But with what?
FRANK: Have you read anything in the papers about—Helen's uncle?
FABIAN: (*gravely*) Yes. He travelled with us in the *Maurevania*.
FRANK: Then look over in the corner there! Through the green light and the smoke. That man alone at the table!
FABIAN: By the newspaper pictures, it looks like Johnson!
FRANK: It *is* Johnson! He's been released. But he's no fool and he knows there's a catch in it.
FABIAN: (*catching his excitement*) What do you want me to do?
FRANK: Go over to that table with me. Whatever I say, play up to it. But be careful; he's about as gentle as a king-cobra.
HELEN: Frank, listen.
FRANK: I won't listen and you've got to get out of here! Please!
HELEN: Frank, wait! Don't go over to... Frank!
(*Sound: voice murmur and accordion up loudly, held for a few seconds. Accordion out. Murmur very faint*)
JOHNSON: Well, well, well! If it isn't Frank Bentley! How are you Bentley?
FRANK: Evening, Mr. Johnson. Surprising you know my name!
JOHNSON: (*offhandedly*) Oh you were pointed out to me. Sit down, both of you! Have some champagne. Who's your friend?
FRANK: Sorry! This is Doctor Fabian, from the *Maurevania.*
JOHNSON: Then sit down—that's it!—unless I'm interrupting a private talk.
FABIAN: (*suavely*) Not at all, Mr. Johnson. Frank was only telling me about an

interesting murder.
JOHNSON: (*bursting out*) Now look here—! I'm tired of this Parker business.
FRANK: No I mean! (*then quietly*) the murder of Jacques Morel at the Turkish bath.
FABIAN: (*playing up*) Jacques Morel! There was something *very* valuable stolen from him. He was robbed.
JOHNSON: (*starting*) *Robbed*?
FABIAN: That wasn't in the paper!
FRANK: No. Monsieur Bo was being crafty. But I was there when I talked to somebody with a fake Southern accent.
FABIAN: What about this robbery?
FRANK: Attached to Morel's wrist was a very small leather pouch. Cut open! There'd been something so valuable it was always carried with him. And what *would* a jewel merchant carry?
FABIAN: Do you know what the jewels were?
FRANK: I was told, yes. They were pearls. And not very many of them.
FABIAN: Then their value wouldn't be…?
FRANK: *These* pearls could be traced back to the Roman Empire in the first Century A.D. They were historic relics. They were…
FABIAN: (*enlightened*) The nine black pearls of Claudius!
FRANK: Right! And worth two fortunes! But how could the murderer dispose of them?
FABIAN: He'd smuggle them out of the country, wouldn't he?
FRANK: Ah, but he couldn't! There was an extra-special guard to search everybody who left Marseilles. He couldn't possibly do it! Unless…
JOHNSON: (*shouting*) Proprietor! More champagne at this table!
PROPRIETOR: (*off*) *Tout de suite, monsieur!*
FABIAN: (*exultant*) How three innocent men can enjoy a talk about crime! You were sayings, Frank?
FRANK: The murderer had an accomplice in America. (*bitterly*) Do you know who it was? It was Frederic Parker's wife! Helen's aunt! A flighty woman who'd fallen for a plausible Don Juan like the murderer. If he could get the pearls over to her…
FABIAN: But he couldn't!
FRANK: He tried, though. Didn't you, Johnson?
JOHNSON: See if you can prove it, Mr. Bentley!
FRANK: Yours. Parker knows *when* he would arrive, and *where* he'd arrive. He was near-sighted; you waylaid him in the hall. You took him into your hotel-room …
JOHNSON: *Into* the room?
FRANK: Naturally! That door wouldn't have been *wide* open if he'd only looked in to ask for directions.
FABIAN: Better not grab the neck of that bottle, Mr. Johnson!

(*Music:* Under, accordion begins softly to play some contemporary tune.)
FRANK: In the room you pulled a gun, and pretended to be a lunatic. You showed him a few sugar-coated pellets, not large, and said you'd kill him unless he swallowed them. The poor devil was scared white; he humored you. Then you made him stand so that English-speaking servants could hear it. Then you made him stand at gunpoint and go through that talk. And you shot him through the head. That was how she heard about the room directions. Understand, Doctor Fabian?
FABIAN: That's how he'd smuggle the pearls to America! In a dead man's body!
FRANK: Yes. In a dead man's body. Which would be sent directly, without delay, to Helen's Aunt.
(*Sound: accordion out as, off, a woman screams. Crowd-chatter grows loud and shrill*)
JOHNSON: What's happening there? Over at the door?
FRANK: It's an operating-table. On wheels. Somebody's pushing it!
PROPRIETOR: (*off, frantic*) Mesdames et messieurs! Rien a craindre! C'est un blague!
ENGLISH VOICE: (*off*) Joke, is it? That's a dead body!

FABIAN; (*close to microphone, almost in a whisper*) And never have I seen a more grotesque sight than that white operating table rolling towards us)—past shrinking guests, and women with mouths frozen in a scream—in the wild green light. Closer It came, and closer, with *something* under a sheet. And Johnson stood up behind the table with a champagne-bottle in his hands. And the bottle fell to the floor...
(*Sound: crash of breaking bottle*)

FRANK: Here's your victim, my friend. What customs-officer, what policeman, would suspect a dead body? It *was* to have been flown home, by Mrs. Parker's order, for embalming and burial.
BO: (*fading on*) But *we* will remove the pearls, Mr. Johnson. Yes, I am Monsieur Bo!
JOHNSON: Remove the...?
BO: Under your own eyes. With sharp knives. Can you watch it?
JOHNSON: No!
BO: Then tell the truth. You killed him!
JOHNSON: I...
BO: You killed him!
JOHNSON: You've got your proof, haven't you? Yes! I did it!
BO: Jules! Maurice! *Tenez les mains!*
FRANK: Wait a moment. That body is only a wax dummy!
BO: (*pleased*) Exactly and precisely. (*raising his voice*) Taisez-vous. Imbeciles! C'est un figurant de cire!

FRANK: (*furious*) Listen, you French Mephistopheles! I agreed to your idea of bringing in the man's body to get a confession. The black pearls were enough I agree—but what's the point if you only bring in a wax dummy.
BO: (*with dignity*) I do it, young man, to pay you back.
FRANK: To pay me back? For what?
BO: For being so confusing, I could murder you. I am Papa Bo. I have indigestion. You tell me the big clue to this crime was something you saw in my office. But you say no more. What *was* it that gave you the idea?
FRANK: (*surprised*) Don't you understand even yet?
BO: No!
FRANK: It was your soda-mint tables, Papa Bo. Your soda-mint tablets! He swallowed the pearls like your tablets.
(*Music: in and behind*)
FABIAN: And so, as I Doctor Fabian of Cabin B-13 end my story. "The Nine Black Reasons", I think you will agree that my title was justified. That was the problem of *why*. Equally curious is the problem of... but let us not anticipate. Next week the *Maurevania* moves only a little way along the Riviera, to anchor in the bay outside Nice. And, as we look from a certain beach to the great gambling-rooms of Monaco, I shall tell you the tale called "The Count of Monte Carlo". Will you join me in *Cabin B-13*?
(*Sound: ship's whistles*)
(*Music: out*)

Notes for the Curious

The story of "The Nine Black Reasons" is unique to *Cabin B-13* although, like an earlier script, it has a minor element in common with "Harem-Scarem", a short, short story published in the (*London*) *Daily Mail* in March 1939. There are also minor points of similarity with "The Third Bullet", which was first published, as by "Carter Dickson", in 1937.

Marseilles' *Rue La Canebière*, the street known as the "rue can of beer" was so-named by American GIs during the second world war.

The protagonist in "The Nine Black Reasons" is Frank Bentley, a "*well-known writer of detective stories*" whose stories "*always begin with some mad situation that turns out to be quite logical*". As such, he is surely another proxy for Carr himself. It is worth noting that another of Carr's detective novelist heroes, Richard Marlowe—who appears in the 1945 stage play *Intruding Shadow*—was the author of a number of mysteries including *The Nine Black Reasons*, which Carr may have had in mind when he came up with the title of this radio play.

Carr had a knack of creating memorable sleuths, even in radio plays, and the Mephistophelian Papa Bo, the *juge d'instruction*—or examining magistrate—who identifies the "nine black reasons" is no exception. It is a great pity that we do not hear or read of him again. He is reminiscent of Carr's first detective, the even more Mephistophelian Henri Bencolin, head of the Paris police and, like Mr. Bo a *juge d'instruction.* Bencolin appears in five novels and several short stories as well as *Grand Guignol*, an early version of *It Walks by Night* (1930) as well as in the framing story for *The New Canterbury Tales* (1927), a set of seven short stories by Carr and the poet and novelist Frederic Prokosch. Bencolin in turn owes something to Hercule Flambeau, a character who appears in several of GK Chesterton's Father Brown detective stories.

The Cavalier's Cup (1953) proved to be Sir Henry Merrivale's final novel but Carr made three subsequent efforts to revive the character. In 1956, he published a novella, "Ministry of Miracles," Also in 1956 he proposed a new Merrivale mystery initially titled *Commander Sir Henry Merrivale*, later *Enter Three Poisoners*, but Carr abandoned the idea in 1958. Then in 1961, he again decided to bring back Merrivale. The new novel was to be titled *The Six Black Reasons* which might mean that the plot would have had something in common with the *Cabin B-13* radio play. However, despite completing eight chapters, Carr never finished *The Six Black Reasons* and the typescript of the eight chapters has long been lost.

The Count of Monte Carlo

(*Sound: a ship's whistle*)
(*Music: in and fades out behind*)
(*Music: in and behind*)
FABIAN: The blue of the Mediterranean, under a noonday sun! As we look out of the sun-lounge—you, a passenger of our luxury-liner *Maurevania*, and I, Doctor Fabian of Cabin B-13—we can see the red-and-white confectionery of houses on the headland above the blue sea. That is Nice, once the playground of the Riviera. The colors seem almost too bright, don't they? As though a painter had overdone it? Nine miles eastwards… follow the coast-line… lies Monte Carlo. And between Nice and Monte Carlo, years ago, I met an adventure whose mystery was compounded of the yellow roses, the woman of the balustrade, and the unseen deaths.

(*Music: fades out*)
(*Sound: theme of jigging/gaiety in and fades behind*)
FABIAN: Do you remember, 18 years ago, how all the world danced and played on the Riviera? In black bars, over banging pianos, they sang the "Maine Stein Song," Behind marble balustrades, overlooking the sea, romances flowered. In the great white Casino, under its artificial-looking palm-trees, the croupier's chant droned endlessly above the roulette-wheel.
(*Sound: faint crowd chatter has come up under*)

CROUPIER: *Faites vos jeux, mesdames et messieurs! Faites vos jeux!*
FABIAN: (*whispering, close to microphone*) Make your bets, ladies and gentlemen. Make your bets!
CROUPIER: *Les jeux sont faits! Rien ne va plus!* (*Sound: the wheel begins to spin, with roulette-ball clicking*).
FABIAN: And the white roulette-ball flickered in the red and-black wheel. And eager faces bent forward. And…
CROUPIER: (*watching*) *Numero… numero…*
FABIAN: It was in that rather tawdry salon, one night in the summer of '30, that I met Barton Stevens. Stevens, young and with money to burn. He was standing by one crowded table, his dinner-jacket rumpled, his face looking… not so much dissipated, as feverish and desperate.
(*Sound: crowd-chatter sustained under.*)
STEVENS: Fabian, old man! You wandering son of a liner!
FABIAN: Hello, Bart! How's your luck at the table?
STEVENS: (*feverishly cheerful*) Terrible, thanks; but who cares? Here, have a handful of these counters!

(*Sound: roulette-counters, of some material like plastic, rattled and riffled*).
CROUPIER: *Faites vos jeux, messieus et mesdames! Faites vos jeux!*
STEVENS: Wait a minute! I'll just lean across the table... *pardon,*
MADAME: *pardon, monsieur* ... and there we are!
FABIAN: What's the stake, Bart? I can't see.
BART: (*pleased*) Ten thousand on number twenty-two. To win *this* time, anyway. How do you like that?
FABIAN: I don't like it. (*as though to a child*) Bart, don't you know you can't win if you back a single number and keep on doubling, when you lose?
BART: What's wrong with it? The wheel's not crooked!
FABIAN: It doesn't have to be. The odds are too heavy in favour of the bank!
CROUPIER: *Les jeux sont faits! Rien ne va plus!*
(*Sound: crowd-chatter sinks to silence. wheel spins.*)
BART: Come on, twenty-two! Come on, twenty-two!—Why didn't you make a bet?
FABIAN: I want to know what's wrong with you, Bart.
BART: (*tensely*) Listen, my boy! I've just finished a love-affair to end all love-affairs. Sky-rockets and thunderbolts! Red fire you could see from here to Tibet!
CROUPIER: *Numero... numero...*
BART: I'm still dizzy. I've wrecked about four lives. And now...
(*Sound: from crowd, noises both of groaning and triumph as wheel stops*).
CROUPIER: *Numero—trois! Manque, rouge, et impair!*
BART: Lost again; lucky in love; and who cares? The police will be here soon anyway...
FABIAN: The police!?
BART: (*grimly*) That's right. French cops—not from Monaco—with white clubs and a nasty look.
FABIAN: (*with authority*) Listen, Bart! We're getting out of here!
BART: (*in friendship*) Good old Fabian! Still helping lame dogs. (*changing tone, bitterly*) Do you think you can help *me*?
FABIAN: If it's what I believe it is, I can have a try. Come on!
BART: (*calling*) *Mesdames et messieurs!* Does anybody want a lot of valuable counters? Here!
(*Sound: counters, falling on top of each other, rattle on heavy felt table top*)
BART: But you'd better work fast, old man. The coppers will be here in fifteen minutes!

(*Music: in and fades behind*)
FABIAN: Outside, on the terrace, it was deserted except for ourselves. I sat opposite Bart Stevens at a table by the balustrade: above gardens and sea, with the Chinese lanterns glowing. His attitude wasn't bravado; it was too deep for that. Judge for yourself!
(*Music: out*)

BART: Excuse me if my hand's not very steady. I'll get this cigarette lighted if it's the last...! There! Got it!
FABIAN: You were saying something about a love-affair?
BART: Lord! *Wasn't I*!
FABIAN: I hate social gossip; and I don't hear much of it. But I did hear you were engaged to Janet Derwent.
BART: (*startled*) This doesn't concern Janet! Except... Anyway, it was another woman. And another kind of—affair. Woman—Her name was Dolores.
FABIAN: Yes. I see.
BART: *Do* you see? She attracted me; it burned up everything like a forest. I couldn't think; I couldn't see; I couldn't reason! I wasn't in love with Dolores. I'm not even sure I liked her. But she hypnotized me with an attractiveness that—now do you understand?
FABIAN: (*wryly*) To my cost, Bart, I've learned. And this—Dolores?
BART: (*impatiently*) That was only what I called her. After Dolores in the poem.
FABIAN: Never mind. Call her that. What's she like?
BART: Young; wealthy; American. I've described her—nature. (*bitterly*) And mine.
FABIAN: What about Janet Derwent?
BART: (*uncertainly*) I can't tell you! I can't tell you!
FABIAN: Does Janet know anything about this?
BART: Know anything? She's been staying at Nice! For two months!
FABIAN: While this was going on?
BART: Yes! What's more, Dolores was engaged to be married to... (*desperately*) Listen, Fabian! *You don't know what's happened.*
FABIAN: I wonder!—Start from the beginning.
(*Music: creeps in behind*)
BART: Both of us, Dolores and I, had the crazy idea that nobody knew; nobody noticed. I'd see her at her villa. Or else we'd meet in a little bar at Nice; a narrow modernistic place, with tables and booths at the back. We'd sit in a booth, in the afternoon, and drink Martinis. It was shadowy there. Over at one side there was a piano...
(*Music: piano emerges very softly with a contemporary tune:* Ain't Misbehavin'. *It continues only a few seconds after Dolores speaks*)

DOLORES: Bart! The first verse of that poem! Tell me again!
BART: (*considering*) I haven't thought about Swinburne for years. At college you think it's great poetry. At thirty you know it's hysterical raving. (*fiercely*) Then I meet somebody like you! And it's *real*.
DOLORES: Bart! Sit closer. Look in my eyes! Now tell me—"Dolores".
BART: "Cold eyelids that hide like a jewel
                    Hard eyes that grow soft for an hour:
                    The slender white limbs, and the cruel

>   Red mouth like a venomous flower;
>   When these are gone by with their glories,
>   What shall rest of thee then, what remain,
>   O mystic and sombre Dolores, Our Lady of Pain?"

DOLORES: Yes! I love that verse.

BART: Even the threat in it?

DOLORES: Yes, darling. It flatters me, I've always thought it meant a special condemnation. In the after-life. Reserved for *me*. I'd like *that*, too!

BART: (*sharply*) Then this isn't the first time you've heard "Dolores?"

DOLORES: No, Bart. Jimmy Westlake used to recite it.—Bart!

BART: Well?

DOLORES: Why did you move away?

BART: I didn't move away!

DOLORES: You did, Bart! (*tenderly*) Was it because I mentioned Jimmy Westlake? (*pleading*) Bart, you must *know* I've met other men before I met you!

BART: I know it, yes. And I admit I'm being completely idiotic! But I hate it!

DOLORES: That's in the past, darling!

BART: It's the past I hate! All the shadowy people I *imagine*.

DOLORES: We're in the present, Bart. (*controlled fury*) And Janet Derwent...

BART: Let's not talk about Janet!

DOLORES: (*thoughtfully*) You know, Bart, I've often wished I'd lived in Renaissance times. They had gay-colored gowns, and fiery jewels. They had poisoned rings, and poisoned gloves, and even—(*she stops; then low voice*) How I loathe that woman!

BART: *You're* engaged too, you know.

DOLORES: Yes. To Jean Ravelle. Do you know what they call him?

BART: I don't *care* what they call him.

DOLORES: They call him "The Count of Monte Carlo." He's as rich, as influential, as any man in France. He's not old; barely fifty; and he's *very* good-looking.— Aren't you jealous, Bart?

BART: Why do you ask that? Because...

DOLORES: Because that's why I got engaged to him. To *make* you jealous. (*still more intensity*) You're not in love with this Janet, are you? *Here* you can say you are, yes! But not when we're—*entirely* alone; can you? You don't love her, do you?

BART: (*bedevilled*) No! Yes! *I* dunno! Maybe not!

DOLORES: As far as I'm concerned, there'll never be anybody except you! You know that, Bart! Sit closer. Put your arms around me. That's it! (*pause*) Bart...

(*Music: Softly, off, the piano begins again with* Ain't Misbehavin'. *This continues for about eight seconds until Ravelle speaks.*)

RAVELLE: (*furious*) Forgive me!

(Sound: Clatter as of cane thrown down on wooden table.)
BART: What the devil?...
DOLORES: Jean! What are you...?
RAVELLE: (*controlled, suave*) Forgive me, my dear, if your fiancé must throw a walking-stick on the table to attract your attention.
DOLORES: (*quick-breathing, but composed*) Quite a surprise seeing you, Jean. Won't you sit down?
RAVELLE: Thank you. I will sit opposite.
BART: You're —Monsieur Ravelle?
RAVELLE: I am. Of Ravelle etc Cie., Cosmetics and Perfumes. (*proudly*) Some call me "The Count of Monte Carlo." No doubt in imitation of Monte Cristor, but still...! I am rather grey, you observe, but not at all the fat bourgeois you pictured.
BART: (*desperately*) Look here, sir! We've got to have a showdown about this. Dolores and I...
RAVELLE: You tell me, in effect that Napoleon is dead.
BART: (*startled*) Then you've known this? But you haven't—?
RAVELLE: (*amused*) Challenged you to a duel? Come, now! (changing tone) Do you imagine I am getting married for love?
BART: Isn't that the usual idea?
RAVELLE: You come from a younger and—forgive me, sir!—less civilized race. No sensible man marries for love.
BART: Then you have older and —forgive me, sir!— less civilized customs!
DOLORES: Be Careful, Bart! Careful what you say!
RAVELLE: (*unheeding*) A sensible man marries for a home. For children. Above all! — for a hostess who will adorn his home and grace the dinner-table. My fiancée there...may I call her Dolores?...has poise, grace, good taste. She loves flowers and the art of living. Her private life is her own, like mine. BUT —
(Sound: flat rap of cane on table.)
RAVELLE: (*quietly fierce*) *I will not be made a fool of.* And this must stop! (*pause*) Pardon me if I lose my temper. My breast-pocket handkerchief! To mop my forehead! I...
(Sound: Very slight rattle, as of small ounce-or-so bottle, flattish, landing on table)
RAVELLE: Clumsy!
DOLORES: (*interested*) Jean! That tiny little bottle in the handkerchief. Is it a new perfume?
RAVELLE: No, my dear. And don't pick it up and put it in your handbag! Give it back...
DOLORES: (*disappointed*) But this is only...!
RAVELLE: Yes. You've seen me carry samples, for my manufactories. And don't sniff at it; it is only a little less dangerous than prussic acid. Hand it back. Thank you. Dolores... if I may call you Dolores...?

DOLORES: Call me what you like! We're not married... yet.
RAVELLE: Those are not your usual manners, my dear. You would divert me from saying; this must stop.
BART: You're right, Monsieur Ravelle. It's gotta stop.
DOLORES: Bart! Don't say that.
RAVELLE: (*tolerantly*) An affair of this kind is excellent (*changing tone*) But don't confuse it with marriage, either of you. (*Ravelle means what he says in the next speech. His logic cannot understand.*) You are actually no more in love with your Dolores than she is with you. You would not... what is your term?... throw over a suitable girl like Miss Derwent? You would not be so foolish. You would not be so imprudent. How would you?
BART: (*stung*) What makes you think I wouldn't?
DOLORES: (*crying out*) Bart! What do you mean?
RAVELLE: No. He does not mean it. This is bravado. If I asked him strighfor-wardly, do you love this— Dolores?
BART: (*losing his head*) I do!
RAVELLE: *You fool*!
BART: What do you mean, fool?
RAVELLE: (*suddenly calm*) I came here, believe me, to settle this matter in a civilized way. I even brought Miss Janet Derwent.
BART: (*startled*) You brought Janet? Where is she?
RAVELLE: At the front of the bar. Stand up and look!
BART: She's not there. (*calling*) Antoine! Ici! Vite!
(*Sound: fade in quick, hurrying footsteps.*)
ANTOINE: (*fading on; fat, breathless*) You called me, *monsieur*?
BART: Yes! A young lady, small, brown hair and eyes. Where is she?
ANTOINE: (*significantly*) She left a moment ago, monsieur. And I think she was crying.
RAVELLE: If you *will* shout like a taxi-driver...
BART: Stop it! —Did she say anything, Antoine?
ANTOINE: Only a few words, monsieur, about this young lady here.
DOLORES: About me? How interesting! What did she say?
ANTOINE: (*grimly*) I hope it was a joke, madame. She says she would like to kill you.
(MUSIC: Sting and down behind.)

BART: You see, Doctor Fabian, this is the story of a murder. Only I didn't know that! It was flying closer, and closer, and then it was there. I don't know why I said what I did, about being in love with Dolores; I don't know what the devil made me say it...
FABIAN: Don't you, Bart? I know.
BART: You know?
FABIAN: Never tell any American, in a tone of challenge, that something

is foolish and imprudent. It's the surest way to make him do it. But the Count of Monte Carlo didn't realize that. Did you mean what you said? That you loved Dolores?
BART: No! As soon as I'd said that, I knew I didn't; But afterwards, in decency, I couldn't approach Janet to... what are you smiling at?
FABIAN: Only in sympathy. Word of Honor.
BART: (*tensely*) Late the next afternoon...funny! that's only today!...I went to Dolores' villa between Nice and Monte Carlo. At the back it has a very small garden with a marble balustrade along the cliff over the sea. (*breaking off*) If I could describe it to you, Fabian...!
FABIAN: Do you want me to describe it, then?
BART: Yes, it'd make things cl... (*suddenly realizing*) Look here, what do you know about this?
(*Music: in softly behind*)

FABIAN: In the garden, on the balustrade, sat Dolores. Dangerously —with her back to the cliffs, and the surf far below. Beside a garden table, facing her, sat...Janet Derwent. On the balustrade, beside Dolores, was a bowl of yellow roses. On the table, beside Janet, was another glass bowl of roses. It was a hot, still day. Not a breath of wind. No noise except the boiling of the surf below...
(*Music: out*)
FABIAN: Nobody heard you enter the house, Bart. A side door led into the garden. But you stood motionless. Because the atmosphere between those two girls, was hatred.
(*Sound: Surf establish then down so that it is hardly heard.*)
DOLORES: ... that's why I say, Janet, it was so nice of you to come here when I phoned.
JANET: It *was* nice of me, wasn't it? I thought so myself. (*bursting out*) Oh, why have we got to keep pretending?
DOLORES: I'm not pretending, dear. *You* are.
JANET: (*slight pause: suddenly*) Yes, you're quite right.
DOLORES: I thought so!
JANET: In front of my family, especially a virtuous brother, I've got to pretend to think Bart Stevens is the lowest of the low. But I *don't* blame him. I've never blamed him. I blame *you*. (*fiercely*) I'd like to...
DOLORES: Yes! You'd like to kill me. And all this time I've been daring you to.
JANET: Daring me? (*startled*) Is that why you've been...?
DOLORES: Sitting on the balustrade? Leaning back like this? Of course! If I fell backwards, now...
JANET: (*instinctively*) For heaven's sake, be careful.
DOLORES:...my body would strike a rock ledge a hundred feet down. Then another rock ledge. Then the sea. You'd like that, wouldn't you?
JANET: No! Not really! Not now!

DOLORES: Didn't you hear what Bart said yesterday?
JANET: Yes, I did.
DOLORES: (*gently*) Do you *enjoy* being slapped in the face, dear?
JANET: No! That's why I'm here today. (*clearly*) Bart didn't mean that; and in your heart you know it. (*pause*) You do know it, don't you?
DOLORES: I love him, Janet.
JANET: For the time being, yes!
DOLORES: Time being or not, it's true and real. I'm sorry you won't *try* to kill me, Janet.
JANET: Sorry? Why?
DOLORES: Because, in the scuffle, *you* might fall.
JANET: (*alarmed but steady*) Stay where you are! There's a stone on the ground here. I could. (*Breaking off*) Who's that standing over by the door?
DOLORES: (*crying out*) Bart!
(*Sound: Fade in slow footsteps on sandy ground with:*)
BART: (*fading on*) Did you mean it, Dolores?
DOLORES: (*clinging-vine again*) Mean what, darling?
BART: "because in the scuffle, you might fall"?
DOLORES: (*sincerely*) No, I didn't mean one word of it. If I killed anyone, darling, it wouldn't be so crude as that. It would be subtle, as the Renaissance was subtle.
BART: (*bursting out*) Look here, Janet! I...
JANET: (*nearly in tears*) Go away, please! Don't speak to me!
DOLORES: You see, Bart, the poor dear is embarrassed. She can't forgive you for overhearing her. (*pleading*) But that doesn't matter to us, does it? Sit down here. Beside me! See the yellow roses in the bowl? There are more on the table by Janet.
JANET: Please go away!
BART: (*bitterly*) I'll go away, all right. I've had enough embarrassment, thanks.
DOLORES: But you'll come back later, Bart. (*significantly*) Won't you?
BART: (*bewildered*) What's *wrong* with us? Have we gone insane, all of a sudden? This talk about murder—!
DOLORES: It's the mad Mediterranean, Bart. It affects even poor Janet.
BART: Suppose somebody *did* kill you?
DOLORES: I won't die, yet, Bart. And if I did—! Don't you remember that verse of "Dolores?"
BART: (*curtly*) No! I've forgotten. (*fade*) And I'd better go now.
(*Sound: footsteps fade under*)
DOLORES: "Thy life shalt not cease though thou doff it,
        Thou shalt live until evil be slain;
      And good shall die first," said thy prophet,
          Our Lady of... of...
(*her voice falters and mouths as though she had been struck dizzy or blinded*) (*in terror*) Help me! Help...
BART: (*shouting off*) Dolores! What's wrong? Dolores!

(*Sound: running footsteps fade in. They are topped by a scream, receding. off; thud as of body against rock; another thud. then splash, surf up loudly then down, distant cry of gulls*).
BART: (*dazed*) She's gone! I saw her strike an edge of the cliff, and then... (*pause*) What happened? My back was turned! What happened?
JANET: (*levelly*) I killed her.
BART: (*staggered*) What are you talking about?
JANET: I said: I killed her.
BART: Don't talk such foolishness! You were sitting beside that table! Where you are now?
JANET: She started to recite, if you noticed. And she stood up.
BART: *Well*?
JANET: All of a sudden her eyes went—crazy. Her mouth writhed. She was going to kill me. On the ground was a stone, a polished stone. When I threw it at her head...yes!...I didn't mean to hit her. I couldn't have hit her if I'd tried; but I did!
(*Sound: crash of surf up momentarily, then down behind*)
JANET: (*bursting out*) Why did you think *I* was so un-approachable? Why did you treat *me* like a—like something in a stained-glass window? Why... (*fade*) Oh, what's the good!
(*Sound: running footsteps, fading off*)
BART: Janet! Come back here! Janet!
RAVELLE: (*fading on*) Do you wonder, Mr. Stevens, if she does not like what we all saw?
BART: (*startled*) Ravelle! How did *you* get here?
RAVELLE: You did not hear me? I thought not. The garden has several doors. (*voice hardening*) From one of them I saw...
BART: (*thinking of Janet*) Saw what?
RAVELLE: I saw *you* throw Dolores from the balustrade.
BART: But—I didn't kill her!
RAVELLE: (*quickly*) Then who did?
BART: (*realizing*) I... I don't know!
RAVELLE: If Miss Derwent...
BART: She doesn't know anything about it!
RAVELLE: I don't like you, sir. Yesterday, perhaps, my voice may have shown more jealousy than I admitted. (*deeply moved and shaken*) When I said I did not love my future wife, that was a lie. Now she is dead. (*swallowing*) You, the right person, must pay for it. I swear on the Cross that the guillotine shall chop your head into the basket as I take this walking-stick between my hands, and...
(*Sound: sharp crack of broken wood*)
RAVELLE: You did it. I saw you. Confess, now! *You* killed her.
BART: (*slight pause*) Yes! I killed her!
RAVELLE: Thank you, my friend. Thank you!

(*Music: sting, and down behind*)
BART: And so, Doctor Fabian, here I am. I went out of that villa like a sleep-walker, after I'd signed a confession for Ravelle. I tried to see Janet, of course...
FABIAN: Would Janet see you?
BART: No... Consequently... (*attempting bravado*)...I changed my clothes and came up here to the Casino.
FABIAN: (*musing*) And we sit here on the terrace. And over there, beyond the French windows, are light and life. (*changing tone*) And I haven't told you the truth!
BART: Told me the truth?
FABIAN: (*grimly*) But I couldn't tell you until I'd heard *your* story. The truth is, Bart, that...
BART: Wait a minute!
FABIAN: What's wrong?
BART: The middle French window! It's Janet... and Ravelle! They're coming out here!
(*Sound: as French window opens, off, crowd-chatter up faintly*)
CROUPIER: (*off*) Les jeux sont fait! Rien ne va plus!
JANET: (*calling, off*) Bart? Are you out here? (*seeing him*) Bart!
(*Sound: crowd-chatter out, as window is closed. No footsteps; the terrace is thick grass*)
JANET: (*fading on*) Bart, help me! He's never let up, never let up, with a mental torture I can't stand any longer!
BART: (*sharply*) Who's been doing this? Ravelle?
RAVELLE: (*fading on*) Yes, young man. And you won't stop me. You will help me. (*through his teeth*) This very foolish girl has confessed to the murder.
BART: Janet!
FABIAN: (*suavely*) I quite agree with you, Monsieur Ravelle. She *was* very foolish.
RAVELLE: (*angrily*) May I ask, sir, who you are?
FABIAN: You may, sir. My name is Fabian.
RAVELLE: You have perhaps some interest in this matter?
FABIAN: Some slight interest. I am the doctor who performed the post-mortem.
RAVELLE: Post-mortem? Dolores?
FABIAN: Yes. The body was washed ashore near Nice. No police-surgeon was available; they summoned *me*. And you were very foolish to speak, Janet Derwent.
JANET: What else could I do? I couldn't let Bart take the blame! I wrote to the police, and—they'll have the letter soon. (*bewildered*) What do you want me to do? Why was I foolish?

FABIAN: Because *you* didn't kill Dolores, Miss Derwent.
JANET: *What did you say?*
FABIAN: You think you killed her. But you didn't. That stone never touched her. (*quickly*) Agreed, Monsieur Ravelle?
RAVELLE: You are a wise man, doctor. A very wise man!
FABIAN: (*almost cajoling*) In that case, sir, let me persuade you to be generous! Drop this charge of murder against Barton Stevens!
RAVELLE: (*taken aback*) You are not a fool, doctor. (*viciously*) Don't talk like one.
FABIAN: Will *nothing* persuade you to drop the charge?
RAVELLE: Nothing in this world!
FABIAN: Then I had better tell you how Dolores *really* died.
RAVELLE: (*fiercely*) She died because he threw her...
FABIAN: *Oh, no!* (*pause*) All of a sudden, you remember, her eyes grew—insane. Her mouth writhed. It was not because she wanted to kill Janet. It was because pain, the searing of agony, burned up through her lungs and throat. Her head swam; her eyesight dimmed; she toppled over the edge unconscious or dead.— She was poisoned.
RAVELLE: *Poisoned?*
FABIAN: Try to remember a talk yesterday, at the back of that bar at Nice. As though a cymbal clanged in memory, hear it—in imagination!—as I described it.
(*Sound: faint clang of cymbals*)

DOLORES: (*filter*) Jean! That tiny little bottle in the handkerchief! Is it a new perfume?
RAVELLE: (*filter*) No, my dear. And don't pick it up and put it into your handbag. Give it back!
DOLORES: (*filter*) But this is only...!
RAVELLE: (*filter*) Yes. You've seen me carry samples, for my manufactories. And don't sniff at it; it is only a little less dangerous than prussic acid.

FABIAN: The liquid in that bottle was nitrobenzene. No layman could get it. Only a technician. Like Monsieur Ravelle.
JANET: Poisoned? But she couldn't have been poisoned.
FABIAN: Why not?
JANET: I was there! She didn't eat or drink anything the whole time!
FABIAN: She didn't need to—nitrobenzene, in its commercial form, is quite harmless. But take the undiluted liquid, as somebody did, and pour it over a large bowl of yellow roses. It only increases their fragrance; that's its purposes The victim, on a hot and airless day, sits for half an hour breathing those fumes beside her. The fumes gather, like unsuspected coal-gas; they take hold of throat and lungs, and then, like my fist on this table, they strike.

FABIAN: (*changing tone*) Will you drop your charge, *now*, friend Ravelle? *Or shall I make mine.*

RAVELLE: (*bewildered*) I drop it! I drop it! Your charge against me is absurd!

BART: Fabian, he can't drop it. He killed Dolores! He's the only one who could have done it!

FABIAN: That's where you're wrong, Bart. He's as innocent as you are. But he had to learn that he couldn't bluff against evidence.

BART: Innocent as... But *somebody* killed Dolores! Who's guilty?

FABIAN: The police told me very little. *You* have the facts. Can't you understand now?

JANET: *I* can't, anyway!

FABIAN: Who *did* talk so much about Renaissance poisoning? Who invited you to the villa, Miss Derwent, for no reason she ever explained? Who gave you a chair at the garden-table, beside *another* bowl of yellow roses?

JANET: But that was...

BART: Dolores! Dolores herself!

FABIAN: She knew about the poison. She knew Ravelle often carried it. She was waiting for an opportunity. And it happened yesterday—when she put the poison in her handbag, and gave him back a harmless bottle.

JANET: Then the whole plot was to kill *me*?

FABIAN: It was. And to put the blame on Ravelle?

RAVELLE: (*in agony*) I deny that! It's impossible!

FABIAN: Her fingerprints alone—ask the police—were on those two glass rose-bowls. But Dolores confused the rose-bowls. Dolores went too far. And she died from her own poison.

JANET: (*bitterly quoting*) "O sanguine and subtle Dolores..."

FABIAN: "Our Lady... of Pain".

(*Music: in and behind*)

FABIAN: And so, as I returned that night to Cabin *B-13*, I took down a work by Doctor C.J.S. Thompson, the British toxicologist; and in his *Poisons and Poisoners*, page 124, I found a case whose medical features were much like those I have been describing. (*Amused*) But I am not a detective. And I know that in the "Miracle Footprint" affair, for instance, I should have been baffled. Does it interest you? Then next week, as we cruise south towards Naples and I tell you the story called "Below Suspicion"[1], will you join me in *Cabin B-13*?

(*Sound: ship's whistles*)

(*Music: fades out*)

---

[1] While the next *Cabin B-13* play is entitled "Below Suspicion"', it is not set in Italy and its plot could not be summarised as the Miracle Footprint affair. However, that would be a reasonable summary of the mystery in the radio play "The Footprint in the Sky", which is set in England and was broadcast in *Cabin B-13* on 7 September 1948. The next *Cabin B-13* play set in Italy is "The Power of Darkness".

Notes for the Curious

The seventh play is another original mystery and, as with some of the other *Cabin B-13* plays, its plot draws on a reference that John Dickson Carr would have found in his extensive library of books on historical crime and the techniques of crime and detection. On this occasion, the specific volume is Doctor Hans Gross's invaluable *System der Kriminalistik* (1904), which Carr regarded as "*the most complete textbook on crime ever compiled*". It was a rich source of ideas for him and his contemporaries.

As well as an interest in the techniques of crime and detection, Carr took a great interest in what is now termed "True Crime." He produced a book-length study of one infamous unsolved seventeenth century crime *The Murder of Sir Edmund Godfrey* (1936) and a short piece considering the case against Nan Patterson, a chorine in a successful musical comedy who was tried—but not convicted—for the murder of her boyfriend in 1904. The complexities of the quest for justice is a regular theme in Carr's work and he was always clear that those guilty of a crime should be spared punishment if the victim deserved what they got.

Carr re-used the central ploy of "The Count of Monte Carlo" in the twentieth Dr Fell novel *In Spite of Thunder* (1960), moving the setting from the Riviera to Geneva, Switzerland, and changing the date from 1930 to 1956.

Poisons and Poisoners (1931) by C. J. S. Thompson, curator of the historical section of the museum of the Royal College of Surgeons in England describes the "*poisoned rings, and poisoned gloves*" of Renaissance times, to which Dolores refers in her conversation with Bart Stevens, and on the page reference given by Carr can be found the following curious story:

> "*The poisoned flowers of mediaeval romance, although they have been discredited in the light of modern science, must not be dismissed as entirely improbable, as evidenced from the following curious case which occurred in London some years ago.*
>
> "*A hawker with a barrow filled with bunches of lavender, was noticed talking wildly in a street in Stockwell. In a few minutes he was seen to fall insensible and was removed to Lambeth Infirmary, where he died shortly afterwards.*
>
> "*The medical officer of the institution said he found the man was suffering from benzaldehyde poisoning, and in his pockets were discovered sev-*

> enteen packets of lavender seeds and a bottle of oil of mirbane which he had evidently used to increase the perfume of the lavender he sold. The doctor stated that in his opinion, the man had been overcome by the vapor of the benzaldehyde he had inhaled from the lavender on his barrow."

"Oil of mirbane" (nitrobenzene) was once used as an inexpensive perfume for soaps, as a cheaper substitute for oil of bitter almonds (benzaldehyde) but by the late nineteenth century both were considered too toxic for any such applications. It is for others to judge whether or not Carr was accurate in suggesting that a large bowl of roses, treated with nitrobenzene on a hot and airless day, would have the same localized toxicity as a similarly treated *"barrow filled with bunches of lavender"*.

The Count of Monte Carlo is the title of a novel *"allegedly based on real-life intrigue and spying… under the surface of European democracy"*, written in 1911 by Jim Blake, the hero of Carr's late novel *The Ghosts' High Noon* (1969). In that book, there are references to a transatlantic liner called the *Mauretania* (sic), which is possibly the same *Mauretania* on which Sir Henry Merrivale sailed to America in the "Carter Dickson" novel *A Graveyard to Let* (1949).

The poem "Dolores", subtitled "Notre-Dame des Sept Douleurs (Our Lady of the Seven Sorrows)" is a poem by Algernon Charles Swinburne whose work Carr quotes in numerous works, including *It Walks by Night* (1930), *To Wake the Dead* (1937), *The Curse of the Bronze Lamp* (1945) and *The Ghosts' High Noon* (1969) as well as the radio play "Who Killed Matthew Corbin?" (1939). Perhaps, Bart Stevens captures something of Carr's own feelings about Swinburne when he says that *"At college you think its great poetry. At thirty you know its hysterical raving. Then I meet somebody like you! And it's* real*."*

Below Suspicion

(*Sound: a ship's whistle*)
ANNOUNCER: *Cabin B-13.*
(*Music: in and behind*)
FABIAN: Look over the railing, here on B Deck tonight, and see how the blue water boils phosphorescent past the *Maurevania's* side! Didn't you recognize me in the darkness? I am Doctor Fabian, our ship's surgeon, from Cabin B-13. But this evening, as we cruise south off the coast of Italy, I wish it were daylight, and I had field-glasses. For over there on the coast, about where I'm pointing, a crime was once committed in which —according to the evidence—the murderer must have walked on air. I wonder if you ever saw Valerie Blake on the stage? As Paula Tanqueray? As Juliet? As Nell Gwynn? You would have to see her to understand that blonde grace, that flashing charm; and we all loved her. Nobody could understand why Valerie Blake — not yet thirty, not at the height of her fame—should suddenly retire from the stage for good. She traveled out with us in the *Maurevania*; it was summer, '28. The whole ship buzzed with gossip. I remember one husband and wife, playing shuffle-board on the top deck. The shuffle-board stick would send that wooden disk slithering across the deck towards the score-board.
(*Music: fades out*)

(*Sound: wooden disk slithers off and strikes hard surface like heavy metal; no ring*)
GEORGE: (*disgustedly*) Missed the score board and hit a ventilator! — What were you saying, my dear?
HARRY: There's something very funny about this Valerie Blake affair.
GEORGE: (*grunting, abstracted*) Don't see anything funny about it. —Watch me get a ten this time!
HETTY: Do you know where she's *going*?
GEORGE Some place in Italy, the paper said.
(*Sound: slither of disk.*)
HETTY: She's taken a little house, with a private beach, on the Italian coast. Miles from anywhere or anybody.
GEORGE: We-ell! The girl's just got married!
HETTY: But to live there *for good!* And — have you met Ralph Garrett? The husband?
GEORGE: I'm afraid I have.
HETTY: My dear! (*Airily satirical*) He's a strong silent man.
GEORGE: (*Growling*) I thought you used to like 'em that way.
HETTY: Strong. Silent. And, oh Lord, how dull. (*changing tone*) Listen, dear. Everybody likes *her*. You can't help it. I don't know why; you just—like

her. And you know they're— stopping the ship?
GEORGE: How do you mean, stopping the ship?
HETTY: A twenty-five-thousand-ton liner, *this* one, is stopping off the coast. So that a motor-launch can pick up Valerie and Ralph Garett. The Company just offered it, that's all. Over to a forsaken beach, where…
GEORGE: Go on! There can't be anything wrong!
HETTY: (ignoring this) She's got a queer, frightened look about her, when she thinks you're not watching. I don't like it.— Oh, let *me* try the shuffle-board.
(*Sound: Disk whizzes across deck, hits ventilator-base and slithers off*)

(*Music: in and behind*)
FABIAN: And well I remember the burning day when we did stop. They had lowered the companion-ladder, which is really a sort of iron staircase against the side, to a waiting motor-launch. Valerie, with her Nell-Gwynn beauty and a huge armful of orchids, was standing outside on the platform. The *Maurevania's* commander, who was then Captain Trevor, shook hands with her; I remember his lean face under the cap with the gold oak-leaves.
(*Music: fades out*)

(*Sound: faint crowd-murmur*)
TREVOR: (*formally*) Good-bye, Miss Blake! I beg your pardon! I should have said "Mrs. Garrett."
VALERIE: It doesn't matter, Captain Trevor! Either name will do.
RALPH: (*off yelling*) Come on down, Valerie! The boat's here!
TREVOR: (*indulgently*) Your husband seems impatient.
VALERIE: (*calling, pleading*) Just a moment, Ralph! I'm only saying good-bye! (*on mike*) I can't begin to thank you, even for these lovely flowers!
TREVOR: Don't thank *me*. Call it: compliments of the Line. (*lightly*) When you go down these iron steps, Mrs. Garrett, the whistle will blow in your honor. And the band will give you a tune. (*hesitates*) I'm not much of a hand at making speeches…
VALERIE: (*too quickly*) Please! It's not necessary!
TREVOR: (*quietly*) But all your acting on the stage has never given as much pleasure as your presence has given us on this voyage. (*slight pause*) God bless you.
VALERIE: (*moved*) I… I don't…
(*Sound: ship's whistle, one long blast. band begins* Auld Lang Syne *continue under.*)
VALERIE: I —I don't want to start crying, do I? On my wedding trip and everything?
RALPH: (*off*) Come on down here! What's keeping you?
VALERIE: Goodbye, Captain Trevor!

(*Sound: fading goodbyes, band music swells up and dies during course of following scene*)
RALPH: Give me your hand, Valerie! Now jump down in the launch... There! — All right, Spaghetti! Let 'er go!
(*Sound: engine of motor launch starts up*)
VALERIE: (*tenderly*) I'm sorry I took so long, darling. But you know how nice they were. And I couldn't be discourteous!
RALPH: (*hard, but a little bored*) Look, Valerie. Who do you think you're kidding?
VALERIE: (*startled*) What do you mean?
RALPH: I always thought ships' captains were fat guys with red faces. *He* wasn't. You knew this Captain Trevor in New York, didn't you?
VALERIE: (*subdued*) Yes. He's a very old friend of mine.
RALPH: Then why couldn't you say so?
VALERIE: Ralph, he once asked me to marry him. A year ago. I thought it would make things easier if we pretended to be just acquaintances!
RALPH: So he's phony too!
VALERIE: (*pleading*) Ralph! It wasn't that! It was only to make things easier! Why do you keep saying that everything and everybody is phony?
RALPH: (*his sincere philosophy*) Because they are, mostly. And it's too bad your other boy-friend couldn't have been aboard too. You know: the one with the Irish name?
VALERIE: Larry Doyle?
RALPH: That's it. Lanky red-headed guy with all the money and the social-column stuff.
VALERIE: Larry's in India. On some kind of hunting trip.
RALPH: (*snarling*) And who *couldn't* be, with his old man's dough? (*correcting himself: casually*) Still! Keep your boy-friends if you want 'em.
VALERIE: (*pleading*) Ralph! Don't you understand?
RALPH: Maybe I do. Maybe I don't.
VALERIE: I have more *affection* for Larry Doyle and Bob Trevor than any two people I know. One is a wild Irish American. The other is stolid British. And they'd both come from the ends of the earth to help you, if you needed it.
RALPH: (*muttering*) Yeah? Try the phonies and see!
VALERIE: But affection's not the same thing as love! Don't turn away and sulk, Ralph! I love you. Don't you know that? Didn't I marry you?
RALPH: (*softened, vanity appeased*) Sure. kid! You stick to me. *I'm* not phony; I'm real. I'll take care of you.
VALERIE: If you look ahead, and in a minute or so, you can see our beach. The house, pink stucco, set back on flat grass. Then the white sand shelving down to the water. And over to the right, on the beach, there's a big rock shaped like a chair.
RALPH: Rock? Shaped like that?

VALERIE: Something like an arm-chair. You can sit in it with your shoulders along the back, and look out to sea. (*changing tone*) Ralph, we *can* be happy here: can't we?
RALPH: (*soothing*) You bet we can, Valerie!
VALERIE: For a year. Maybe more. Until...
RALPH: Forget it, baby! It's gonna be all right.
VALERIE: (*in terror*) I wonder if I can face that! I wonder if I can face it!

(*Music: up with sinister effect: then segue softly into languor with theme suggesting* Santa Lucia—*down behind*)
FABIAN: For a year they lived in that house. Tides swept softly up the beach; tides rippled past the stone arm-chair, and flooded up to the grass bank; tides retreated, and left the chair in a great area of mud-grey sand. Languorous was sunny Italy, of the heavy grape-vines and the drowsy guitars. Valerie and Ralph should have been happy there. And yet, if you looked late one afternoon into the long windows of the drawing-room facing the sea ...
(*Music: fades out*)

ANNE: (*calling, off*) Valerie! Valerie!
VALERIE: (*raising her voice*) Yes, Anne?
ANNE: (*fading on, agitated*) I'm sorry to burst in like this; I know I'm only your secretary; but... (*stopping short*) Oh! I thought you were talking to somebody.
VALERIE: No, Anne. I was only using the phonograph-recording machine. Some of my old scenes, to know how they sounded. I've put it back in the corner now.
ANNE: Valerie, I've *got* to talk to you!
VALERIE: I want to talk to *you*, Anne.
ANNE: (*quickly*) Oh? What about?
VALERIE: Don't look startled! It isn't... (*hesitates*) Anne, how long have you been my secretary?
ANNE: Well! (*slight pause*) I came out from home about eight months ago.
VALERIE: Ralph sent for you, didn't he?
ANNE: (*slight pause; harsher tone*) Look, Valerie, You weren't what I thought you'd be. I thought I'd hate you. But I don't. And I swore to myself, if you ever asked me, I'd tell you.
VALERIE: Then you and Ralph...?
ANNE: Yes! (*hesitates*) Oh, I took a secretarial course once! I've done your correspondence pretty well, haven't I?
VALERIE: What little of it there is, yes. They've forgotten me, mostly.
ANNE: (*harshly*) But we're in show-business, all three of us. You're high-hat. Ralph and I are just —show-business. I used to help him with his act on the stage; yes, and I could do the routine as well as he could. He's got

his faults. But I'd do *anything* for him.

VALERIE: (*quietly*) I only wanted to tell you, Anne, that—you can have him.

ANNE: (*amazed*) You mean you don't…?

VALERIE: (*ironically; voice rising*) Love him?

ANNE: Yes! I thought…

VALERIE: After a month or so, Anne, it was only a kind of indifference. (*meaningly*) And I'm not—cold in any way, Anne. (*bursting out*) Now I'm sick! And fed up! And frightened! Every time I see his face… that sneer! that eternal sneer!… I want to start screaming.

ANNE: Shh! Keep your voice down! He's in the next room!

VALERIE: Not loving him wouldn't matter so much. I married him; I wouldn't go crying for a divorce. But he played a trick on me so filthy, so… do you know what it was? —No, I can see you don't. And I'm glad! (*abruptly*) Anne, I'm leaving here.

ANNE: (*startled*) Leaving? When?

VALERIE: As soon as I can pack my things. Or—or muster up the nerve!

ANNE: (*grimly*) I wish you *could* leave, kid. Don't I, though! But you can't leave. And you'd better get used to it.

VALERIE: (*crying out*) *Why* can't I leave?

ANNE: He'd stop you.

VALERIE: But why should he stop me?

ANNE: (*expostulating*) It's his vanity, kid. (*fiercely, protectively*) He's like — like a little boy!

VALERIE: (*hollow irony*) Little boy! Lord help us!

ANNE: Look, Valerie. You're all right. (*quietly*) But don't make any cracks about Ralph!

VALERIE: (*contemptuously*) He's your idea of a "man", isn't he?

ANNE: He's tough, kid. They don't make 'em any tougher. If Ralph Garrett says it goes, then nobody can make him say different. Don't think I don't want him to myself! I do! But if he tells me to keep you here…

VALERIE: You'd do it?

ANNE: Sorry. That's the way it is.

VALERIE: (*near tears*) You know, Anne, it's funny.

ANNE: (*on edge*) What's funny?

VALERIE: A long time ago—weeks ago!—I sent two letters. Oh, not through you! I didn't deserve an answer. I know that. But I kept on hoping! I … what's the matter with you?

ANNE: That's what I had to see you about! (*intensely*) Were those letters addressed to a man named Larry Doyle and another named Captain Trevor?

VALERIE: Yes! Why?

ANNE: Because they're both here now. (*menacing*) So watch your step, Valerie, dear!

VALERIE: (*hope soaring*) *They're here?* Where are they?

ANNE: If you look out the front windows, you can see them coming up the lawn now.

(*Music: very softly, sneak-in with auld syne. it registers before Valerie speaks, and holds* under)

VALERIE: (*again near tears*) Larry Doyle used to say he had two ambitions in life: to get a ten-foot tiger, and to write a great poem. Bob Trevor's ambition, if he has any, is to command the White Planet's biggest liner. It's been only a year since I've seen them. No! It's been longer than a year since I've seen Larry. But it seems... it seems...

(*Music: fades out*)

(*Sound: door opens, on.*)

VALERIE: Larry!

LARRY: How are you, Valerie?

TREVOR: Always at your service, my dear.

VALERIE: Bob! Give me your hand! You too, Larry! (*swallowing*) Did you... did you get the tiger? Or write the poem?

LARRY: I regret to say, Valerie, that I didn't do either. The tigers were too scarce in the Simla, and the booze was too plentiful at Bombay. Anyway—I got your letter.

TREVOR: (*as though musing*) You know, Doyle: I think we've got rats in this house.

LARRY: Yes. A big rat, in the next room. Throwing down a whisky-bottle on a hearth-stone.

(*Sound: off, door opens and closes*)

RALPH: (*fade in*) Hel-lo, Doyle! Hel-lo, Trevor! Make yourselves at home!

LARRY: I'm afraid we've got to, Ralph. We drove out from Rome in an old rattletrap that went dead a mile back. (*sharply*) Valerie!

VALERIE: Yes, Larry?

LARRY: We're very fond of your company. *And* Miss Webster's, of course. But you might like to leave us for a little while.

RALPH: Yeah. That's a good idea. (*furious*) Get out! Both of you! (*controlled; merely sneering*) Tha-at's it! That's better. *I'll* have a talk with your swell friends.

LARRY: Now's your chance, Ralph.

RALPH: (*pause, then*) I was just standing here wondering why I hate you two so much.

LARRY: It's because you hate everything on earth, except yourself. You can't stand the world as it is.

RALPH: (*slowly firing up*) Yeah. Maybe you're right. Wait till we get a Soviet New Order in America!

LARRY: That wouldn't help you, Ralph. You'd be just as thick-headed then as you are now.

RALPH: (*not loudly*) Do you want some trouble, Doyle?

LARRY: I'm looking for it. I'm longing for it. How do *you* feel, Trevor?

TREVOR: Just the same way. Shall we spin a coin to see who gets him?
RALPH: I'm not gonna bother with you. Not when I've got a hip pocket—and *this* in my hand. Easy! It's a .38. (*snarling*) Do you know what I am?
TREVOR: You practically force us to tell you.
RALPH: I had an act, see? Trick stunts with a gun and a blacksnake whip. But it wasn't phony. I *could* whip a cigarette out of somebody's mouth at ten or twelve yards. I *could* drill the ace of hearts at twice the distance. So don't move while I've got the gun. (*pause*) You want to stay here? Okay! But you don't take Valerie, because I say you don't. As long as I've got *this*. I'm boss. (*fade*) Think it over, while I catch a drink!
(*Sound: door opens and closes off*).
TREVOR: (*grimly*) Well, you were right. He's got artillery. Did you—?
LARRY: Oh, yes. I had him covered from a side-pocket. But I don't want to use a gun, Trevor. It's too easy.
TREVOR: (*suppressed wrath*) I agree with you! Then let's go in there and...
LARRY: Take him apart? Oh, no! Wait a minute!
TREVOR: If you meet trouble, young fellow, walk up and hit it straightaway. Or it turns into worse trouble.
LARRY: Not this time! (*emotion showing*) That letter from Valerie—didn't say much. But can you guess what kind of life she's had?
TREVOR: Yes! That's why...
LARRY: I want to work slowly. I want to watch him squirm. (*pleasantly*) *Then* we stick him in the ash-can.
TREVOR: (*abruptly*) I don't like it!
LARRY: Why not?
TREVOR: (*groping*) That fellow is nearly out of his mind. I'd like to know why. What's more, Valerie made a certain remark that... (*stops*) There's some deadly danger, some *other* danger, we don't understand. Let's take Valerie and clear out now!
LARRY: We couldn't go if we wanted to! The car's broken down and there's no phone here.
TREVOR: I don't like it!
LARRY: Nothing's going to happen, old man! Leave it to me!

FABIAN: (*abrupt—flatly*) Larry Doyle was wrong.
(*Music: hits hard, then down behind*)
FABIAN: Only once did I, Doctor Fabian of the *Maurevania*, hear Captain Trevor tell that story before he was transferred to command the *Queen Victoria*. He said he slept that night in an upstairs room, overlooking beach and sea. It was thick, hot weather, the brilliance of a Mediterranean moon, with dreams that drugged him without *quite* bringing sleep. Once or twice, in the night he thought he heard someone practicing with a .22 rifle...
(*Sound: far off, noise like .22 rifle*).

FABIAN: And again, as he tossed and turned...
(*Sound: repeated*)
FABIAN: At dawn, under a leaden sky heavy with coming thunder, he was asleep.
(*Music: sting and out*)

(*Sound: sharp rapping on door, which opens*).
DOYLE: (*calling, off*) Trevor!
TREVOR: (*only mumbling the words*) Eh? What's that?
DOYLE: (*fading, horror-stricken*) Trevor! Wake up!
TREVOR: (*gathering wits*) Oh! It's you, Larry. Wait till I sit up in bed. I... (*suddenly clear-headed*) What is it? Don't stand there like a wild man! What is it?
DOYLE: Valerie's dead. She's been strangled.
TREVOR: She's been...?
(*Sound: a long roll of thunder*)
DOYLE: (*bursting out*) Don't put your head in your hands! I'm responsible! Say it!
TREVOR: (*repressed*) You're not responsible, Larry. What happened?
LARRY: (*near breaking*) Poor... little...
TREVOR: You've never lost your nerve yet! Don't lose it now! What happened?
LARRY: She... (*pulling himself together*) Sorry; I'm all right!
TREVOR: Well?
LARRY: You remember that fat Italian woman, the cook, who tried to keep us out of the back door last night? And we walked round to the front door?
TREVOR: Yes; what about it?
LARRY: This morning, at daybreak, Valerie walked out of the house. She walked down the grass to the beach. On the beach she turned left, and walked along the wet sand to that rock shaped like an arm-chair.
TREVOR: Valerie told us she went there every morning. Well?
LARRY: *I* got up—oh, twenty minutes ago. Couldn't sleep, Maria, that's the Italian cook, told me where Valerie'd gone. I followed, across the grass. I looked out over the beach, and...
TREVOR: Hold up, now! Go on!
LARRY: Valerie was lying across one of the chair-arms. Face upwards; head hanging over. Her face was—black. She'd been strangled with a heavy scarf; something like that. *But!*—and this is what you won't believe...
TREVOR: Never mind what I believe!
LARRY: The tide was out. That chair stood in the middle of a big area of wet sand. More than thirty, maybe forty feet in any direction! (*clearly*) But there were no footprints in the sand except Valerie's.
(*Sound: roll of thunder*)
TREVOR: Hold on, now! Are you telling me that...?

LARRY: Somebody went out there. Strangled Valerie. Took away the weapon; and came back. But there's not a mark of any kind on the sand!
TREVOR: That's impossible!
LARRY: I admit it! But it happened.
TREVOR: You were shocked; upset! You weren't in any condition to...
LARRY: Wasn't I? Listen! I started to rush out on the sand. Then I realized: this was a trap. They'd think *I* killed her. So I called Maria to show her there were *no* marks before I went out. You know who did this, don't you? Ralph Garrett! But *how* did he do it?
TREVOR: As soon as I get into some clothes, we're going to find out something!
LARRY: Where? Down on the beach?
TREVOR: (*as though remembering*) No. Downstairs in the living-room!
(*Music: bridge to*)
LARRY: (*a little off*) (*puzzled, on edge*) But what are we doing here in the living-room?
TREVOR: (*on*) Where's the voice-machine—whatever-you-call-it!—that makes the records?
LARRY: It's over here! I'm standing beside it.
TREVOR: And here's a radio-gramophone. We're looking for a home-made record with a mark on the label.
LARRY: What kind of mark?
TREVOR: Any kind! Don't you remember what Valerie said about records?
LARRY: (*waking up*) "If I ever die or anything" —that's what she said; — "you might like to have them."
TREVOR: Right!
LARRY: She was warning us! She didn't dare say any more, but... wait a minute!
TREVOR: Have you got anything?
LARRY: There's a record with a little blue cross in ink. But the writing only says, "Juliet. Balcony scene."
TREVOR: Bring it here, will you?... Thanks! Now we'll open the lid... put the record on the turn-table... switch on... set the needle... Steady, now!
(*Sound: needle on turning record*)
VALERIE: (*filter*) Dost thou love me? I know thou wilt say, "Ay", And I will take thy word; yet if thou swear'st, Thou mayst prove false; at lovers' perjuries, They say, Jove laughs. O gentle Romeo, If thou dost love, pronounce it faithfully!—(*break off*)
(*Sound: a click*)
LARRY: (*repressed*) Sorry, Trevor. I can't stand any more.
TREVOR: I'm sorry too. Because I've got to turn it on again.
(*Sound: another click, turntable spins—needle goes on as they speak; but no voice*).
LARRY: (*turning on him*) What's the matter with you? Haven't you got *any* human feeling?

TREVOR: Yes. Too much. But it's got to be done!
LARRY: (*suddenly*) She's not speaking! Is the needle all right?
TREVOR: Yes. And she wouldn't stop in the middle of the scene. *Would she?*
VALERIE: (*filter*) For Larry Doyle and Bob Trevor. In case —Ralph kills me. (*slight pause*)
TREVOR: (*in the pause*) Take it easy, Larry.
VALERIE: (*filter, unsteady*) There's only one thing I can't forgive him. In New York, before we were married, he found a fake doctor and fake X-ray plates. They told me I was ill with...anyway, it couldn't be cured. They said most people didn't suffer pain, but I would; horribly after a year. Ralph said we'd better live abroad, where a foreign doctor would—put me out. He only did it to keep me away from people; to use what money I had. While he was away I went to a doctor in Rome. There's nothing wrong with me. But if Ralph guesses I *know*, he'll think I'd charge him with —what is it? —conspiracy. (*faltering*) The j-joke is that *I* won't give him away; I just can't; I once thought I was in love. (*breaking down*) I can't talk any more.
(*Sound: needle on record. Then a click. Silence*)
TREVOR: (*sharply*) Larry, where are you going?
LARRY: I've got a little business to settle with Ralph. *Now!*
TREVOR: Oh no, you don't.
LARRY: Last night *you* wanted action!
TREVOR: Last night we didn't have a murder. You can beat him up, yes! But he can laugh at us, he can laugh at the whole Italian police, unless we know *how* he killed her!
LARRY: But surely a jury...?
TREVOR: The defense would say, "Show us, please. How did he go across all the unmarked sand?"—Finish!
LARRY: (*bitterly*) And I thought he didn't have any brains!
TREVOR: So did I. And I still think so! Because... (*groaning*) If I could only get the facts in order!
LARRY: (*bitter but friendly*) Ship-shape and Bristol-fashion! One born to the sea!
TREVOR: (*retorting*) I was born in South Africa. At fifteen I drove a wagon-team of ten yoked oxen. I didn't join the Merchant Service until ... (*pause: suddenly*) South Africa! I've got it!
LARRY: You know how she was killed?
TREVOR: Yes! But Garrett ...
(*Sound: door opens and closes, off*)
RALPH: (*a little off*) Did somebody mention my name?
LARRY: (*softly sinister*) Yes, Ralph! Come on in!
RALPH: (*fading on*) Can't stay. Got a little trip to — (*stops*) Now if this ain't nice! Playing records, eh? By this time both you mugs ought to be able to recite Romeo to my wife. Don't *I* rate a recitation of some kind?

(*Music: hits hard, then down and under narration*)
FABIAN: Wait! We shall see what happened! But imagine yourself, just an hour later, standing on the edge of the grass facing out over the beach. Ahead of you but a good distance away, is the back of the stone arm-chair. It has no grisly occupant now, but—something else. Under a storm-darkening sky, Larry Doyle and Captain Trevor stand on the grass edge... and Trevor has a small suitcase in his hand.
(*Music: fades out*)

(*Sound: roll of thunder. the tide, which is just coming in, can be heard only very faintly at any time*)
TREVOR: (*grimly*) You understand what we've done, Larry?
LARRY: Are you worried about the law? Forget it!
TREVOR: We've moved Valerie's body. We haven't tried to reach the police. If this doesn't work we're for it! Who's the one in the trap now?
LARRY: Then we're for it. (*exultant*) I never set a tiger-trap like this!
TREVOR: (*low voice, quickly*) Where's the tig—let's say our quarry! Where's our quarry now?
LARRY: Coming out of the house. Walking towards us! What did you tell the—person in question?
TREVOR: Only to meet us here at this time. Now play your part. I hope I can play mine.
LARRY: (*loudly*) Look here: what have you got in that suit-case?
TREVOR: I've got the weapon that killed Valerie.
LARRY: Then open the case! Let's have a look!
TREVOR: There! —Did you ever see *this* before?
LARRY: Yes; I've seen it. On the stage! At the circus!
TREVOR: It's a blacksnake whip. Coiled now, but more than thirty feet long. Watch me! I turn my back to the sea, and aim at nothing. I throw the whip its full length...
(*Sound: like that of .22 rifle-shot*)
TREVOR: And at a distance the whip-crack sounds just like. a .22 rifle. (*low voice*) Where's the person we're waiting for *now*?
LARRY: (*low voice*) Still walking towards us. (*loudly*) Ralph Garrett told us he could lash a cigarette out of somebody's mouth at twelve yards: thirty-six feet!
TREVOR: I turn back to the beach, coiling up the rope. Look at the stone chair out there! Describe it!
LARRY: Somebody's propped up a wooden post. With stones, maybe. The top of the post is like...
TREVOR: Like the head and neck of someone sitting there. Yes. What *else* have you seen whip-throwers do?
LARRY: They can coil the whip three times round a woman's neck without

hurting her!

TREVOR: Imagine that post is the back of someone's head and neck. South African drivers used to lash a fly off the lead-oxen at this distance. I'm thirty years out of practice; I'll probably miss by yards: but...

(*Sound: heavy whip-crack, really noise of .22*)

LARRY: Three times round!

TREVOR: She's wedged in the chair. If I wanted to strangle her...

LARRY: You'd only have to pull tighter at the whip. Tighter! Tighter! Tighter!...

TREVOR: A couple of flicks...you've seen it done—the whip's dislodged. I throw it *up and back*, like this; and it lands behind me without touching sand. *But*... where's the murderer now, Larry?

LARRY: There! Just beside you!

TREVOR: Ralph Garrett hasn't the brains to think of a murder like this. But somebody once helped him on the stage, and could do the trick as well as he could.... Didn't you kill her — *Miss Anne Webster?*

(*Sound: roll of thunder*)

ANNE: (*tense but shaky*) Yes, I suggested the whip trick. And he persuaded *me* to do it. Then, he started to run out and let *me* take the blame if the cops guessed.

LARRY: He won't run anywhere, Anne Anne Webster. He's an accessory before and after the fact!

ANNE: I thought he was—everything. And when you three were in the living-room. Mr. Doyle just took his gun away and beat him senseless. (*suddenly*) I don't care what happens to me! But I liked her. I didn't want to hurt her! If she could hear me, I'd tell her that!

LARRY: If she could hear us!

ANNE: Maybe she *can* hear us! (*almost hysterically*) I deserve to die, Valerie!

LARRY: (*exalted, Celtic fervor*) It won't bring you back, Valerie! It won't ease the hurt. But wherever you are, Valerie...

TREVOR: (*slowly*) We have kept the faith.

(*Sound:* Auld Lang Syne, *comes up and fades during Fabian's final narration*)

FABIAN: And so, I end my story. Anne Webster was "Below Suspicion", never thought of, as Doyle and Trevor were *above* suspicion. Or did *you* think of her? In any event, I hope that next week —when we shall have touched at Naples, and our scene is Rome — you will be made a little uneasy by "Last Night In Ghost-Land"[1]. By the way, next week I shall be speaking to you at a different day. Will you join me, then, in *Cabin B-13*?

(*Music: in and behind*)
(*Sound: ship's whistles*)
(*Music: fades out*)

---
[1] The next play in *Cabin B-13* is "The Power of Darkness" and Carr never used the title "Last Night in Ghost-Land" in *Cabin B-13* or anywhere else.

Notes for the Curious

"Below Suspicion", another original story, shares its title—but nothing more—with the 18th Dr. Fell novel, published in 1949 which features the roguish barrister and "*damned Irishman*" Patrick Butler. Butler, the self-styled "*Great Defender*", is almost the exact opposite of Dr. Fell. While the academic is precise and measured, capable of humility as well as genius, the lawyer is brash and above all arrogant, given to proclaiming that "*I am never wrong*". But he is an admirable detective and would go on to appear in *Patrick Butler for the Defence* (1956) in which Dr. Fell is merely mentioned in passing. In 1956, Carr planned a second novel with Patrick Butler, provisionally titled *Look upon the Prisoner*, but the project was abandoned.

John Dickson Carr told his family that he based the lawyer on Adrian Conan Doyle, with whom he had collaborated on *The Exploits of Sherlock Holmes* (1954). There is no reason to disbelieve this but it is also likely that he was inspired by a defence lawyer called Patrick Butler who appears in one of G.K. Chesterton's Father Brown stories, "The Man in the Passage".

Blake is another of Carr's favorite names. As well as Valerie Blake in this radio play, there is Kenwood Blake, who acts as "Watson" to the "Holmes" of Sir Henry Merrivale in several of Carr's early "Carter Dickson" novels. And there is also the journalist James Buchanan Blake, the main protagonist of Carr's late historical mystery *The Ghosts' High Noon* (1969), where the newsman is identified as the author of *The Count of Monte Carlo*, echoing the *Cabin B-13* script of the that name.

Carr re-used the central ploy of "Below Suspicion" in the Dr. Fell story "King Arthur's Chair" (1957), changing the setting from Italy to North Cornwall in England. The short story was first published, as by "Carter Dickson", in *Lilliput* magazine in August 1957.

The Power of Darkness

(*Sound: a ship's whistle*)
ANNOUNCER: *Cabin B-13.*
(*Music: in and behind*)
FABIAN: Rome, 1937. City of contrasts: of marble vying with slums, of washing hung above the mud-colored Tiber; and the great dome of St. Peter's ageless under its spell of history. In the midst of modern Rome there stand—a vaster area than we might think—the ruins of that ancient city which once ruled the world. I remember saying good-bye in Rome to young Alan Stannard, whose family had millions but who had just taken his Ph.D. in history; I remember the calm, very pretty face of Ruth Gale, his *fiancée*. For myself, I put up at my usual quiet little hotel off the Via Cavour morning after breakfast as I sat in the quiet little writing-room ...

(*Sound: twitter of birds in cages comes up as music fades under narration.*)
FABIAN: They weren't good for concentration on writing letters, which I was doing. Then some impulse —was it a sense of disturbance or shock?—made me swing my chair round...
(*Sound: noise of bird-song, up and for the moment out*)
RUTH: (*fading on*) Doctor Fabian!
FABIAN: Hullo! Surely you're not...?
RUTH: Don't you recognize me, Doctor Fabian? I'm Ruth Gale. I travelled with you in the *Maurevania*!
FABIAN: (*heartily*) Of course I recognize you, Ruth! I was a little startled at...
RUTH: At the way I look? —No, please don't get up! I'll sit down beside the desk. I know I'm as pale as that writing-paper! I know I look like nothing on earth!
FABIAN: (*telling lies soothingly*) By "startled", Ruth, I meant startled at seeing you here. Will you give me your hand please?
RUTH: Thanks, Doctor Fabian. But I know my pulse isn't—right. Alan...
FABIAN: Where *is* Alan, by the way?
RUTH: I don't know! That's why I'm here! (*swallowing*) And another thing, Doctor Fabian. Do you believe I'm sane? Reasonably intelligent? Or at least—sensible? *Do you*?
FABIAN: Far more sensible than that *fiancé* of yours. (*lightly*) Alan's got to behave himself, now that he's supposed to be a learned historian... I see I've said the wrong thing! What is it?
RUTH: (*slowly but tensely*) Last night, Doctor Fabian, I travelled back three hundred years in time. I saw things through a dead man's eyes.
(*Sound: song of birds in cages comes up, hold for a moment or two; then down and out.*)
RUTH: You won't believe that, naturally!

FABIAN: If you say it's true, Helen, of course I believe it. Just tell me.
RUTH: It started three days ago. At Naples, when Alan and I—well, all of us! — had got into the train for Rome. Do you remember Alan's eldest sister? Helen? The flighty one? She stayed behind to visit somebody at Capri.
FABIAN: I remember her perfectly.
RUTH: (*satirically*) It was one of the *Duce's* trains, which notoriously start on time.
(*Music: sneaks in and backs narration briefly*)
RUTH: Alan and I were standing at one compartment-window, looking out at the platform. Just at the last-minute Helen came rushing along the platform with her hat over one ear. Doors were slamming along the train, and the guard was having a fit…

(*Sound: doors slam, receding effect*).
RAILWAY GUARD: (*off, shouting in agony*) Presto tempo! Il traino departite! Presto tempo!
HELEN: (*fading on, half breathless*) Alan! Ruth! Wait a minute!
ALAN: It's all right, Helen. We haven't started yet. (*amused*) Have you forgotten something *else*?
HELEN: (*abject*) Alan dear, I'm afraid I have! This is for *you*. It's a big box of English cigarettes.
ALAN: (*pleased but puzzled*) Well! Thanks very much. But I've already put in a supply of American cigarettes, and…
HELEN: No, silly! These aren't from *me*!
RUTH: Not from you?
HELEN: No, Ruth. They're from a very dear friend of mine. And you *must* call on her!
RUTH: In Rome? Who is she?
HELEN: (*rattling on*) She's a very dear friend of mine, though of course I only met her for a few hours in New York. And you mustn't mind if she's terribly, terribly religious. There's a clergyman there most of the time.
ALAN: Isn't that rather extreme? In keeping sin at bay?
HELEN: (*impatiently*) Alan! Listen to me! Her name is Bianca da Carpi.
ALAN: (*startled*) Bianca da Carpi!
RUTH: You sound as though you knew her, Alan.
ALAN: I've never met her, no. But—(*he stops*)
(*Sound: several quick agonized blasts on a whistle*)
RAILWAY GUARD: (*more agony*) Il traino departite!
HELEN: Bianca's got a lovely villa out on the other side of the Aventine Hill. They've built a horrible new suburb straight up to it, Bianca says. But the villa once belonged to one of those people who were always stabbing other people. You *must* see her!
RUTH: Does she speak English, Helen?
HELEN: Darling! She's American! A widow! Beautiful! Not exactly beautiful;

but... Oh, Alan, that reminds me. I ought to warn you!
ALAN: (*quickly*) Warn me? About what?
HELEN: You mustn't let her persuade you ... oh dear!
(*Sound: chug of the engine and the grind of wheels getting under way; this comes up fairly loudly as the train moves.*)
ALAN: (*calling*) What did you say? I mustn't let her persuade me ... (*as though listening*) What?
RAILWAY GUARD: (*dramatic ecstasy of triumph*) Il traino — departite!
(*Sound: train noise up; then out into music; music is held under Ruth's speech*)

RUTH: The next day late in the afternoon, Alan and I set out to explore the ruins of ancient Rome. (*pause*) I never knew how large they were. How silent! How deserted even of tourists! The hot sunlight seemed to heighten a sense of eeriness among broken columns and temples; At dusk we came to the Coliseum — where they held the beast-fights and the gladiator-shows. Those huge oval walls, broken, against a reddish-purple sky! Inside it, of course, most of the benches and galleries have gone. But you can climb up fairly high. Under arches, and up dim sloping inclines...
(*Sound: scene is now on echo; we are in an enclosed space sloping up; a rattle of small stones, as though dislodged by a foot*)
ALAN: Are you all right, Ruth? Shall I give you a hand?
RUTH: (*trying to be amused*) I'm all right, Alan. It's as easy as walking up the ramp of a modern stadium!
ALAN: (*impressed*) Yes! It *is* like that. This passage leads out on one of the galleries, where we can look down on the arena. See the daylight ahead?
RUTH: (*hesitant*) There isn't much daylight left, is there?
ALAN: (*pause, then exclaiming*) You know, Ruth, I must be the most inconsiderate hound on earth!
RUTH: No, Please! I didn't mean it that way!
ALAN: Five hours! Six hours! I've been dragging you...
RUTH: Do you think I *mind* being dragged, Alan?
ALAN: Well! Just because *I'm* fascinated by all this...
RUTH: You can drag me anywhere, Alan. (*half humorous*) Through bramble-bushes, if you want to. But may I ask you a question?
ALAN: (*faintly on guard*) Of course. What's wrong?
RUTH: Ever since this morning, Alan, you've been nervous and on edge. You jump when somebody speaks to you. Why?
ALAN: I haven't been nervous! At least, I haven't noticed it.
RUTH: (*quietly*) Isn't that an English cigarette you're smoking? From the gift that woman "Bianca" sent?
ALAN: (*slight pause*) Yes. I — think so. (*changing tone*) It *is* getting dark. Shall we go back down?
RUTH: No! Please! I *want* to go on!

ALAN: Then we've got only a few stops more.
(*Sound: footsteps on stone are heard under next speech*)
ALAN: When you get outside, don't be afraid of the gallery. There's a stone balustrade round it; and they've put iron railings where the masonry's crumbled. Now! Into the open!
(*Sound: off echo*)
ALAN: Turn to the left — careful! — walk along by the balustrade to... here. Now look down.
RUTH: The Coliseum! In twilight!
ALAN: Lonely, isn't it?
RUTH: (*uneasy*) *Horribly* lonely!
ALAN: A lion, down there, would look as small as a toy.
RUTH: Alan, is this the place we always associate with Nero?
ALAN: No angel. Good old Nero was dead when they built this. There was just as much butchery, of course. (*suddenly*) How would you like it if we stirred up some ghosts?
RUTH: (*startled*) Ghosts? What ghosts?
ALAN: (*feverish excitement growing*) Look! There's a good-sized pebble here on the balustrade. I'll wind up and throw straight ahead. *Now!*
(*Sound: off, heavy pebble strikes stone, bounces as though down rough stone slope, rolls; and noise fades*)
ALAN: There! It must have rolled into the arena. The ghosts ought to reply — even if they don't. Here's another bit of rock; let's heave it out into the gallery below. There!— but the dead audience won't answer either! They're lost in time; withered; gone away! But the villa where the Duke Nicolo. If we want ghosts, Ruth, we've got to — (*stops, abruptly, startled*)
RUTH: Alan! What's wrong *now*?
ALAN: That stone I just threw. (*slight pause*) It didn't land anywhere. There was no sound.
RUTH: No! There wasn't.
ALAN: And the whole Coliseum is as quiet as a tomb.
RUTH: Then where did it go?
ALAN: That's what I want to find out! It fell into the gallery out and below us!
RUTH: You're not going to climb down there?
ALAN: I don't have to climb down! I can go by one of the passages!
RUTH: Alan! Listen! I'd rather you didn't...
ALAN: You stay here, my dear. I'll be back in two minutes.
RUTH: (*crying out*) Alan!
(*Music: sinister bridge*)
ALAN: (*muttering*) Hardly any red left in the sky. Only black walls with empty windows. But the stone landed in this gallery! It landed... it landed...
PIETRO: Just about here, *signore*? Where I am sitting? Yes?
ALAN: Who spoke then?

PIETRO: *I* spoke, *signore.* (*humbly*) Only poor Pietro, fat Pietro. Yet a man of more ability than my poor clothes would show. I doff my hat — so. (*dismally*) *Ecco*, there are holes in it! I put it on again.
ALAN: Excuse me, Signor Pietro; but I'm looking for...
PIETRO: A stone, yes? It is here. I caught it.
ALAN: You caught it? Why?
PIETRO: We-el! I think you are the sort of man —what-do-you-call — impetuous. Who will come to seek it? And I would speak to you, Signor Alan Stannard, when your fiancé is not present.
ALAN: Look here, who are you? Have you been following us?
PIETRO: (*brushing it away*) *Scusatemi!* (*voice hardening*) This morning, at the Excelsior Hotel, you received a letter from the *Signora da Carpi.* Yes?
ALAN: The *Signora da...* (*meaning, "so you know that too!"*)
PIETRO: You call her Bianca. The lovely and pious lady, attended by a Church-of-England parson, who lives in the marble villa. (*sharply*) She send you a letter; yes?
ALAN: All right; what about it!
PIETRO: (*cooing*) You must see her, she begs. Tonight, at ten o'clock, limousine will call for you. But her poor heart! She regret! You must go alone. — (*urging*) And you *will* go, *Signore*?
ALAN: Oh, yes. I intend to go.
PIETRO: (*softly exultant*) Excellent! *Bravissimo!* You are wise!
ALAN: (*puzzled*) How do you mean, wise?
PIETRO: (*reproachful*) *Signore*! She is beautiful! A blonde Venus. I, poor Pietro, have my head swim when I think of her! And she is not at all ... no, no!... as pious as she look.
ALAN: (*low voice; astonished*) Wait a minute! You think ... I'm interested in Bianca?
PIETRO: (*quickly*) *Pardone*? I did not hear!
ALAN: Pietro, you old satyr, I've done it again!
PIETRO: *Signore*, you confuse me! Talk what is sense!
ALAN: I get so wrapped up in doctoral research that I never notice what people think! I ... Ruth must have noticed that letter! And thought — what you think.
PIETRO: We-el! A little jealousy—!
ALAN: Look, Pietro. I don't want to meet that woman out at the villa. I don't care two hoots for any woman except Ruth!
PIETRO: (*staggered*) You don't want to ...?
ALAN: No! But that villa, more than three hundred years ago, was the hunting-lodge of a certain —Duke Nicolo. He was a royal murderer who died pretty horribly himself. The villa is supposed to be malignantly haunted.
PIETRO: Haunted! (*pouncing on a new lure*) You seek a ghost? Is that it?
ALAN: Yes! That's why I couldn't show Ruth the letter, or take her with me. I don't believe in—evil spirits. But if something *did* happen ...

PIETRO: *Bene!* You are right! Miss Ruth must not go!
ALAN: Oh, yes she will! I'm not going to have any *more* misunderstanding! I'll explain the whole thing; and Ruth goes with me.
PIETRO: (*he means every word*) *Signore!* In dead earnest! Don't do it!
ALAN: Why not? What's *your* reason?
PIETRO: I am not a religious man, *signore*. But here, in the Coliseum, I make the Sign of the Cross! Don't take her there!
ALAN: It *is* haunted, then?
PIETRO: I can't explain! I only warn you! Don't take her to that villa!
(*Music: hits hard, then holds under next speech*)

RUTH: And so, Doctor Fabian, an hour later I was driving out to that villa, in Bianca da Carpi's limousine. (*fiercely*) I *had* seen that letter with the initials on the sealing-wax! I *was* jealous! But... (*pause, changing tone*) we drove at last through a noisy suburb—whose main avenue... street-cars! bicycle-bells! ... ran almost to the front door of that white marble villa. We were admitted by a dark-faced servant who didn't speak a word. Inside there was one long corridor; it ran crossways through the villa, instead of front-to-back. Down on the left there was a partly opened door, with light inside. I had a glimpse of a book-lined room, with windows facing out on the noise and glare of the suburb. Then I heard—
GOODLAW: (*off, but not far off*) One tries to do one's duty, *Signora*. But you won't accept advice either from the Church or from a friend. To take a practical consideration, now...!
BIANCA: Practical considerations have always bored me, Mr. Goodlaw.
RUTH: (*on; whispering*) Alan! Is that —?
ALAN: (*on; whispering*) Our hostess? Must be!
GOODLAW: If you go into a slum at night, you're in danger of being robbed or killed. It is the same, believe me, in the realm of the spirit. And if you call evil forces ...
BIANCA: I *have* called them. Duke Nicolo will be here before midnight.
RUTH: (*frightened; whispering*) Alan!
ALAN: Shh! Take it easy!
GOODLAW: Another consideration then. Your heart won't stand it. Oh, you look healthy enough!
BIANCA: (*langourous*) A blonde Venus, should you say?
GOODLAW: No such vulgarism, I thank you. But your heart is weak. As a final consideration...
BIANCA: Well, Mr. Goodlaw?
GOODLAW: You endanger your soul! I forbid it!
BIANCA: (*triumph*) You're too late.
GOODLAW: (*controlled*) One moment. (*fussed*) My eye-glasses! Isn't there someone at the door?

(*Sound: a faint clangor of traffic as though through windows*)

ALAN: (*suavely*) Forgive me for coming into the library, sir. The butler just—disappeared. I imagine you're the Reverend Mr. Goodlaw?

GOODLAW: (*foggily*) Yes! Certainly! Yes, yes, yes! Er—may I present...?

BIANCA: (*exuding appeal*) You don't need to. I'll introduce myself. I've heard so much about you, Mr. Stannard, that—(*stops, taken aback*) Oh!

ALAN: This is my fiancée, Miss Ruth Gale.

BIANCA: Oh. I see. How do you do, Miss Gale?

RUTH: I'm well, thanks. (*faint but meaning inflection*) And you?

BIANCA: (*sudden intensity*) Did you two, either of you, hear what we were saying a moment ago?

ALAN: Yes. Both of us heard.

BIANCA: Then we mustn't stand on ceremony, must we? Will you look at the portrait over the fireplace, please?

GOODLAW: A thin face! A handsome face! A cruel face!

BIANCA: That is Nicolo Orsini, Duke of Urbania. He was hacked to death, by his own servants, in October of 1621.

ALAN: Yes. I've read about him. Has he been...seen?

BIANCA: We've seen him many times, yes. But never *inside* the house.

ALAN: (*quickly*) Where have you seen him? When?

BIANCA: At twilight. Peering in through the long windows. With the dagger-wounds in his face.

RUTH: (*badly frightened*) I— I don't understand this, *Signora*. But for some reason you keep looking at *me*. If he's *outside* the house...

BIANCA: *Why doesn't he get in*? Is that it?

RUTH: Yes!

GOODLAW: Because he can't! Unless you invite him. No evil force can!

BIANCA: Not in *his* case anyway. Now look at those tall windows! And the suburb crowding up! Where those houses stand, it was only open fields in Nicolo's time. Open fields, and a mud path leading to a forest. Now...noise. Eternal, stupid people!

GOODLAW: Shall I push the leaves of the windows shut, my dear? And close the curtains?

BIANCA: (*real charm*) Would you do that, Mr. Goodlaw? We can't keep out noise altogether. But... How Nicolo must hate it!

ALAN: Let's get our facts straight, even if they're only mad facts. Where did Nicolo die?

BIANCA: Out there. Just beyond those windows.

ALAN: But Capello's history says...

BIANCA: They struck him down in the open field, yes! Ten daggers. They left him for dead. But he had... I don't know...a kind of diabolism! I love it! He started to crawl...

RUTH: Towards the windows?

BIANCA: Yes.

(*Sound: heavy curtains are suddenly swept together with noise of many small hook-rings sliding on metal bar*)
BIANCA: (*starting*) What's that?
GOODLAW: (*off, soothingly*) I'm only closing the curtains, you know. This red velvet is as heavy as lead... Now the other curtains.
(*Sound: sound follows*)
GOODLAW: (*fading on, pleading*) Miss Gale! Mr. Stannard! Since you've heard what I said... a word more. This lady is in great danger.
BIANCA: (*trying to laugh, quick breathing*) How very silly of you! I'm quite all right.
GOODLAW: If she were an honest psychic researcher, it would be dangerous enough. But she's exhausted everything in life she calls "thrill." Now she has turned to these forces only for...
BIANCA: Yes! The thrill!
GOODLAW: To bring an evil spirit *inside* the house...
BIANCA: I've called him, Mr. Goodlaw. There's only one more thing to do, and he'll be here. Will you follow me, please? All of you?
RUTH: (*instinctively*) No! That is...
ALAN: Where do you want us to go?
BIANCA: Out into the corridor. Only a little way. we'll be back here immediately. Don't hesitate, please! Follow me!

(*Music: sinister music up and down, holding under next speech*)
RUTH: In the corridor we turned left, on thick padded carpet. She left the library door open; it was the only light. We walked straight along, to a little staircase at the end. The steps led—down. That was where I nearly... anyway, we didn't stay long in that old cellar. She left us behind her, even the little parson in his clerical collar, when she went into another room. I don't know what she did. There was a noise like...
(*Sound: through music, grind of key turning in lock*)
RUTH: Like an old key in a lock. When she came back, she had something hidden in her closed hand. We went upstairs. It was a relief even to see that library door on the left, and the portrait inside, and the red-curtained windows. We sat down, all of us. And then—nobody spoke. For what seemed like hours, nobody spoke. It went on, and on! And on, and on! Until...
(*Music: comes out with a sting*)

ALAN: If nobody's going to ask the question, *I* will! What have you got in your hand, *signora*? What did you bring up here?
BIANCA: A gold coin. A heavy coin. *This*. It's been polished you see. But I throw it on the table...
(*Sound: coin falls on wooden surface*)
BIANCA: It was the talisman of Duke Nicolo.

ALAN: (*strung up*) Talisman! In the modern sense of a luck-charm?
BIANCA: Of course, dear Alan! He wasn't wearing it when they stabbed him. So he—crawled back to those windows there.
ALAN: To get the charm? Even when he knew he was dying?
BIANCA: Why not? It might save him. He got to the house; he clawed at those heavy vine-stems to stand up; he knocked at the window. But he was too weak to open or smash the window. The servants stood where we are, and laughed when he fell and died. But — he wanted this luck-charm. He still wants it. Here!—I'll spin it in the air!—
(*Sound: coin falls rattling on table, and rolls off*)
BIANCA: Will you come for it *now*, dead Nicolo!?
RUTH: (*suddenly, half hypnotized*) Wait! There's something wrong with the room.
GOODLAW: In the room, or outside?
RUTH: That's it there's not a sound from outside. Not a noise in that suburb!
ALAN: Ruth, I was just thinking the same thing! They must go to bed very early! Or else...
BIANCA: Or else what?
ALAN: (*trying to laugh*) Nothing! Nothing at all! Do you mind if I open the curtains for a minute?
BIANCA: No-o, Alan! Please do!
ALAN: (*fading off*) Not a sound of a street-car. Not a taxi-horn. No voices. Not—
(*Sound: curtains flung back*)
ALAN: Not even a street-light! It's so dark I can't see anything.
RUTH: But... the moon was up! I noticed it!
ALAN: Yes, but there's a black cloud. Hold on! The clouds are moving. The moon is... (*whispering*) Lord Almighty!
GOODLAW: (*rapt monotone*) Thou shalt not be afraid for the terror by night; nor for the arrow that flieth by day; not for...
RUTH: (*crying out*) Alan! What is it!
ALAN: (*fading on*) I don't want you to think I'm crazy, But—*there aren't any houses*!
BIANCA: (*low voice: quick breathing*) This is the first time it's happened. Because *I* called this morning; and tapped on the window with that coin. What else did you see?
ALAN: (*blankly*) Open fields. A mud road towards a forest.
BIANCA: Anything else?
ALAN: No. Only a bundle of clothes on the ground. Bundle of clothes!
BIANCA: (*savoring triumph*) Yes, Alan!
GOODLAW: (*now off: loud but calm*) The bundle of clothes—is moving. It's crawling towards the villa.
BIANCA: We'll see now what the servants watched. We're seeing through dead men's eyes.
GOODLAW: I locked the windows long ago. Now I'll close the curtains again

and...
(*Sound: curtains swept shut*).
ALAN: This isn't real! We're all drugged or hypnotized! Mr. Goodlaw! What do *you* say?
GOODLAW: (*fading on*) Young man, I am of what dissenters call the High Church. Such forces exist. But the shell-of-death won't get in. There are words to keep it out.
BIANCA: You *will* let him in!
GOODLAW: Your heart won't stand it!
RUTH: Listen! What's that?
(*Sound: a tearing as of heavy branches or vine-stems*)
RUTH: It sounds like...
BIANCA: He's outside the window! He's clawing at the vine-stems. In another second...
GOODLAW: He won't get in, Bianca!
ALAN: Why not?
GOODLAW: Do you know your Vulgate, the Latin Bible? Well! *Illa magas artes Aeaeaque carmina nouit inque caput...*
(*Sound: three knocks on glass, as from heavy but weak fist*).
BIANCA: Open the curtains! You'll see his face!
ALAN: (*crying out*) Mr. Goodlaw! Mr... what's your first name?
GOODLAW: It's Septimus. Why?
ALAN: Well, Mr. Septimus Goodlaw... you're not a real clergyman!
GOODLAW: *What's that?*
(*Sound: three heavier knocks*).
ALAN: When you quote Latin, don't say it's the Bible when it's really a line from Ovid. And if there's anything outside that window... I challenge it! Enter!
(*Sound: crash of breaking glass. then music hits hard, and is held briefly as Ruth speaks*).

RUTH: That's all I can tell you. *I* was the one who couldn't stand it; I fainted. The red curtains bulged out, and that's all I remember until... (*voice growing dizzy*)... until...
(*Sound: bird-song from cages then down and finally out*).
FABIAN: Ruth! Open your eyes! Do you know where you are?
RUTH: (*dazed*) Yes! I...
FABIAN: I'm Doctor Fabian of the *Maurevania*. You're in the writing-room of my hotel, sitting beside my desk, where you started to tell your story. Right?
RUTH: Yes! I'm sorry. It was—remembering. That supernatural horror!
FABIAN: That's what I want to tell you, Ruth. (*gently but with authority*) There was nothing supernatural in anything you saw or heard. Do you understand?

RUTH: *Nothing ... supernatural?*
FABIAN: You were fooled by a pair of clever swindlers, that's all. The fake parson and the blonde with the so-called "weak heart." It was only a new version of an old confidence-game.
RUTH: But who'd play a confidence-game on *me*?
FABIAN: Not you, Ruth. They didn't want *you*. You nearly wrecked their scheme. Remember their behavior?
RUTH: (*thinking*) Yes! That's true! But...
FABIAN: It was all directed at Alan. Didn't you tell me he was very wealthy? Yes! Now suppose a young and wealthy American, far less clever than Alan, had gone to that villa last night?
RUTH: Well? Tell me!
FABIAN: He would have overheard, as Alan overheard and was meant to, a talk in the library about ghosts and a weak heart. Then the net of terror would be woven. *Then* they would have staged their show—and you can't deny it was effective! —with the aid of a servant outside. At the height of the terror...
RUTH: Go on! What happens?
FABIAN: (*satirically*) The blonde Venus drops dead. Of a weak heart.
RUTH: (*beginning to realize*) And the wealthy young man is ...
FABIAN: He's frantic! He's in no condition to realize the woman isn't dead. Then the kindly old clergyman, taking pity on him, says they *can* hush it up if they bribe the police. But where is *he*, the poor-devil parson, to get a lot of money?
RUTH: Money! Of course! The victim would have paid *anything* to that fake parson!
FABIAN: Their blonde Venus, of course, was the bait. But their new confidence-twist was the supernatural. They made up a good part of their history; don't you remember how Alan tried to correct them?
RUTH: They may be clever, Doctor Fabian; but they're not wizards. They couldn't make a whole suburb disappear!
FABIAN: Oh, yes, they could! Quite easily.
ALAN: (*calling, off*) Doctor Fabian! (*fading on*) They told me you were... Ruth! At last! Thank the lord!
RUTH: (*near tears*) Alan!
ALAN: (*soothing her*) It's all right, now! It's all right!
RUTH: Where *were* you, Alan? I—I woke up at dawn, in a chair in some other room at that villa. There was nobody in the house. Where did you go?
ALAN: We were all at the police-station! I spent the night there! When that window smashed and nothing happened, that fake blonde fell over, apparently dead. Then "Goodlaw" tried, to get money out of me. At that minute about fifty cops came pouring in...
PIETRO: (*fading on*) If you will introduce *me, signore?*
ALAN: (*not pleased*) Yes! This is Inspector Rossi of the Civil Police. (*bitterly*)

Known to *me* as Poor Pietro of the Coliseum!

PIETRO: (*hurt*) *Signore*! We want to trap these confidence-people. They cheat tourists too often. We are always interested in letters to rich Americans with the initials B.D.C. on the sealing wax. I must make sure you are the victim, and use you as what-you-call stalking- 'orse.

ALAN: (*angrily*) But you told me...

PIETRO: I nearly faint when you say you will take Miss Ruth! Maybe it spoil their game!

RUTH: Please, never mind their game! How did they make a whole suburb disappear?

FABIAN: Ruth, think back! You were in the library. just before you all went downstairs to get that gold coin. Do you remember?

RUTH: Of course I remember!

FABIAN: You went out of the library, and turned left. You walked along a straight corridor to a staircase at the end. Presently you came back. What had happened?

RUTH: How do you mean, happened?

FABIAN: You were facing in the opposite direction, weren't you? The library door should have been on your right. But, as you told me, the lighted door was at your left!

RUTH: *You mean she took us to a different room*!?

FABIAN: Just across the corridor, yes! A room furnished exactly like the library at the front. A room opened and lighted in your absence. But where would the windows of *this* room be?

RUTH: At the back of the house! Of course!

FABIAN: You knew this was an outermost suburb. When Alan opened the curtains, what *should* he see but open fields and a path leading to a wood?

RUTH: Then the whole supernatural nightmare could be worked because ...

ALAN: We were looking out of the back windows instead of the front windows!

FABIAN: (*perplexed*) Look here, wasn't it obvious? As I keep telling everybody... I am not a detective*!*

(*Music: in and behind*)

FABIAN: And so, as the *Maurevania* weighs anchor in the port of Naples to set her course for Greece, I muse on the subject of those two swindlers,. Have I met criminals more clever? Oh, yes. One of them actually hoaxed us into believing that... but let it wait for next week. And, when I tell you the story called "Nobody's Hand"[1] will you join me in *Cabin B-13*?

(*Sound: ship's whistle*)
(*Music: fades out*

---

[1] The next play in *Cabin B-13* is "The Footprint in the Sky" and Carr never used the title "Nobody's Hand" in *Cabin B-13* or elsewhere.

Notes for the Curious

For the ninth play in *Cabin B-13* John Dickson Carr devised one of his most audacious impossibilities. In almost every book he wrote there is presented one baffling enigma after another but none, surely, is more daring and baffling than that with which "The Power of Darkness" is concerned. As Carr cheerfully confessed:

> *"That I, of all people, should complain of improbable solutions would be like Satan rebuking sin or St. Vitus objecting to the twist."*

In his work, the impossible is *always* possible. In *It Walks by Night* (1930), the murderer must be invisible. In *The Three Coffins* (1935) the killer appears to be able to fly. And in *The Devil in Velvet* (1951) ... even when Carr stepped outside the physical world, as he did in two of his most famous books, he did so brilliantly. His explanation of how the crimes were committed in *The Crooked Hinge* (1938) is genuinely impossible and, while he offers a practical solution in *The Burning Court* (1937) it is the *other* solution, outlined on the final pages, that gives the novel its enduring power.

Carr revised the script as "The Villa of the Damned", first broadcast on 23 August, 1955 in the ninth and final series of the BBC program *Appointment with Fear*. Carr had planned to call the later version of the story "The Dark of the Moon" but abandoned that idea because of the risk of confusion with a stage play of the same title. Nevertheless, he retained a fondness for the title and it re-surfaced for the final Dr. Fell novel, *Dark of the Moon* (1967). *The Power of Darkness* was Carr's original title for the historical adventure mystery published as *The Bride of Newgate* (1950).

The Footprint in the Sky

(*Sound: a ship's whistle*)
(*Music: in and fades out behind*)
ANNOUNCER: *Cabin B-13*. Tonight: "The Footprint in the Sky".
FABIAN: A storm at sea, did you say? (*amused*) No. Our luxury-liner *Maurevania*, on this world-cruise, won't find much of a storm in these Mediterranean latitudes. But I, Doctor Fabian, our ship's surgeon from Cabin B-13, remember a storm at sea that... Yes! It brought to light the story of Marcia Tate, who disastrously loved two men, and how guilt left a footprint where no human being ever walked.
(*Music: begins quietly but suggesting a storm, softly behind*)
FABIAN: It was towards the end of January, 1938. We were on a North Atlantic run, from Bermuda back to England. Three days out of Southampton— Lord, how cold it was! — The gale whistled in ahead of the gale-warning. There was no danger, of course, to a liner like this. But the wild effect of the gale was that of a luxury-hotel swung in space. At first you could stand at the front of the promenade deck.
(*Music: fades out*)
(*Sound: whistle of wind, then rise and pitch of ship follows under speech.*)
FABIAN: You could feel in your stomach the upward surge of the bows, then the crash as they plunged deck-deep into whitened water...
(*Sound: lash of gale on glass: storm sounds behind*)
FABIAN: And the heavy lash of water against glass, Later, most of the decks became too dangerous. All over the ship, like a haunted hotel with so many passengers in their cabins, you might have heard voices...

PURSER: Hello! Hello! Bridge?
SECOND OFFICER: (*on filter*) Bridge here. Second officer speaking.
PURSER: This is the purser's office. That last little dip smashed a lifeboat on number three station. Tell the old man, will you?
SECOND OFFICER: (*weary impatience*) Listen, my bucko. *Do you think the captain doesn't know that*? (*slight pause*) What do you really want?
PURSER: All right! There's been trouble! — The grand piano broke loose in the palm-lounge!
SECOND OFFICER: (*hollow noises of amusement*) Loud cheers!
PURSER: (*bitterly*) A thousand pounds' worth of damage, and you think it's funny! A grand piano's like a runaway cannon. One young fool of a passenger got in front and tried to stop it...
SECOND OFFICER: (*changing tone*) Passenger? Is he hurt?
PURSER: I want you to tell the old man I'm not responsible!
SECOND OFFICER: I said: is he hurt?
PURSER: Yes. He's in the doctor's surgery now.

(*Sound: sea and wind come up, then down under*)
FABIAN: (*gentle heartiness*) There young fellow. That dressing ought to do. You were lucky to get off with five stitches in the head, after falling under a runaway piano.
(*Sound: off, phone rings*)
FABIAN: (*turning away*) Nurse! Will you answer that?
NURSE: (*off*) Certainly Doctor Fabian.
FABIAN: And... (*suddenly back to mike*) No, young fellow! Don't get up! Sit back... now *lie* back... on the cot. You're too dazed to speak now! This gale...
(*Sound: another plunge. heavy chair crashes against wall as though having slipped without sound across rubber flooring*)
FABIAN: There goes *my* chair against the wall!
NURSE: (*off*) Doctor Fabian! Will you come to the 'phone, please?
FABIAN: Thank you, nurse. (*pause*) — Hello!
STEWARDESS: (*filter, agitated*) Doctor Fabian! Cabin-stewardess in charge of C-14 to C-30! Can you come down to C-24 at once?
FABIAN: Yes; what is it?
STEWARDESS: It's the young lady here, sir! She's out of 'er mind!
FABIAN: Shock, you mean? A fall?
STEWARDESS: It wasn't a fall, sir. But she doesn't know where she is or how she got here! She thinks it's Christmas over a year ago! And...
FABIAN: Speak up! I can't hear you!
STEWARDESS: She wants to know why she hasn't been hanged for murder!

(*Music: up, then down and fades out under narration*)
FABIAN: In C-24; a large double-cabin whose rosewood-paneled walls creaked like wickerwork, the girl we shall call Marcia sat back against pillows in the left-hand bed. I shall not forget, as I opened the door, the wide-spaced blue eyes and the gentle face white with terror. The stewardess was with her. When I had been there for some minutes...
MARCIA: (*English, 25, high strung but soft-voiced*) Really and truly, Doctor, that hypodermic-sedative won't do any good! It won't! I know!
FABIAN: We-ell! Then we must try something else. Just sit back against the pillows!
MARCIA: All right! If you insist! But...
FABIAN: (*interrupting quickly*) As I understand it, you haven't *completely* lost your memory.
MARCIA: No! Of course not! My name is Marcia Tate. I live... or did live... with my parents.
FABIAN: Where?
MARCIA: At Brent; near Richmond. By the river. About ten miles from London. — But why am I on this ship? And this is a double cabin; who's with me? (*appealing*) Stewardess!
STEWARDESS: (*distressed*) Please, ma'am! Who *should* be with you but your...

FABIAN: (*sharply*) Stewardess?
STEWARDESS: Yes, Doctor?
FABIAN: I've written something on this prescription-pad.
(*Sound: leaf torn out from pad on dotted line*)
FABIAN: Would you mind taking it up to the nurse in my surgery?
STEWARDESS: Very good, sir.
MARCIA: (*in terror*) Was she going to say—my husband? *Was she*?
(*Sound: off, door opens and closes as ship pitches*)
FABIAN: Listen, Miss Tate. I'm going to try to bring back your memory. Just trust me. What's the last thing you *do* remember?
MARCIA: I remember—words. "You've killed—"
FABIAN: Wait! What's the last *happy* memory?
MARCIA: (*slight pause; almost caressingly*) Five o'clock in the afternoon. Two days before Christmas. The studio!
FABIAN: What studio?
MARCIA: At home we've got a deep back garden that stretches down to the river. There was an old stone-coach-house. My father had it remodeled into one big studio-room with a north skylight. I—I only dabble at painting; I'm not much good. But it was a lovely — retreat!
FABIAN: (*steady insistence*) Two days before Christmas. Five o'clock in the afternoon. You were in the studio…
(*Music: creeps in behind next speech*)
MARCIA: Outside it was cold. Bitter cold! But inside the studio there was a huge log fire burning in the rough-stone fireplace. The velvet sofa was in front of it. All around were the curios that my father—he's a retired Colonel—brought back from other countries. In one corner there was the grand piano…
FABIAN: (*muttering*) Grand piano! (*aloud*) Go on!
MARCIA: It was getting dark; only bright firelight.
(*Music: fades out*)
MARCIA: I was sitting at the piano. Ted—Ted Benson was there. And I've never been happier, never!— than when…

(*Sound: piano, on, with "Hark The Herald Angels Sing" a Christmas song which is being played joyously; then piano continues softly under.*)
MARCIA: (*deeply in love*) Ted, darling!
TED: (*a little off*) Yes, Marcia?
MARCIA: I won't look 'round; I want to imagine you. Where are you now?
TED: I was admiring this painting on the easel. And the other canvases here!
MARCIA: (*happily*) I can't paint for toffee; I know it; and I don't care! But it *is* nice of you to say that!
TED: It isn't "nice". It's true! What's more… (*interested*) Marcia: this big brass gong in the corner by the curtain! It looks Chinese. There's a padded stick here to…

MARCIA: (*suddenly*) Ted! Please don't sound that gong!
TED: (*surprised*) Of course not, if you say so. But why not?
MARCIA: Dad got it from some Buddhist monks. If you sound the gong, it's, supposed to mean death and destruction, I know it's only a silly superstition, but—we don't touch it.
TED: Then I won't touch it either.
(*Sound: piano, which has been almost inaudible, begins* "Good King Wenceslas.")
TED: No, wait! Turn around! Look up at me!
(*Sound: piano stops*)
TED: You've known me for just two weeks. Your father likes me, yes! Because I'm a gunner-officer and his old regiment at that! (*grimly*) But your mother ...
MARCIA: Mother's got a kind of crush on Barry Stoner herself. *And* his money.
TED: (*abject*) *I* haven't got any money, you know. I'm only a two-for-a penny captain, just promoted from subaltern, whose pay wouldn't...
MARCIA: Ted! Who cares?
TED: You were engaged to Barry Stonor for nearly a year. You *must* have loved him!
MARCIA: I thought I did, yes! I didn't know anything different. (*tenderly satirical*) This is England, dear. I'm a 'well-brought-up-young lady'. How *could* I know anything different?
TED: But if you still love him, Marcia, I don't want to...
MARCIA: Ted, kiss me. As hard as you kissed me the first time we met. As...
(*pause*)
TED: I'm an Army man too, remember. I've been stationed in too many out-of-the-way places to ... (*changing tone; huge amusement*) Lord help us!
MARCIA: (*not pleased*) Ted! What's so very funny?
TED: This silver statuette! On the table behind the sofa. I never heard *you* were a gymnastics-champion!
(*Sound: piano jangles and stops*)
TED: The inscription says, 'June 3rd, 1936. Won by Barry Stonor for—' (*stops*) (*embarrassed*) Oh. Sorry!
MARCIA: Ted, *I'm* sorry! I meant to take that out of here!
TED: No! Why should you? But... (*with intensity*) No, don't get up. (*fading on*) I'll come over and put my hands on your shoulders. Marcia, are you *sure*? About us?
MARCIA: So sure, Ted—so terribly sure!—that ...
(*Sound: piano strikes emotionally into song beginning*: "When The Dawn Flames In The Sky"...)
MARCIA: Darling. (*unsteadily*) Now you'd better go, or I shall begin crying and say you're responsible. (*suddenly realizing*) Ted! That War Office

man who's staying at Richmond! When are you supposed to met him?
TED: Four o'clock.
MARCIA: What time is it now?
TED: Quarter past five. *And who cares*?
MARCIA: Darling, *I* care! For *your* sake! He's a higher-up at the War Office!
TED: Old Corky? We're only going to have some drinks.
MARCIA: But he's Lord Avon, dear! You know all these people, and yet it never once enters your head to … never mind! I want you as you are. Here's your greatcoat — those shoulder-buttons want polishing! — and I'll hold the coat. There! Now your cap. I'll practically *throw* you out.
(*Sound: on, door opens*)
MARCIA: (*wavering*) Ted …
TED: (*quietly; deep earnest*) I love you, Marcia.
MARCIA: (*same earnestness*) Do I need to say it, Ted? Good night.
(*Sound: door slowly closes*)
MARCIA: (*to herself*) Always and always, Ted. Always and always! Until…
(*Sound: heavy note from flat brass gong*)
BARRY: If this gong is struck, Marcia, it's supposed to mean death. (*ironically*) Sorry!
MARCIA: Barry Stonor!
BARRY: (*fading on*) Your ex-fiancé, Marcia. In cosy firelight!
MARCIA: How did you get in here?
BARRY: With a key. The key you gave me. I remained behind the curtain there until …
MARCIA: You said you lost that key! So you lied to me again!
BARRY: (*agreeably*) Women, my pet, invariably love men who lie to them. That's how I've scored many of my successes.
MARCIA: (*controlled*) I hate to remind you, Barry. But you didn't have much success with *me*.
BARRY: In a way you're thinking, no. But then you're a very funny girl, Marcia.
MARCIA: (*frightened*) How do you mean?
BARRY: The face of a Burne-Jones angel and yet all the passion of … for Ted Benson, anyway! Does he know *everything* about you?
MARCIA: (*crying out*) You can't say I ever—
BARRY: No, I mean you're *rather* neurotic. Has your father told Benson about your fainting-spells? Or walking in your sleep? They're bad symptoms, Marcia.
MARCIA: (*through her teeth*) Will you please get out of here? *Now*?!
BARRY: The answer is no. I will not.
MARCIA: Why do you hate me so much for breaking off our engagement. *Why*?
BARRY: You can't throw *me* over, Marcia. And get away with it.
MARCIA: Throw you… (*suddenly realizing*) I've hurt your conceit! Isn't that it?
BARRY: (*ignoring this*) You *were* very fond of me, you know.

MARCIA: Yes. I wonder why!

BARRY: (*complacently*) It was my charm, Marcia. I've got charm; why should I deny it? (*changing tone*) In those days you were a powerful letter-writer. All ecstasy and purple patches. Anyone who read it all would think for certain...

MARCIA: Are you trying to...

BARRY: Come off it, my pet! I'm no blackmailer. (*pleasantly*) I'm going to give those letters, free of charge and with my compliments, to Ted Benson. Do you see the game?

MARCIA: There's nothing ... at least... Ted won't mind!

BARRY: He'll *say* he doesn't mind. But he will. Your worrying, on top of that, will poison your marriage in six weeks... And you know it.

MARCIA: Ted wouldn't even...!

BARRY: He wouldn't even read the letters? He'd throw 'em in the fire? Is that what you mean?

MARCIA: Yes! It is!

BARRY: If he's that sort of fool, which he may be, he'll always wonder what was in them. You'll try to reassure him. And it will poison your marriage, better still.

MARCIA: (*breaking*) Barry, listen! Is it any good *appealing* to you?

BARRY: (*amused*) You can try.

MARCIA: I wish you were dead! I wish ...

BARRY: (*interested*) Now why are you backing away towards that table behind the sofa? Why are you ... Here! It's the silver statuette *I* won!

MARCIA: Yes, Barry. It is!

BARRY: (*enjoying himself*) Hold it by the head, as you're doing; and the base is a murderous weapon. You could smash a man's skull with that. Wouldn't you like to smash *my* head?

MARCIA: Yes! If I had the nerve!

BARRY: (*gently*) Neurotic. You see?

(*Sound: statuette falls with a thud on cloth-cover of table*)

BARRY: (*amused*) I've only to say "neurotic", and you drop the weapon. No, you're not dangerous.

MARCIA: What are you going to *do*?

BARRY: Stay here. Make up the fire. Sit on the sofa, with my back to the door and all draughts blowing. It's going to snow, too. At about half-past eleven I'll ring up Ted Benson ...

MARCIA: (*fiercely*) You know what he'll do to you?

BARRY: I'm a fairly well-known athlete, Marcia, He wouldn't stand a chance. (*snarling*) — What do you see in the fellow, anyway?

MARCIA: I'd do *anything* for him. That's all.

BARRY: Benson and I are both tall; we're both light-haired; we... Interesting! Maybe you love *me* — in *his* image.

Marcia: *Stop it! Stop it!*
Barry: You're in a corner, my pet. (*fading a little off*) (*contemptuously*) As for your "death-gong" over here …
(*Sound: gong, angrily*)
Barry: There you are! And again!
    (*Sound: gong*)
Barry: (*fading on*) But you can't throw *me* over, Marcia. And get away with it!

(*Music: up. for a moment*)
(*Sound: the crash of the sea; but sea-noise out as music holds under.*)
Marcia: That night, Doctor Fabian, I dreamed. (*pause*) How I faced dinner at home, with my father and mother at the table, I don't know. After dinner I ran upstairs. I just couldn't face anything more. I took two sleeping-pills. My bedroom's at the back of the house. When I raised the windows, getting drowsy already, I felt a snowflake sting my face. I vaguely, remember putting my fur coat over the bed, in case there weren't enough blankets. My slippers—they're Red-Indian moccasins; small ones—were near the bed. I won't tell you what. I dreamed, because it was too horribly real. Then, all of a sudden…
(*Music: comes out into cymbal-thrumming, which continues under speech*)
Marcia: It was grey daylight. I was in my bedroom, yes! But I was sitting in an arm-chair hear the unlighted gas-fire. And my mother… she's tall and thin, like my father… was looking down at me. And I saw her eyes.
(*Music: cymbal-sting*)

Blanche: (*50, trying to be brisk but fearful*) Marcia! Marcia dear!
Marcia: (*dazed*) Oh! Hullo, mother! I thought…
Blanche: Marcia. Give me that fur coat! And the moccasins!
Marcia: What fur coat!
Blanche: The one you're wearing over your pajamas, dear! And the moccasins… they're still damp!. Get up, please! That's it! Give them to me!
Marcia: (*still blankly; seizing on trifles*) Mother! The—the windows are closed!
Blanche: (*brisk but breathless*) Yes, dear. We've looked in here once before.
Marcia: Who looked in?
Blanche: Your father and I. (*fading off*) Now I'll just take these things over to the wardrobe. Neatness! That's what your grandmother always used to say. Neatness! There! (*fading on*) Now here's a quilted dressing-gown, and another pair of slippers. Put them on. Quickly, please!
Marcia: (*has suddenly realized that it mightn't have been a dream*) *Mother*! What's wrong?
Blanche: Now, dear. You mustn't excite yourself. Sit down. That's it! But the fact is…

MARCIA: Well?
BLANCHE: There's a police-officer downstairs. A divisional detective-inspector.
MARCIA: Detective... What does he want?
BLANCHE: Hadn't you better talk to your father, Marcia? He'll be up here in a moment!
MARCIA: One question! And now about the police-officer! (*slight pause*) Is he dead?
BLANCHE: (*taken aback*) Is *who* dead?
MARCIA: (*far away*) He was sitting on the sofa. His back to the door. His head outlined against firelight. The statuette gleamed. You could creep up, ever so softly...
BLANCHE: Marcia! How do you know that?
MARCIA: I dreamed it! Or thought I did!
BLANCHE: Then this sleep-walking — (*stops abruptly*) Did you... in your dream, dear! of course!... hear anything like the gong?
MARCIA: No! I don't think so! *Why*?
BLANCHE: Well, dear. A policeman heard it. Out in the road. After midnight. Very faintly. The studio door was open. That poor boy in the studio...
MARCIA: Go on! *Please!*
BLANCHE: He'd managed to crawl over to the gong. Inch by inch. His head was — all bloody. He was trying to summon help. Then he collapsed.
MARCIA: Is he...?
BLANCHE: He's in the hospital. Dying.
MARCIA: (*bursting out*) I didn't do it! It was only a dream!
(*Sound: off, door opens and closes.*)
MARCIA: (*she is her father's favorite.*) Dad!
COLONEL: (*gruffly*) Hello there, kitten.
MARCIA: Dad! Come and help me! What do they say?
COLONEL: (*fading on*) I won't lie to you, kitten. It's bad. Pretty bad. But don't worry. Give your Dad time to think; the old Colonel's no fool; and we'll fake this evidence from here to bloody-end-all!
BLANCHE: (*shrilly*) Do you want to get us all in trouble, George Tate?
COLONEL: Woman, shut up — (*worried*) Now look here, Marcia. There's only one bit of evidence I *can't* get round. *Can't!* That's your footprints in the snow.
MARCIA: (*groping*) Snow! *Yes!* I seem to remember...
COLONEL: (*heavily embarrassed*) *Did* you do it, kitten? *I* don't give a curse! But you'd better tell me.
MARCIA: Dad, I don't know! I was dreaming!
COLONEL: Last night it started to snow about nine-thirty. Not a heavy fall; only a light coating. It'd stopped by eleven, they tell me.
MARCIA: And *I*...?
COLONEL: Somebody in your moccasins, walked out from our back door to the

studio. Then walked back here again.
BLANCHE: And there are no other footprints except the policeman's!
COLONEL: (*desperate*) D'ye *see*, kitten?
MARCIA: But if somebody took the moccasin.
COLONEL: Could have been an outsider. We never lock the back door. *But* —
MARCIA: Go on!
COLONEL: Not a soul in this house, not a single man you know, could possibly have worn those moccasins! We're all too big! Number nine or ten shoe. If you didn't make those tracks, nobody else could have.
MARCIA: I didn't do it, I tell you!
COLONEL: (*not steady*) Come over to the window for a minute. Come on; eh? To please *me*? Good girl! That's it. Now look... (*breaking off*) Who are those people in Preston's back-garden?
BLANCHE: Carol-singers, George. Practising. It's the day before Christmas.
COLONEL: Never mind! Let's have the window up!
(*Sound: window raised*)
COLONEL: You see, kitten...
(*Sound: a few carol-singers, with the toy xylophone they always carry, can be heard far off*)
CHORUS: *Good King Wen-ce-las looked out On the feast of Stephen, When the snow lay round a-bout, Deep and crisp and even. Brightly shone* —
(*Sound: window closed heavily*)
COLONEL: You see, Marcia? There're the footprints. There's the very high laurel-hedge, with the arch in it, across the garden. The footprints go under the arch. Then out to the studio: Then back towards...Stop a bit! There's something devilish queer about that laurel-hedge! It's too thin; a cat couldn't walk on top. And yet...
MARCIA: (*eagerly*) Dad! What is it?
COLONEL: Dunno. Got to think. But don't worry!
BLANCHE: (*so nervous she is angry*) You *ought* to say that, George Tate! Since it's all your fault!
COLONEL: It's all my fault again, eh.
BLANCHE: The girl's been neurotic for years. You knew that!
COLONEL: Marcia's my daughter! She's as sound as a bell!
BLANCHE: (*satirically*) And in your eyes, of course, she simply can't do any wrong!
COLONEL: Very well, she can't! (*changing tone; gruffly*) Look here, kitten. D'ye love Ted Benson a good deal?
MARCIA: He's everything in the world.
COLONEL: That's the blasted torture! If it had only been the other fellow, that swine, who got his head bashed in...
BLANCHE: But it wasn't, George!
COLONEL: Benson and Stonor are both tall; they're both got light hair. If you saw one sitting there, with his back turned, you'd think...

MARCIA: (*growing horror*) Dad! What are you saying?
COLONEL: (*taken aback*) Didn't your mother tell you?
MARCIA: No!
BLANCHE: Barry wasn't there, dear. *You've killed Ted Benson!*
(*Music: hits hard with first bars of "Good King Wenceslas", then into different theme and held under —*)

(*Sound: sea-noises*)
FABIAN: And so I, Doctor Fabian, sat at the foot of Marcia's bed in Cabin C-24 of the *Maurevania*. The last mumbled words died on her lips. Her head fell back against propped-up pillows; her eyes closed, The nurse, from my surgery on A Deck, stood beside me. I waited, with my eyes on my watch. Three minutes...five minutes...ten minutes... until the nurse could keep silent no longer...
NURSE: Doctor Fabian!
FABIAN: Yes, nurse?
NURSE: You sent up a prescription-blank by the stewardess. But all it said was to come down here, and bring the man who —
FABIAN: (*interrupting; on edge*) I wanted to get rid of the stewardess. She talked too much! Did she tell *you* anything?
NURSE: She said you gave the young lady a hypodermic-injection.
FABIAN: I did. But not the kind Marcia thought. I gave her 55 cc. Sodium Evipan.
NURSE: You mean the —?
FABIAN: Medically, nurse, it's wrong to speak of Evipan as a "truth" drug. It opens the subconscious mind when the patient's in a nearly-waking state. If we have any luck we'll bring back her memory for good!
NURSE: And — solve the mystery. Didn't you read about it in the papers?
FABIAN: Nonsense! The police solved that 'studio-mystery' over a year ago. Marcia knows the truth.
NURSE: Then—excuse me, Doctor—it won't be a very happy memory! She killed the man she was in love with. (*remembering*) And — the husband! Aboard this ship! Her husband may be...
FABIAN: (*sharply*) Wait!
NURSE: (*stolid again*) Yes! Her lips are moving.
FABIAN: Fifteen minutes' unconsciousness; and now she's waking. Marcia! Can you hear me?
MARCIA: (*only half-hypnotized*) Of course I can hear you! Why do you ask?
NURSE: Imagine you're back, now, in what used to be your own bedroom at home. Thin snow on the ground! Footprints. Carol-singers! Your mother has just told you...
MARCIA: (*shuddering*) Yes! She said I killed Ted!
FABIAN: (*persuasively*) Easy! Why are you shuddering? It wasn't true, was it? You *weren't* guilty, were you?

MARCIA: (*radiant relief*) No! Of course not! The police proved that.
FABIAN: You didn't walk in your sleep, did you? Not after two sleeping-pills! You never left that room all night!
MARCIA: No! Never!
FABIAN: It was all a murderous trick, Marcia. What was the last clue that gave the game away?
MARCIA: It was the laurel hedge! A tall, thin laurel hedge, with an arch cut in it, across our garden. The top and upper sides were powdered with snow.
FABIAN: Your father noticed something *on* that hedge. What did he notice?
MARCIA: It was a footprint. A very large footprint.
FABIAN: Where *was* the footprint, exactly?
MARCIA: On the side of the hedge. High up! Above the arch!
FABIAN: But nobody could have walked there. It was like a ghost-footprint. What the press called "The Footprint in the Sky." How did it get there? What did the real criminal do?
MARCIA: The real criminal, with my moccasins, crept out of our back door. The real criminal...
FABIAN: (*sharply*) Who *was* the real criminal?
MARCIA: It was Barry Stonor.
(*Sound: plunge of ship, with crash and hiss of water. furniture rattles.*)
FABIAN: That's it, nurse! Hold her head and shoulders. Steady while the ship steadies!...And it was Barry Stonor!
NURSE: (*low voice*) Doctor, that's impossible! This man Stonor couldn't have worn her slippers!
FABIAN: No! But...tell us what he did, Marcia!
MARCIA: (*emotion showing*) He — he never intended to give Ted any letters. He wanted to kill Ted and make *me* suffer for it. He...
FABIAN: Go on!
MARCIA: At ten o'clock he 'phoned Ted at the hotel. With an urgent message from me. But he said I might be delayed. He knew Ted would rush over to the studio. He knew Ted would wait there. Ted didn't make any footprints; it was snowing.
FABIAN: And what did Barry Stonor do? Just before then?
MARCIA: He — he came over and hid in our house. He waited until the snow stopped. Then he slipped upstairs; I was drugged, asleep; and took my moccasins. He couldn't have worn them in the way *you* mean. But Barry — he's a champion gymnast. He won that silver trophy for it. And...
FABIAN: And he wore the moccasins...on his hands!
MARCIA: All he did, you see, was walk over and back on his hands afterwards he lifted *me* into a chair with the fur-coat and moccasins, and left by the front door. But, when he walked over to the studio on his hands, and got near that laurel-hedge...
FABIAN: His right shoe touched the snow over the arch. And he left the footprint that trapped him! (*muttering*) The drug's wearing off, nurse!

NURSE: (*muttering*) I know, Doctor!
FABIAN: You're not neurotic, Marcia; or you'd never have *feared* being neurotic. Many people walk in their sleep; there's no harm in it. And you didn't lose your memory more than a year ago. You lost it only an hour ago. Aboard this ship!
MARCIA: (*fainter now*) I couldn't have! I...
FABIAN: Think! You were in the palm-lounge! At the grand piano!
MARCIA: (*bewildered*) I don't remember! I...
FABIAN: The piano broke loose. It struck somebody down. You saw the blood on his head; and the shock blotted out your memory!
MARCIA: *No*! And yet...wait...I seem to re—
FABIAN: You know Ted Benson didn't die last Christmas, despite Stonor's beating! Ted's alive now. And if you doubt what I say... (*moving a little off*)...I'll just open this door.
(*Sound: door opens*)
FABIAN: May I introduce you to your husband, Mrs. Benson?
TED: (*fading on, shakily*) I'm sorry, I played the fool, Marcia, and got in front of that piano especially on our honeymoon but Doctor Fabian fixed me up! (*trying to laugh*) However, I'm all right; this old skull can stand anything. (*pleading*) Don't you recognize me?
MARCIA: (*pause: then crying out*) Ted! Ted! Ted!
(*Music: up to final narration*)

FABIAN: And so, as I end my story, I might mention that the drug Evipan was used on Rudolf Hess during his stay in England. It is described in a book called *The Case Of Rudolf Hess,* by Doctor J.R. Rees; and a friend of mine, a low hound named Carr, gave some very slight assistance to Doctor Rees. Next week we shall be in Athens. When I say that next week's story is called "*The Eyes of the Blind*"[1], it means only that a clue may be too obvious to be seen. If you doubt me, will you accept the challenge and join me in *Cabin B-13*?
(*Sound: ship's whistles*)
(*Music: fades out*)

---

[1] While it does feature "*a clue too obvious to be seen*", the next play in *Cabin B-13* was titled "The Man with the Iron Chest"; Carr never used the title "The Eyes of the Blind" in *Cabin B-13* or elsewhere.

Notes for the Curious

Like much of John Dickson Carr's post-war work, "The Footprint in the Sky" is set just before the outbreak of the Second World War. Carr and his family were directly affected by the war and the bombing of the German *Luftwaffe*, losing two houses; Carr was at the Savage Club (where Carr was a member) when a bomb sheared off a wall of the Club's premises in Carlton Terrace early in the morning of 15 October, 1940. Perhaps unsurprisingly, Carr yearned for the time before the coming of the air raids and the bombing that destroyed so much of the physical and social infrastructure of the United Kingdom. Eventually, this nostalgia led him to return to a new strand of writing, the historical mystery.

Other than juvenilia, his first substantive historical story is *Devil Kinsmere* (1934), a novel published under the pseudonym "Roger Fairbairn", and he went on to write other novels like *The Bride of Newgate* (1950), set in the Regency, the Scotland Yard trilogy—*Fire, Burn!* (1957), *Scandal at High Chimneys* (1959) and *The Witch of the Low-Tide* (1961)— as well as *Captain Cut-Throat* (1955), a mystery set in the Napoleonic period like his early radio serial, "Speak of the Devil" (1941).

The play is a revised version of 'The Gong Cried Murder', first broadcast on 14 December 1944 in the fourth series of the BBC program *Appointment with Fear*. The plays use the central ploy of the *Department of Queer Complaints* short story 'Clue in the Snow', first published in the *Strand* magazine in January 1940. A Marcia Tate is the main character in both of the radio plays and Carr seems to have associated the name with wintry weather for in the Carter Dickson novel, *The White Priory Murders* (1934), a Marcia Tait (*sic*) is found dead in a folly surrounded on all sides by ice and unmarked snow; other than this homophone, the novel and the radio plays do not have anything else in common.

In the script Carr references *The Case of Rudolf Hess; A Problem in Diagnosis and Forensic Psychiatry* (1948), edited by Jack Rawlings Rees. [London, William Heinemann, 1947]. Rees's introduction thanks Carr and others for having "*spent much time and thought in helping to improve the book.*" In July 1947, Hitler's deputy Rudolph Hess had been transferred to Spandau Prison in West Berlin after being found guilty of crimes against peace and conspiracy with other German leaders to commit crimes. After landing by parachute near Glasgow in Scotland, Hess was held briefly in the Tower of London, where he was seen by a number of psychologists. These included Rees, latterly President of the World Federation on Mental Health.

Evipan is a commercial form of the drug hexobarbital—also known as hexobarbitone—a *barbiturate* derivative with *hypnotic* and *sedative* effects. Evipan was used to murder women prisoners at Ravensbrück concentration camp and after the second world war for inducing *anaesthesia* for surgery and as a rapid-acting, short-lasting hypnotic.

The Man with the Iron Chest

(*Sound: a ship's whistle*)
(*Music: in and behind*)
ANNOUNCER: *Cabin B-13*. Tonight: "The Man with the Iron Chest".
FABIAN: Yes, the *Maurevania's* engines have stopped. This is the Modern Piraeus, the port of Athens. It's badly damaged, you notice. But I, Doctor Fabian of Cabin B-13, ship's surgeon on our cruise 'round the world, would tell you of drowsier pre-war days. How out of a locked and sealed room, the man called John Gronov make an iron chest and a hundred diamonds vanish as though they had never existed?

(*Music: up, and held under narration.*)
FABIAN: Over there, on our left, the yellow sunset is darkening behind Salamis. Six miles north is Athens, spreading and sprawling round the high crag of the Acropolis. But don't, I urge you, cherish too many romantic illusions; Joyce Allison, the American girl who had recently married a likeable young fellow from the British Embassy, cherished such illusions. Well do I remember the morning—it was February, '39—when we docked here at the *Piraeus*...
(*Music: fades out*)

(*Sound: crowd-murmur up and down.*)
JOYCE: Good-bye, Doctor Fabian.
FABIAN: Good-bye, Joyce. But why the hurry? You'll get crushed to death in this mob!
JOYCE: Don's here! My husband! He's down on the wharf!
FABIAN: (*tolerantly*) And—how long since you saw him last?
JOYCE: (*seriously*) It's almost three weeks!
FABIAN: Ah, yes. These lengthy absences can be bitter. All the best, Joyce! But remember what I told you!
JOYCE: About Athens?
FABIAN: Yes! It's one of the finest cities in the world. But...
JOYCE: (*as though rattling through a lesson*) But it's also the noisiest. And most good Athenians keep chickens, and the chickens make more noise than the street-cars. And the noblest building on the new road is a brewery. And I don't care! (*hesitating*) But I do feel a little disappointed already.
FABIAN: Oh? How so?
JOYCE: Because I've got to wear a coat. It's *cold!*
FABIAN: My dear Joyce, this is early February. Did you think Athens was always languorously warm?
JOYCE: I suppose I did, really. Never mind! The...(*startled*) Doctor Fabian!

There! Pushing through, the crowd.
DON: (*off, declaiming*) The mountains look on Marathon, and Marathon looks on the sea...!
JOYCE: *Don!*
DON: (*fading on*) How are you, Joyce! Let's lift you up in the air—high!—and down again. Joyce!
JOYCE: (*pause; breathless*) Don! How on earth did you get aboard ship?
DON: I used Embassy credentials. I said I was meeting the Chancellor of the Exchequer; and they shot me aboard like a Greek catapult.
JOYCE: Doctor Fabian, this is my husband. Mr. Donald Allison, Doctor Fabian.
FABIAN: Have you been in Athens for a long time, Mr. Allison?
DON: 'Fraid not, sir. Just stationed here. I came out ahead to swot up on Greek and get us a place to live. Then, naturally, there's been a lot to see...
JOYCE: (*eagerly*) Doctor Fabian! What do you advise us to do?
DON: (*seriously*) After the first few days, of course!
JOYCE: (*just as seriously*) Yes, of course!...What's so funny?
FABIAN: (*as though shocked*) Funny, Joyce? You mistake my professional sternness! (*considering*) You want a romantic evening; is that it?
JOYCE: Something completely unlike New York or London!
(*Music: creeps in under*)
FABIAN: Well! Hire one of those open carriages, and drive out Kifissia Street past the palace. That's the fashionable section; no poultry. Drive back from Kifissia late at night. Ahead of you, high up, you'll see the temples on the Acropolis in full moonlight. There won't be a sound, hardly a light. And, as the horses hoofs clop along that road...
(*Music: out into—*)

(*Sound: steady clopping of single horse's hoofs, drawing an open carriage along a good road*)
JOYCE: (*dreamily*) Doctor Fabian was right, Don! It's perfect.
DON: Completely and absolutely! So are you, Joyce. Have a cigarette?
JOYCE: No, thanks. Not now.—*Don*, wouldn't it be wonderful, if we had some kind of adventure?
DON: Out of a novel, you mean? *I* know!
JOYCE: "The temples on the Acropolis, in full moonlight." And Mount Lycabettus, over on our right! And Don, what are the houses on each side of the road? With modern balconies?
DON: They're luxury flats, mostly. That's where I've been trying to get a flat for *us*.
JOYCE: If there weren't any street-lights, they'd look like houses in old Athens. A moonlit scene for something unearthly; nothing modern at all! A street as deserted and silent as...
(*Sound: off, the dinning clangor of a burglar-alarm—preferably in bursts rather than a continuous sound. It continues under—*)

DON: (*sharply*) Driver! Pull up!
(*Sound: carriage stops, but horse is nervous; we hear clatter of hoofs.*)
JOYCE: Don! What is it?
DON: (*thoroughly awake*) That, Joyce, is a very modern burglar-alarm.
JOYCE: They don't have burglar-alarms in these apartment-houses, do they?
DON: No! But look across the street! About thirty yards back!
JOYCE: (*nervous now*) It—it looks like a jeweler's!
DON: It is! (*excitement growing*) And Athens is a big diamond-market! And those men over there, closing in as quietly as ghosts, are police.
(*Sound: horse rears and clatters.*)
DON: Driver! Steady the horse!
DRIVER: (*in agony*) Dan borno na to cratiso![1]
JOYCE: Darling, listen! This isn't the sort of adventure I meant!
DON: I know, Joyce. But over there—standing bang in the middle of the street—is a man I know pretty well. You don't mind if I jump out of the carriage?
(*Sound: thud as he jumps*)
DON: There! I'll be back in half a tick!
JOYCE: Don, who *is* your friend?
DON: His name is Melis; and he speaks English better than we do. He's the head of a Greek government department that corresponds to our Home Office. He... back in half a tick, Joyce.
JOYCE: (*fade off with cue below*) Don! Wait! I'd rather...
(*Sound: microphone follows Don, in running footsteps on asphalt. Burglar-alarm grows louder.*)
DON: (*calling*) Mr. Melis! Mr. Melis!
(*Sound: burglar alarm stops.*)
MELIS: (*fading on as footsteps stop; grimly pleased*) A very good evening, my young friend. Or, if you prefer it, a very good morning.
DON: I thought I recognized that long lean figure of yours!
MELIS: And also, I daresay, what you so often call my eagle beak. Well! I won't correct you!
DON: You sound pleased, Mr. Melis.
MELIS: I *am* pleased, young man. The burglar-alarm has stopped. Our men are in the jeweler's shop. By this time they have arrested—don't misunderstand!—the man with the *Iron chest.*
DON: (*puzzled*) Iron chest?
MELIS: Call it a box! Call it a coffer! Call it anything that is made of iron, lined with lead, two feet long and nearly as deep. Now this man—attend me!—is no common burglar. He is the best jewel-thief in the trade. Yet when-

---

[1] Translation: An English translation of the phrase "Dan borno na to cratiso" is not possible. Carr may have meant ευχαριστώ για το τίποτα which is normally rendered in English lettering as efcharistó gia to típota and meaning "Thanks for nothing!"

ever he robs a jeweler, he takes with him an iron chest weighing sixty *pounds*!
DON: But what the devil for? To carry the loot?
MELIS: (*almost pityingly*) My friend! The loot is jewelery; he can put it in his pocket.
DON: What about a burglar's kit, then?
MELIS: His only burglar's tools are his ten fingers. No, no, no! He goes and returns with an *empty* iron chest!
DON: But *why*?
MELIS: That, Mr. Allison, is what the police of seven cities want to know.
DON: The feller's scatty, that's all. Anyway, how do you know so much about the chest?
MELIS: In Amsterdam they nearly caught him. He dropped the chest and had to leave it. On two later occasions he was seen carrying a chest just like the first. Elaborate! With—and this is insult!—monkeys heads carved on the iron bands.
DON: I tell you, sir, the fellow's loony!
MELIS: I do not think so.
DON: But why should he load himself with a weight like that?
MELIS: In any case, we shall soon know.
DON: What did you do? Set a trap?
MELIS: Yes. And Mr. X fell into it. In a few seconds, now, you will hear...
JOYCE: (*crying out, off*) Don! Don!...Help!
(*Sound: two revolver shots. neighing of frightened horse; clatter of hoofs, then gallop, which gradually fades under next*)
MELIS: Who called then?
DON: My wife! And the horse has bolted with the carriage! Come on!
(*Sound: running steps on asphalt. microphone follows Don and Melis*)
JOYCE: (*cue: fading on*) (*terrified*) I'm all right, Don! I—I got out of the carriage to follow you. But...
(*Sound: steps to stop as—*)
DON: (*contrite*) Easy, Joyce! I was a triple-dyed fool to leave you! What happened?
JOYCE: (*bewildered*) I—I'm not quite sure. But I think he fired the shots at me.
MELIS: (*quickly*) Who fired the shots, madam?
JOYCE: Some man who slipped across the street while you two were up there. I didn't see any gun. He—he was carrying some kind of iron chest.
DON: Iron chest!
MELIS: By the six horns of Satan, we've lost him!
DON: Joyce, where did he go?
JOYCE: (*even more puzzled*) I don't know that, either. He just seemed to disappear in the moonlight or the trees along the sidewalk.
MELIS: (*bitterly*) Since we hunt again, I had better call back my men. (*shout-

ing, off) *Elaté olé opiso!*
DON: (*urgently*) Mr. Melis! Haven't you got any description of this man?
MELIS: I regret: not a word! No living person has seen his face.
JOYCE: But...*I* saw him! I can describe him!
MELIS: *You*, Mrs. Allison?
JOYCE: Yes! I wouldn't have noticed his face, actually. I was looking at that queer chest with the heads on it. But he ran just under a street-light, looked 'round.
MELIS: *What* did he look like?
JOYCE: Red hair, but dark eyes. High cheekbones, but a long face. He seemed to be... laughing.
MELIS: Would you know him, do you think, if you saw him?
JOYCE: Yes! I'm sure of it!
MELIS: Forgive me if I, whom they describe with irreverence as Old Eagle Beak, ask a more grim question. Would *he* know *you*?
JOYCE: (*realizing what this might mean*) I... I don't know!
DON: (*also realizing*) Has he ever used a gun before, Mr. Melis?
MELIS: A little. He has killed three people.

(*Music: up, then down and under narration.*)
FABIAN: *Now* why *does* a thief, for no apparent reason, weigh himself down with an empty iron chest? And yet, when one is young and happy, fear brushes as lightly as a spider-touch. By the next morning, when Joyce and Don were having a late breakfast in their hotel-room at the Grande Bretagne, they considered it only half a dream unrelated to themselves! And at the breakfast table, while a pretty maidservant dusted the room...
(*Music: out*)

JOYCE: Do you know what the man stole, Don? A hundred diamonds!
DON: Now look here, Joyce; you're not going to pretend you can read that Greek newspaper?
JOYCE: Darling, no! but the maid there—Eirini—wrote out a translation. (*calling*) Didn't you, Erini?
EIRINI: (*off*) I do what I can, nice Missus (*anxiously*) It is not good, yes?
JOYCE: It's very good, Erini. (*apologetically*) I've changed a little of the grammar, that's all.
DON: Read it, angel! I've got to get along to the Embassy!
JOYCE: (*reading*) One hundred large uncut diamonds, the property of a maharaja from India whose name was not disclosed—
DON: (*muttering*) Must be worth fifty thousand quid!
JOYCE: —were stolen last night from the premises of Mr. Ioannis Paniros, the famous jeweler and diamond-cutter of Kifissia Street. The stones were left with Mr. Paniros to be weighed and cut and polished.

(*Sound: off, phone rings.*)
DON: (*fading off*) I'll answer it, Joyce! Go on reading!
JOYCE: "A clever thief, the police say, would think the gems less well-guarded before they had been cut. A trap was set, but failed. We understand, however, that a full description of him has been given by Mrs. Donald Allison, now staying at the Grande Bretagne Hotel while in search of living-accommodations in..."
DON: (*fading on, excited*) Joyce! Forget everything! All our troubles are over!
JOYCE: Troubles? How?
DON: (*exuberant*) That was the letting-agent on the 'phone, my pet! He's found us a place to live!
JOYCE: (*just as exuberant*) Don, that's wonderful! What kind of place?
DON: It's a flat. And we don't need any keys; we just open the door and walk in. It's—wait a minute!—second floor, Flat D, 212 Kifissia Street.
(*Sound: small crash as of china figure dropped.*)
JOYCE: (*puzzled*) Eirini! What's wrong?
EIRINI: Nice Missus. I could weep! I have knocked St. Luke off the mantlepiece and break him!
DON: (*also puzzled*) Never mind, Eirini! I'll say *I* did it. But why did you jump just then?
EIRINI: Sir! I have an older sister who is—chairlady!—clean-woman!—at that place. 212 Kifissia Street. I think it is funny, that's all!
DON: (*eagerly*) Now listen, Joyce! I've got to turn up at work or the Old Man'll wring my neck. But the Embassy's in the same street. I'll meet you... Here! What are you doing?
JOYCE: I'm getting my hat, darling! If I don't go and camp in that flat, somebody else'll get it. And I'm going *now*!

(*Music: hits hard; then under during the whole of the following scene*)

FABIAN: (*sharply*) Be careful, Joyce! (*pause*) On the second floor of that block of flats A carpeted corridor, no windows; yellow stucco walls sickly under electric light. Chilly. Suddenly lonely! I wish that I, Doctor Fabian of the *Maurevania*, could have spoken to you then; could have answered the thought that suddenly, like a tiny knife, dug into your nerves. You were thinking...
JOYCE: (*on filter*) Red hair, but dark eyes. High cheekbones, but a long face. The eyes seemed... oh, this is ridiculous!
FABIAN: *Is* it so ridiculous, Joyce?
JOYCE: (*on filter*) After all, Don was *looking* for a flat in this district. Why be suspicious of a 'phone call?—Wait! I turn left here!
FABIAN: A short corridor, now. A green painted door with the Greek letter D. Your hand hesitates on the doorknob, Joyce. You don't want to open it. You're thinking...

JOYCE: (*on filter*) Of course I'll open it!. But... quietly. Not a sound!
FABIAN: A square room, like an office, lighted by a bright coal fire. There's a man sitting at a flat-top desk, with his back turned to the door. The top of the desk is covered with red velvet; and on the velvet is the iron chest; and near the chest are ranged all the stolen diamonds. And the man at the desk—turns around.
JOYCE: (*on filter; terrified*) Red hair. Dark eyes. High cheek-bones...*No!*
FABIAN: He's running towards you, Joyce! Jump back! That's it! Jump! P—
(*Sound: in quick succession thus: woman's scream; slam of door; bolt shot into socket*)
(*Music: comes out with a sting.*)
MELIS: (*calling, off*) Mrs. Allison! Mrs. Allison!
JOYCE: I'm here in the corridor! Outside the door of Flat D! (*slight pause*) Mr. Melis! What are *you* doing here?
MELIS: (*fading on, rather breathless*) I am not here by accident, believe me. (*sharply*) Have you seen him?
JOYCE: Yes! He's in this flat!
MELIS: So! Did he try to...?
JOYCE: Hurt me? No! He just slammed the door in my face, and *bolted* the door!—If you hurry, if you've got men here, you can catch him! This flat...
MELIS: (*grimly*) It's not a flat, Mrs. Allison.
JOYCE: Not a flat?
MELIS: No! It is only one room; he rents it as an office under the name of Gronov. The only exit is this door.
JOYCE: But the windows! He'll get out through the windows!
MELIS: I think not, dear lady. Two of my men have been watching the windows for an hour.
JOYCE: Then you've more than caught him, Mr. Melis! You've got the diamonds!
MELIS: *Diamonds!?*
JOYCE: Yes! I saw them! And the iron chest too!
MELIS: (*over his shoulder*) Inspector Glyptis! Cover this door! (*muttering*) Gronov! Gronov!
JOYCE: Is that his name: Gronov? Is he from this country?
MELIS: God forbid; he was born in Russia. He is now, or claims to be, an American citizen. (*to himself*) Gronov!
JOYCE: Listen! I think he's coming to the door!
(*Sound: bolt shot back. door opens*)
GRONOV: (*heartily*) *Hel*-lo, you two! And also welcome! Did someone mention my name?
MELIS: (*still half-incredulous*) Red hair! Dark eyes!—Is this the man you saw last night, Mrs. Allison?
JOYCE: Yes! Definitely!
GRONOV: I can't help my face, you know. I can even make it worse. Like this! (*then laughs*) But I don't want to frighten the lady. Eh?

MELIS: Are you Mr. John Gronov?
GRONOV: I am, sir. Very much at your service.
MELIS: What is your profession, Mr. Gronov?
GRONOV: I'm a Bible-salesman. (*laughs, then serious*) Don't glare at me; I really am! I purvey the gospel, in all texts and all languages, at very modest prices. Would you like to see my samples?
MELIS: I should prefer to see the diamonds.
GRONOV: (*astonished*) Diamonds? What diamonds?
MELIS: Here is my card, sir. I am technically, if not in actual practice, the head of the national police... You will shortly be arrested on a charge of robbery...
GRONOV: *Robbery?*
MELIS:... and probably extradited for murder. At this moment you have in your office the diamonds stolen from Paniros, the jeweler; and an iron chest with raised bands in the design of—monkey's heads.
GRONOV: (*starting to chuckle*) Monkey's heads, eh?
MELIS: (*over his shoulder, quietly furious*) Inspector! Have you got your handcuffs?
GRONOV: (*sharply*) Wait a minute! (*then amiably persuasive*) I don't want any trouble, friend Melis. I didn't mean to hurt your dignity. But this is a mistake! You claim I've got all this stuff in my office? Then come in and search, please. Come on in! (*Gronov begins to laugh. He is still laughing when...*)
(*Music: comes up under Fabian's brief narration*)
FABIAN: One hour! Two hours! Two hours and ten minutes of frantic searching. An office grotesquely littered with Bibles and dismembered furniture...
(*Music: creeps out*)
FABIAN: *But there were no diamonds. And there was no iron chest.*
(*Sound: crash of plaster bust smashed.*)
GRONOV: The only thing left, good friends, was the plaster bust of Socrates. And you've just smashed *that*. Are you satisfied *now*? (*he starts to laugh*)
JOYCE: (*half-hysterical*) Stop that! Stop it!
GRONOV: All right, ma'am. But this stuff couldn't have disappeared into thin air; now could it?
JOYCE: (*helplessly*) I don't know! Ask Mr. Melis!
GRONOV: It couldn't have gone out the door; the Inspector was there. It couldn't have gone out the windows; two men were watching. It couldn't have gone up the chimney; they had the fire raked out and then found an iron grating in the flue. There's no other door. It couldn't have got out of here, could it?
JOYCE: No! I suppose not!
GRONOV: Just as you like, ma'am. I'm a good Christian and honest man. So I don't hold any malice. But all this stuff couldn't have disappeared into

thin air; now could it?

JOYCE: (*helplessly*) I don't know!

GRONOV: (*persuasive*) Take a look at the door over there. It couldn't have gone out the door; Inspector What's-his-name has been standing there ever since you came in here.

JOYCE: I admit it didn't go out the door!

GRONOV: It couldn't have gone out the windows. Two policemen, they tell me, were watching the windows before you even got to this building.

JOYCE: All right! It's true!

GRONOV: Finally, the lost chest and diamonds didn't go up the chimney. Your friend Melis got the charwoman to rake out the fire; and then found an iron grating in the chimney-flue. The stuff just couldn't have got out of this room; and you ought to know it!

JOYCE: I do know it! You've hidden the chest and the diamonds!

GRONOV: Where?

JOYCE: Well! If you have a secret hiding-place…

GRONOV: *Where?*

JOYCE: Don't keep saying, "Where?" I'm not a detective!

GRONOV: This wrecking crew of cops… look at 'em… They've torn my office to pieces. Walls, floor, ceiling: all solid. No secret cavity; nothing in the furniture; no place that would as much as hide a dime. (*persuasive*) Now don't get hysterical, Mrs. Allison…

JOYCE: *I'm not hysterical in the least!*

GRONOV: (*drily*) Doesn't sound much like that, does it?

JOYCE: I admit the diamonds can't be hidden here! But it's still a trick!

GRONOV: (*honeyed*) Come over here for just a minute, Mrs. Allison… Mind! Don't step on that Bible!

JOYCE: What do you want?

GRONOV: Only a word in private. One American to another. (*earnestly*) Don't get these Greeks mad at you. It's not healthy.

JOYCE: Are you trying to tell me Mr. Melis doesn't believe a word I say?

GRONOV: Would *you* believe it? If *I* said it? Come on! would you?

JOYCE: No, I certainly wouldn't!

GRONOV: They're not going to believe you, Mrs. Allison. Just take my tip, and don't trust Melis too far. Do you see what they've done now?

JOYCE: They haven't done anything at all!

GRONOV: Oh, yes. They've put my desk back together again, all neat and tidy. As though they wanted to apologize. Now if I were a betting man—which I'm not—I'd give you ten to one you're in plenty of trouble right now. It *may* mean jail, though of course I like to look on the cheerful side. What does your friend Melis *say*? But this wrecking-crew of cops… Look at 'em seething!… they've torn my office to pieces. Walls, floor, ceiling: no secret cavity. Now where would I hide a hundred diamonds and a chest two feet long?

JOYCE: I don't know, I tell you!
GRONOV: At least they've had the decency to put my desk together again. But our friend Melis...
JOYCE: He won't *say* anything! He just stands there looking down at the red-velvet cover on the desk. He won't *say* anything!
MELIS: I could say much, Mrs. Allison. But there is only one question.— Are you *sure* these things were ever in the room?
JOYCE: (*taken aback*) Am I... Yes, of course I'm sure! (*hesitating*) That is...
MELIS: (*pressing her*) Are you even sure—come now!—that Mr. Gronov was the man you saw last night?
GRONOV: That's better! That's *much* better!
MELIS: Look, please, at the velvet desk-cover with the gold fringe. It bears an inkstand... a small paper-weight... a desk blotter. I lift the little paper-weight; and you see a mark in the smooth velvet. (*clearly*) If an iron chest had stood there, even for a few minutes, there would have been a deep mark in the velvet. When we entered this room, there was no such mark!
GRONOV: That's what I keep telling you! There was no such chest!
JOYCE: (*crying out*) Do you think I'm crazy? Or just telling lies?
MELIS: (*deprecating*) Not lies, my dear lady. But a witness who is shocked—! A witness who is hysterical—!
GRONOV: (*persuasive*) Go on home, ma'am. Get some sleep! (*beginning to laugh*) Monkey's heads, eh?
MELIS: (*snapping*) Do you know, sir, that *you* resemble a large, red monkey? Smirking and laughing amid the Bibles?
GRONOV: I don't like insults, Mr. Melis.
MELIS: I don't like sneers, Mr. Gronov.
GRONOV: (*temper showing*) If it comes to that, old man, the damage you've done to my office...
MELIS: You will be repaid. In your own coin.
GRONOV: (*quickly*) American money?
MELIS: You are a Russian, aren't you?
GRONOV: I'm an American citizen now; just ask at the consulate. What's more, I'm going there now to lodge a complaint. Are you going to stop me?
MELIS: No. You may go.— Let him pass, there!
JOYCE: (*desperate*) Mr. Melis, you can't do it! Stop him! Stop him before he gets away! I wasn't hysterical and I wasn't dreaming! You've *got* to believe *me*!
MELIS: (*quietly*) I do believe you, my dear. Forgive my pretense in front of Gronov.
JOYCE: You... *do* believe me? Then why didn't you arrest him?
MELIS: First, because I have a plan for tonight. Second, because I would play

chess and win. Third, because I saw too late how the chest and the diamonds were made to *vanish*!
JOYCE: But that's what I want to know! How *did* they vanish?
MELIS: By a method so obvious that we never even thought of it!

(*Music: hits hard, then under narration.*)
FABIAN: The dock-side of the Piraeus, its squalor softened under a full moon. Those narrow streets with so many shuttered houses, *seem* placid enough. Behind drawn curtains on the ground floor men sit with dark beards worried in a fevered eye. In one such street, at past midnight, two familiar figures lurk waiting under an archway...
(*Music: out into—*)

(*Sound: one or two boat-whistles, very faint.*)
DON: So they're a pretty tough lot, eh? These blokes in the cafes?
MELIS: Yes, Donald Allison. You will be useful to me if trouble starts.
DON: But what are we *doing* here?
MELIS: We meet Gronov. It is kill or be killed.— Do you understand the game he played against your wife?
DON: I know he sent us a fake telephone call about an apartment. The police were guarding Joyce; they traced the call, and go to Gronov's office before Joyce did. But he led the coppers straight to himself! He must have known he would! Why did he do *it*?
MELIS: Your wife alone could identify him as the burglar! *Yes*?
DON: Yes! But even so!
MELIS: Don't you understand? Your wife is invited to the office, and allowed to see the diamonds. She tells us, of course! We search the office, and what she says is impossible. Her whole value as a witness is smashed. Dare we put her in court to identify him *then*?
DON: No! They'd have said she was hysterical! This Gronov is the cleverest...
MELIS: (*Almost admiring*) He is subtle! He strikes like a fer-de-lance. (*soft ferocity*) But it is Greek against Russian; let us see who wins!
(*Sound: off, some person whistles three different notes.*)
MELIS: Our signal, our friend Gronov is in the Paradise Cafe. Come on.
(*Sound: Signal repeated*)
DON: Which way do we turn?
MELIS: To the right. That's it! Walk slowly along the pavement past the colored curtains of the cafes. They will not know us at the Paradise.
DON: Listen!
(*Sound: there begins and grows louder the music of the hassarika or the sloviko[2], mandolin and guitar. Steady stamping and jumping as of three*

---

[2] The nature of the musical instruments Carr describes as a "hassarika" and a "sloviko" is unclear...

men on a board floor, in time to music.)
MELIS: It's only our friends in the Paradise. They are dancing.
DON: Dancing!
MELIS: While they wait. Ceremonial dances as old as Olympus. Here's a chink in the curtains at the Paradise. Look through the glass! You will see three of them...
DON: Jumping; stamping! Jumping; stamping! Their shadows moving on the wall like apes. And over at that table—it must be Gronov!
MELIS: Yes. And the girl who is with him? Pretty; dark hair; red cheeks?
DON: (*startled*) That's Eirine! The maid who looks after our room at the hotel! Is *she* mixed up in this?
MELIS: Not criminally, no. Now one word before we enter! Most of these people are not criminals. But all have been drinking heavily. Most have been smoking hashish. Take care, you won't get your pocket picked, but you might get your throat cut. In you go!
(*Sound: music, dancing, come up for a moment; then stop under a burst of applause. Then thick crowd murmur in background*)
DON: Smoke! Wine-bottles! Moustaches! (*voice hard*) Never mind the crowd, Melis. This is a personal matter with me. Do you mind what I say to Gronov?
MELIS: Not in the least.
DON: Hello, Eirini!
EIRINE: (*startled*) Mr. Allison! (*quickly, pleading*) Sir, I am not here for why-you-think. I...
DON: And this is the clever Gronov. What are you drinking, old boy?
GRONOV: Red wine; rough wine. In big goblets. (*faintly irritated*) That's right. Pick one of 'em up!
DON: Thanks; I will. You've done a lot of things at my wife's expense, haven't you?
GRONOV: (*coolly*) I don't know what you're talking about.
DON: Then you won't mind if I throw the wine in your face. *Like this*!
GRONOV: (*bursting out*) You—
(*Sound: crowd—murmur stops abruptly; dead silence.*)
MELIS: (*pleased*) This warms my blood. My ancestors would have approved. (*fiercely*) Now sit down! All of you! Good. I came here, Mr. Gronov, to play a game of criminal chess. Do you play?
GRONOV: I'm a little tight. I'm a little reckless. I play!
(*Sound: crowd-murmur slowly begins*)
MELIS: My first move is to ask why you, or Mr. X, must always carry to robberies an empty iron chest.
GRONOV: I move, too. There couldn't be a reason!
MELIS: Oh, yes! There could. If the chest were not so heavy and clumsy it would be an excellent disguise.

DON: Disguise? How do you mean?
MELIS: Every witness—remember?—has looked at that queer chest; and never noticed his face. Your own wife said so! He distracted attention, that's *all*!
EIRINI: Wit' anyt'ing else, yes! But a big heavy chest...!
MELIS: How do we know it was heavy?
DON: What's that?
MELIS: Only because, in Amsterdam, he deliberately left a chest behind him. But afterwards? What sort of chest did he carry then? Who touched the chest? Who opened it? Who saw it except in dim light? He was carrying it last night, when he ran from the jeweler's. Yet he could instantly draw a gun and fire two shots. Today the chest stood on smooth velvet. Yet it left not a single mark.—It was made of cardboard.
DON: *Cardboard?*
MELIS: Skillfully painted, with raised bends and animal-faces and a cardboard padlock. If you look beside you, Mr. Gronov, you will now see, Inspector Glyptis. He is carrying... look at it! We made it ourselves!
EIRINI: An iron chest!
GRONOV: No, Erinini. They've built their own cardboard chest. So what?
MELIS: How easy to make a chest vanish! When Gronov was alone for five minutes in a locked room, he put it...
DON: *Into the fire!*
MELIS: Into the fire, of course. And that is also where he poured the diamonds.
DON: Yes! Diamonds can resist almost any heat!
MELIS: These diamonds, recall, were uncut stones. Grey-colored; rough; unpolished. In the small coal fire they would be coated black. When we had the fire raked out, they would look like small bits of half-burnt coal. Eirini's sister...
EIRINI: My sister—I tell you so!—is charlady-cleanwoman! She carry the ashes to the cellar! This Gronov tries to get them; but he is watched. He threaten my sister! She send me to tell him what she don' dare to say—The police have got the diamonds!
MELIS: Here are a few of them now.
(*Sound: rattle as of heavy pebbles on table-top*)
GRONOV: Then it's *my* move, Old Sherlock!
(*Sound: crowd-murmur again stops dead.*)
GRONOV: This is a thirty-eight automatic! None of you has got a gun; I can tell by your clothes. So I'll take what's a good haul anyway.
MELIS: You think you can cry checkmate?
GRONOV: I know it!
MELIS: Inspector! *Now!*
(*Sound: thud and cry, shout from crowd, falling body.*)
DON: (*bewildered*) What the devil happened?
MELIS: Didn't you see?

Don: The Inspector slammed that cardboard chest in his face! Gronov went over like a ninepin!
Melis: *This* cardboard cheat was real iron! (*softly fierce*) Checkmate, my Russian friend!
(*Music: up to final narration.*)

Fabian: And so, with a rattle of deck-winches, the *Maurevania* weighs anchor to leave the Piraeus. Next time—under hotter, bluer skies—we shall touch at Port Said: gateway to Egypt and to darker mystery, as the *Maurevania* continues our cruise 'round the world. Our scene is Cairo; our theme will be ancient magic versus modern magic. Do you believe that there *could* be a curse on the rifled tomb? That the girl who touched the lamp *could* be "blown to dust as though she had never existed"? That is why, when I tell you the story called "The Curse of the Bronze Lamp"[3], I challenge you to join me in *Cabin B-13*.
(*Sound: ship's whistles.*)
(*Music: out*)

---

[3] The next play is set in Cairo but it is titled "The Street of the Seven Daggers". "The Curse of the Bronze Lamp" was not broadcast until 14 November 1948.

Notes for the Curious

The final play in the first series of *Cabin B-13*, "The Man with the Iron Chest" would appear to owe something to the traditions of stage magic which John Dickson Carr considered a *"fine art"*, on a par only with friendship. He was fascinated by the way that magicians managed to bring about apparent impossibilities by comparatively simple means— as he said in an article to promote a radio program he had written about the world of magic and magicians:

> *"Would you believe that a dismembered body could put itself together and walk off the stage? Or a lady could disappear in full lights and in full sight of the audience? Or a severed hand could play dominoes? Such things could be done and were done."*

And *"such things"* crop up again and again in the work of John Dickson Carr. In the 'Carter Dickson' novel *The Gilded Man* (1942), Sir Henry Merrivale impersonates a magician and magicians of one kind or another appear in the novels *The Three Coffins* (1935), *The Red Widow Murders* (1935), *He Wouldn't Kill Patience* (1944) and *Below Suspicion* (1949), as well as the radio play "Lord of the Witch Doctors" (1941).

Carr re-used the central ploy of "The Man with the Iron Chest" in the twenty-second Sir Henry Merrivale novel, *Behind the Crimson Blind* (1952), which is set in Tangier rather than Athens.

The Street of the Seven Daggers

(*Sound: a ship's whistle*)
(*Music: up and behind*)
ANNOUNCER: *Cabin B-13*. Tonight: "The Street of the Seven Daggers".
FABIAN: Yes, our world cruise has come to the great harbor of Alexandria. Watch the green water turn Nile-yellow against the piers, and the modern warehouses outlined on a blue Egyptian sky. But I, Doctor Fabian, ship's surgeon of our luxury-liner *Maurevania*, hesitate to say, "modern", especially here in my cabin, B-13. For I would tell you of drowsier pre-war days, and how a certain street in Cairo was said to mean death to Edmund Parrish or anyone who walked in it after midnight. There! We've warped in against the pier. It was here in Cabin B-13 of the *Maurevania*, beside the dock at Alexandria, that I first met Betty Parrish. I knew, of course, that Edmund G. Parrish... the American shipping-magnate... was travelling on the *Maurevania* with two secretaries, his brother, and his daughter. Then, as I was packing a bag to join the passengers and catch the afternoon for Cairo...
(*Music: fades out*)

(*Sound: crowd-murmur, which comes up and down as though heard through open port-holes; then out into* a knock at the door)
FABIAN: Yes? Come in!
(*Sound: door opens and closes.*)
BETTY: (*American: frightened but anxious to explain*) I'm terribly sorry to intrude, Doctor Fabian. You don't know me, but I've heard a lot about you. I'm...
FABIAN: You're Miss Betty Parrish, aren't you?
BETTY: (*wryly*) It's the newspaper-pictures, I suppose?
FABIAN: Yes. They don't do you justice. (*as though she had flinched*) Wait: that wasn't meant as flattery! (*thoughtfully*) Your pictures tend to show you as arrogant, and you're not arrogant at all, are you?
BETTY: Yes, it was difficult to come here, Doctor Fabian. When you're the daughter of a very wealthy man, people think you ought to walk the earth as though you owned it. But you can't. Or at least I can't. From the time you're a child they teach you to distrust everybody so much that—that—
FABIAN: In the end you distrust even yourself.
BETTY: How did you know that?
FABIAN: Because you're lonely, that's all. But for some reason you think you can trust me. (*half-humorously*) As a matter of fact, you can. What's wrong?
BETTY: Doctor Fabian, listen! You *are* going to Cairo today?

FABIAN: As you see by the state of my packing: yes.
BETTY: Now a horribly impertinent question. *Why* are you going?
FABIAN: To meet a lady.
BETTY: (*taken aback*) Oh! I'm sorry! I didn't mean to...
FABIAN: (*drily*) *This* lady, Miss Parrish, is over seventy. She keeps a musical instrument shop near the railway station. Every year I take her five pounds of American marshmallows. In return, she tells me some story of crime—usually an ugly story—from her own ugly past.
BETTY: Then you wouldn't mind helping...
FABIAN: With what?
BETTY: It's my father! He'll die tonight! He'll be murdered! Unless you stop it!
FABIAN: Murdered? Who wants to kill him?
BETTY: (*controlled voice*) Nobody wants to kill him.
FABIAN: Well! Then who's *going* to kill him?
BETTY: Nobody. Nobody at all.
FABIAN: Are you sure we've got this straight?
BETTY: Oh, I know it sounds mad or hysterical or both! But it's the literal truth! Nobody will kill him, and yet he'll be stabbed through the back!
(*Sound: blast of ship's whistle.*)
BETTY: (*startled*) What's that whistle for?
FABIAN: It's to muster the crew. All passengers are supposed to have gone.
BETTY: Then I've got to *run*! Dad will be furious!
FABIAN: Is your father such a dragon as all that?
BETTY: (*backing a little off*) He isn't a dragon at all! He's a stocky little man, with grey hair and a vile temper, who struts about whistling "Oh, Susannah." But he's... he's... (*now desperate to leave*). Doctor Fabian, where can I reach you in Cairo? Where are you staying?
FABIAN: At the Continental-Savoy Hotel. It's...
BETTY: I know! We're staying at the same place. Will you meet me there tonight! Ten o'clock!
FABIAN: Yes, of course. But if you'd only explain...
(*Sound: a little off, door opens.*)
BETTY: (*suddenly*) Wait! There's something I almost forgot! And it's terribly important!
FABIAN: Oh? What is it?
BETTY: In my handbag here... Oh, I wish my fingers weren't all thumbs!... I've got a mirror. Not a big one, but it'll do. I think I can detach it. Yes! I'm going to throw this mirror on the floor and smash it!
(*Sound: crash of small mirror breaking.*)
BETTY: There! (*deeply sincere*) Doctor Fabian... *do you mind my doing that*?
FABIAN: (*bewildered*) Not in the least. But I'll mind still less if you tell me what this is all about!
BETTY: Tonight! Ten o'clock! Continental-Savoy Hotel'.

(*Music: hits hard, then down and under in oriental theme*)
FABIAN: Cairo, 1934. (*pause*) The night in Egypt comes at one stride, into a violet sky shimmering with stars. Against that sky, southwards, the minarets seem as white as the houses underneath. Even the Modern Quarter—despite its daylight babble of beggars, camels, donkeys, lunatic tradesmen—is touched with that same blue magic. On this particular night, at the Continental-Savoy, I waited for a message from Betty Parrish. There was a masquerade-ball at the hotel, with firework-illuminations in the garden behind. The first skyrocket went up at ten o'clock…
(*Sound: hiss of ascending rocket, very quickly followed by a few exploding stars.*)
FABIAN:… and exploded in red and yellow stars above masked figures in the garden, when…
(*Sound: phone rings and is picked up.*)
FABIAN Yes? Hello?
GERALD: (*filter*) (*pleasant, cultured*) Doctor Fabian?
FABIAN: Yes! Speaking!
GERALD: This is Gerald Parrish, Doctor Fabian. I'm the brother of Edmund G. Parrish. (*drily*) You may have heard of him?
FABIAN: Yes. I've heard of him.
GERALD: He's on his way up to see you now. And he's in a foul temper.—Wait, please! I can almost hear you freeze over the telephone. Don't be offended. The good Edmund G. doesn't mean his bad manners. He's got a great admiration for you.
FABIAN: For *me*?
GERALD: Yes! So if you hear an unexpected knock at your door…
FABIAN: My door isn't closed, except for the little tropical swing-doors. But I was supposed to get a message from…
GERALD: Betty? You will. In the meantime, you can always tell the approach of Edmund G.; he whistles "Oh, Susannah" whether he's pleased or furious. See you later.
(*Sound: click of phone at the other end.*)
FABIAN: But look here, Mr. Gerald Parrish! I…
(*Sound: hiss and bang-bang-bang of skyrocket. As this begins, we hear off but approaching someone whistling "Oh, Susannah." This fades on and stops only when Fabian speaks.*)
FABIAN: (*pleasant irony*) (*cue*) Come in! Make yourself at home!
PARRISH: (*less truculent than swaggering*) Thanks, Doctor. I already have.
FABIAN: You're Mr. Edmund Parrish, aren't you?
PARRISH: That's right. Don't be fooled by this masquerade clown's suit, or the toy balloon in my hand. Jerry—that's my brother—says I've got no sense of humor. Maybe not! But a man's got a right to a *little* fun, hasn't he? On the night he's going to die? (*laughs heartily*)
(*Sound: hiss of sky-rocket and bursting of stars.*)

PARRISH: (*changing tone*) Anyway, Doctor Fabian, I just wanted to get a look at you.
FABIAN: Oh? Why?
PARRISH: (*interested*) You're the fellow who'll go half way 'round the world, and pay his own expenses at that, just to find the solution of some crazy mystery. Where's the cash-value? What do *you* get out of it?
FABIAN: I am never bored, Mr. Parrish. You say the same.
PARRISH: Yes! Of course I can say... (*bursting out*) No; I'm a cock-eyed liar! And what's more (*as though bitterly defiant*) I like you for it. Because *my* hobby is the same, only a little different. I'm a superstition-breaker.
FABIAN: How do you mean, superstition-breaker?
PARRISH: Spilled salt! Broken mirrors! Walking under ladder! Those are the simplest ones.
FABIAN: You make war on popular superstitions; is that it?
PARRISH: Make war? Look! This toy balloon in my left hand is a superstition. This lighted cigar in my right hand is common-sense. I bring 'em together, like this...
(*Sound: pop of exploding balloon*)
PARRISH: Where's your superstition *now*? (*pause*) Everyman alive has *some* superstition, and he won't be a free man until he gets rid of it!
FABIAN: Aren't you making too much of harmless things?
PARRISH: (*fiercely*) You call 'em harmless?
FABIAN: In most cases, yes.
PARRISH: Listen, Fabian. This Old Slabsides in the clown suit—meaning me—would go ten thousand miles or spend ten thousand dollars to burst one superstition. Why, there was that place in Germany, where blood was supposed to come through the floor; *I* fixed *that*. There was...
FABIAN: (*quickly*) Ah, if you're talking about group-superstitions! That's different! That can be dangerous!
PARRISH: (*grimly*) Then you ought to be on my side tonight. D'jever hear, in Cairo, of a little alley called the Street of the Seven Daggers?
FABIAN: No. What about it?
PARRISH: (*jeering*) If you walk through the street, after midnight and alone, you're supposed to die.
FABIAN: How do you die?
PARRISH: With a dagger through the back. The street's full of invisible people.
FABIAN: Invisible people?
PARRISH: (*satirically*) Yes. Even if you've got a witness there, he can't see anyone stab you. (*chuckling but grim*) *I'll show 'em!*
FABIAN: Then that's why Betty said... Where *is* your daughter, Mr. Parrish. You've locked her in her room, I imagine.
PARRISH: Yes, I have! (*changing tone*) How did you know that?
FABIAN: Forgive me, sir: you're the sort of man who would.

PARRISH: (*flaring out*) Now look here, Fabian. If you think you can talk to me like…
BETTY: (*fading on, appealing*) Dad!
PARRISH: (*growling*) So you're out making trouble again, eh, Betty?
BETTY: If you want to call it that, yes.
PARRISH: Sweeping through those swing-doors; all dolled up in a gold gown your mother would have had a fit at…!
BETTY: (*uncertain*) I'm trying to keep as much dignity as I can, thanks, after being treated like—never mind! Doctor Fabian! Have you persuaded him?
PARRISH: To keep away from that street? Ho! I've got a date there in less than an hour.
FABIAN: (*quickly*) Maybe he's right, Miss Parrish! Before you judge, let's hear all the facts!
PARRISH: Now there's a man who's got some sense!
FABIAN: Why was it called the Street of the Seven Daggers? Where did its murderous legend get its start?
PARRISH: It was superstition!
FABIAN: But it must have had a starting-point!
PARRISH: Well! (*hesitating*) Umpteen years B.C. and after that—Jerry's got the documents!—it was the street of the hired killers. If you wanted a murderer, you Just went there and hired one.
BETTY: And three hundred years ago, under Turkish rule, some bigwig got annoyed about hired assassins. He had them executed in front of their houses; and burnt out the street. Then… people began to die.
FABIAN: When was the last time a death occurred there?
BETTY: Less than fifty years ago, that's all! A young Frenchman made a bet. His friends stood at the mouth of the street—it's only a little dead-end alley twelve feet across—and held up lights. He got about twenty feet away. And…
FABIAN: *Go on!*
BETTY: They could see him. Nobody could have touched him. Nobody could have thrown a dagger. But it just—*appeared* in his back. And he screamed and fell.
(*Sound: rush of skyrocket, its fairly loud explosions timed to correspond with the end of this speech and the beginning of the next*)
GERALD: (*fading on, and with mock-heroic loudness*) And behold the entrance of Satan!
BETTY: (*crying out*) Uncle Jerry!
PARRISH: (*snapping*) Fabian, this is my brother. All dressed up in a red devil's suit. Only five years younger than I am; future head of the Black Bell Steamship Line; and he thinks that's funny!
GERALD: (*patiently*) And I didn't think it was funny. I didn't mean to startle anybody. I only came up here to bring this portfolio, with the documents…

FABIAN: About the Street of the Seven Daggers?
GERALD: Yes! Would you like to see them?
FABIAN: Very much!—Thank you. Now where *is* this street?
BETTY: *You're* not going there?
FABIAN: Never mind, please. Where is it?
BETTY: It's in what's now a modern part of Cairo. North. Near Midan-el-Mahatta.—Doctor Fabian! Why did you jump just then?
FABIAN: Did I jump? I wasn't aware of it. But I can give Mr. Edward G. Parrish some good advice.
PARRISH: Wait till I get off this clown's rig over the dinner-jacket. Now! (*sharply*) What's the advice?
FABIAN: Don't go!
PARRISH: (*astounded*) Don't... Have you gone superstitious too?
FABIAN: No. But your life's in great danger.
PARRISH: (*exploding*) Danger, my...!
FABIAN: (*cutting in*) Betty here thinks you have no enemies. Is that true! Here in Cairo, for instance?
PARRISH: Cairo? (*snorts with a sound like "Ho!"*) There's one Egyptian business-man; three, *four*; Arif Bey's the worst; cut my throat and drink the blood. But what's that got to do with *this*. Nobody knows about it!
FABIAN: (*hits hard but likes him*) Will you take my advice?
PARRISH: (*not loudly; soft ferocity, but likes Fabian*) I wouldn't take your advice for a million dollars!
FABIAN: Will you make me a promise, then?
PARRISH: I never make promises. If I do, I mean to break 'em.
FABIAN: Then you don't dare risk one hour?
PARRISH: One hour? What for?
FABIAN: I want to visit a friend of mine. I'll leave this hotel and 'phone back inside an hour. Will you stay here until then?
PARRISH: (*as though suggesting*) A trade's a trade, Doc.
FABIAN: Right!
PARRISH: What do I get in exchange?
FABIAN: Your worthless life!
PARRISH: (*beginning to chuckle; he enjoys this*) All right. I promise.

(*Music: up, sinister oriental, then down and backing narration*)
FABIAN: Far ahead of me, as I walked beside the wall in the dimness, the great railway station loomed grotesque above palm-trees. Past me moved shapeless figures, the woolen-hooded burnoose of the Arab, sometimes a red-tasseled cap against a street-lamp, in one endless pad-shuffle of slippered feet...

(*Sound: bring in Fabian's occidental footsteps, then Betty's hurrying steps fade in as Fabian continues*)

FABIAN: I was hurrying towards the square called Midan-el Mahatta, in an area where there had been only sand and grass a century ago. Now the houses threw heavy shadows. Then...
(*Sound: footsteps stop as—*)

BETTY: Doctor Fabian! Wait!
FABIAN: Betty! What the devil are *you* doing here?
BETTY: You guessed I'd follow, didn't you? Especially when I knew where you were going!
FABIAN: (*surprised*) You knew where I was going?
BETTY: To the Street of the Seven Daggers! It's only about twenty feet ahead now. On the night!
FABIAN: (*grimly*) Is it, by George?
BETTY: Didn't you know that?
FABIAN: I knew it was somewhere close to here, of course. (*changing tone*) But it's not where I'm going, Betty. And I wish you hadn't come.
BETTY: (*three different moods in three speeches*) Where are you going? (*slight pause*) You've got to take me with you! (*slight pause*) Is it dangerous?
FABIAN: Yes.
(*Sound: their footsteps behind.*)
FABIAN: Come on; straight ahead; and we'll have a look at the dagger-alley as we go past.
BETTY: Doctor Fabian, I didn't mean any harm!
FABIAN: Neither does your father; actually, I like the old pirate; I can't help liking him. But sometimes I could kill him.
BETTY: He'll keep his promise *this* time, you know!
FABIAN: For his own sake, he'd better. Where's the dagger-alley?
BETTY: Here! With the street-lamp just in front of it! Look to your right!
(*Sound: footsteps stop.*)
FABIAN: I see.
BETTY: There's nothing left of the old street, of course. Just a big brick warehouse on each side of the alley, and a brick wall at the end.
FABIAN: (*badly worried*) Betty, this is impossible.
BETTY: What's impossible?
FABIAN: High brick walls, almost black. No windows; not an opening! And the street-lamp shines in. You couldn't kill a man in there without being seen!
BETTY: (*frightened*) Let's go on! Please! Let's go on where you were taking me!
FABIAN: Very well. Straight ahead; same direction.
(*Sound: steps begin again.*)
BETTY: You say "impossible". But I—I could have sworn you had some idea what all this meant.
FABIAN: Perhaps I do know part of it, yes. But the real tangle is: how can a

murderer attack in front of witnesses? And yet this one means to try!

BETTY: I—I couldn't have stood in front of that alley any longer. It wasn't that it was filthy and foul-smelling; lots of the streets are that. But it seemed *evil*. I...

FABIAN: (*sharply*) Listen!

BETTY: What is it?

(*Sound: footsteps stop.*)

(*Sound: slight pause: then we hear the whistling of, "Oh Susannah"; beginning far off, and gradually getting closer under ensuing speeches.*)

BETTY: (*horrified*) That... isn't who I think it is?

FABIAN: If it is, he deserves what he may get.

BETTY: Don't *say* that! (*looking round, bewildered*) Where *is* he?

FABIAN: I don't know. I can't tell the direction of the sound!

BETTY: Wait! I think I can see him!

FABIAN: Where?

BETTY: Walking in the same direction *we* came from! The street-lamp back there... his black dinner-jacket coming near it... Yes! He's at the mouth of the alley.

(*Sound: whistling stops*)

FABIAN: (*calling*) Mr. Parrish! Wait! Stop there!

PARRISH: (*calling, off*) Never keep a promise, Fabian! (*triumphant*) I *thought* I could get to this place without being stopped!

FABIAN: But I only wanted to tell you that—

PARRISH: Here I go into the dagger-street!

(*Sound: whistling again, this time slowly moving off as Parrish enters the alley; it continues under—*)

BETTY: (*not calling; speech to Fabian*) Don't let me down, Doctor Fabian! Please don't let me down!

(*Sound: two sets of running footsteps, briefly; quick stop.*)

FABIAN: Here's the mouth of the alley, but where's your father? I can't see him in the alley!

BETTY: There! Walking beside the right-hand wall about twenty feet down!

FABIAN: What's more, there's a Sudanese policeman just behind us. Officer!

POLICEMAN: (*Sudanese: slight English accent*) Yes, sir? Can I help you?

(*Sound: off, the whistling stops*)

FABIAN: Cover the entrance while I run in there! We—

(*Sound: off, there is a man's loud scream of terror or agony. Slight pause; then fall of body on earth floor of passage.*)

BETTY: No! It can't be! I was watching him!

FABIAN: (*quietly*) Quiet, Betty. Officer! Have you got your electric lamp?

POLICEMAN: Just switching it on, sir!

FABIAN: Then flash it into the alley...that's it! Up, and down! Sideways; back! Rake every inch of walls and ground. Can you see anybody there except—? (*he stops*)

POLICEMAN: Nobody, sir. Except the man with the knife in his back.
FABIAN: Officer! Hold the light steady on him How long should it take before that ambulance gets here?
POLICEMAN: They're very quick, sir. And I telephoned five minutes ago.
FABIAN: (*rapidly considering*) He's spread-eagled on his face; I daren't touch the knife; there might be a hemorrhage. In the meantime, I can only keep a pulse-count... weak and reedy... but he'll probably live.
BETTY: (*low-voiced; frightened of the alley*) Pulse-count! Does that mean he's...?
FABIAN: Has regained his suavity. I greatly fear, Betty, that your respected parent may live.
BETTY: (*like a prayer*) Live!
FABIAN: I should like to hold out hope for a speedy death; but it's beyond my power. We must take what fate sends.
BETTY: If he lives, Doctor Fabian, I'll never again laugh at what they call "superstition". I'll obey the least little one of them. Don't you believe now?
FABIAN: (*drily*) No.
BETTY: *Then how was he stabbed*?
POLICEMAN: (*shaken; English speech thickening*) Doctor, sir!
FABIAN: Yes, Officer?
POLICEMAN: I am a Christian and the Good Father knows it. But in what lady says there is much truth. You see me as police-officer; what am I to tell in my report?
FABIAN: Tell them what you saw!
POLICEMAN: But what I saw cannot be! Unless...
BETTY: Unless a dead assassin came up out of the ground like smoke. (*in a daze*) And the invisible people are all around us now!
FABIAN: (*sharply*) Betty! This is got to stop!
BETTY: Please! Don't... don't shake me! I'm all right!
FABIAN: (*steadily*) Look at your father. Look—don't flinch!—at the knife. From what we can see of it, it's painted all black: light filigree handle and heavy blade. Now look at his right hand. When he came into this street, why should he have been carrying his own wallet full of bank-notes?
BETTY: His—wallet? Was he carrying it then?
FABIAN: I didn't notice. But it's in his right hand now, bright red and stamped with his initials. What's more, in his pocket he's carrying a *second* wallet full of money. Two wallets, Betty. *Why*?
(*Sound: clang of ambulance bell approaches.*)
BETTY: There's the ambulance! You're going to the hospital with us, of course!
FABIAN: (*low-voice*) I can't. I must go somewhere else, for the final evidence. Lower your voice when you answer!
BETTY: Is it the place you were going when I stopped you tonight? And—I've been thinking. You said this morning you knew an old woman, with a long criminal record, who kept a musical-instrument shop near the rail-

way station. Is *that* the place?
FABIAN: (*inwardly alarmed*) If it is, Betty, you mustn't tell anyone I've gone there tonight. Or any night! Do you understand that?
BETTY: Is it... as important as that?
FABIAN: (*cynically*) Not important, perhaps. *But it may mean my life.* Will you promise not to tell anyone?
BETTY: All right, of course! I promise!

(*Music: up, then down and held under.*)
FABIAN: I was uneasy—I admit it—when I entered the shop of Old Mother Gizeh. It looked harmless enough; but it was the spider-web of half the crime in Cairo. There was the little room, rank with smoke and lamp-oil, the broken musical instruments on the walls. In the middle of the floor, as usual, sat Mother Gizeh in her hooded robe, with a stringed musical instrument before her.
(*Music: out*)

FABIAN: (*greeting*) *Naharak said*, Mother Gizeh![1]
GIZEZ: *Naharak said umbarak, o hakim!*[2]
FABIAN: (*after a pause*) Your eyes watch me under the hood, Mother Gizeh. Your hands move snake-veined above the strings. Do you say no word?
(*Sound: Mother Gizeh slowly begins to play, "Oh Susannah" on the zither. it is halfway through the tune when a hand is swept across the strings as though in wrath.*)
FABIAN: Your spies have heard the whistle, Mother Gizeh.
GIZEH: (*her voice is old and grating, though not unpleasant when she is pleasant, but she is not pleased now.*) My spies have everything. You have always been our friend, *hakim*. Because you have betrayed no secrets. But now—You have entered my home tonight.
FABIAN: Have I betrayed a secret now?
GIZEH: I do not say it! But one man is slain, with a knife in the back, at no great walk from my poor shop. The police will follow you, if only from curiosity. That is not good. Behind the bead curtain there are Abou Owad and his friends. And...
(*Sound: a sharp click as knife is opened, off.*)
GIZEH: That is Abou Owad opening his knife.
FABIAN: (*contemptuously*) Your tactics are childish, Mother Gizeh. (*amused*) Marshmallows or war!
(*Sound: angry sweep across strings of zither.*
FABIAN: You say there has been friendship in this house?
GIZEH: *Wallah!* That is true!
FABIAN: And has friendship no word to explain?

---
[1] Translation: "Good day, Mother Gizeh.
[1] Translation: "*A very* good day, wise sir."

GIZEH: Speak!
FABIAN: I came here to bring a portfolio. *This* portfolio. It contains documents about a so-called "Street of the Seven Daggers." Here is an order, signed by a Turkish Commandant three hundred years ago, for the execution of certain hired assassins. (*like a courtier*) Now Mother Gizeh, in her long war against the dogs of the law, is highly skilled in the craft of forgery.
GIZEH: (*pleased, almost chuckling*) *Wallah*! That is true, too?
FABIAN: Then take this document. Tell me if it is true or forged.
GIZEH: I would oblige the *hakim*. Give it to me: But! you swear no one knows you are in my house tonight?
FABIAN: Only one person; and she would not speak.
GIZEH: You swear you were not followed?
FABIAN: I swear it!
GERALD: (*calling, off*) Fabian, old man! Are you inside this house with the filthy curtain across the door? Fabian!
(*Sound: irregularly, three sharp clicks.*)
FABIAN: Open your knives! As many as you like! But admit this man!
GIZEH: (*furious*) Who is he?
FABIAN: He is a young-old man; of grey hair, but lean figure and fine presence. He was the brother of the man nearly killed; and his name is Gerald Parrish.— Come in, Mr. Parrish!
GERALD: (*fading in*) Apparently all you've got to do is push the curtain aside, and…(*slight pause*) I only came here, Doctor, to tell you poor old Ed…(*impatiently*) Fabian, what are you *doing* here?
FABIAN: May I present you to Mother Gizeh?
GERALD: (*carelessly*) Hel-lo, my wicked old crone! *Well*?
FABIAN: I came to prove that her Egyptian countrymen had no hand in this— attempted murder.
GERALD: Are you off your head again? Of course these Egyptian business-fellows were behind it! You asked us about 'em yourself!
FABIAN: I did, sir. Because I knew they were certain to get the blame for the plot. They were meant to get the blame.
GERALD: What plot about the Street of the Seven Daggers?
FABIAN: "The Street of the Seven Daggers"—never existed.
GERALD: Never existed!?
FABIAN: No. When Betty told me where it was supposed to be located, I jumped. Old Cairo is to the south. *This* whole area is to the north. It was only a waste of grass and sand a century ago. B.C. No street *could* have existed here.— Mother Gizeh!
GIZEH: (*subtly gloating*) At your service, good *hakim*!
FABIAN: That order signed by the Turkish Commandant three hundred years ago: what do you make of it?
GIZEH: The paper is perhaps ten years old. Well aged, of course. But still! Has it been shown to the Cairo Museum?

FABIAN: No! It's been shown to nobody! All these documents, forged, were collected and vouched for by one man. No Egyptian would have made such mistakes.
GERALD: *Then who did it?*
FABIAN: You did, Mr. Gerald Parrish. It was part of the plot to kill your brother.
(Sound: irregularly, three sharp clicks.)
GERALD: (*sharply*) What were those noises just then?
FABIAN: Egyptian reactions, that's all. Shall we talk about your brother?
GERALD: I didn't have any reason to kill poor Ed!
FABIAN: You inherited the Black Bell Steamship Line; he told us so himself!
GERALD: But this was a... a miracle murder! Nobody can explain it.
FABIAN: Oh, yes! Dull-witted as I am, *I* can explain it. You chose some nameless little alley between two high warehouses. You spun 'round it this whole superstitious romance to lure your brother here. But I didn't know how you killed him until I found the two wallets. Why did he carry two wallets?
GERALD: Answer your own question! *Why*?
FABIAN: He didn't.— Let's look back at that little alley, partly lighted by the street lamp, just as your brother entered.
(Sound: zither, very softly begins with "Oh, Susannah"; it registers before Fabian speaks, and continues under)
FABIAN: Betty and the policeman and I were at the mouth of the alley. Your brother was difficult to see, because he wore a black dinner-suit and hat against a black wall. But what had *you* done, Gerald Parrish?
GERALD: Well? Tell me!
FABIAN: Before that time, you had burgled the right-hand warehouse. And you had gone up to the flat roof.
GERALD: (*in a corner*) The roof?
FABIAN: Yes. From there you dropped into the alley a bright-red wallet against a brown earth floor. When your brother saw a red wallet stuffed with money, what did he do? What would *anybody* do? He bent down to pick it up. And, as he bent over with his back parallel to the ground...you *dropped* a black knife.
(Sound: "Oh Susannah" ends with sweep of hand across zither.)
FABIAN: Betty and I had turned for one instant to speak to the policeman. Even if we'd been looking straight at the victim, we shouldn't have seen the fall of a black dagger, with a heavy blade and a light handle, against a black wall.
GIZEH: (*crying out*) Abou Owad! Hassan! In front of the doorway!
FABIAN: (*suavely*) Have I your leave to go, Mother Gizeh?
GIZEH: Of course, noble *hakim*. But the other gentleman... (*subdued ferocity*) We must discuss whether or not I am a "crone".
(Music: up to final narration.)

Fabian: Oh, no, Gerald Parrish wasn't killed but even as Betty and I left, I knew we were powerless to help him, even by summoning the police, against the vengeance of Mother Gizeh and her band whom he had tried to betray. His punishment was better than having his brother know the truth; better than prison or disgrace. Indeed, tonight's story is the least violent which I, Doctor Fabian, ship's surgeon of the *Maurevania*, shall have to tell you in these latitudes. For next week, we shall look towards Port Said; Port Said, which twenty years ago was the world's cesspool of devilment and evil. And so, when I tell you of intrigue and murder in a story called "The Dancer From Stamboul", will you join me in *Cabin B-13*?
(*Sound: ship's whistles*)
(*Music: out*)

Notes for the Curious

While they have nothing in common, the alliterative title of the opening play in the second series of *Cabin B-13* recalls one of Carr's earliest short stories "The Inn of the Seven Swords", a historical romance published in his college magazine, *The Haverfordian*, in April 1927.

Carr was a writer from a very early age, and his earliest known work appears to be "The Ruby of Rameses", a detective story written for his high school magazine *Maroon and White* when Carr was around 15 years of age. Other mystery stories followed as well as poems and, at 16, Carr had a regular column for his local newspaper the *Uniontown Daily News Standard*. At college he wrote a number of historical romances and created his first great detective, Henri Bencolin, for a series of short stories, all but one of which were collected in *The Door to Doom and Other Detections* (1980).

For "The Street of the Seven Daggers", Carr re-used the central ploy of the short story "The Silver Curtain", first published in the *Strand* magazine in August 1939. While "The Silver Curtain" is also set in the 1930s, the story is largely different and it is set in France rather than Cairo.

The Dancer from Stamboul

(*Sound: a ship's whistle*)
(*Music: in and behind*)
ANNOUNCER: *Cabin B-13*. Tonight: "The Dancer from Stamboul".

FABIAN: Port Said, at the gateway to the Suez Canal! Nowadays it is… tolerably respectable. Our luxury-liner *Maurevania*. on its cruise round the world, lies here in harbor before we enter the canal. But I, Doctor Fabian, of Cabin B-13, remember an adventure in Port Said twenty-five years ago. She *was* alluring, Madame Almah, that dancer from Stamboul. And, when the sword-blades crossed in that lost fencing-room, who *could* have dropped poison into the glass?
(*Music: a fantastic rather than oriental theme, up, down and backing narration.*)
FABIAN: Port Said, from the harbor, looks like a French provincial town. The French built it; their influence has been strong. In those old days, when so many ships took on coal at the port, you were deafened by the never-ceasing din.
(*Music: continues but is covered by:*)
(*Sound: roar of coal descending very large chutes into hold of ship*)
(*Music: again behind*)
FABIAN: As coal roared down through the hatches; and ships grew invisible in a fog of black dust. Along the waterfront-promenade jostled Egyptians, Turks, Syrians, Greeks: past grey French buildings; and, as a mark of British respectability, a huge gilt sign advertising Tea. One night in Port, I was sitting inside one of those waterfront cafes apparently alone while a ship loaded coal nearby…
(*Music: out*)
(*Sound: roar of coal down chute.*)

JIM: (*American, well-mannered but an underlying toughness, now a little worried*) Doctor Fabian!
FABIAN: (*surprised and pleased*) Jim Canfield! What are *you* doing in this place?
JIM: I was sitting in a dark corner over there. I thought you wouldn't mind if I brought my drink over to your table.
FABIAN: Mind!? Didn't we travel out from New York together?
JIM: (*a little hesitant*) Yes. But I haven't been exactly frank. I…
FABIAN: Sit down, man! Sit down!
JIM: Thanks.
(*Sound: clink of glass on marble-topped table*)
JIM: I didn't say much about myself, did I? I wonder if you can guess what

my job is?
FABIAN: I think so. You're a New York detective-lieutenant, Homicide Squad. You've come out here with extradition-papers to take somebody back.
JIM: How the devil did you know that?
FABIAN: Jim, I wish I could astonish you with my brilliant deductions. (*changing tone*) As a matter of fact, the purser told me.
JIM: (*puzzled*) But you didn't ask any questions!
FABIAN: It wasn't my business to ask questions. (*self-mockery*) I'm British, you see.
JIM: (*earnestly*) Doctor Fabian, you know Port Said as well as you know New York or Singapore. And I could use a lot of advice.
FABIAN: I'm at your service, Jim. Who's the fugitive from justice?
JIM: Her name is Lydia White. She's a missionary's daughter, believe it or not. Only twenty-two years old. Outwardly she's what's called a lady; inwardly she's vicious in any way you can think of.
FABIAN: What's the charge against her?
JIM: Murder. Each one by poison: potassium cyanide.
FABIAN: So! And what's the lady's—profession?
JIM: Men. She's a dark-eyed brunette with a pink-and-white figure that...
(*Sound: rattle of saucer and small ice-bucket on marble-tapped table.*)
WAITER: *Un Cinzano à l'eau, monsieur. Un peu de glace aussi!*[1]
FABIAN: *Merci, mon gars*[2]. About her figure, Jim: you were saying?
JIM: Well! It's caused at least three murders. Lydia likes to get presents, especially jewelery: then she likes the fun of watching men die by poison. (*fiercely*) Yes; she's like that! I've got an indictment for one murder; New York City; that's all I need. (*grimly*) But I haven't got Lydia.
FABIAN: You mean the Egyptian authorities won't—?
JIM: Oh, the extradition's all right! They'll cooperate, But I've never seen Lydia; no cop has. There's not a single known photograph of her. All I've got is a verbal description.
FABIAN: Look here, Jim! If they sent you on a hunt like this, one of those people she killed must have been...
JIM: (*drily*) Politically important? He was!
FABIAN: How do you know she's in Port Said at all?
JIM: We *know* that; I'll explain later; but we *know*. And if I can't find a full-blown charmer like Lydia, in as small a city as this, I ought to be pounding a beat in the sticks. But if she's masquerading...
(*Sound: faint crowd-murmur, which we have heard once or twice in this scene, begins slowly to grow louder in wrath under speeches*)
FABIAN: She's clever, I take it?
JIM: She's as clever as Satan's wife. Where *is* she, Doctor Fabian? Where would

---
[1] Translation: "A Cinzano with water; and a little ice."
[2] Translation: "Thank you, waiter."

you look for her?

FABIAN: If you want to find the woman, look for the man. I think I can take you to a place where you *will* get a lead.

JIM: That's what I hoped you'd say. Where is it?

FABIAN: Finish your drink and come along. It ought to be just about time for… things to start.

(*Sound: crowd-noise up to a boiling of furious speeches, all indistinguishable. one voice cleaves it.*)

VOICE: *Ma hala ya ma hala kobal en—*

(*Sound: roar of coal down chute, drowning voice: crowd-noise a little down.*)

JIM: What was that fellow shouting out there? Just before the coal went down?

FABIAN: It was Arabic. Something about, "Oh, how sweet it is to kill—!"

(*Sound: crash as of large cafe window broken by stone.*)

WAITER: (*fading on and off, running*) (*maddened*) *Voila le fils de putain qui caisse toujours les fenetres!*[3]

JIM: Now they're smashing the cafe windows! (*puzzled*) Is everybody nuts in this part of the world?

FABIAN: (*sharply warning*) You're in Port Said, Jim! It's in the air, in the atmosphere: people do crazy things. Before this adventure's ended, you may do crazy things too.

JIM: (*amused*) I haven't got much to recommend me, Fabian. But I'm pretty level-headed. Let's go!

(*Music: up sharply in bridge, first suggesting violence; then softly sinister*)

FABIAN: This, you see, is like a street in France. Except that it's dirtier and less well-lighted. The door we want is on the left… *here*, Jim.

JIM: What's inside?

FABIAN: Read the sign up over the door!

JIM: (*puzzling*) "*Salle d'armes!*" That means "Room of weapons," doesn't it, Fabian?

FABIAN: Say, in a looser sense, *fencing-room.*

JIM: Fencing-room! (*as though reading*) "Founded by J. Moreau, 1868. Present fencing-master: Rene Moreau."

FABIAN: In this lost corner, Jim; you can see better fencing than any in the world. European champions make a pilgrimage here, to say they've visited old Moreau's.

JIM: But what's this got to do with Lydia White?

FABIAN: There's a new British-made King on the throne of Egypt. Turkey will soon declare a Republic. The Balkans are full of European notables—men with money!—who come here to watch fine fencing. Men with money, Jim!

JIM: I see. Lydia's natural friends. (*sharply*) Wait a minute.

---

[3] Translation: "Look at those sonsofbitches smashing all the windows."

FABIAN: What's wrong?

JIM: (*troubled*) There's nothing *wrong*. But that big advertising poster! On the wooden board to the left of the door! (*muttering; considering*) Big enlargement of bad photograph. Woman in a Moslem half-veil and not much else. Lettering across the poster in Arabic, French—*and* English. Wait till I strike *a match*!

(*Sound: match struck*)

JIM: (*reading*) "Every night at Maxim's Club, which is much same as Chez Maxim in Paris…"

FABIAN: What an infernal lie *that* is!

JIM: "—the so-famous dancer Almah from Stamboul or Constantinople will perform her so-captivating dance." (*suddenly*) Fabian! You don't suppose…?

FABIAN: No! Never. We've got her whole record! In this verbal description, did you get any distinguishing marks?

JIM: Only a little scar over the right eyebrow. And she could hide that with make-up. (*exclamation of pain*) Hold on! Another match!

(*Sound: match struck*)

FABIAN: Then why the inspiration about the photograph?

JIM: Because this picture looks just as I'd imagined her. (*changing mood*) Oh, it's only a wild hunch! It's impossible! It's…

(*Sound: whish of thrown knife, and thud of point in wood*)

JIM: (*long breath; then grimly*) That's the first time I ever had a match put out by knife-throwing. (*furious*) Knives, eh?

FABIAN: Easy, Jim! Don't reach for your gun!

JIM: (*snarling*) Why not? If they want to play marbles, I can play too!

FABIAN: Whoever threw that knife didn't aim at either of us. Look here at the photograph!

JIM: What about it?

FABIAN: The knife-point struck just above her right eyebrow.

JIM: (*slight pause*) (*muttering now*) Right eyebrow! Old scar! Then that means… (*Jim doesn't know himself*)

FABIAN: Our voices carry in this Street. Somebody's calling your attention to the dancer from Stamboul.

JIM: Wait! There's a little rat of a man coming across the street now. Head on one side, all fawning…

FABIAN: It's only one of the so-called "guides". (*suddenly reflecting*) But there might be…

JIM: Information?

FABIAN: Yes. (*calling*) Come here, O dissolute one, and earn honest money for once!

GOHA: (*no known nationality, indeterminate age; thin voice, insinuating, wheedling tone, not much accent*) (*fading on*) Would the kind gentle-

men, the rich gentlemen, care to see something very interesting? I am only poor Goha; but I am named for the great Goha of the *Arabian Nights*.
JIM: Never mind that, Goha! Here's my billfold, and here's a hundred-piastre note. Take it! It's yours!
GOHA: (*staggered*) This gentleman is indeed a gentleman!
JIM: What do you know about a woman named Almah? A dancer from Constantinople?
GOHA: (*quickly*) You wish to see her? I will take you! But it is too early! The club is not yet open!
FABIAN: That's not the point, Goha. Is she really Turkish?
JIM: (*slight pause*) You don't have to take a look all around before you answer. *Is* she Turkish?
GOHA: (*almost pityingly*) Sir! She is no more Turkish than I am. And heaven knows what blood is in *my* veins. Her dance is not Turkish either.
FABIAN: You're quite sure of that?
GOHA: *I*? Who have spent six, seven year in Stamboul? No, no, no! A gentleman who has seen this dance told me it is something like he has seen in—where is it? Malay!
JIM: Malay! (*realizing*) And Lydia's parents were missionaries. Lydia being Lydia, she'd have learned that dance as a young girl!
FABIAN: Yes! I think you've got it. But... What else can you tell us, Goha?
GOHA: A big secret; yes! Madame has two men in love with her, the Italian baron and the French fencing-master. But the big secret is a joke. (*chuckles*) True! I will tell you. The joke is...
(*Sound: whish of knife, but thud as though into flesh.*)
GOHA: (*cries out; then his heavy gasps can heard under the next two speeches.*)
JIM: Fabian! Grab his other arm! Hold him up!
FABIAN: I've got him. But whoever threw the first knife won't have missed his heart with the second even through the back. Steady. My watch crystal near the mouth.
JIM: Well?
FABIAN: The knife didn't miss. Lower him to the ground.
JIM: I've got a sight-line to where that knife was thrown. Now here's what we'll do! I'll close in on the right...
FABIAN: Wait a minute, Jim! You can't report this man's death.
JIM: I'm a cop, Fabian. Not report his death? I've got my papers, why not?
FABIAN: Because you'll probably be arrested by somebody who can't read and spend the night in jail yourself.
JIM: Maybe you're right. I think I know where to find Lydia White.
FABIAN: You're partly right. But that knife thrower has been following you! Who sent him? Doesn't it seem too easy that this trail should lead straight to...
JIM: To Maxim's Club and that's where we are going for an interview with a dancer from Stamboul. To—this Maxim's club. Yes!

FABIAN: To Maxim's Club! And an interview with the dancer from Stamboul!
(*Music: up, with a theme suggesting slow heavy drums, then down and under narration*)

FABIAN: The club, as Goha had said, was not yet open. But we entered, by the front door, into a dark fusty-smelling cavern pierced by only one thin light. Out between the curtains, stepped a girl. She wore the baggy red trousers, and loose white blouse of the Turkish upper-servant. Her smile, her olive skin, and dark eyes, seemed to gleam and glow with vitality. Then, as we spoke to her...
(*Music: out*)
BELKIS: (*Turkish with French accent; bouncing sprightly; great sex-appeal, which she uses always*) (*laughing*) Pardon, Monsieur. But it is so very funny!
JIM: What's so funny?
BELKIS: My name is Belkis, monsieur. I am the maid of Madame Almah. Often people say to me, "Are you the great danseuse?" (*delighted*) And I am so pleased I squirm like theese.
JIM: But what's your nationality? Don't talk about jokes. The last person who did —(*he stops.*)
BELKIS: (*puzzled*) Pardon, monsieur?
JIM: Forget it! What were you saying?
BELKIS: I, Belkis, am *really* Turkish. Madame is—what madame says she is. But I am Turkish. My French—very good!—and my English—not so good!—I learn at the school at Jaffa in Syria.
FABIAN: (*quickly*) What language does *madame* speak?
BELKIS: English! And she make everybody else speak it or she get mad.
JIM: She's American, isn't she?
BELKIS: (*yearning*) Monsieur! *I* will ask a question. Do you think I am nice?
JIM: Well! Yes! But—
BELKIS: (*all stops out*) Don't you think I am nice?
JIM: (*driven too far*) Look, Belkin. If you get any closer, if you keep on using your eyes like that, I'll take you at your word, and...
FABIAN: (*musing*) Remember how level-headed you are, Jim!
JIM: Yes! What's the matter with me? (*changing tone*) Look, Belkis! My friend and I want to see Madame Almah!
BELKIS: (*very curtly*) I regret! She is in her dressing-room now. But you can't see her!
JIM: Why not?
BELKIS: First, because I am mad! I hate you! Second, because... (*as though shrugging*)... Eh bien, because the Baron da Scali is with her now.
FABIAN: That's her Italian admirer, isn't it?
BELKIS: Yes, monsieur. He is tall and blond; from Milan; he go to Oxford and

has much money. Everybody call him just "Carlo."
FABIAN: And her French admirer, I imagine, is young Rene Moreau? The fencing-master from Eugenie Street?
BELKIS: Yes. May Allah defend us if those two ever meet!
FABIAN: You mean they *haven't* met?
BELKIS: No! They would *keel* each other. Each thinks that madame…well! only *likes* the other. Each is a famous swordsman. If Rene Moreau knew Carlo was with Madame now, he would—(*stops with a gasp*)
FABIAN: What's the matter? Why are you looking so horrified?
BELKIS: Rene Moreau! he has just come in the front door! I wonder if he heard me.
(*Sound: from off, steps approach slowly across a hardwood dance-floor, close to microphone, in a whisper, over steps*)
BELKIS: Look at heem! He is nice too, like Carlo; but he—*brrrh*!—he make eyes like a black wolf. He is too *serieux*, what you call too serious! *Did* he hear me?
(*Sound: footsteps stop.*)
MOREAU: (*35, harsh, but not unsympathetic, very little French accent*) Yes, Belkis. I heard you. (*fiercely*) Stand away from those curtains.
BELKIS: Monsieur! Please!
FABIAN: (*quickly*) Forgive me, Mr. Moreau; but do you happen to remember *me?* Doctor Fabian, of the *Maurevania?*
MOREAU: Sir, I regret I have no time to…(*recollection strikes him; pause: almost smile in voice*) Doctor Fabian! Shake hands! What brings *you* here?
FABIAN: To find old friends in strange places. This is Mr. James Canfield, from New York. May I offer a word of advice?
MOREAU: (*bitterly*) About Madame Almah? And the fool I have made of myself?
FABIAN: Moreau, we all do that! But you're in no state of mind to see either of them.
MOREAU: (*controlled fury*) Thank you; I disagree. Here is this Carlo, rich and polished from Oxford and Milan. Here am, I, the blue-chinned provincial, from the mud-flats in the smoke. How Port Said must laugh! But strike me dead if they laugh another day!
FABIAN: The woman's responsible! You know that?
MOREAU: There you are wrong. (*fervently*) She would be a saint out of heaven, if *he* let her alone!— Come to the dressing room! all of you!

(*Music: hits hard, then down and under narration*)
FABIAN: In the meantime, though we didn't know it then, there had already been trouble in that dressing-room between Carlo, Baron da Scali, and the woman who called herself Almah. Look into the dressing room a minute or two before we entered. A small room, almost filled with exotic

flowers sent by Carlo. Carlo, tall and light-haired, hat and gloves in hand, sat on the edge of a dressing-table before a mirror ringed with lights. Almah, in a flamboyant red dressing-gown, should have been in one of her smiling moods.

(*Music out*)

ALMAH: *You—!*
(*Sound: crash of some small object striking metallic surface without breaking.*)
CARLO: (*English accent, strong, suave*) Almah, my pet! Do you need to throw a hair-brush at the looking-glass, merely because I ask whether you love me?
ALMAH: (*slow-speaking, cultured, American, with much sex-appeal*) I do love you, Carlo. But don't ask me so often!
CARLO: It's fortunate for your dance tonight that you didn't break the mirror. You couldn't see to undress.
ALMAH: That's the sort of witticism I don't like.
CARLO: No, Almah! Because you are prudish and wanton all in one. (*bursting out*) I don't understand you!
ALMAH: That's best, Carlo, (*cryptic tone*) Then you won't understand what a complete joke my life is!
CARLO: You call it a joke? *I* don't.
ALMAH: Poor Carlo!
(*Sound: slap as of gloves against edge of dressing-table*)
CARLO: Don't say that!
ALMAH: (*lightly mocking*) How he slashes the gloves against the edge of the dressing-table! Say what?
CARLO: Never say "Poor Somebody!" to any man. That means liking; not love. If you don't love me, Almah, please accept me as an enemy.
ALMAH: And now how he postures! Oh, these romantic Italians!
CARLO: (*slightly different tone*) *This* romantic Italian is quite desperately in love with you. *I* don't care what you do, Almah. I want you anyway. But never think I don't see through you.
ALMAH: (*abruptly*) What do you mean by that?
CARLO: My intelligence tells me you are an American wanted by the police. Probably for murder committed with potassium cyanide.
ALMAH: Did they teach you to write romances at Oxford?
CARLO: On this dressing table here, among a lot of bottles and jars, there's a little corked bottle labelled "nail-varnish." Clever! That label explains any faint scent or bitter almonds. A quick-acting poison, cyanide!
ALMAH: I know nothing about that bottle.
CARLO: (*angry but distressed*) *Almah mio!* An American detective landed here today!
ALMAH: (*starting*) How do you know that?

CARLO: How does the grapevine-telegraph work in the jungle? Everybody here knows it! If that detective should call on you tonight...
(*Sound: sharp knocking at door, which opens*)
CARLO: (*icy dignity*) Good evening, Mr. Rene Moreau!
MOREAU: (*fading on*) Good evening, Baron da Scali.— Almah! If I can get past all the flowers Baron da Scali has sent you, I want you to meet two visitors.
CARLO: (*realizing what this may mean*) Visitors, eh?
MOREAU: Almah! This is my friend Doctor Fabian, from the liner *Maurevania*.
ALMAH: (*slight pause*) Oh! A ship's doctor. (*then all charm*) I'm flattered, Doctor Fabian, that someone who saw me dance would wish to see *me*.
FABIAN: We must all admire an artist, Madame. Doesn't the name "Almah," in Arabic, mean "learned"?
ALMAH: (*significantly*) There are many branches of knowledge, Doctor Fabian.
FABIAN: And Madame no doubt is mistress of them all. (*changing tone*) But that little scar over your right eyebrow. Surely it's a recent one?
ALMAH: Yes, of course. (*suddenly confused*) I mean—! Yes, it is! (*quickly*) Who is with you here?
FABIAN: Forgive me. This is Mr. Canfield, from America.
ALMAH: America!
CARLO: (*not sarcasm for Almah: draws fire on himself*) Come, my pet! Surely, you've heard of America. It was discovered some years ago by a countryman of mine. Of course, Moreau here...
MOREAU: (*murderously quiet, inviting*) You spoke to *me*, Baron?
CARLO: I did, Moreau. Perhaps even you, on your mudflats at Port Said, have heard of the place?
MOREAU: (*bursting out*) You posturing *swine*!
CARLO: These gloves, sir, are new and soft. I hope you won't mind them...
(*Sound: slash of gloves across face.*)
CARLO: ...across your face!
BELKIS: Carlo! You are one beeg fool! He has beaten every European champion!
ALMAH: Be quiet, Belkis!
MOREAU: (*still murderously quiet*) Will tomorrow morning suit you... (*mimicking*)... Carlo? At my fencing-room? No toy fencing-foil or epee; but the cup-hilt rapier, fashioned by craftsmen three hundred years ago. (*snapping*) Agreed.
CARLO: Agreed! (*irrepressibly*) *Viva l'Italia!*
MOREAU: No one except ourselves must know of this. I will save the reputation of a saint and an angel! Doctor Fabian! Will you act as my second?
FABIAN: If you insist, yes. I have no choice.
CARLO: (*careless enthusiasm*) And Mr... er... the American! Will *you* act for *me*?
JIM: I don't know anything about duels. But if this is a fair fight: why not? (*sug-

gesting) Maybe Madame Almah will come along too?
ALMAH: All men are fools. Belkis is right. Yes! Tomorrow I will watch you fight—and kill. But first, tonight, you shall watch me dance!

(*Music: hits hard, then down behind -*)
FABIAN: Only an hour later, when Jim and I sat in one of those imitation-stone stage-boxes which copy the old Maxim's... with only darkness beyond the spotlight, and a shadow of the dancer writhing... I tried to reason with Jim Canfield, while the drum throbbed for the dance.
(*Sound: music has come out into only the throb of a heavy drum—very softly heard—as in rhythm for a barbaric dance. This continues under the dialogue*)

FABIAN: I don't want to insult you, Jim. But have you got any idea what's *really* going on here?
JIM: (*grimly*) I've got a pretty good idea; yes, Fabian.
FABIAN: How's your eye for subtlety, Jim?
JIM: Subtlety isn't much in my line, thanks.
FABIAN: I know! Therefore you can't see the pattern of deviltry underneath. *Nothing in this case is quite what it seems*. What'll happen tomorrow? I'll tell you. Murder.
JIM: (*conscience fuming*) I'm a cop! I oughtn't to allow it. But if these guys fight on the level—
FABIAN: I wasn't talking about murder with a dueling-sword.
JIM: Then what *were* you talking about?
FABIAN: Poison. There's one thing you promised to tell me, and never did. How did you know Lydia White was at port Said?
JIM: When a woman skips the country, keep an eye on her girl-friend's correspondence. If she's doing well abroad, she'll write to the girl-friend and brag about it.
FABIAN: Well?
JIM: Lydia White... look at her dance down there! Makes your head swim!
FABIAN: Go on! You were saying!?
JIM: Lydia had a friend named Hazel Waring; quite a charmer too; but Hazel disappeared on us. Then there was a girl named Milly Fisk. Lydia wrote to Milly from here. Said she had a "fine position," and "at least one rich follower."
FABIAN: Meaning Carlo?
JIM: Must be! Whatever your subtleties are, Fabian, I think we agree Lydia White is this dancer from Stamboul. I'll nab her tomorrow, as soon as I've seen the commissioner...
FABIAN: About this duel, Jim...
JIM: I don't know how to act as second!

FABIAN: You don't have to know. This fencing-room—don't look at the dancer; listen to me!—this fencing-room is like a small gymnasium. Got that? There'll be a gymnasium-mat for the duelists to stand on. Old Captain Conover...
JIM: Who's Conover?
(*Sound: the drum-beat begins to fade.*)
FABIAN: Moreau's assistant. Former British officer; broken. He'll act as referee.
(*Music: music creeps in behind and backs narration.*)
FABIAN: You and I will stand behind Conover, all of us close to the mat. The duelists, in white shirts and with needle-sharp rapiers, will stand fidgeting. Across the room, facing you and me, Madame Almah will sit in a special chair. Then old Conover will give the word.
(*Music: comes out with a sting.*)

CONOVER: Are you ready, gentlemen?—Mr. Moreau?
MOREAU: (*with loving hate*) Most murderously ready, Captain Conover!
CONOVER: Baron da Scali?
CARLO: A long life and a merry one! (*calling*) What do *you* think, Almah?
ALMAH: (*off*) I mustn't take sides, must I? But I'll drink the health of you both in a minute.— Belkis, stop crying and sit down over there!
BELKIS: (*off*) I do as you wish, Madame. But I think...
CONOVER: Now, gentlemen! You will not attack until I say engage! When blood is drawn, serious wound or not, I will strike up the blades with *this* sword in *my* hand.
MOREAU: One of us, Captain, will not leave the mat alive.
CARLO: (*insulting*) Which one, little Frenchman?
CONOVER: Attention!... Salute! Engage!
(*Sound: the tick-tick, tick-ting of the two blade-ends circling round each other! behind.*)
FABIAN: (*low*) Look at them, Jim! The fencer's stance, knees bent. That noise is only the points circling round each other: feeling for an opening, waiting to lunge...
JIM: (*low*) Do they fight all over the room? The way they do in films?
FABIAN: (*contemptuously*) This is *swordplay*, Jim. They won't move three feet. The play will be only in short bursts, like...
(*Sound: thrust-parry, thrust-parry, in a short sharp burst as described. just before the blades tick again at engage-disengage.*)
FABIAN: (*low*) Lord!
JIM: What is it, Fabian?
FABIAN: Moreau lunged straight for the heart. Carlo was slow on his *riposte*. Moreau's out for a kill in thirty seconds. He's...
(*Sound: swords begin again: sharp exchange continued.*)

FABIAN: They're both playing for the heart! Every thrust at *quarte!*
JIM: Fabian! Look at Almah's face over there. Beyond the crossed line of the swords!
FABIAN: Yes, I see... (*breaking off, galvanized*) Where did she get that wine-glass in her hand?
JIM: (*surprised*) Moreau gave her the drink when we first came in here. She's been nursing it for twenty minutes! Didn't you notice?
FABIAN: No! What's *in* the glass?
JIM: Cherry brandy. She's taking a drink now. She—
FABIAN: (*calling*) Don't drink that brandy! (*back again*) Strike up the swords! End this duel!
(*Sound: clash as sword strikes up other two; noises cease.*)
CONOVER: (*furious*) Are you mad, sir? I had to stop play, or an accident would...
ALMAH: (*off, screaming in agony*) Carlo! Rene! My throat is burning! I... (*voice trails away*)
JIM: Over there! Quick!
(*Sound: running footsteps merge into Jim's next speech*)
JIM: Here's the glass she drank from. (*realizing*) Cherry brandy! It'd hide the smell of almonds. Cyanide!
MOREAU: (*panting heavily*) She lies back in the chair! Is there nothing we can do?
FABIAN: Yes, Moreau! You and Carlo carry her into the anteroom. Artificial respiration, as in drowning. 'Phone the nearest doctor for a stomach-tube. Pick her up, now!
JIM: That's it!
CARLO: (*also panting*) This direction, I think? Yes!
JIM: Has she got *any* chance against potassium cyanide?
FABIAN: Almost none. She's unconscious now, with foam at the mouth. And I was the fool who could have prevented this! If I'd known about the drink!
JIM: (*bitterly*) You mean *I* was the fool, don't you? She knew I was after her, so she killed herself!
FABIAN: Oh, no, Jim! She was murdered.
JIM: *Murdered?*
FABIAN: Yes. Didn't it strike you from the first that—for a clever woman—Lydia White was acting like an idiot? (*slight pause*) She danced in public; Her photograph was everywhere. She insisted on everybody speaking English. Wasn't it just a little too easy to track her down?
JIM: I still don't get it!
FABIAN: When I spoke to her about an obviously *new* scar above her right eyebrow, where Lydia had an old scar, she lost her head and admitted it *was* new. No, Jim! That woman who was poisoned, the dancer, *was not Lydia White.* And I'll prove it by the testimony of her own maid.— Belkis! Come here!
BELKIS: (*fading on*) I know very little, Monsieur! I prepare thees big jar of

flowers for madame, and now madame is dead!
FABIAN: Come, Belkis! Why don't you drop your fake accent?
BELKIS: (*exclaiming*) Fake accent?
FABIAN: Yes, Belkis. *You're the real Lydia White, aren't you*?
(*Sound: crash as heavy flower-jar drops and smashes.*)
FABIAN: (*sharply*) Take care of that broken flower-jar, Lieutenant Canfield! The poison-bottle may be in it!
BELKIS: This man they call doctor! He talk what is imbecile!
FABIAN: You knew the American police were after you. You knew they'd get you sooner or later. Unless you—anticipated. So you brought a friend of yours out here.
JIM: Hazel Waring! The brunette charmer who "disappeared"!
FABIAN: And you put her forward, with the only foreign dance you could teach, as the "Lady from Stamboul." *She* would get the money and the applause. *You*, in a walnut-juice complexion, would play the maid and be the brains of the partnership. She knew she was playing your game; she agreed to have a scar over her eyebrow. This dancer was only your bait for the American police. When Jim grew certain she was the woman, she intended to prove her identity but you poisoned her. That was your whole plan. Jim would think Lydia White had killed herself as he did. And you would be forever free.
BELKIS: (*fury bursting; foreign accent gone*) Shut up, you blasted—
JIM: *That's* dropping an accent, Lydia!
BELKIS: Let it go! Who cares?
JIM: You admit all this?
BELKIS: I'm proud of it. That rattle-brained dancer knew I was wanted for murder; she wouldn't give me away unless *she* was in a corner. But everything Doctor Fabian told her really applied to *me*.
FABIAN: Oh? How was that?
BELKIS: (*pride and nonchalance*) After all, dear doctor, I *am* an artist!
(*Music: up to final narration —behind.*)

FABIAN: And two last glimpses I had, as I left that fencing-room. Lydia White, in handcuffs, sulky or furious. And in the anteroom, somber beside their somber dead, the Frenchman and the Italian reaching out to shake hands. (*change of mood; almost chuckle*) But scenes change! And next week—when our luxury-liner *Maurevania* has passed through the Suez Canal into the Red Sea—I have a story called "Death in the Desert." If I tell you only that its background is a little steamboat on the River Nile, and the great Sudanese Desert with its Dervish-riflemen in 1895, will you join me in *Cabin B-13*?
(*Sound: ship's whistles*)
(*Music: out*)

Notes for the Curious

As would happen more often than not in the second series of *Cabin B-13*, John Dickson Carr adapted an earlier script. For "The Dancer from Stamboul", Carr re-used the central ploy of the short story "Death in the Dressing Room", first published in the *Strand* magazine in March 1939. As usual he changed the setting—from the Orient Club in London to Maxim's in Port Said—and also the time—from the 1930s to the 1920s.

After Carr had written his first radio play for the BBC, an excellent three-part mystery entitled "Who Killed Matthew Corbin?" (1939) and a few other mystery scripts, he worked mainly on writing scripts that were mostly aimed at boosting morale among the population or raising awareness of the effects of Nazi occupation. But on his return to the United States he concentrated on writing mystery plays in earnest. The first of these was "Will You Make a Bet with Death?", written for the immensely popular CBS program *Suspense* and thereafter Carr wrote for *Suspense* on American radio and *Appointment with Fear* on British radio and adapting the scripts that he had written for the former to suit the format of the latter and vice versa.

Carr also adapted some of his favorite thrillers for the radio, including short stories by Ambrose Bierce, G.K. Chesterton, Sir Arthur Conan Doyle, Edgar Allan Poe, Melville Davisson Post and Robert Louis Stevenson.

Death in the Desert

(*Sound: a ship's whistle*)
(*Music: in and behind*)
ANNOUNCER: *Cabin B-13*. Tonight: "Death in the Desert".
FABIAN: Under a white-hot sky, our luxury-liner *Maurevania* moves almost without noise through the Red Sea. You—a passenger on our world cruise—and I, Doctor Fabian, ship's surgeon from Cabin B-13—can see very little that's inspiring. On our left is the coast of Arabia. On our right... well, that's the coast of the Anglo-Egyptian Sudan, where so much blood was spilled in desert-fighting many years ago. Forget the *Maurevania*. Let me tell you a story out of my parents' time: of the Sudanese desert, of an American girl who kept faith there, and of a murderer you may not suspect.

(*Music: out*)
FABIAN: (*cold*) December! 1895!
(*Music: begins with a few bars of "Sweet Rosie O'Grady"; but almost immediately changes to sinister theme under*)
FABIAN: The 1890s, when men's moustaches were heavy and ladies' dresses were long, now glitter only by far-off gaslight. But the city of Cairo, in '95, was restless. In the desert far southwards, there was firing as red-turbaned Dervishes circled and melted away. All over the British Empire disquiet stirred. There was tension between Britain and the United States. If we could have listened to a talk, in Cairo, over that fairly new instrument, the telephone...
TIMES: (*English, on filter*) Yes! This is the Cairo correspondent of the *London Times!*
RECORD: (*American*) Hello, Tom. This is the *New York Record*, just across the street from you. Have you seen the latest cables from the States?
TIMES: (*on filter*) I've got some on my desk here. Haven't looked at 'em.
RECORD: President Cleveland's sent a message to Congress.
TIMES: (*on filter*) About Venezuela?
RECORD: Yes. If you British intervene in Venezuela, without arbitration, he says America ought to consider it cause for war.
TIMES: (*on filter*) This'll blow over! It always does.
RECORD: Not if my paper can help it; that's orders. (*chuckling; grimly amused*) Anyway, there's one good story we can't get. Do you know those little steamboats, like a glorified houseboat with a big paddle-wheel at the back, that make excursion-trips up the Nile?
TIMES: (*on filter*) Naturally! What about 'em?
RECORD: One boat, called the *Joy-bringer*, sails tomorrow. Over six hundred

miles up the Nile to Wadi Halfa.
TIMES: (*on filter*)Anybody important on board?
RECORD: No. But the only passengers are two Americans, three British, and one German. (*amused*) What's going to happen when the Yanks and the Limeys hear about *this* possible war?

FABIAN: (*line delivered cold*) One thing that happened, late that same night before the steamboat had even sailed, was...
(*Sound: off, a muffled revolver-shot*)
(*Music: hits hard, then down under.*)
FABIAN: No one, in the darkness beside the river Nile, heard that muffled revolver-shot. No one saw a body, heavily weighted, sink into the water. When the six passengers went on board the *Joy-bringer* next morning, one of them was a murderer.
(*Sound: thrashing of old-fashioned paddle-wheel; river boat whistle*)
FABIAN: The paddle-wheel churned in a milk-coffee river. Three days later, at sunset, two passengers sat on camp-stools on the after-deck. One was the Herr Professor Bauer, with his thick body and his thick-lensed glasses. The other was that stately spinster—puffed shoulder-sleeves; straw hat with green sun-veil—Miss Emily Conroy of Baltimore.

EMILY: If you *must* know, Herr Professor Bauer, this book is my diary.
BAUER: (*German accent: 50 years old*) (*enlightened*) So! You study the old tombs, Miss Emily! The great authority on old Egypt is Mommsen. He is a German.
EMILY: Pardon me, Herr Professor. It's not about old tombs. (*dignified pride*) Shall I read you what I've just written?
BAUER: It would be a pleasure, Miss Emily!
EMILY: Well! Then! (*reading, rather self-consciously*) "Sunset, now, leaves a long crimson glow over the Libyan Desert."
BAUER: *Ja*. That is accurate!
EMILY: (*dignified snap*) I know it's accurate, Herr Professor! I was trying to make it picturesque!
BAUER: For that, Miss Emily, you must come to Germany.
EMILY: (*reading*) "The river runs as smooth as quicksilver. On the Arabian side it is blue-black, until an edge of the moon shines over—" (*suddenly*) Good heavens, it *is* getting dark! I wonder where Louise is?
BAUER: *Ach*, your pretty niece! (*gravely*) Miss Emily! I do not say what is in my mind about your niece and Mr. Brent...
EMILY: Louise is a modern girl, Herr Professor!
BAUER: *Ja, ja!* (*more confidentially*) But I ask you this. Don't you feel there is something queer, something odd, about this whole journey?
EMILY: (*meaning the opposite*) I don't understand you!

BAUER: Something is not good. Something prowls. We are glad when the oil-lamps are lighted.
EMILY: Stuff and nonsense! I never heard such—(*changing tone*) Very well: yes! I *have* felt it! But why should it be here?
BAUER: These English people. This Colonel Legget and his wife! Do you trust them?
EMILY: (*amazed*) Colonel and Mrs. Legget?
BAUER: We-el! Since your two countries will soon be at war...
EMILY: (*loftily*) With the Leggets, Herr Professor, I do not discuss war. Nor do they, being well-bred, mention it to me. They are an elderly retired couple...
BAUER: Look ahead, Miss Emily. Along the tiny little deck to starboard! A lamp is lighted in the saloon-lounge. It throws Mrs. Legget's shadow out across the water, and she is sitting down at the piano. Her husband is with her.
EMILY: And what of *that*, please? Mrs. Legget often plays the piano.
BAUER: (*fiercely confidential*) You and I sit here, yes! But if someone went along the little deck... (*fading*)—near that window and near the piano.
(*Sound: paddle wheel fades with him. Just before his voice becomes inaudible, piano begins—on—with* "After the Ball is Over")

COLONEL AND CONSTANCE: (*singing*) "After the ball is o-ver,
            After the break of morn,
            After the dan-cers' leaving.
            After the stars are gone;
            Many a heart is aaa-ching... "
        COLONEL: Hold on! Stop a bit!
(*Sound: piano out*)
CONSTANCE: Please, Colonel Legget! After all these years! You're not too dignified to sing?
COLONEL: Dignity me foot, Mrs. Legget! It's standin' here at attention, shoulders back, and mouth open like the Cheddar Caves, moustache quiverin' all the way out to the points. Makes me feel as much of a blasted fool as... (*breaking off; then, rather guiltily, dropping all formality*) I say! Connie!
CONSTANCE: Yes, Bill? You don't seem—yourself.
COLONEL: I'm not. I've had a devilish odd feeling—had it all the way from Cairo!—that somebody on this boat is going to get stabbed in the back.
CONSTANCE: *Stabbed in the back?*
COLONEL: Maybe only a touch of liver; but there it is. I had the same feeling in the Sudan campaign, in '85. They were sneakin' up and knifin' our sentries every night. You couldn't see anything; but you could feel *eyes.*—You're worried too, m'dear.
CONSTANCE: Yes. About two things. One of them...
(*Music: three notes struck on piano; as in hesitation.*)

CONSTANCE: (*bursting out*) Bill, it's this nice American girl! Louise! I wish her Aunt Emily would take better care of her. She's in love with our so-called "Mr. Brent."
COLONEL: (*uncomfortable*) Now, Connie! Easy, now!
CONSTANCE: Who *is* Mr. Brent?
COLONEL: Whoever he is, old girl, it's his own affair.
CONSTANCE: (*uneasy*) Maybe I misjudge him. I never saw a man who looked so—so *hounded;* so ill; in spite of all his swagger. He's British; he's got "Army" stamped all over him; but he's "Mr. Denis Brent." And this girl Louise is so infatuated that...
COLONEL: Brent's all right, tell you! Seems quite a decent sort!
CONSTANCE: Do you know how much he drinks? At this moment, I'll wager you, he's sitting in the dining-saloon at the front of the boat. Sitting at one of the little tables. Rattling a glass against an empty bottle to call the waiter! (*begins to fade*) Rattling a glass against an empty bottle...
(*Sound: rattle of bottle on glass comes up.*)

BRENT: (*English, late 30's; not drunk only greater politeness, sudden anger*) (*calling*) Waiter! Waiter!
WAITER: (*Egyptian*) Yess-sare-Mr. Brent?
BRENT: Will you be good enough to fetch me another bottle of brandy, please?
WAITER: (*hesitating*) Another bottle, sare?
BRENT: (*furious*) Hop it, confound you! (*controlling himself*) Wait! Just a moment!
WAITER: Yess-sare?
BRENT: (*sincerely*) I shouldn't have said that. I sincerely beg your pardon. Here's a pound note; keep the change.— That's all, thanks.
(*Sound:* (*off slightly*)
LOUISE: Good evening, Mr. Brent.
BRENT: (*on the defensive*) Good evening, Miss Louise.
LOUISE: I—I was admiring the scenery by night. I—saw the lights in here in the dining room.
(*Sound: off, the wailing cry of a jackal.*)
LOUISE: (*startled*) What was that?
BRENT: Only a jackal, Miss Louise. On the right bank of the river. Won't you come in?
(*Sound: door closes*)
LOUISE: (*fading on*) May I sit down at your table?
BRENT: (*light tone*) Of course, if you'll forgive me for not getting up. My speech is quite clear, you notice. My brain is, or seems to be, unusually acute. But—curious fact!—I can't walk.
LOUISE: (*quietly*) Is that a second bottle you've ordered?

BRENT: Yes.— Put it here, waiter!
LOUISE: Do you mind if I drink with you?
BRENT: (*startled*) Drink wi... (*suave again*) Not at all, if you feel inclined. American girls have even more freedom than I'd heard. Waiter! Another glass!
WAITER: I have one here, sir.
LOUISE: Fill the tumbler half full of brandy, will you?
(*Sound: liquid poured.*)
LOUISE: Thanks.
BRENT: (*harshly*) You can't drink that stuff; and you know it!
LOUISE: (*voice rising*) Maybe I'll *have* to drink it. In order to tell you what I'm going to tell you.
BRENT: Oh? What's that?
LOUISE: I ought to be coy, and arch, and with all the graces of our modern year '95. (*mimicking*) "Yes, Mr. Brent!" "How true, Mr. Brent!" "In two days, sir, we reach the outpost of civilization."—But I can't do it; and I won't: (*fiercely pleading*) Darling, what's *wrong*?
BRENT: (*pause*) I... I told you. I can't walk.
LOUISE: (*near tears*) I'm sorry. I shouldn't have asked.
BRENT: Drunk or sober, Louise, I won't see you with tears running down your face!— What do they say about me?
LOUISE: Oh, only that you were court-martialled or something! Who *cares*?
BRENT: Well: They're quite right. I *was* a Major; Indian Army. Served in the Sudan before that. And I *was* court-martialled. Do you know the charge against me?
LOUISE: No... All right! What was it?
BRENT: (*calmly*) Cowardice.— Where's *my* glass?
(*Sound: liquid poured.*)
BRENT: You don't ask whether the charge was true.
LOUISE: I... *was* it true?
BRENT: Oddly enough, no. (*bursting out*) No, by the living... (*partly checks himself; but rushes on*) But can you guess what "cowardice" means, even if it's not proved, to a man whose whole career is the Army? His life? His friends? His soul? (*controlling himself, mocking*) Any emotion you may see, my dear, comes entirely from that bottle.
LOUISE: Oh, stop it!
BRENT: Stop what?
LOUISE: (*pleading*) Stop pretending you don't care! Stop holding yourself in! It's killing you!— Why did they charge you with—(*she stops*).
BRENT: The story doesn't matter. My closest friend, Matt Griffith, told lies to save himself; and a sergeant-major backed him up.
LOUISE: What did you say in reply?
BRENT: Say in reply? Nothing.

LOUISE: You didn't defend yourself? Why not?

BRENT: I think it was contempt. Plain, ordinary contempt. Contempt for this friend of mine; maybe contempt for the world.

LOUISE: (*again fear tears*) Denis Brent, you *fool*!

BRENT: The funniest thing—real comedy—was the court martial. Officially, there weren't any "findings." They didn't believe the charge; but there were the witnesses. (*satirically*) So it was a British compromise.

LOUISE: How?

BRENT: They said to me, "Now look here, Brent. You've got a secret job of work to do; take six months' leave and finish it. Then we'll transfer you somewhere as—well! junior subaltern." (*satiric loathing*) In other words, second lieutenant.

(*Sound: bang of fist on table.*)

LOUISE: Strike your fist on the table! Do anything! But—talk to me! What was this "secret work?"

BRENT: Ah! That's where I can hit back at 'em! Do you know what a Maxim-gun is?

LOUISE: Well! It's... (*helplessly*) No; I don't know.

BRENT: It's a quick-firing gun. What some people now call a machine-gun. Every British regiment has a Maxim-gun section. But the gun's not effective yet.

LOUISE: How do you mean?

BRENT: It's too heavy. It usually jams. The water in the cooling-jacket boils after ninety seconds' use. *But* if you could make it lighter; if you could stop it from jamming as a rule; if you could keep it firing without boiling or blowing up.

LOUISE: And you've been working at that?

BRENT: I've done it, Louise. *I've done it*!

LOUISE: The completed gun?

BRENT: I hope so. I'm taking it out now, for a secret test under the hottest possible sun. If it works—

LOUISE: You can go back to England and clear yourself?

BRENT: Clear myself? (*grimly amused*) That's really funny!

LOUISE: (*alarmed*) What are you going to do?

BRENT: I can say to—never mind names—I can say: "The court-martial wouldn't find 'Not Guilty', or, 'Guilty, get out!' No! You still had a use for me. All right: here's your gun completed. Here's my resignation as (*loathing*) second lieutenant. In conclusion, sir, here is one in the jaw for *you*."

(*Sound: bang of fist on table.*)

LOUISE: And these people you talk about... Denis! Listen!

(*Sound: off, cry of a jackal.*)

BRENT: It's only another jackal, Louise.

LOUISE: No! Before that! Somebody very softly opened and closed the door to the deck. It was so—I don't know—*stealthy*! Is this new gun... valuable?
BRENT: Slightly! (*incredulous*) I'd thought of that too. But can you imagine any more harmless group than Professor Bauer, and Colonel and Mrs. Legget, and your Aunt Emily?
LOUISE: (*low voice*) Denis! I think there's someone outside the door now!
BRENT: (*low voice, rapidly*) I *can* walk, you know if I have to. Ugh! It's in my *head* now. Wasn't there a tiny little lamp on one of these tables?
LOUISE: Yes! Here!
BRENT: Give it to me. Thanks, Now over to the door. Softly! No noise! I'll turn the knob, and...
(*Sound: door opens quickly.*)
BRENT: (*ordinary voice*) Nobody! Stand back while I step out on the so-called "deck".
(*Sound: faintly—from aft—noise of paddle wheel. lapping of water, cry of jackal rises.*)
BRENT: There's nobody here, Louise. Only the sound of the paddle-wheel aft, and the jackal over there. You were imagining things!
(*Sound: off, a revolver shot.*)
LOUISE: Denis!
BRENT: (*grimly*) Not bad shooting. Blew the glass shade off the lamp and numbed my hand like frostbite.
LOUISE: (*crying out*) Who fired at you, Denis? Who did it?
(*Music: hits hard, then down and under.*)

FABIAN: On up the Nile; and on. Puffing black smoke, at only five knots, the river-boat thrashed its way. Now eeriness, even danger, pressed in like the thick heat. They were between Assouan and Wadi Haifa: the raiding-ground of the Dervishes. I can only imagine three of the passengers—Aunt Emily, Professor Bauer, Colonel Legget—as they sat the next night, under large clear stars, in the rounded bow of the *Joy-bringer*. Of course, as Aunt Emily said...
(*Sound: paddle wheels. behind—*)

EMILY: Stuff and nonsense! There Isn't a Dervish within three hundred miles! Or we wouldn't have been allowed to come on this trip. Don't you agree, Herr Professor?
BAUER: *Ja*, I agree. This journey last year was forbidden And thank Heaven there are no Dervishes!
EMILY: (*despite herself*) What do they look like?
BAUER: They wear red turbans and wool robes. They are silent, like ghosts, on swift-loping camels; you hear nothing until the first *crack* of a Remington rifle. Do I speak the truth, Colonel Legget?

COLONEL: Yes. They're first-class fighters. Bad strategists; always ride slap-bang in frontal attack. (*voice rising*) But look here! (*on edge; showing it*) what I want to know is, what's scaring my wife?
EMILY: (*catching some of the panic*) If we face it, Colonel Legget, it's what scares all of us. A murderer.
COLONEL: (*fiercely*) Madam, you're imaginin' things! (*deflated*) All the same, why did Mrs. Legget scream in the middle of the night?
EMILY: (*startled*) Did she scream?
BAUER: That is true. I heard her! It was something about her brother.
COLONEL: (*testily*) Her brother's a bank-manager in London! She was having nightmares all night. Hasn't been out of the cabin today.
EMILY: It wasn't a touch of liver, as you call it, that someone fired a shot at Mr. Brent!
BAUER: (*deep conviction*) Don't trust the British, Miss Emily!—*Ach*, Colonel Legget, pardon me! I would not speak so of *you*. But who is to say Mr. Brent did not fire the shot himself? As a blind?
EMILY: (*all dignity*) I happen to like Mr. Brent, Herr Professor. If a gentleman cares to take a—a beverage now and then—
BAUER: Now and then!
EMILY: I happen to know he has not been in the dining-room today, except at meal-times.
BAUER: Miss Emily! Do you know where your niece is now? With Mr. Brent! On the starboard deck. In the dark, outside the lounge windows. In Germany, for that, they would be married. (*brooding*) Brent! Brent! *Ach*, we go to our cabins now! But I would give much to hear what he says!
(*Music: sharp, very brief, bridge.*)

BRENT: Now, listen, Louise. I didn't want to tell you this, but I've got to. Or you'll be alarmed when it happens. I'm going to disappear.
LOUISE: Disappear? How do you mean, Denis?
BRENT: We reach Wadi Halfa tomorrow morning. That's the last outpost in the desert, as you said. But *I* leave the boat just before daylight.
LOUISE: (*puzzled; growing uneasy*) Denis! Isn't the Army garrison at Wadi Haifa?
BRENT: (*through his teeth*) I wouldn't touch the Army garrison with a barge-pole!
LOUISE: But aren't they expecting you?
BRENT: Oh, yes.— Now here's what I've arranged. Can anybody hear us?
LOUISE: I—I don't think so. There's only the lounge behind us, with the piano under one window. Everything's dark.
BRENT: About two miles this side of Wadi Haifa, there's a little mud village. Castor-oil plantation; belt of palm-trees: we've touched at a dozen like it. I've got an old friend there.

LOUISE: Who is it?
BRENT: He's a big Nubian named Comus. Used to be a Corporal in the 10th Nubian Battalion; speaks good English. Comus will be waiting with mules for desert-travel. Just before daylight—it's arranged with the skipper—this boat noses into the mud-bank. Over goes the gangway. *I* slip ashore with the gun in separate pieces. Nobody will notice.
LOUISE: Denis, where are you going in the desert? How far?
BRENT: Not far! And there's no danger. It's a deserted British camp, with a fully equipped rifle-range. Everything I need to test the gun.
(*Sound: faintly, noise of piano key as of someone accidentally brushing keys.*)
LOUISE: Listen! Didn't that sound like...
BRENT: (*too engrossed to notice anything*) Like what?
LOUISE: Like somebody brushing the piano keys! In the lounge!
BRENT: *I* didn't hear anything!— But I had to tell you, Louise. Now remember, even with mule-travel, I can come back and reach Wadi Halfa tomorrow evening.
LOUISE: Denis. (*pause*) Take me with you!
BRENT: (*startled*) Take... Now look here! I couldn't do that!
LOUISE: Why not? Just tell me why not?
BRENT: Well! These Dervishes...
LOUISE: There aren't any Dervishes! You know that. I could leave a note for Aunt Emily. You said yourself you could reach Wadi Haifa by evening. (*softly*) Don't you want me to go?
BRENT: Yes! I do!
LOUISE: Please, Denis!
BRENT: All right. We'll risk it. But if there *should* be any Dervishes...

(*Music: hits hard, then down and under narration.*)
FABIAN: On the desert, that morning, the sunlight smote as though caught by a burning-glass. Sandhill after yellow sandhill, with outcroppings of black rock, rolled away to a sand horizon. Southwards lay Dervish country, ruled under the black flag of the Khalifa. Here, there was only stillness, utter stillness, as figures moved: the white sun-helmet of Denis Brent, the khaki and straw hat of Comus the Nubian, the girl riding sidesaddle. Then they reached it: the deserted Army camp. Its barracks in ruins. The only building intact was a yellow-white church—built by missionaries, not yet consecrated—with a large bell in the low tower. Beside that church, under the shadow of the great bell, Denis Brent assembled the clumsy machine-gun...

BRENT: (*tension*) (*deep breath*) There! That's got it! It's mounted on a low tripod and swivel, you see. How do you like the *new* product, Louise?
LOUISE: (*on filter*) — I don't like it. I'm thinking that I hate guns! I'm terrified

of them! But if your life is the Army, so is mine.

BRENT: If *she* won't speak, Comus, what do *you* think?

COMUS: (*slightly slurred: not American Negro*) In my day, we had only the Gatling-gun with the crank-handle. Times change, Major!

BRENT: (*snarling*) Don't call me Major! (*controlling himself*) Sorry, Comus; there isn't time to explain. You understand what you have to do?

LOUISE: There isn't time to explain? Denis! Why isn't there time?

BRENT: (*ignoring this*) *This*, on the left of the gun, is the feed-block. The belt of cartridges... have you got the ammunition-book open?

(*Sound: vultures, high up, faint, through —*)

COMUS: Yes, Major. (*fiercely*) You are Major to *me*!

BRENT: The belt of cartridges—two hundred and fifty rounds in each belt—is drawn through to the right. When I press the trigger, *here*, you feed the belt evenly... evenly...!

LOUISE: Denis! What are those huge birds flapping and circling high up?

COMUS: (*rather loudly*) They are vultures, miss.

LOUISE: Vultures!?

BRENT: (*grimly*) Comus wants to break it gently, and not scare you. (*now drawn up: authoritative*) Comus! What's your estimate?

COMUS: I think, sir, the desert is clear for five hundred yards. Beyond that, there is a Dervish sharpshooter behind every black rock.

BRENT: I think so too. Where's the main force of camel-riders?

COMUS: I think, Major, behind the long sand-rise about two thousand yards away.

BRENT: Right!—Louise!

LOUISE: I'm all right, Denis! It's this... *silence*!

BRENT: Walk into the church, Slowly. Comus! Go with her as a shield; carry the ammunition-box in front of you. Don't show a cartridge-belt or we'll draw fire.

COMUS: I go, Major! I...

(*Sound: off, revolver shot...*)

COMUS: (*cries out*)

LOUISE: Comus! Comus!

(*Sound: pause: vultures: then fade.*)

BRENT: That wasn't a rifle-shot. It was a revolver, fired close to us. And it hit him between the eyes.

LOUISE: There's someone coming round the edge of the church. With a revolver! (*incredulous*) But it's...

LEGGET: (*fading on: not too close*) That's right, m'dear. I'm the fellow you call Colonel Legget!

BRENT: *Are* you Colonel Legget?

LEGGET: I'm his brother, anyway. No, never in the Army! I had to get rid of Bill on the night before we sailed. But what better disguise—for a brother who looks like him!—than an elderly Colonel travelling with his wife?

BRENT: You couldn't fool *Mrs.* Legget, could you?

LEGGET: No; but I could scare her. I've practically grown up with Connie. Even when we could be overheard on that boat, I hinted about a knife in the back if she didn't keep her mouth shut. Then she got hysterical and screamed I was Bill's brother; but she's under drugs now. And you, ex-Major Brent! Couldn't you guess there's a Dervish spy at every village? I've had two hundred Dervishes following you since morning!

BRENT: (*amazed*) You've had...?

LEGGET: Do you doubt my authority? I raise my left hand, like this...

(*Sound: rifle-shot, bullet richoceting off edge of church.*)

LEGGET: That was fired high and wide. Just as a warning!

BRENT: Who's *your* chief? The Khalifa of the Dervishes?

LEGGET: The Khalifa is at war with Britain. And how he sneers at your Army! This is war!

BRENT: It is for *them*. Not for you. What do you want?

LEGGET: I want that machine-gun!

BRENT: Come and get it!

LEGGET: (*close*) I don't want to shoot you. I want you as adviser about the gun. Do you still doubt I rule those Dervishes out there? Revolver in my left hand now; my right hand's going up to signal three shots close to you. Like this!

(*Sound: three rifle shots.*)

LEGGET: (*cries out*)

BRENT: That Dervish was a bad marksman, Legget. He's got *you* through the chest—Louise!

LOUISE: Here, Denis! I'm too scared to be anything but calm!

BRENT: Into the church, and up in the bell-tower! That's the only place we can make a stand!

LOUISE: I think I could carry the cartridge-belts!

BRENT: Get 'em, then! I'll take the gun. (*measured ferocity*) So the Khalifa sneers at the Army, eh?

(*Music: sharp musical effect, possibly drum; very short bridge.*)

BRENT: This bell takes up most of the room in the tower. Machine-gun over the parapet; tripod steady as a rock. Gun locked; cartridge-belt in place...

LOUISE: It's as still as death out there, Denis! Why don't they come *on*?!

BRENT: Keep your head down under the parapet!

LOUISE: I heard what you said to Comus! *I* can feed the gun! Just keep the belt steady!

BRENT: You can still do that and keep your head down!

LOUISE: *But why don't they...?* (*she means "come on."*)

BRENT: The leader beyond the sand-ridge doesn't know what's happened;

Wait! There's a red turban and a camel up over the skyline! Gone now! In one moment they'll come pouring over that ridge in one long mass. No sound except rifle-fire!— Get ready: here they come!

(*Sound: a fusillade of rifle-shots, heavy but irregular. some bullets strike or glance off the bell. Rifles continue, getting closer.*)

LOUISE: Denis! Why aren't *you* firing?

BRENT: Not at two thousand yards. Fifteen hundred. What's that row behind me?

LOUISE: It's the bell! They're hitting the bell!

BRENT: Just one second now, and... *So the Khalifa sneers at the Army!?*

(*Sound: maxim-gun begins, on; and continues in steady bursts all through the next speeches.*

BRENT: Come on, whiskers! Come on, red-turban! We can look to the left... we can look to the right...

LOUISE: Denis!! Suppose they get behind us?

BRENT: They won't. Dervishes ride bang in a frontal attack!

LOUISE: What chance have we got?

BRENT: If they get too close, we're done. If the gun jams, we're done. (*sheer joy*) But it won't happen, my angle-pet-sweetheart!

LOUISE: (*galvanized*) What did you call me?

BRENT: You don't like it, whiskers! It's breaking you to blazes! Come on! Meet the baby!

(*Sound: Rifles and machine gun again.*)

BRENT: Louise! Get away from this gun and crawl towards the tower stairs. Don't ask why! Do it!

LOUISE: The gun's so hot I can't touch it! But this cartridge belt—

BRENT: I can feed it myself. Go on!

LOUISE: What are they doing?

BRENT: A lot on foot now. Trying to get near the church-door! (*pouncing*) No, you don't!—*Or* you!

LOUISE: (*a little up*) Denis! There's steam pouring out of the gun.

BRENT: That's all right! Water-cooled jacket. Escape-valve!

LOUISE: But not as much steam as *that*!

BRENT: Keep back, Louise!— They're circling; re-forming...

LOUISE: The water's evaporated! Stop, Denis! The gun'll blow up in your face! (*Sound: loud bullet-noise on bell.*)

BRENT: Good old bell! I wish we could hoist a Union Jack. Come on, whiskers!

LOUISE: Stop the gun! Stop it!

BRENT: I've fired four belts, a thousand rounds, and I'll get through six!

LOUISE: It won't last five seconds more! It won't.

BRENT: Two more belts on the Khalifa's chest. And the Khalifa sneered...

(*Sound: off, man's voice shouting something of which the words are indistinguishable. Rifle-fire instantly ceases, so does the machine-gun fire*)

LOUISE: (*pause*) (*crying out*) What is it?
BRENT: (*no triumph; high emotion gone*) They're retreating, Louise. What's left of 'em. And the gun's... all right.
(*Sound: off, British bugle-call of "advance".*)
BRENT: (*starting*) Bugle? But the British garrison couldn't have heard of this! Wait! Other side of the belfry!— Yes!
LOUISE: (*fading on*) Who are they?
BRENT: A little patrol of the Camel Corps, coming up fast. (*hatred gathering*) And a young pink cheeked lieutenant, outranking me, in fine clean khaki and white helmet. How very interesting!
LOUISE: (*near tears*) Denis—before you insult that officer—and you want to—try to think of today! Look into your heart, if you've got one! You're stubborn, that's all. You're intolerable. But I love you... What will you say to that officer?
BRENT: Well! I—
LOUISE: You know you could be reinstated, if you wanted to be. *What will you say to that officer?*
BRENT: (*pause*) (*calling clearly*) Lieutenant Brent reporting, sir! The position—has been held!
(*Music: up to final narration.*)

FABIAN: And so, as I end my story of the nineties, we aboard the *Maurevania* can look over at a place where the Nile runs roughly parallel with the Red Sea. Here in the Red Sea it is not very exciting, until next week we come to a certain place—off the coast of Abyssinia—which has one name on the map and a more evil one in my casebook. And so, when I tell you the story called "The Island of Coffins", will you join me in *Cabin B-13*?
(*Sound: ship's whistles*)
(*Music: out*)

Notes for the Curious

For the next play in *Cabin B-13*, John Dickson Carr decided to write an imperialist adventure rather than a mystery or detective story. He had done this before with the radio play "Lord of the Witch Doctors" (1941), written for the BBC as by "Robert Southwell", and later adapted for *Suspense* (1942). Carr's adventure stories owe something to Sir Arthur Conan Doyle, whose biography he was researching in parallel with writing the *Cabin B-13* plays and which would be published as *The Life of Sir Arthur Conan Doyle* (1949).

Conan Doyle's life was astonishing by any means, taking in experiences as diverse as ship's surgeon on the *Hope*, a Greenland whaler, at the age of twenty, keeping goal for the English soccer team now known as Portsmouth FC and friendship with the likes of Harry Houdini. Carr admired Conan Doyle immensely and at one time even considered a novel in which the creator of Sherlock Holmes would himself play detective.

While the story of "Death in the Desert" is unique to *Cabin B-13* it shares its setting and some of its characters with *The Tragedy of the Korosko* (1898) by Sir Arthur Conan Doyle. Twenty years later, in his late novel *Papa La-Bas* (1969), Carr would re-use a device from "Death in the Desert" to mis-direct the reader away from identifying the murderer.

Carr's original title for this play was "Four Ways to Danger", which he may have abandoned because of the similarity to "Death has Four Faces".

The Island of Coffins

(*Sound: a ship's whistle*)
(*Music: in and behind*)
FABIAN: Shade your eyes against the hot sun, now, as our luxury-liner *Maurevania* moves through the Red Sea towards the Gulf of Aden. I, Doctor Fabian, from Cabin B-13, our ship's surgeon on this cruise round the world, have a reason for asking you to look everywhere. Those brown plateaus, rising into mountains from the sandy plain, are the table-lands of Abyssinia. Below them you can make out the port of Massawa, and the group of islands between Massawa and this ship. On one of those islands—Hadar, it's called—occurred as terrifying an adventure as I can remember. *Could* the dead sleep in Mrs. Almack's house?
ANNOUNCER: CBS presents John Dickson Carr's famous Doctor Fabian—ship's surgeon, world traveler and teller of strange and incredible tales of mystery and murder, directed by John Dietz.

FABIAN: Hadar Island: that's it! You notice, through field-glasses, how luxuriant the trees are, almost a miracle in this arid place? Many a traveler had told me it ought to be called "The Island of Coffins"—a tantalizing phrase— sandpaper to the curiosity. Yet I never knew why until three years ago, after the war, at the end of '45. Late that night, the *Maurevania* was passing just this point off the Abyssinian Coast. I was sitting in Cabin B-13, reading, when...
(*Music: out, into—*)

(*Sound: knock on door, off.*)
FABIAN: Yes? Come in!
(*Sound: door opens and closes.*)
NURSE: (*fading on*) Sorry to disturb you, Doctor Fabian.
FABIAN: Not at all, Nurse. (*puzzled*) But if we've got a patient in the middle of the night, why didn't you 'phone me?
NURSE: It's all so odd and—Don't you notice the ship's slowing down?
FABIAN: Yes! So it is!
NURSE: The Captain says, through Mr. MacCleary, could you go over to Hadar Island at once?
(*Sound: large book closed abruptly.*)
NURSE: You close the book very quickly, Doctor Fabian!
FABIAN: Yes, nurse! I... Hadar Island! What's happened?
NURSE: Mr. MacCleary was on the bridge. All of a sudden a ship's lamp, a signaling-lamp with a shutter, began flashing over the trees on that island. It signaled, "*Maurevania*". The bridge answered. Then it signaled,

in English... Well! Mr. MacCleary wrote it down. Here!

FABIAN: (*reading*) "Vital you send doctor at once. Life and death. Life and death."

NURSE: They didn't like it; but they couldn't ignore it. Will you go?

FABIAN: Yes, of course! But I've got to be prepared. Did MacCleary ask the nature of the case?

NURSE: Yes, Doctor. They said—serious bullet-wound.

FABIAN: An intensely hot night; black, yet with a bright moon silvering the water, as the motor-lifeboat carried me across to Hadar. The island—giant sycamore-trees, date-palms, juniper, laurel—towered up like a jungle. I remember that old Tom Yardley, the A.B. at the engine, was humming "Blow the Man Down" as he always did: but he was humming it rather loudly when he ran the boat up on the beach in darkness. Then someone was swinging a lantern against the line of trees. It was a girl not more than twenty-two or three; but she wore her yellow hair in a curious style, and her blue dress puzzled me.

JANICE: (*hesitant, soft, frightened, sounds younger than age*) Are you —are you the doctor from the ship?

FABIAN: Yes. My name is Fabian. (*gently*) You don't need to be frightened of me, you know.

JANICE: (*quickly*) Oh, it isn't that! At least—! (*changing mood*) Will you follow me quickly, please? There's a path through the trees. It's narrow, but you don't need to be afraid of snakes or anything.

FABIAN: I've got an electric torch here. Lead on, Miss...?

JANICE: I'm Janice March. Please call me Janice. Everyone does. —Mind the tree branches!

(*Sound: occasional brushing of foliage, through—*)

FABIAN: Do you mind my saying, Miss Janice, that the blue dress becomes you?

JANICE: (*naively pleased*) Does it really? *I* thought so, but of course I didn't know.

FABIAN: (*questing*) It was made, I dare guess, in Paris. It's quite new...

JANICE: (*naively indignant*) New! I should think it was new! It's the very latest fashion for 1920!

FABIAN: 1920! (*collecting himself*) Yes, of course. (*lightly*) You don't by any chance mean 1945?

JANICE: Really, Doctor Fabian! I can't tell what people will be wearing a quarter of a century from now! (*as though realizing*) Oh! I'm sorry! That must be one of your jokes from the Other World.

FABIAN: My dear young lady! You talk as though I were a ghost!

JANICE: (*almost laughing*) I didn't mean *that*, of course. —The path turns here—I mean: from the outside world. The evil place.

FABIAN: Haven't you ever been in this Other World?
JANICE: (*as though starting*) No! Of course not! I don't think I was born here; but I don't remember any other place. David and Harry—they're the boys—just dimly remember; but David is twenty-six and Harry must be thirty.
FABIAN: Did you ever hear, for instance, of a man named —Adolf Hitler?
JANICE: No; I don't think so. (*voice rising*) Sometimes I get so *horribly* curious about the Other World that... (*exclamation, as though stumbling*) I *would* stumble over a tree root! —And I don't really mean what I said about the outside world. I wouldn't go there if I could! Let's not talk about it!
FABIAN: Gently, now! —Your message from the island said, "Life and death". "A serious bullet-wound."
JANICE: I mustn't talk about that, either! We're nearly at the house now. Beyond those two big sycamores!
FABIAN: It isn't a large island, then?
JANICE: Oh, no! You could walk across Hadar in ten minutes—Now! Into the clearing! I'll hold up this lantern... You look astonished!
FABIAN: I *am* astonished, believe me. This house is a palace!
JANICE: (*as though meeting a joke*) Really, Doctor Fabian! It couldn't be that! I've seen palaces in books!
FABIAN: (*muttering*) Black unpolished marble... not as high as the trees; well hidden!... no lights at the front... (*suddenly*) Janice!
JANICE: Yes?
FABIAN: Follow the beam of this electric torch. Over to the right. There's a conservatory, or glass enclosure of some kind, built out from the house. Those objects inside, ranged all in a line: are they what I think they are?
JANICE: (*matter of fact*) *Those* things?
FABIAN: Yes!
JANICE: Oh, those are only the coffins!... This is the front door.

(*Music: in, sinister, and behind—*)
FABIAN: "Only the coffins". (*slight pause*) Imagine entering, as I did, a low marble hall furnished with the luxury of a quarter-century ago. Even in this heat there was no sign of insects, dry-rot, any tropical pest. A little calendar on one table gave the date as November 12th, 1920. (*pause*) Beyond it, where Janice urged me, was the open door of a big room lined with books. In the doorway, with his back to us, stood a young man of about thirty. In a big chair, blood-spattered, sat an elderly, strong-faced lady who had once been very beautiful. Her dress was of older fashion than Janice's, with rows of small glass beads across the bodice: one row of beads torn from right to left, towards a left arm with a blood-stained bandage. When she spoke, it was to the young man in the doorway.
(*Music: out*)

HENRIETTA: (*harsh, yet hurt*) You understand, Harry, that you forced your grandmother into the course she took?
HARRY: (*horrified*) To try to kill yourself?
HENRIETTA: When *you* desert me, Harry...
HARRY: Grandmother, listen! If I said I wanted to leave this island, I didn't mean it! But I don't remember saying that!
HENRIETTA: Your own words? In this library?
HARRY: (*bewildered*) I can't remember much *about* today! That's just it! I must have had a drug or something!
JANICE: (*off, calling*) Mrs. Almack! Mrs. Almack!
HENRIETTA: Janice? Did you bring the doctor?
JANICE: Yes, Mrs. Almack! He's here now.
HENRIETTA: Then be good enough to show him in. Good evening, Doctor. (*casual haughtiness*) I am Henrietta Almack.
FABIAN: (*fading in*) How do you do, Mrs. Almack?
HENRIETTA: I regret having to inconvenience your ship. I regret still more having to tell the untruth that this was a matter of life and death.
FABIAN: Are you sure, Mrs. Almack, there's no matter of life and death here?
HENRIETTA: (*fierce contempt*) A bullet in the arm. Will-power, ordinary will-power, can ignore a little pain or a bone smash above the elbow. Unfortunately, will-power can't mend it.
FABIAN: Don't try to move the arm! Just let me look at it!
HENRIETTA: Thank you, Doctor. Is there anything you need, before I send Harry and Janice away?
JANICE: (*cutting in*) Harry! I never saw you look so white; Are you all right?
HARRY: (*still groping*) Janice, I don't know. I never make trouble. Give me music-studies; give me the things we have here; I'm satisfied. You know that.
JANICE: Of course I know, dear!
HARRY:Last night I must have fallen asleep with a lighted cigarette in my fingers. But that won't account for the burn on the back of my hand, below the thumb. Today, for some reason—I can swear it! —I slept until evening. And yet...
JANICE: Let me help you up to your room! How do you feel?
HARRY: (*quoting slowly*): "As one who on a lonesome road
Doth walk in fear and dread;
And, having once looked round, goes on,
And turns no more his head:
Because he knows... "(*stops*)
HENRIETTA: (*defiantly*) Have you forgotten your Coleridge, Harry? (*challenging*) Go on!
FABIAN: "Because he knows a frightful fiend
Doth close behind him tread." —Hot water and towels, please!
(*Music: sharp, sinister bridge; short.*)

FABIAN: There, Mrs. Almack! That ought to do. If you won't move from that chair, here's a blanket for your shoulders. A sedative, now...
HENRIETTA: (*grimly*) No sedatives, Doctor Fabian! But do you understand *now* how it's possible to keep away from the world?
FABIAN: (*troubled, wondering*) You brought the children to this island twenty years ago. Is that correct?
HENRIETTA: Yes —And speak out! We're alone here!
FABIAN: All their parents were dead then. The only one related to you is your grandson Harry. But if they don't know what's happening outside... do you?
HENRIETTA: Oh, yes. By a hidden radio (*controlled; but ferocious triumph*) And was I right, my dear sir, to anticipate what I *did* anticipate? Look at the world as it is! Dare you call it "civilization"?
FABIAN: No. There I agree with you.
HENRIETTA: When I left it, did I go to some tropical paradise? No! That's the course of the weakling who wants to forget *himself*; not the world! *I* chose a forsaken place miles off the Abyssinian coast. Nobody looks; nobody cares! When we first came here, this island was only scrub and vermin. Look 'round the room now! What do you see?
FABIAN: (*growing feeling of some secret duel with her*) A very fine library; I envy you. For music, an automatic organ built into the wall...
HENRIETTA: More than that! If I touched one of these switches here, on the table, you would hear the organ play. (*as though pointing*) And what do you see *there*, Doctor Fabian?
FABIAN: A wall of windows. A terrace outside...
HENRIETTA: We're on high ground here. From that terrace, concrete stairs lead down to a landing-stage. Each month a little steamer—it belongs to me—brings us everything we need. Everything! And when we first came here, I turned back the calendar to the year 1900.
FABIAN: Why did you do that, Mrs. Almack? *Why*?
HENRIETTA: (*her obsession*) It was to live again—even in imagination — through the only years that were worth living. (*pause*) Let me touch *this* switch on the table.
(*Sound: sharp click. organ begins very softly playing.*)
(*Music: the "Merry Widow Waltz"; it registers before.*)
HENRIETTA: (*in a dream— on cue*) When "social problems" had little meaning. When women's pleasure was to be attractive. When the lamps were bright; when there was laughter without irony. When leisure—culture—good manners—still existed on this earth.
(*Sound: sharp click.*)
(*Music: out*)
HENRIETTA: (*pleading*) *Can you understand that?*
FABIAN: I can more than understand, Mrs. Almack. I can sympathize: with *you*. But what about the young people?

HENRIETTA: (*deeply sincere*) I love those children! All of them!
FABIAN: Yet you keep them here like prisoners?
HENRIETTA: (*inflexibly*) I won't have them face what is outside!
FABIAN: Haven't they the right to judge for themselves?
HENRIETTA: No. (*curtly*) You've heard what happened today.
FABIAN: On the contrary, I haven't heard! *Did* Harry threaten to leave the island?
HENRIETTA: Not this time, no.
FABIAN: (*puzzled*) Not this time?
HENRIETTA: Yesterday Harry remarked—very casually!—that it might be pleasant to study music in Italy. That thought would grow, unless I rooted it out. Well! Last night Grimm and I...
FABIAN: (*cutting in sharply*) Forgive me: who is "Grimm?"
HENRIETTA: He's my last servant from the old days. And a famous wrestler, my dear sir! He could break the backs of any two men.
FABIAN: Is that a threat, Mrs. Almack?
HENRIETTA: (*graciously*) Not at all, Doctor Fabian. (*changing tone, grimly*) Last night we gave Harry a strong drug. He was still asleep this afternoon. So I took my late husband's revolver... *this* revolver...
FABIAN: You've kept it pushed down in the chair beside you, I see.
HENRIETTA: Always close at hand, Doctor! It's an old revolver; it has a "back-fire" of powder-grains; but it's useful. This afternoon, I put the muzzle against my left arm, and...
FABIAN: (*cutting in sharply*) What did you gain by that?
HENRIETTA: Harry *thinks* he came in here and made a scene. He *thinks* I tried to kill myself, and failed. He won't think of leaving here again.
(*Sound: rattle of heavy pistol on table.*)
HENRIETTA: There's the revolver on the table. — And you're looking at me very strangely, Doctor Fabian!
FABIAN: Yes. I have reason to. I was thinking...
HENRIETTA: *What?*
FABIAN: Among other things: you're heading for a smash.
HENRIETTA: (*snapping*) Why should I be?
FABIAN: There's an ocean-liner close to this island, Mrs. Almack.
HENRIETTA: Ships in the Red Sea are as common as flies!
FABIAN: (*as though continuing* speech) And down on the other side of this house, old Tom Yardley is sitting in a motor-boat waiting for me, and humming "Blow the Man Down." You've unsettled your prisoners, Mrs. Almack! Even Janice! I haven't met the one you call David...
(*Sound: off, sharp knocking at door: it opens and closes.*)
DAVID: (*fading on; nervous; trying to be determined*) I'm sorry to intrude, Mrs. Almack. I beg leave to ask a question.
HENRIETTA: (*the Grande Dame*) Certainly, David. But...

DAVID: (*formally*) Yes, Mrs. Almack?
HENRIETTA: You and Janice used to call me "grandmother." Just as Harry does.
DAVID: I'm sorry, Mrs. Almack. I can't do it.
HENRIETTA: May I ask why not?
DAVID: (*on edge*) I don't know! Everything you've taught us has been out of books. Maybe the reason's in a book. But I can't do it!
HENRIETTA: Just as you like, David. What question do you want to ask?
DAVID: (*steeling himself*) Did you play a trick on Harry today?
HENRIETTA: In what way you mean trick?
DAVID: (*blurting it out*) Did you drug him and then tell lies? (*realizing its effect on her*) I mean—!
HENRIETTA: Your manners, David...!
DAVID: (*half-cowed*) You're picking up that revolver; putting it down again; picking it up...
(*Sound: for a few seconds we hear the revolver put down on the table; each time harder between very brief pauses, as of rage gathering.*)
DAVID: (*bursting out*) Why don't you *say* something?
HENRIETTA: How long has it been since Grimm flogged you?
DAVID: Not since I was 18! And if he tries it now—!
HENRIETTA: (*casually*) What will you do, David? You're strong enough; so is Harry. But you wouldn't last ten seconds against Grimm. (*pouncing fiercely*) And you know that! *Don't you?*
DAVID: (*quietly*) Yes; God help me.
HENRIETTA: (*mocking*) You've been very bold, David, since you've thought you were in love with Janice. Harry's in love with Janice too. Now go to your room! *Go*! That's it... don't stumble.
DAVID: (*off, not clearly*) I've learned what I wanted to know, Mrs. Almack.
HENRIETTA: (*scenting rebellion*) What did you say? *Speak up!*
DAVID: (*hitting back, clearly*) With all respect: I've learned what I want to know!
(*Sound: door opens and closes sharply.*)
HENRIETTA: (*furious; trying to conceal it*) That boy needs a lesson. Where's the buzzer to call Grimm? Here!
(*Sound: far off, buzzer sounds several times.*)
FABIAN: What are you going to do?
HENRIETTA: You'll see, Doctor Fabian. We won't need one of our coffins. David won't try to leave here. He wouldn't go without Janice... the man in the motor-boat wouldn't take him without orders...
FABIAN: What about your signal-lamp?
HENRIETTA: That's on the roof. In a black concrete hut with an iron door. And *I've* got the only key. I always keep it, for emergencies, here on a key-ring in the pocket of... (*faltering*)... in the pocket of...
FABIAN: Your key-ring's gone: is that it? Somebody's taken your keys?

HENRIETTA: Yes!
FABIAN: (*dominating*) Now listen to me, Mrs. Almack! From what you've told me, and from what I've seen and heard, I can guess more than you think. Don't be a fool any longer! Above everything, don't you see the danger if David and Harry are both in love with Janice?
HENRIETTA: (*amazed*) That? Adolescent nonsense that...
FABIAN: (*cutting in*) They're not adolescents! They're—
(*Sound: sharp knocking at door.*)
HENRIETTA: That's Grimm! (*calling*) Come in, Grimm!
(*Sound: door opens.*)
HENRIETTA: He's no beauty; but he fills the doorway. —What are you staring at, Doctor Fabian?
FABIAN: First at his color. Then at the bluish tinge of his lips...
HENRIETTA: Get your horse-whip, Grimm!
FABIAN: For the last time, will you listen?
HENRIETTA: Get your horse-whip, Grimm! You'll need it!

(*Music: hits hard, then down under—*)
FABIAN: And at that same time, as I afterwards learned, a door was open on the roof of that house. The iron door to the concrete hut—it housed the big signal-lamp—stood wide open. The beam of the lamp, blinding white, was turned on towards the *Maurevania* two miles away. Inside the hut, dark except for an edge of that white glow, David Barton struggled with the shutter of the light.
(*Music: out into—*)

(*Sound: metallic clashing, as of opening and closing of big shutters across light. These follow morse code as David speaks in time with them*)
DAVID: (*nervous; to himself*) Short...Short...short. There! That's "S". Now what's "O"? Wait a minute! It's...
JANICE: (*a little off*) David!
DAVID: *Who's there?*
JANICE: (*fading on*) It's only Janice! (*terrified*) You know we're never allowed in here! What are you doing?
DAVID: I've read about the Morse code. There's a book on the table with the code in it. One little signal, "S.O.S.," means "help".
JANICE: But—why do you want that?
DAVID: I've got to get you off this island, Janice! She's—
JANICE: She's—what? And how did you get in here?
DAVID: I stole her keys this evening. I made one last effort to convince myself she isn't... (*breaking off*) I can't remember the signal for the letter "O"! Get me that book off the table!
JANICE: All right! If I can manage to see it!

DAVID: And—Janice. Those coffins downstairs…
JANICE: But they've been there since I can remember! *I* never minded them!
DAVID: Do you remember, in the old days, what she said was in them?
JANICE: The bodies of people who tried to leave the island. But she laughed! It was only pretending! (*pleading to be told otherwise*)
DAVID: That's what I thought. Until a few months ago. Then I read a description of modern coffins. Inside the wooden shell there's a lead sheathing: air-tight! And another wooden coffin inside the lead. Air-tight! You *could* keep… (*breaking off*) Where's that code-book!
JANICE: Here! (*almost whispering*) But, David—!
DAVID: Get it near the light, and… The letter "O" is—of course! And I've got to hurry, or—
JANICE: Listen! There's somebody on the roof! Somebody with a whip.
(*Sound: a little off, sharp crack of horse-whip.*)
JANICE: (*again trying to convince herself*) But Grimm's fond of us! Grimm wouldn't hurt us!… Would you, Grimm?
GRIMM: (*deep voice, polyglot accent; pleading but implacable*) I don' want to 'urt you, Miss Janice. I don' want to 'urt Mr. David. But if Mrs. shall order me, I do it.
DAVID: Get to the Devil and take your whip too!
(*Sound: metallic clashes begin in time as David speaks again.*)
DAVID: Three Shorts—Three Long!… Long! Lo—
(*Sound: crack of whip. David gives stifled cry. clashing stops.*)
GRIMM: I don' want to 'it you across the face!—like that! No! Don' make me! There is another reason why I don' want to! Go down to the library, Mr. David!
DAVID: I won't do it!
GRIMM: Go!
(*Sound: whip-crack.*)
GRIMM: Go!
(*Sound: whip-crack.*)
GRIMM: *Go!*
(*Sound: another whip-crack.*)
(*Music: hits hard, and into bridge of sinister effect.*)

HENRIETTA: I believe there's nothing more, Doctor Fabian. That is the story of the coffins. Sealed and airtight with their human contents.
FABIAN: I see, Mrs. Almack.
HENRIETTA: Quite a few persons have come and gone from this island, of course. Laborers for the irrigation system; workmen when the electric plant goes wrong; those with new methods who have almost rid us of insects. All well enough paid for their future silence. (*changing tone*) But the tutor who promises to stay, and won't; the maidservant who changes

her mind; anyone who betrays me... anyone who betrays me...
(*Sound: off, door opened with the effect of a bang.*)
GRIMM: (*loudly, off*) You will go in library first, Mr. David! Then you, Miss Janice! I follow!
HENRIETTA: (*pleased*) So, David! You didn't go to your room after all!
FABIAN: (*surprised; growing furious*) That red mark across his face! — Grimm! *Did* you flog him?
HENRIETTA: What did you expect, Doctor Fabian? What made you think Grimm wouldn't? As for *you*, David...
DAVID: You've broken my nerve, if that's what you want. And it is what you want! It always has been! (*despair*) Go on: gloat! Janice here...
JANICE: I don't think I ever hated you, Mrs. Almack, until I saw that whip go across his eyes. And he couldn't see the signal-lamp. (*near tears; but voice rising*) And he groped 'round that little room, until... Have we *got* to stand this forever? Isn't there *any* help?
FABIAN: (*a little off, but very sharply*) Oh, yes, Janice! There's help!
HENRIETTA: (*suddenly*) Doctor Fabian! (*viciousness; faint alarm*) What are you doing near those bookshelves?
FABIAN: When I first came in here, I noticed a book strangely bound for these shelves. It's here. It's...
HENRIETTA: Close that book! Put it back!
FABIAN: (*coming closer*) And you can take courage, Janice! So can you, David! The tyrants aren't always so powerful as they think.
HENRIETTA: (*boiling; trying to conceal it*) Aren't they, Doctor Fabian? Here's the revolver beside me; and it's good to the touch when I pick it up. Grimm! Put away your whip! That is for the children. Do you challenge me, Doctor Fabian?
FABIAN: Yes, I challenge you.
HENRIETTA: One revolver-bullet,...
FABIAN: If you were insane, as you like to pretend, you might fire. But you're very coldly sane, Mrs. Almack. And this is too small an island.
JANICE: Don't challenge her! Look at her face!
FABIAN: If you fire a shot, my good tyrant, Tom Yardley in the motor-boat would hear it. He knows there's trouble already; I came here to treat a bullet-wound. He'd go back to the *Maurevania* for armed help. Whether you kill me or whether you don't you'll leave your island paradise in handcuffs... I am at your service, Mrs. Almack. Fire!
(*Sound: pause. revolver put down on table.*)
HENRIETTA: Grimm!
GRIMM: (*rather hoarsely*) Yes, Mrs.? I do what you tell me!
HENRIETTA: (*cry with rage*) We won't dispose of him just yet. Just break his arm and strike him unconscious. *That* makes no sound.
DAVID: (*crying out*) Doctor Fabian!

FABIAN: Yes, David?
DAVID: I don't know who you are; but you've put life and blood and soul into me. If that man-mountain tackles you, I'll go for him too!
FABIAN: Thanks, David. But I don't need help. —Come on, Grimm! Try a wrestling-fall!
JANICE: (*short pause*) (*astounded*) What's the *matter* with Grimm?
FABIAN: Yes, Grimm! What's the matter? Your shoulders are sagging. (*changing tone*) It's heart-disease, isn't it?
HENRIETTA: (*exclaiming*) Heart-disease?
FABIAN: Yes, Mrs. Almack. You didn't notice the color of his face, or the bluish tinge in his lips. There are far more advanced symptoms than that. Did he want to use the whip, David?
DAVID: No! He said…
JANICE: He said there was another reason!
FABIAN: He's exerted himself too much already. A wrestling-fall would kill him. —Will you try to break my arm, Grimm, before you're a dead man?
GRIMM: (b*ursting out, in agony*) Mrs.! I am sorry. Old Grimm sorry! Last doctor has told me! But I don't tell you! I…
FABIAN: (*sharply*) *David*!
DAVID: (*snarling*) What do you want?
FABIAN: There's murder behind that red mark across your face. I know how you feel! But in the outer world there's something called sportsmanship. You know you can beat him! Now let him alone! —for you, Mrs. Almack…
HENRIETTA: I can still use the revolver, Doctor Fabian!
(*Sound: off ship's whistles.*)
HENRIETTA: What was that?
FABIAN: It was the *Maurevania* signaling. Mrs. Almack. A ship's time is money. This delay means hundreds of pounds. You've kept me too long here already.
JANICE: Is that true, Doctor Fabian?
FABIAN: Now they're worried about what's happened. Now they will come here. And you're finished, Mrs. Almack, whether I act or not.
HENRIETTA: But how you must hate me!
FABIAN: Because I know the secret you've been hiding for twenty years. You didn't fire that bullet into your arm.
HENRIETTA: That's a lie!
JANICE: Doctor Fabian, what are you saying. She didn't…?
FABIAN: No, Janice. Look at the row of glass beads across her dress. One of them is torn from right to left, ending in the new bandage on her arm. There was a struggle, you see. Somebody tried to kill her with the revolved held at very close range. She knocked the gun aside just as it was fired.
JANICE: But who tried to kill her?
FABIAN: The revolver, she mentioned, has a bad "back-fire" of flash and pow-

der-grains. There is no powder grain on *her*. She's been gripping the revolver. There is no pain at all. There is only one person...
HENRIETTA: (*bursting out, pleading*) Stop! In the name of pity and mercy, stop!
FABIAN: There is only one person in this house with a burn on his hand like that.
JANICE: *Harry! Harry Almack!*
DAVID: But it couldn't be Harry; He's too fond of her!
FABIAN: Harry doesn't remember doing it. He attacked the person he liked best. Homicidal maniacs usually do.
JANICE: *Homicidal maniacs!*
FABIAN: You knew the boy was criminally mad. Mrs. Almack knew it when he was ten years old. There's his medical-case-history, by a certain Doctor Wilson. But you knew they'd lock him up. And you couldn't stand that! So you brought him here, with Janice and David for companions. And an ex-wrestler to control him when he had attacks.
JANICE: But, Doctor Fabian! Those coffins!
FABIAN: The coffins are empty.
HENRIETTA: (*broken*) No. No. *No!*
FABIAN: The coffins are empty. They're only false terrorism, to keep people here—and you'd rather have everybody think you were mad than have them suspicious of Harry. When Harry went berserk, he never remembered his fits of violence afterwards he slept. And now...
HENRIETTA: (*terror*) What are you going to do to Harry? Take him away?
FABIAN: I'm afraid there's no other course, Mrs. Almack. Grimm has been faithful, Mrs. Almack, even when you lost your head with power and authority. But now...
HENRIETTA: That empty lie of trying to kill myself. With this very revolver in my hand. Let's make it a reality.
FABIAN: (*suddenly suspicious*) After what?
HENRIETTA: (*quickly*) After I turn the gun on myself!
FABIAN: No, Mrs. Almack!
(*Sound: at the same time as his speech, revolver-shot.*)
HENRIETTA: (*furious*) Why did you strike my hand away?
FABIAN: Not from pious motives, believe me. But would you desert Harry at the very time he needs you most?
HENRIETTA: (*conquering something like a sob*) No. You're right! And I will go with him. (*contemptuously*) If there be any punishment for me in the outside world...
FABIAN: There is.
HENRIETTA: (*fiercely*) I did what I thought was right! But... I was thinking of a quotation from an old play...
FABIAN: Yes? What was it?
HENRIETTA: (*slowly*) Oh, God, turn back thy clock again.
(*Sound: sharp click of a switch. "The Merry Widow Waltz" is heard being played on an organ and registers*)

HENRIETTA: *... and give me yesterday!*
(*Sound: organ with "Merry Widow Waltz" rises higher! and then into curtain with full orchestra, into*)
(*Music: up and behind for final narration.*)

FABIAN: Henrietta Almack died not long afterwards; let conventional notions be satisfied. Janice and David were happy; and Harry, in the place where they cared well for him, was at least... content. (*changing mood*) But next week when the *Maurevenia* takes us near enough for a glimpse of Kenya, in British East Africa, you might care to hear of a different kind of I remember a lion-hunt, and an unknown criminal with an express-rifle. And so, if you would like to hear a story called "The Man Eaters"[1], will you join me, Doctor Fabian, in *Cabin B-13*?
(*Sound: ship's whistles*)
(*Music: out*)

---

[1] Carr never used the title "The Man-Eaters" in *Cabin B-13* or elsewhere and he does not seem to have ever completed the script featuring "a lion hunt and an unknown criminal with an express rifle". The next play in *Cabin B-13* was a repeated broadcast of "The Man Who Couldn't Be Photographed".

Notes for the Curious

"The Island of Coffins" is the most extraordinary story in *Cabin B-13*, from its setting, the fictional island of Hadar, whose unusual climate suggests it benefits from something like the Gulf Stream, to the island's inhabitants who recollect the islanders in one of Shakespeare's late plays as well as the protagonist of *The Phantom of the Opera* by Gaston Leroux. Leroux was one of Carr's great heroes and his novel *The Mystery of the Yellow Room* (1907), with its impossible crime and duplicitous characters, was as much of an influence on the young writer as Chesterton, Poe, Conan Doyle, and Thomas and Mary Hanshew, the chroniclers of the adventures of Hamilton Cleek, "the Man of the Forty Faces".

When the central character in "The Island of Coffins" observes that the 1920s and 30s were *"the only years that were worth living"* Carr would have sympathized. Carr's biographer, Douglas G. Greene, has observed that at this time the writer was becoming increasingly estranged from much of the modern world. His yearning would eventually lead him to focus on historical mysteries and the three time-slip novels, *The Devil in Velvet* (1951), *Fire, Burn!* (1957) and *Fear is the Same* (1956), the latter published as by "Carter Dickson", which might also have been inspired by the so-called Time Plays of his friend J.B. Priestley, the most famous of which, *An Inspector Calls*, was first performed in July 1945.

While the story of "The Island of Coffins" is unique to *Cabin B-13*, Henrietta Almack's motive is the same as that of Count Kohary in Carr's radio play "The Devil's Saint" (1943), first broadcast on *Suspense*.

As is suitable for a story concerned with time, Hadar Island is named for the third month of the Abyssinian calendar.

The Most Respectable Murder

(*Sound: a ship's whistle*)
(*Music: in and behind*)
ANNOUNCER: *Cabin B-13*. Tonight: "The Most Respectable Murder".
FABIAN: Tonight, in the *Maurevania's* dining room, the orchestra played a selection from *Pagliacci*. To my fellow-diners, it was only a background for an excellent meal. But to me, Doctor Fabian, it brought the sharp, shocking memory of a night at the Paris Opera— of two friends, quarreling bitterly and of how within a few hours, their whole future hung on my answering the question, "How did a murderer get out of the locked room?"

(*Sound: in and behind—end of Pagliacci "Laugh, Clown"*[1])
FABIAN: The Opera at Paris. (*slight pause*) I was sitting that night in a box on the lowest tier, with my friend Vautrelle, and his wife, and young Charles D'Arville. Towards the end of the first act of *Pagliacci*—when the famous song of "Laugh, Clown" rose to its end—

(*Sound: the music concludes, to be followed by applause rises and fades into faint crowd-murmur*)

VAUTRELLE: (*mid 30's but seems older: cynically humorous*) There's nothing like a box at the opera, Doctor Fabian, to make us feel superior. Are you enjoying *Pagliacci*?
FABIAN: I always enjoy it, my dear Vautrelle.
VAUTRELLE: So do I. (*tensity creeping in*) "Laugh, Clown!" You've been betrayed by a woman. By the way, I noticed your look of surprise.
FABIAN: My look of surprise?
VAUTRELLE: Oh, now! I meant ten or fifteen minutes ago. When Ninette—my wife slipped out of this box with young Charles D'Arville... May I read your thoughts, Fabian?
FABIAN: Yes! If I may read yours. Look at you, Vautrelle!
VAUTRELLE: (*grimacing: half-humorous*) A hopeless sight, I'm afraid!
FABIAN: The decorations, for instance, across the left side of your evening-clothes. The Ribbon of the Institute, France's highest academic award. The Grand Cross of the Legion of Honour. The Cross of War. The...
VAUTRELLE: (*he is amused at the decorations*) I wore this nonsense, believe me, only because Ninette insisted.
FABIAN: You call those decorations nonsense?
VAUTRELLE: (*deeply sincere*) With all my heart!

---
[1] "Vesti la giubba", the tenor aria from Leoncavallo's 1892 opera *Pagliacci*.

FABIAN: Then another thing! This Charles, this... decorative man-about-Paris... You call him "young" Charles, as though you yourself were elderly at thirty-six! (*insistently*) Don't you see that your wife, being very young, likes glamor—a certain gaiety?

(*Sound: door opens hurriedly.*)

NINETTE: (*fading on, hurriedly*) Hello, Michel! Hello, Doctor Fabian:

FABIAN: Madame Vautrelle!

VAUTRELLE: Where's Charles, Ninette?

(*Sound: door closes.*)

CHARLES: (*fading on*) Here, sir. Pardon us. It was very warm in here. I thought perhaps: some air, or a glass of sherbet for Ninette...

NINETTE: Oh, why pretend any longer! (*as though wanting not to hurt him*) Michel, we must talk to you.

VAUTRELLE: *Ninette! One moment!*

NINETTE: (*taken aback*) Michel! I never heard you speak like that!

VAUTRELLE: (*good-humor again*) Your face is flushed, my dear. You breathe as though you'd been running. (*quiet warning*) Whatever you were going to say, don't say it.

NINETTE: Why not?

(*Sound: crowd murmur while the orchestra tunes up*)

VAUTRELLE: We're in public, Ninette. Look at the white shirt-fronts and the elaborate gowns out there! This is the Paris Opera, holy of holies.

NINETTE: (*bursting out*) You and your respectability, I hate your respectability!... Charles, I want you to give me a divorce.

FABIAN: If you don't mind, Vautrelle, it *is* a little warm in here. If you'll excuse me now...

VAUTRELLE: Sit down, Fabian. Sit down, Ninette!

CHARLES: If you'd allow *me* to say a word, sir?

NINETTE: Yes, Charles. Tell him!

CHARLES: This isn't a sudden impulse, sir. It isn't new. We know what we're doing. We've wanted to tell you for a long time. But Ninette...

NINETTE: (*also meaning it*) I couldn't bear to hurt you, Michel. That's true! You know how much I love you!

VAUTRELLE: (*without inflection*) Yes, my dear. You've just been telling me.

NINETTE: I didn't mean that, and you know it! I *am* fond of you. But...

CHARLES: Do you ever take her out to dinner, sir? Or send her flowers? Or pay her compliments? I'm not very intelligent, Professor Vautrelle. *I* don't know anything about books. But you don't seem to know anything else.

NINETTE: (*maddened*) Books! I wish I could burn every book that... I can't stand it! I won't!

VAUTRELLE: (*bursting out*) For the love of heaven, will you stop making a scene? —Have you a programme, Fabian?

FABIAN: Yes; here at hand.

VAUTRELLE: The house-lights die away. The orchestra-leader lifts his baton. By the way, have you noticed the dark-haired woman who sings "Nedda?"
CHARLES: Can't you give us some answer, sir? (*suddenly*) What are you thinking?
VAUTRELLE: It would surprise you to know!
(*Sound: a bar or so of* "Laugh, Clown!" *then down softly, backing narration.*)

FABIAN: Not a word more was said at the opera. Afterwards, when Vautrelle's car carried us through the pale lamps of Paris out to his home in a very respectable suburb near the Forest of Marly, the silence of these people was like powder packed into a cartridge. Presently we stood in Vautrelle's library. I couldn't guess, *then*, it would lead to murder.
(*Music: heavy beat in music as it comes out on word* "Murder.")

CHARLES: (*on his dignity*) If nobody's going to say anything, perhaps I'd better go back to Paris!
NINETTE: (*agitated*) No, Charles! Darling: wait! (*tenderly*) Michel!
VAUTRELLE: (*grimly*) Say what you have to say, Ninette! Doctor Fabian here is our witness.
FABIAN: An unwilling witness, I assure you! (*distaste*) But continue!
NINETTE: (*pleading*) Michel, I didn't mean to behave so badly at the opera tonight. I—I can't think why I made a scene like that!
VAUTRELLE: (*suave, pleasant*) Can't you, Ninette? *I* can. Look at the big globe-map in front of me, on the heavy wooden stand. A touch sets the globe moving. If I strike it with my hand…
(*Sound: hand struck on globe-map; turning and creaking of globe on central pivot.*)
VAUTRELLE:—it whirls round and round so that colors and names flash past without meaning. Like your wits, Ninette.
CHARLES: (*fiercely*) Do you think we're not serious? Do you think we don't mean it?
VAUTRELLE: Of course you mean it. At the moment.
CHARLES: Will you, or won't you, give Ninette a divorce?
VAUTRELLE: Certainly I will. (*quieting their burst of relief*) Did it never occur to you, Ninette, that I might be as bored with your company as you are with mine?
NINETTE: (*crying out*) Michel!
VAUTRELLE: That *I* might be interested in another woman? That *my* wits, to take the comparison of the globe-map here…
(*Sound: hand struck on globe-map; again it spins and creaks.*)
VAUTRELLE:—might whirl and spin like that? (*quietly*) Hasn't it occurred to you?
NINETTE: (*dumbfounded*) Well! I… No, I never thought… (*quickly*) Who is she?

VAUTRELLE: Come, my dear! What difference does that make?
CHARLES: (*radiant relief*) Of course it doesn't make any difference! It solves everything! (*suddenly*) Why do *you* care, Ninette?
NINETTE: I—I don't care, of course! I'm completely indifferent! But I... I *am* fond of Michel. You know that. He's unworldly; he's a man of books. I don't want to see him make a fool of himself with... who is she?
VAUTRELLE: I pointed her out to you tonight, my dear. She sang Nedda in *Pagliacci*. A dark-haired, very enticing woman.
NINETTE: (*amazed*) Not Claudine Duclos?
VAUTRELLE: That's the woman, my dear. You never look at opera-programmes, or you'd have noticed. Claudine lives, if you recall, not five minutes' walk from here. In the Forest of Marly.
NINETTE: That woman Michel, she's *notorious*!
VAUTRELLE: (*placidly*) That's just it, my dear. (*critically*) Now you: no matter what you pretend you're not worldly.
NINETTE: Not worldly as *she* is! I should hope not!
VAUTRELLE: Claudine understands all the moods of love. Magnificently! There's a spirit of gaiety and of the carefree about her you can never understand. (*warming up*) You have no idea how a man, especially a man of books who can find intelligence elsewhere, craves for these things.
NINETTE: (*bursting out*) She ought to be killed:
CHARLES: (*also wrought up*) No. It's your husband who ought to be killed!
VAUTRELLE: (*mocking*) Why are *you* so shocked, Charles? Everybody knows you as the conqueror of foolish women, the Don Juan of the...
CHARLES: I don't pretend to be what I'm not! Your so-called "respectability"...
VAUTRELLE: You're jealous, Charles. Your own wits, like this globe-map—!
(*Sound: hand, and creaking spin of globe.*)
VAUTRELLE: Jealousy's the root of your character. As for Ninette, here...
NINETTE: If you'll excuse me, I have a violent headache and I'm going upstairs. Charles, darling! I'll 'phone you in the morning. (*fading off*) Now excuse me, please.
(*Sound: off, door opens.*)
VAUTRELLE: (*calling softly*) Ninette!
NINETTE: (*very coldly*) Yes, Michel?
VAUTRELLE: Presently, my dear, I'm going for a walk in the Forest of Marly. Near the clay-pigeon range and the bridle-path. You don't mind if I'm rather late?
NINETTE: (*icy indifference*) I don't in the least mind what you do, Michel. (*bursting out, near tears*) *I hate you*! Good night!
(*Sound: door slams.*)
VAUTRELLE: As for you, Charles, it's getting late. You'd better drive my car

back to Paris and return it in the morning.
CHARLES: (*furious*) You think you're a strategist, don't you?
VAUTRELLE: (*hitting back*) On the contrary, Charles. *You're* the strategist.
CHARLES: What do you mean by that?
VAUTRELLE: You appear, unexpectedly, in our box at the opera. You're dressed informally; wearing a topcoat; and the travelling cap you're twisting in your hands now. Clearly, young man, you're "going away forever." Or you tell Ninette so. *She* dissolves in tears, and… *You'd better leave now, Charles!*
CHARLES: Thanks! I'll come back tomorrow morning. (*fading*) Don't trouble to show me out!
(*Sound: door opens and closes sharply.*)
VAUTRELLE: (*abruptly; steeling himself; nearly breaking down*) God help me! I couldn't have kept up that pretense much longer!
(*Sound: pack of cards riffled together, then straightened out and tapped on wooden table.*)
FABIAN: No. I don't think you could have.
VAUTRELLE: (*bitterly: towards himself*) And all this unpleasant time, Fabian, you've been sitting at that table with a pack of cards. Listening! As I asked you to! Because… *could* you see through my little game?
FABIAN: I think so. This dark-haired opera-singer, this Claudine Duclos…
VAUTRELLE: *I never met the woman in my life!*
FABIAN: You pretend to be in love with Claudine, and watch its effect on Ninette?
VAUTRELLE: Yes! What else can I do? I love Ninette! (*hesitating*) It may be Charles is right. I really *am* the dull stodgy, respectable…
FABIAN: (*cutting in*) It takes a good man, my friend, to have as little conceit as *you* have!
VAUTRELLE: (*puzzled*) What's conceit got to do with it? I love her. I can only… give me that pack of cards, with you? Thanks. Once, Fabian…
(*Sound: sharp riffle of cards.*)
VAUTRELLE: Once I was a fair amateur at sleight-of-hand. Observe, now! The five changes to the ace; the ace to—the black knave. Curse the cards!
(*Sound: the cards fly outwards, as though pressed and released by finger and thumb.*)
VAUTRELLE: I can only play my poor tricks like the clown. Now where's my hat? I must go over to Claudine's villa in the Forest of Marly!
FABIAN: Were you serious about that? *Why* must you go?
VAUTRELLE: Because Claudine knows nothing about this! She's got to know. If she lives up to her reputation, she'll think it's a great joke. If necessary, I'll bribe her.
FABIAN: Suppose she isn't there?
VAUTRELLE: She *is* there. I've made careful inquiries at the Opera. She's re-

hearsing "Juliet"—"with," they told me, "a property dagger covered with false jewels." (*agitated*) Where's my hat?

FABIAN: (*also agitated*) Listen to me, Michel. *Don't go!*

VAUTRELLE: Why not?

FABIAN: Because I think all four of you are headed for disaster!

(*Music: chord.*)

FABIAN: And, on that same night, disaster struck.

(*Music: hits hard, then down and behind.*)

FABIAN: In my bedroom, at Vautrelle's house, I couldn't sleep. I saw the dawn come up in mist. At that hushed hour I dressed and went downstairs. You know these premonitions! Some workmen, in the Forest of Marly, told me where to find Claudine Duclos' villa. I emerged into a large open space, amid mist-hung trees; there was a clay-pigeon range, beyond it a bridle path, beyond the bridle-path a small villa with its back towards me. There were three pairs of long windows at the back. Even as I ran forward, I could see Michel Vautrelle standing outside one window. I could hear his fist pounding against the glass...

(*Music: out.*)

(*Sound: off, fist pounding glass; and Vautrelle's voice.*)

VAUTRELLE: (*calling, off*) Claudine! Answer me! Are you all right?

(*Sound: glass-pounding fades on as though microphone approached with Fabian*)

VAUTRELLE: Claudine! Answer me! Are you all right?

FABIAN: Gently, man! Gently!

VAUTRELLE: (*startled*) Fabian! What the devil are *you* doing here?

FABIAN: For your own sake, what are *you* doing here? Have you been here all night?

VAUTRELLE: (*surprised*) Did I... No! Can't you see I've changed my evening clothes for this suit? I came back here only ten minutes ago!

FABIAN: Why did you come back here at all?

VAUTRELLE: (*pause*) I can't tell you that. There's a—a fact you *didn't* notice last night. And there's something wrong at this villa now! Look at the windows!

FABIAN: What about them?

VAUTRELLE: They're all locked on the inside. The folding shutters, very thin steel, are closed inside that! But you can see bright light in the tiny slits of the shutters. Every room is still lighted in there! Besides, Claudine's mood last night...

FABIAN: (*pressing him*) Ah! Your meeting with her last night. What did you say to Claudine?

VAUTRELLE: (*on edge*) I can't understand these temperamental singers!

FABIAN: Never mind! What happened?
VAUTRELLE: When I got here, she was in one of her suicidal moods. They'd warned me about that at the Opera. Wanted to kill herself; no reason at all! Box of sleeping tablets; a sharp knife as well as that stage dagger. Then—all of a sudden—she was as gay as Mistinguett! Coy... smiling...
FABIAN: (*urgency of friendship; not of anger*) You're not telling the whole truth, Vautrelle! *What is it?*
VAUTRELLE: Well, she took quite a fancy to me. She gave me—if you laugh I'll kill you!—She gave me a key to the front door of this villa.
FABIAN: A key to the front door?!
VAUTRELLE: Yes!
FABIAN: But if you've got a key to the front door, then why were you—(*stops abruptly; then sharply*) Never mind! Round to the front door! Hurry!
(*Music: short, sharp musical bridge*)
(*Sound: steps on hardwood*)
VAUTRELLE: This is the main hall of the villa, Fabian. Now, straight ahead, at the back! That's the door of the sitting-room. Where I talked to her! And there's a thread of light under the door-sill!
(*Sound: footsteps stop.*)
VAUTRELLE: Try the knob!
(*Sound: knob turned and rattled.*)
FABIAN: It's locked, all right! On the inside. It's an ordinary housekey, not a Yale lock. Wait till I stoop down—Yes; the key's in the look!
VAUTRELLE: Can you—see anything inside the room?
FABIAN: No; not with the key in the lock! Now we'll open this door by... That's curious! You've got a newspaper in your coat pocket!
VAUTRELLE: What's curious about that? It's yesterday's paper!
(*Sound: newspaper business: behind, to follow.*)
FABIAN: (*dismissing it*) Anyway! I want you to open up the newspaper... That's it! Now take one sheet of the paper, and push it under the sill of the door into the room. —Only a little way! That's it!
VAUTRELLE: What are you going to do?
FABIAN: I take *this* pencil; watch! I press it against the end of the key from outside... I push it through the lock towards the inside...
(*Sound: rattle as of medium-heavy key falling on newspaper against the floor.*)
FABIAN: And the key falls inside: *on* the newspaper. Now draw the newspaper towards you, and you'll draw the key under the door into your hand. Gently! That's it. Have you got the key?
VAUTRELLE: Yes! Here you are! But, Fabian! Listen to me!
FABIAN: Key in the lock; turned—!
(*Sound: rattle of key; click of lock.*)
VAUTRELLE: She was gay enough when *I* left her! She meant to go horseback-riding this morning. She—

FABIAN: (*door opens*)
VAUTRELLE: Name of the name of heaven! *No!*

(*Music: sharp chord; then softly under.*)
FABIAN: Facing us, sitting bolt upright in an armchair, her eyes wide open, was a small dark-haired woman in a flowered dressing gown. The glass jewels on the handle of a dagger, projecting from the dressing-gown just over her heart, glittered red and blue. Behind her—as we looked into those wide-open dead eyes—were the two windows with their steel shutters barred on the inside.
(*Music: out*)

FABIAN: Vautrelle! This *is* Claudine Duclos?
VAUTRELLE: Yes. (*controlled, strong, easy voice*) And I won't writhe with uncertainty now; because I *know*. She killed herself!
FABIAN: I don't think she did! (*sharply forestalling objection*) Wait! One moment! (*as though concentrating*) Walls of the room papered dark-red. Thick carpet. Grand piano. Chairs; and across one chair...
VAUTRELLE: Those are only her riding clothes! She brought them in here last night!
FABIAN: (*considering*) Leather boots, jodhpurs, tweed coat, large cap. Nothing here.
VAUTRELLE: I ask you a sincere question, Fabian!
FABIAN: Ask it, then!
VAUTRELLE: This room has one door and two windows. All are securely locked on the inside. Then why do you say this is—murder?
FABIAN: Look at the woman's body! She was killed with the stage dagger; see its false jewels gleam! You saw the dagger last night?
VAUTRELLE: Yes! I told you so!
FABIAN: Was the dagger sharp?
VAUTRELLE: No; naturally not! Such things are...
FABIAN: (*cutting in*) You said she had in her possession a box of sleeping tablets and also a sharp knife. Having those things, would anybody commit suicide with a blunt dagger?
VAUTRELLE: That may be clever! It's not evidence!
FABIAN: True! But just over here, on the top of the grand piano...
VAUTRELLE: There's nothing on the top of the grand piano!
FABIAN: Oh, yes! (*slight pause*) Many particles of—iron-filings! Yes! Certainly iron-filings. And beside them—a large file.
(*Sound: loud jangle from keys of piano, as though someone had stumbled and put a hand on keyboard.*)
VAUTRELLE: (*tense coolness*) Forgive me, my dear sir! I slipped and fell against the piano!

FABIAN: A slip? Yes. —Someone in haste forgot this file and the soft iron-filings. If it means what I think it means, the murderer could leave behind him a room locked up on the inside. And it was done in a completely new way!
VAUTRELLE: You seem to admire the murderer's intelligence!
FABIAN: I do. But... (*dropping his guard; appealing*) Vautrelle, I'm your friend! I want to help you! *I* won't betray you!—Did you kill her?
VAUTRELLE: (*steadfastly*) No, I did not.
FABIAN: Are you shielding anyone who did?
(*Sound: sharp rapping on glass, as though beyond thin shutters.*)
VAUTRELLE: There's someone rapping on the window beyond those shutters. You're not going to...?
FABIAN: Open the window? Of course. Come along with me. —Now! We'll lift the light bar...fold back the shutters to see who's outside...
(*Sound: both shutters are of bars of such very thin metal—as in all French houses—that there is only a creak and scrape.*)
VAUTRELLE: It's Ninette! Don't unlock the window!
(*Sound: French window unlocked; pushed open.*)
NINETTE: Thank you, Doctor Fabian.
VAUTRELLE: (*agitated*) Ninette, have you completely gone out of your mind?
(*Sound: horses, three or four, galloping off, fading in behind—*)
NINETTE: Yes! Completely! That's why I'm here! (*forcing calm*) I want to see her.
VAUTRELLE: That's impossible!
NINETTE: (*calmly*) Let me enter, please. (*breaking off, startled*) What's that?
(*Sound: horses in, then fading*)
VAUTRELLE: It's only a few early-morning horsemen. Galloping on a bridle-path where they shouldn't. (*raising voice*) Keep away from this villa, you fools!
FABIAN: Come; they're women! From the neckties and bowler hats, I thought they were—(*he stops suddenly*) Ye-es!
NINETTE: Will you let me come in, Michel?
VAUTRELLE: (*despairing*) If you insist. Yes!
NINETTE: You don't know how hard it is for a woman to meet—the other one. You feel you've got the right on your side; you rage until you're nearly blind; and yet—(*stops; quiet voice*) I came here to tell her, very simply, that if she sees Michel again I'll kill her. I'll...
VAUTRELLE: Ninette! Keep away from that armchair! Don't look at what's in the arm-chair!
NINETTE: (*recoiling; horror*) Oh, no—no!
FABIAN: She's been stabbed through the heart, madame. You notice?
NINETTE: I...let go my arm, Doctor Fabian! Please!
FABIAN: And not much blood. That means a direct, savage heart-wound. —

Didn't you *want* to kill her, a moment ago?
(*Sound: faintly, off, two horses trot past window.*)
NINETTE: (*no pause*) I...I thought I did, yes! Just as I thought I was in love with Charles D'Arville. But I'm not. I never was! (*breaking*) *Michel! Darling! Why did you have to kill her?*
VICTOR: (*slightly off*) Exactly and precisely, madame! Why *did* he have to kill her?
NINETTE: (*presumably back turned*) *Who spoke then?*
VICTOR: (*fading in*) I spoke, madame. Your husband knows me well. I am Alphonse Victor. The Commissary of Police for this district.
(*Sound: far off, report of shotgun; pause, then another shot for second barrel*)
VICTOR: (*sharply*) Be calm, madame. That noise was only some early sportsmen practicing at clay-pigeons. (*grimly amused*) *Clay* pigeons, eh? Real pigeons. (*swelling*) I, the Commissary of Police—
VAUTRELLE: (*weary*) It's all right, Victor! Do what you have to do! But...do you always wear your tri-colored sash at six o'clock in the morning?
VICTOR: I do, Professor Vautrelle, when someone telephones me at five-thirty—
NINETTE: (*startled*) Telephones you?
VICTOR: —and informs me there is death at this villa. But I don't approach openly; not I! Not when I see Professor Vautrelle rapping on the window. And this Doctor Fabian following him! I wait. I listen. I follow you both through the front door to here. I have heard every word you said!
NINETTE: What are you going to do?
VICTOR: I must arrest your husband, Madame Vautrelle.
VAUTRELLE: I didn't kill her. On my word of honor, I didn't kill her! (*as though thinking aloud, but clearly spoken*) A suicide: that's bad enough! But the scandal of a murder, with Ninette involved in it...!
VICTOR: (*cynically*) The good professor is very, very respectable! But a case of murder—
FABIAN: (*hitting hard*) Can you prove it was murder, Mr. Commissary?
VICTOR: (*taken aback*) What's that, Doctor Fabian? You yourself said it was murder!
FABIAN: I said it; true! But can you prove it? You can't convict this man, or anybody else, until you can show how he killed a woman in a locked room!
VICTOR: Do *you* know how?
FABIAN: Yes! I think I do.
VICTOR: (*beginning threat, swelling*) For obstructing justice, here in France...!
FABIAN: You shall have your justice! If you grant me an hour or two before you arrest him! In return, I'll give you two very large clues, like... like that double-barreled shotgun out there!
VICTOR: (*in agony*) Well! I...(*barking*) What are the two large clues?

FABIAN: First, the heavy file and the iron-filings over on the piano. It's soft iron, remember; not steel! Now search the room for the head of the key.
VICTOR: (*bewildered, angry*) Now what the devil can I make of *that*? Give me your second clue!
FABIAN: Does a woman in France ever wear a cloth cap with riding clothes? —Both barrels, Mr. Commissary!
(*Sound: off, two reports of shotgun spaced, then… two whacks of a fist on a table, spaced like reports of shotgun.*)
VICTOR: (*after fist has been heard*) One—two! Like my fist on this table, Doctor Fabian! Your clues are not good sense!
FABIAN: Don't get excited, Mr. Commissary!

VICTOR: We sit, now, in the fine library of Professor Vautrelle. It is evening! You ask for "an hour or two" to investigate; and it's evening! What have you been doing?
FABIAN: I was watching the horseback-riding. Excellent evidence!
VICTOR: (*end of patience*) This goes too far!
FABIAN: (*fiercely*) Victor, I'm not joking! Listen to me! Vautrelle, and Ninette, and young Charles D'Arville; he's the—well! admirer…
VICTOR: (*crushing*) The police too hear gossip, good doctor!
FABIAN: They're out in the hall now. There's another emotional row; Ninette is frantic. Before they come in here… Can you guess who telephoned you this morning? And told you there was death at the villa?
VICTOR: No! Only a disguised voice! Who did telephone?
FABIAN: Vautrelle himself.
VICTOR: (*amazed*) Vautrelle?
FABIAN: Think for a moment! When *I* arrived there, he was pounding at the window and saying there was something wrong in the villa. But if he had *really* wanted to find out, he had a front-door key in his pocket. No, no, Victor! The poor devil lost his head. He telephoned you, he finally chose me, because…
VICTOR: I don't see it! *Why*?
FABIAN: Because he needed a witness, he needed a dupe, when his "locked room" was opened!
VICTOR: Then he *is* the murderer!
FABIAN: (*instantly*) Did I say he was the murderer?
(*Sound: off, door opens, with effect of bang.*)
NINETTE: (*fading a little on*) Charles, don't follow me! Please! I have nothing more to say!
CHARLES: (*nearly frantic*) I want an explanation, that's all! I'm entitled to one, Ninette! Why have you changed your mind? What's wrong? (*abruptly*) Oh! I didn't know there was anybody in the room.
FABIAN: Come over here to the table. Both of you! —That's it!

NINETTE: (*uneasily*) What do you want?
FABIAN: I have here...
(*Sound: medium-weight key lands on wooden table.*)
FABIAN: An ordinary indoor key. It's a type common here; and in England or America. It will fit any door inside the house.
NINETTE: Is it from...*that woman's* villa?
FABIAN: Yes. It is. Now I show you a second key...
(*Sound: rattle on table.*)
FABIAN: A second key, just like the first. Except for—what's wrong with it? Speak up, Charles!
CHARLES: (*fascinated but puzzled*) Well! The second key hasn't got a head. Nothing to turn it with! It looks as though the head has been filed off.
NINETTE: *Filed*?
FABIAN: Yes, madame! It's soft iron. (*sharply*) Last night, madame, your husband found himself alone in a murder-room with a dead woman. He wanted, desperately wanted, to prove her death was suicide. How did he try to prove it?
NINETTE: He *didn't!*
FABIAN: Oh, yes. The real key of that room was already there. He took a second key—from another room in the villa—and filed off the head. It was a dummy key. Do you follow that?
VICTOR: But what was the purpose?
FABIAN: He went out of the murder-room, and closed the door. He locked the door from outside, and put the real key in his pocket.
CHARLES: But in that case... there was no key in the lock!
FABIAN: Exactly! So he took the dummy key, without a head, and pushed it through the lock into place. From outside it looked exactly like a real key!
VICTOR: (*triumphant*) And now, doctor, I *do* understand!
FABIAN: When Vautrelle and I examined the door this morning, I thought it was the real key. He even *asked* me if I saw anything? He was all prepared, newspaper in coat-pocket, for the obvious way to open the door. When I pressed at the key with a pencil, the dummy key fell inside. When he drew the newspaper under the door, he palmed the dummy key and handed me the real one. As he showed me with cards, he's very good at sleight-of-hand!
NINETTE: But he didn't kill her. I know he didn't! (*crying out*) Michel! Darling! Where's Michel?
VAUTRELLE: (*fading on*) I am here, my dear. I have been listening. (*bitterly*) I went across to see Claudine last night; and if they insist I killed her—
FABIAN: Nonsense! You know she was already dead when you got there!
VICTOR: *What's that?*
FABIAN: Somebody got to the villa before he did. And so, on the spur of the moment, he invented this locked room to shield the murderer!

VICTOR: (*sinister*) There is only one person he would shield!
NINETTE: (*pause*) (*terrified*) Stop! Don't look at *me*? Why are you all looking at *me*?
FABIAN: Tell me, madame. Do women, in France, ever wear a cloth cap with riding clothes?
NINETTE: (*hesitation; then blurting*) No! Of course not!
FABIAN: True! I noticed the bowler hats when those women galloped past the window. But on Claudine's riding-clothes—remember, Vautrelle?—lay a large cap. Claudine, with her small head, could never have worn it. It was a man's cap: left behind, unnoticed! Here's the cap now, with a name inside!
NINETTE: But only one person wore a cap last night! That cap belongs to…
FABIAN: To the real murder. *Mr. Charles D'Arville*!
(*Sound: thud of globe overturned.*)
VAUTRELLE: (*cynically bitter*) Don't kick over the globe-map, Charles. We all know your tantrums!
CHARLES: Vautrelle, you swine! You knew what Claudine and I had been to each other. (*he stops*) You knew that all the time!
VAUTRELLE: Of course! That was the great joke! When I said I was in love with another woman, you were all approval until I told her name. Then you went half-mad. You killed her out of jealousy, even though you'd left her for Ninette. I told you the root of your character was jealousy. But I didn't realize you'd kill her. Then, I had to shield you because Ninette might have been talked about.
FABIAN: Your cap was there, Charles. Your front-door key was still in the spring-lock…
VAUTRELLE: And I forgot everything, because I'm not a good criminal! I tried to manage the least scandal, the most respectable suicide. But I couldn't even manage…
FABIAN: The most respectable murder!
(*Music up to closing narration.*)

FABIAN: And when he told that story in a French witness-box, Michel Vautrelle received only applause. Such sensitivity for the highly-respectable is deeply cherished in France. (*changing mood*) But next week, as our luxury-liner *Maurevania* sails on, I shall glance back to another story I remember from Egypt. Of invisible death, apparently supernatural, that—again apparently—destroyed a girl as though she had never existed. And so, when I tell you the tale called "The Curse of the Bronze Lamp" will you join me in *Cabin B-13*?

(*Sound: ship's whistles*)
(*Music: out*)

Notes for the Curious

This play is centered on a theme that Carr would return to throughout his career, the twists and turns of love.

Carr's own love life was sometimes more complicated than it should have been and a man torn between the love of his wife and the love of another woman features in many of his stories *"There is one woman he loves. There is another he desires"*. In 1954, Carr planned a "Carter Dickson" novel with this dilemma at its core. In the novel, to be titled *The Other Dear Charmer*, a present-day actor decides to mount a new production of a nineteenth century play, opting for one of the old "blood and thunder" thrillers on the basis that, as Carr put it, *"pathos and comedy differ in different generations but fear is much the same at any time"*. On the opening night, the actor would make *"his entrance: to a burst of applause, yes, and on the proper set; but amid actors he has never seen before, and under the scorching heat of gas footlights"*. Somehow the actor has been transported in time, and Carr's intention was then to embroil him in a *"mystery he must solve to save his own neck"* while juggling relationships with *"two women, one his wife and one his leading lady in the play"*. Some elements of this planned novel, including the double relationship, were carried into *Fear Is the Same* (1956), set in the 18th century.

While the story of "The Most Respectable Murder" is unique to *Cabin B-13*, Professor Michel Vautrelle is perhaps related to Edouard Vautrelle whose mysterious death was investigated by Henri Bencolin in Carr's first novel *It Walks by Night* (1930).

Carr would incorporate the locked-room gimmick and the relationships between the characters of the *Cabin B-13* radio play in *The Dead Man's Knock* (1958), a Dr Fell novel which also incorporates some elements of the *Appointment with Fear* radio play with that title, first broadcast in 1955.

The Curse of the Bronze Lamp

(*Sound: a ship's whistle*)
(*Music: in and behind*)
ANNOUNCER: *Cabin B-13.* Tonight, from his notebooks of mystery and murder, ship's surgeon Dr Fabian tells you the story of "The Curse of the Bronze Lamp".

(*Music: accent and continue*)
FABIAN: A curse on an Egyptian tomb? We've heard that before. But many have forgotten their terror when the ancient tomb of Herihor was opened—when one man lay dead—another man, near death—and a girl, Helen Loring, was apparently blown to dust as though she never existed!
(*Music: fades behind*)

FABIAN: On that day in 1939, Doctor Gilray, of Cambridge, was the first person who entered that tomb. As he opened the it, Doctor Gilray was stung in the hand by a scorpion. That was why—in the sitting room of a suite at the Mena House Hotel, on the edge of the desert near the Great Pyramid—Helen Loring and Chris Farrell waited uneasily in the yellow dusk, for the telephone to ring.
CHRIS: (*on edge; but soothing her*) Helen!
HELEN: Yes, Chris?
CHRIS: I wish you'd sit down, my dear. And don't keep looking at the 'phone!
HELEN: Whatever you say, Chris. But if anything did happen to Doctor Gilray...
CHRIS: (*almost amused*) Helen! A scorpion-bite!
HELEN: I know!
CHRIS: Most people get their ideas of scorpion-bites from fiction. Actually it's no more dangerous than...(*he himself is muddled: on edge*)... well, I can't think of a comparison! It's unpleasant; but not dangerous.
HELEN: Have you seen the newspapers, dear?
CHRIS: Have I *seen* them? They're all over the floor!
HELEN: Chris, look here. This is what the *Cairo Times* quotes my own father as saying!
(*Sound: rustle of someone searching among papers*)
HELEN: Listen, Chris! (*reading*) "The Earl of Severn, interviewed today, stated that all the objects found in the tomb of Herihor, priest-king of Egypt at the end of the Twentieth Dynasty, were now at the Cairo Museum. The..."
CHRIS: (*grimly*) Do they mention any exception to that? The little lamp here

on the table now??

HELEN: Yes, they do! (*reading*) "The single exception is a low bronze lamp, shaped like a flattish gravy-bowl, in which the ancient Egyptians put oil and a floating wick. This lamp was presented by the Egyptian Government to Lady Helen Loring, Lord Severn's daughter. No danger or curse, he hopes and believes"... (*accenting it*) *hopes* and believes, Chris!... "attaches to..."

(*Sound: paper crumpled up.*)

HELEN: Oh, it's so *idiotic!*

CHRIS: I know it's idiotic, Helen! That's why you mustn't let it upset you!

HELEN: (*earnestly*) It doesn't upset me, really. Look at the lamp on the table now!

CHRIS: It's no beauty, is it?

HELEN: It's old, and ugly, and withered-looking. It's no more deadly than an ordinary lamp. But...

CHRIS: (*quickly*) But what?

HELEN: Do you think I ought to go back to England now? With Doctor Gilray in the hospital?

CHRIS: There's no good you can do here! You know that! Your father and I will follow in a week!

HELEN: Chris, you can book a reservation for tomorrow's plane. (*appealing*) Will you go back with me?

CHRIS: There's nothing on earth I'd like better! But we have some business to wind up in Cairo...

HELEN: (*much in love*) Chris, do you really love me? (*mocking, but tender*) Or do you, as a good Yankee, object to marrying the daughter of a British peer?

CHRIS: (*desperately serious, but quiet*) Listen, Helen. When you talk about my being in love with you...

HELEN: Yes, darling?

CHRIS: Don't ever joke about it. I'm so much in love with you that I haven't even got a sense of humor left. (*fiercely*) If anything ever—(*he stops abruptly*)

HELEN: Were you thinking: "what if anything ever happened to me?"

CHRIS: (*recovering*) No! Of course not! (*puzzled*) Why are we talking like this, anyway? Doctor Gilray's all right! He'll be out of the hospital this evening!

(*Sound: slightly off: phone rings: double-ringing tone.*)

HELEN: That'll be... my father. From the hospital.

CHRIS: Wait, Helen! Stay where you are! I'll get it!

(*Sound: phone picked up.*)

CHRIS: Hello! Lord Severn?

SEVERN: (*filter: elderly, clear but tired*) Yes. Is that you, Chris?

CHRIS: Yes, sir! What's the news?

SEVERN: (*pause*) Doctor Gilray is dead.
(*Sound: a little off, thud as of some smallish but heavy object striking floor.*)
CHRIS: (*away from phone*) Helen! Did that bronze lamp fall off the table?
HELEN: (*a little off*) Only because I yanked at the table-cover! I heard what Dad said!
CHRIS: Lord Severn, that's impossible! A scorpion-bite?
SEVERN: (*wearily*) It's a question of what the doctors call the toleratory condition.
CHRIS: Toleratory condition? How do you mean?
SEVERN: Some people can throw it off as no worse than a bad sting by a wasp. Others can't. Poor Gilray couldn't.
HELEN: (*fading on*) Chris, let me speak to him! —Dad!
SEVERN: (*blankly*) Poor Gilray! Poor old Gilray!
HELEN: (*anguished*) I know, Dad! —And do you realize what they'll say *now*?
SEVERN: They're already saying it, my dear. Danger to *you*. (*satirically*) And— "the curse of the bronze lamp".
HELEN: Chris, this has got to stop! It's got to stop!

(*Music: in and behind.*)
FABIAN: And that, next morning, was what Helen said when she and Chris Parrell stood on the portable steps of the big Imperial Airways plane. The four-engined plane, gleaming silver at Cairo Airport, was besieged by so many reporters that Bill Hastings, of Argus News Service, acted as spokesman.
(*Music: out, into*)

(*Sound: plane-engines are idling, off; mutter of voices in background, coming up or down at times with approval or mirth*)
HASTINGS: (*40, polite tenacious, no fool*) (*slightly off*) Just a couple more questions, Lady Helen! And you too, Mr. Farrell!
CHRIS: (*addressing all, urgently*) Look, boys! could you hurry it up? They want to take way these steps and get us into the plane!
HASTINGS: Okay, Mr. Farrell! —Lady Helen! Could we have a picture of you holding up the bronze lamp?
(*Sound: hum of approval.*)
HELEN: (*addressing them all*) I'm sorry, gentlemen! The bronze lamp is packed away in my luggage!
HASTINGS: What are your plans when you get back to England, Lady Helen?
HELEN: I—I'm going to open Severn Hall.
HASTINGS: Severn Hall? That's the ancestral mansion? Has it been closed?
HELEN: Yes! It's been closed for two years. (*eager, to get away from subject of bronze lamp*) The only person there is old Benson; he's the butler; but I expect he can get together some kind of staff!

HASTINGS: But your father's staying here in Cairo. Is that it?
HELEN: He's following later! He...
HASTINGS: Is there any truth in the report, Lady Helen, that your father's too sick to be moved?
CHRIS: (*dumbfounded*) He's not sick at all! Only worried! Don't make things worse for the sake of a newspaper story!
HASTINGS: We won't, Mr. Farrell. But I can quote you as saying: things *are* pretty bad?
(*Sound: plane motors rev up—then way down, as.*)
HELEN: (*frantic, near tears*) Gentlemen! Listen to me! (*wait for motors down*) You can quote *me* as saying there is no truth in *any* report. You can also quote me as saying...
CHRIS: (*low voice*) Helen, please get into the plane!
HELEN: (*unheeding*) What I want to see most, when I get back to England, is my own room at Severn Hall. I'm going to put the bronze lamp on the mantelpiece. I'm going to write an account of the real facts. When I get back to that room...
ALIM BEY: (*loud, sinister, 45, French accent*) You will never reach that room, mademoiselle.
HELEN: (*startled*) Who spoke then?
(*Sound: group mutter rises with a sort of "what-the-hell-who's-this?" intonation—then three footsteps up wooden steps.*)
ALIM BEY: (*close on*) Forgive me, mademoiselle, if I walk up three steps; and tower over you like a vulture in a red tarboosh. It is for your own good!
HELEN: Are you—are you from a French newspaper, or something?
ALIM BEY: (*wryly humorous*) Alas, no, I am Alim Bey. A poor scholar of—let us say—mixed blood. (*changing tone*) And I entreat you not to take this stolen relic from Egypt!
HELEN: (*amazed*) Stolen relic?
ALIM BEY: Could your archaeologist-friend Mr. Farrell decipher the inscription on the lamp?
CHRIS: Yes. And I'm sick of it! It only says...
ALIM BEY: (*towering: quoting*) "Rich in years, strong in victories, Lord of the Diadems." (*breaking off*) This man whose tomb you rifled, *mademoiselle*, was no mere king. He was a high-priest of Ammon, skilled in dark arts. He will follow you.
(*Sound: crowd-mutter rises, with one suggestion of suppressed guffaw of mirth*)
HASTINGS: (*feeling this is too much*) Now take it easy, Alim Bey!
ALIM BEY: (*voice lifting*) You smile, gentlemen of the press. You will not smile, I tell you, when this young lady is blown to dust as though she had never existed.
HELEN: (*crying out*) It's all nonsense! I'll *prove* it's all nonsense!

CHRIS: (*grimly*) Will you get off these steps, Alim Bey, or shall I throw you off?
ALIM BEY: She will never reach that room alive!
(*Sound: plane engines throb to life, then die away*)

FABIAN: No untoward incident marked Helen's and Chris' journey to England, From Croydon, they went to London and spent three days there. Then… Ancient Severn Hall, in Gloucestershire. Five o'clock on a dark April afternoon, with rain falling. Helen's car, with Chris Farrell at the wheel and Helen beside him—still, clutching the bronze lamp!—turned in past the lodge-gates. Up the long driveway, through trees, towards Severn Hall under a flicker of lightning…

(*Sound: car driving very faintly under, and slow tick-tick of windshield wiper.*)
HELEN: Only a few minutes, Chris! Only a few minutes now!
CHRIS: (*cold: aloof*) Yes, Helen. Then you'll be home. (*half bursting out*) Blast this windshield-wiper! It sounds like a—like a clock ticking.
HELEN: (*suddenly: pleading*) Chris, what's wrong? What have I done to offend you?
CHRIS: (*telling the lie coldly*) There's nothing wrong, Helen.
HELEN: Darling, there *is*!
CHRIS: (*with an effort*) I suppose you don't remember what happened in London. You don't realize you scared me green!
HELEN: (*wretchedly*) I know, Chris! But—(*she stops*)
CHRIS: (*on edge*) When we got to London, *I* thought you wanted to come straight on here. Oh, no! We stay at the Savoy. The next morning, I 'phone your room; and you've disappeared.
HELEN: Chris, I left a note for you! I said I'd come back!
CHRIS: (*unheeding*) You stay away for three days. Then, this morning, you turn up in your hotel-room again. Pale as death! Won't say where you've been. What do you think *I* was imagining, all that time?
HELEN: Chris, I'm so sorry! But there was something—I had to learn. (*floundering*) What *did* you imagine?
CHRIS: First about that lamp you've got in your hands. Then—well! Some love-affair or other…
HELEN: (*amazed*) Some… You *know* that's not true!
CHRIS: (*deflated*) Yes. I'm the one who ought to apologize. It's nerves. But… look ahead! There's Severn Hall!
HELEN: (*nostalgia*) Lights shining out on wet ivy… towers lost up in the rain… home!
CHRIS: You're safe, Helen!
HELEN: (*soothing him*) Of course, my dear!
CHRIS: Nothing could possibly hurt you now!
ALIM BEY: (*filter*) She will be blown to dust as though she had never existed.

CHRIS: (*trying to laugh*) Don't stare at me, Helen. It was just something I heard in my imagination. *You're* looking very uneasy!
HELEN: (*suddenly*) I was—I was thinking of Benson. (*also trying to laugh*) *You* know him! He looks like a butler in a comic-paper, bald head and corporation and all. But he's been a second father to me ever since I can remember. And I forgot to send him a telegram and say we were coming!
CHRIS: Well? Is that bad?
HELEN: (*expostulating*) Oh, Chris! —He'll want to line up the servants in the main hall, everybody from the chauffeur to the kitchen-maid, to welcome us! He'll be so shocked that...
CHRIS: (*almost amused*) Never mind the formalities, Helen! —Round in front of the terrace; and here we are.
(*Sound: car stops. rain can now be heard distinctly.*)
HELEN: (*in triumph*) I said I was going to accomplish it, Chris...
(*Sound: car door opens; light footsteps jump out on gravel; car door closes.*)
CHRIS: Easy, now! Why jump out like that?
HELEN: I'm going to run straight up to my room! I'm going to put this bronze lamp on the mantelpiece! (*fading off*) And then, Chris... then—!
CHRIS: Helen, wait! I've only got to get the luggage out of the car! Wait!
(*Sound: kicking—not heavily—at heavy door.*)
CHRIS: (*calling*) Won't *somebody* open this front door, even if I have to kick at it? I'm loaded down with suitcases. I... Ah, that's better?
(*Sound: heavy knob is turned; large door, suggesting oak door thick and high, is opened.*)
CHRIS: (*affectionately*) Hel-lo, Benson! How are you?
BENSON: (*astonished but pleased*) Mr. Chris, sir! This is a real pleasure!
CHRIS: Same to you, Benson! Would you mind giving me a hand with these suitcases?
BENSON: (*quickly; reproachfully*) Mr. Chris! Allow me!
CHRIS: You do enough work, Benson. Just take the two under my arms; and we'll put 'em down on the floor... there!... while I close the front door.
(*Sound: front door closed. Sound is now on echo.*)
CHRIS: Same old stone hall like a cathedral-vault! Only—mummy-cases instead of armor!
BENSON: Yes, sir. But... Lady Helen?
CHRIS: Helen? What about her?
BENSON: (*taken aback*) Well, sir—where is she?
CHRIS: *Where is she*?
BENSON: Yes, sir!
CHRIS: But she walked in through this door just before I did!
BENSON: Forgive me, Mr. Chris; but... she didn't.
CHRIS: (*suddenly; trying not to get rattled*) Now wait a minute, Benson!

Let's get this straight! As soon as we drove up here, Helen rushed into the house with that bronze lamp...

BENSON: (*breathing relief*) Then... that explains it, sir!

CHRIS: Explains what?

BENSON: Well, sir! (*with dignity*) I fear I had no intimation of your arrival...

CHRIS: I know; I'm sorry!

BENSON: And I was in my pantry, without collar or tie, when the gate-keeper 'phoned from the lodge. He said a car was coming up the drive. It was a minute or two before I reached this hall.

CHRIS: And Helen must have gone up before you get here?

BENSON: Exactly, sir! (*shaken*) But I confess with all this talk in the newspapers...

CHRIS: You were scared? So was I! You ought to have seen her clutch that lamp, Benson! She wouldn't have dropped it, she wouldn't have let go, if all the gods in Egypt had grabbed her. She... (*pause, then exclamation*) Benson!

BENSON: (*jumping slightly*) Yes, sir!

CHRIS: Look there. On the table by the window! Where the lightning just flared through!

BENSON: (*slight pause*) Sir, it couldn't be...?

CHRIS: That's the bronze lamp! Where's Helen?

(*Sound: short, heavy peal of thunder.*)

CHRIS: (*fiercely, to convince himself*) Now we mustn't lose our heads, Benson! It's all right!

ALIM BEY: (*filter*) She will never reach that room alive!

FABIAN: One hour of searching for a vanished girl... two hours... three hours... and then, as Chris Farrell sat in the great drawing-room, with only firelight and the white eye of the lightning through pointed windows...

(*Sound: a long peal of thunder.*)

BENSON: (*fading on*) Mr. Chris!

CHRIS: Well, Benson? What's the news?

BENSON: (*shaken*) I'm glad I could persuade you to stop searching, Mr. Chris. The fact is...

CHRIS: Well? Go on!

BENSON: May I ask, sir, whether you noticed the gardeners working on the lawns?

CHRIS: I didn't notice anything except Helen!

BENSON: I employed a great number of odd-jobs men—just for the week, sir! —to put the grounds in order. Some were working; some were under the over-hanging roof out of the rain. Every door and window of this house has been under observation at all times.

CHRIS: (*quickly*) Oh? And what did the workmen say?
BENSON: Lady Helen came into this house, Mr. Chris. That's certain! She did not leave the house at any time. That's also certain!
CHRIS: *I* could have guessed that! What about it?
BENSON: (*bracing himself*) Unfortunately, sir... Lady Helen is not *in* the house either!
(*Sound: short peal of thunder, dying away as—*)
CHRIS: (*to himself, muttering*) It's dark in here. Cold, too. Over to the fire. Mummy cases round the wall, just as in the hall out there...(*suddenly bursting out*) Benson, this is sheer lunacy!
BENSON: No one knows that better than I, sir!
CHRIS: It's impossible! She's *got* to be here!
BENSON: (*heavy pleading*) I've known Severn Hall since I was a boy, sir. The chauffeur and I—there's not an inch of this house we haven't searched!
CHRIS: I'll find her, Benson! If I have to tear this place to pieces!
BENSON: (*bearing*) Mr. Chris, that was why I begged you to stop searching before! You're in no fit state of mind!
CHRIS: (*hitting back*) I'm a human being, if that's what you mean! *I'm* not British! *I'm* not stolid!
BENSON: (*steadily, as though looking him in the eyes*) If you'll forgive the liberty, sir: could you call Lady Helen—stolid?
CHRIS: (*deflated*) No. I shouldn't have said that. (*as though with sudden hope*) Here! Here in my pocket! Here's the envelope and note she left me when she went away from the Savoy Hotel. But that wasn't like *this*! The note's no good now! Into the fire with it!
BENSON: ... (*horrified*) Mr. Chris!
CHRIS: (*astonished*) What's the matter with you? You're shaking like a whole mountain!
BENSON: (*recovering*) I... I only hesitated, sir, before giving you more bad news. Someone has telephoned the press about this. Also the police.
CHRIS: (*galvanized*) Telephoned the newspapers? About Helen's disappearance? Who did it?
BENSON: I don't know, sir. But there are several reporters down at the lodge-gates now.
CHRIS: I can't see any reporters! If this story gets out, it'll confirm every rumor about the bronze lamp!
BENSON: Yes, sir. But we can't keep the police out, I'm afraid. Superintendent Gates is in the hall now.
CHRIS: Benson, the police have no right here! No crime's been committed! (*wondering*) Or... what does the Superintendent want? Why did he come here?
BENSON: Well, sir. (*hesitating; bracing himself*) He's looking for Lady Helen's dead body.

(*Sound: clock bell, far off as though in a tower, with three strokes like a funeral bell.*)
CHRIS: (*counting*) Ten… eleven… twelve. That's midnight, Superintendent Gates!
GATES: (*his accent has a touch of Gloucester, on guard but sympathetic*) (*assenting*) Ah, Mr. Farrell. Midnight. That clock in the east tower always did keep good time.
CHRIS: You and your men have been here for hours! Won't you answer just *one* question?
GATES: (*uncomfortable*) I know, lad! It's 'ard for you! You ken me, all beef and bowler hat, keeping my lip buttoned as a copper should. *But*—!
CHRIS: (*cutting in*) Why do you think Helen's dead? Why?
GATES: Her ladyship didn't leave 'ere. I accept that. My man can't find her…
CHRIS: But *somebody* must have seen Helen when she came in! What about the servants?
GATES: They were all having tea together at the back of the house. Except the kitchen-maid; but she took the day off! No testimony!
CHRIS: None from *anybody*?
GATES: (*satiric*) Except your butler, there. I'm a plain man, Mr. Farrell. Don't you see the plain answer?
CHRIS: No! I don't!
GATES: Parts of Severn Hall are as old as—! There's a secret hiding-place; that's what!
BENSON: (*off, urgently*) Mr. Chris, may *I* speak!?
CHRIS: Naturally, Benson! What's on your mind?
BENSON: (*fading on*) I keep telling this man; there is no secret hiding-place at Severn Hall!
GATES: (*snap of hostility*) *You* say that; ah! Maybe you've got a reason to say it.
BENSON: (*quickly; on dignity*) Meaning what, Superintendent?
GATES: Lady Helen never vanished of 'er own free will; now did she?
BENSON: (*swallowing*) No.
GATES: (*hitting again*) Her own uncle, Mr. Fred, was with that fancy crowd when they opened a tomb in 1922. And old Mr. Fred—'e died!
BENSON: It was a natural death!
GATES: Yes; but what'd they do? The *News of the World*, every rag from here to the States, makes people think it's "vengeance from Egypt;" look! *I've* not seen Lady 'Elen since she was a little girl; but I know about 'er. She hates this daft superstition; she wouldn't encourage it of 'er own free will. No, m'son! She's dead. (*significantly*) And somebody, maybe… somebody who's been acting funny and sneaky-like…
BENSON: (*staggered*) Do you think *I* would hurt her! (*fury*) You incompetent fool!

GATES: (*snarling*) Are you getting larky with me, bald-head?
BENSON: If I were even *ten* years younger, Superintendent...
GATES: (*sneering*) Yes, Mr. 'igh-and-Mighty?
BENSON: (*losing his head*) *I'd knock your bleeding face off!*
CHRIS: Benson! Wait! Who's in no-fit-state-of-mind *now*?
BENSON: (*waking up*) Mr. Chris! I... I don't know what...
GATES: (*half ashamed but gruff*) We're all like that. *My* fault! Lost me temper! Shouldn't 'a' done it! All nerves over this. (*turning grim*) But—!
RUTHERFORD: (*calling, off 35; brisk, cultured*) No, Sergeant! Stay there! I don't need you any longer!
CHRIS: Who's that? Who's out in the hall?
GATES: (*grim triumph*) That's Mr. Rutherford, lad! The architect! I brought 'im with me. If there's any secret hiding-place, he can find it!
BENSON: Suppose there isn't any?
GATES: There's got to be! She couldn't 'a vanished like a soap bubble! It's the only solution left! (*calling*) Mr. Rutherford! Have you finished?
RUTHERFORD: (*fading on*) Yes, Mr. Gates. All finished now.
GATES: (*pouncing*) Well, sir? What did you find?
RUTHERFORD: You're wasting your time, Superintendent. There is no secret hiding-place!
(*Sound: short, heavy peal of thunder, which merges into—*)

FABIAN: How did Helen Loring vanish? Where was she? (*pause*) Next morning, when the press of three continents exploded into headlines, a dead priest of Egypt loomed over England and cast his shadow. *Could* a girl be blown to dust? *Was* it possible? That evening, again one of incessant rain, a murmur of new voices filled Severn Hall. Benson and Superintendent Gates, no longer enemies, met outside the archway of the drawing-room.

(*Sound: crowd-murmur, rather like cocktail party is now heard faintly off.*)
CHRIS: You couldn't give me another shock. I hit an all-time low. Last night. When you were both talking about—Helen's dead body, I was so stunned I couldn't say much. (*fiercely*) But I'm all right now! *Do you hear?*
BENSON: (*soothing him*) Of course, sir!
CHRIS: And in our own troubles, Benson, we've forgotten something else. What about Helen's father?
BENSON: Yes, sir. I *had* thought of it.
GATES: *Is* Lord Severn very ill, Mr. Farrell? Near death? Like they say?
CHRIS: No, Superintendent! But he's not young any more; his heart's not good. To learn about Helen...
GATES: If 'e dies—well! They'll say it's the third victim!

CHRIS: Listen, Benson! He'll telephone from Cairo. You know that. (*half frantic*) What am I going to tell him?

BENSON: I shouldn't worry about it, sir! They've probably kept the newspapers from him. I feel sure he won't...

(*Sound: off, telephone rings: double-ringing tone.*)

BENSON: (*fading off*) Excuse me, sir.

(*Sound: off, 'phone picked up.*)

BENSON: (*off*) Yes? (*slight pause*) Yes, that is the number. (*pause*) Cairo? I see.

CHRIS: Benson! Is it—?

BENSON: (*off*) What you expected, sir. Shall I—shall I say you're not here?

CHRIS: (*half-loathing*) No, Benson! I'm responsible for Helen. I was supposed to take care of her. That's funny, isn't it? Give me the 'phone!... Hello? Lord Severn?

SEVERN: (*filter*) (*emotionless*) Yes, Chris. And I have only one question to ask.—It is true?

CHRIS: (*slight pause: flatly*) Yes, sir.

SEVERN: A prophecy, I hear, was made by a man here named Alim Bey...

CHRIS: Alim Bey's a fake! You and I know his racket! He just made a prophecy, in front of newspapermen; and hoped there'd be an accident. Even if Helen had only sprained her ankle, he'd have said it was "vengeance." That's how these miracle-mongers work!

SEVERN: Doctor Gilray—dead. Helen—vanished. And I, they say, will be the next to go. (*he starts to laugh in rising chuckles*)

CHRIS: (*alarmed*) Lord Severn! Are you all right? Are you *laughing*? Or—?

SEVERN: I was laughing, Chris. It's very funny. Good-night. (*laughter, uncanny and sounding half-mad on filter, rises again, out as—*)

(*Sound: phone click on opposite end.*)

CHRIS: (*crying out*) Lord Severn!

GATES: (*off*) I think that 'phone's dead, Mr. Farrell.

(*Sound: phone put down.*)

CHRIS: Yes, Superintendent; it's dead. So is reason! So is common-sense! So is anything like happiness!

GATES: (*growing alarm*) Now take it easy, lad!

CHRIS: I'm only coming back to the table, where you are. Here's the bronze lamp! Exudes poison, doesn't it? Exudes evil? Let's throw it at something!

GATES: There's people just across the 'all, lad! Don't *you* go daft!

CHRIS: (*unheeding*) Mummy-cases round the walls. And... (*suddenly*) Benson! Where's Benson?

GATES: Benson slipped out of 'ere, through the drawn curtains, while you were at the phone!

CHRIS: Curtains, yes! Look at the mummy-case on the right of the curtains; "wooden-coffin", we call it. Painted black, gold, orange, brown, with a witless face. See the magic symbols on the forehead? Let's throw the lamp at him!

GATES: Don't throw that lamp! Don't—

(*Sound: crash as lamp strikes wooden shell; two parts of shell, light wood clatter down.*)

CHRIS: And the shell comes apart and clatters down! And the mummy bows at us and falls. And... (*astonished*) by all the gods of murder!—There's Benson coming back through the curtains!

BENSON: (*speaking strongly*) Yes, Mr. Chris. I've got to end this nightmare!

GATES: End it? How?

BENSON: You've searched every inch of this house, Superintendent! Can you swear Lady Helen isn't here?

GATES: Yes! I swear it!

BENSON: Then let me draw back these curtains!

(*Sound: curtains swept back.*)

BENSON: Look at *this* slatternly girl with the draggled hair. Have you ever seen her before?

GATES: That's Annie—the kitchen-maid!

HELEN: (*crying out*) No, Superintendent! I'm Helen Loring. I've been masquerading as kitchen-maid in my own house! (*pleading, strong emotion*) Chris, I had to do it! But Benson and I—we couldn't keep it up. Do you hate me very much?

CHRIS: (*groping*) You've got it all wrong, Helen! I love you. But if you'd only told me something about it...

HELEN: Darling, I did! I slipped a note in your coat-pocket because I didn't want you to stop me! But you thought it was an old note, and you threw it in the fire!

BENSON: You did, Mr. Chris! And Lord Severn was warned by airmail; that was why he laughed. The Superintendent here...

GATES: I'm a p'lice-officer, m'lady! *I* want to know *how—why*—?

HELEN: I got the idea from Alim Bey. At the Cairo airport.

CHRIS: (*startled*) Cairo airport?

HELEN: I'd been talking about Benson, and Benson finding a whole new staff of servants. The servants wouldn't know me! And in a big place like this there are some servants—the kitchen-maid, for one—never seen by any guest! The police wouldn't know me; even Mr. Gates hasn't seen me for years!

CHRIS: (*suddenly*) I remember something else at Cairo! Before the plane took off. You said...

HELEN: I said, "It's all nonsense! I'll prove it's all nonsense!" Then, when we got to London, and I "disappeared" from the hotel...

CHRIS: You came down here! Is that it?

HELEN: Yes, Chris. Benson installed me as Annie, the kitchen-maid. Three days later, I took the night-train to London; I was ready to drive back here, with you, in my real character. All I did when I "vanished" was change my clothes for Annie's clothes, and go to the servants' hall!

BENSON: (*dryly*) If you remember, sir, the kitchen-maid had the day off. And clothes make the woman.

CHRIS: But this telephoning the papers...getting the police...!

HELEN: (*growing exalted*) I wanted to build this superstition as high as heaven! And then smash it like a china plate. (*pleading*) Don't you see what I can say to the world now?

CHRIS: Yes! I do see!

HELEN: "There's your supernatural disappearance," I can say. "Only a little trick that any woman could have worked!" You swore it couldn't have a natural explanation. But it has! No dead king can strike with lightning out of a tomb. There's no such thing as a curse that works harm! It's all in your imagination; and, if you believe it, it can poison your life as it almost poisoned mine! Now please stop talking about Egyptian magic or any other magic!

CHRIS: (*exalted*) Benson!

BENSON: Yes, sir?

CHRIS: (*happy triumph*) Bring in the reporters!

(*Sound: theme up to final narration*)

FABIAN: And so ends my little story, with, perhaps, something of a moral. But next week...ah! There I remember a human puzzle just as troublesome. A certain important man, let us say, is so well-guarded that no person can possibly kill him. And yet...if you care to hear my story called "The Dead Man's Knock"[1], will you join me again next week in *Cabin B-13*?

(*Sound: ship's whistles*)
(*Sound: theme fade*)

---

[1] While a play with the title "The Dead Man's Knock" was broadcast in *Cabin B-13* on 28 November 1948, this seems unlikely to have been the plot Carr had in mind involving "*certain important man... so well-guarded that no person can possibly kill him*".

Notes for the Curious

For "The Curse of the Bronze Lamp", Carr drew inspiration from two sources, one factual and one fictional, though the central trick in the story is one he had been experimenting with since his college days.

While the fictional source will be discussed in the "Notes for the Curious" for this story, the factual one will be immediately apparent. On 29 November, 1922, a team led by Howard Carter discovered and opened the tomb of *Tutankhamun* in the Valley of the Kings and just over four months later, Carter's financial backer Lord Carnarvon, died of pneumonia. Six weeks later, another one of the first people to enter the tomb also died and around the world there began to circulate talk of a curse that would strike down everyone associated with the discovery. This was fueled by the British media, including the *News of the World* newspaper, the novelist Marie Corelli and none other than Sir Arthur Conan Doyle who in an interview with an American journalist claimed that a mummy in the British Museum had been guarded by "elementals" which, he claimed, had also brought about Carnarvon's death.

The British Museum denied Doyle's story of an "unlucky mummy" but not long after this the tomb was visited by one Philip A. Poe, a self-professed descendant of Edgar Allan Poe, who fell ill shortly after and claimed to have been struck down by the "curse". Then Woolf Joel, the son of a South African millionaire, visited the tomb and died from a fractured skull a few days later when he fell down the companion stairway of the *Patroclus*, a liner on which he had been due to sail from Egypt. And *then* Lord Carnarvon's half-brother, who had been at the opening of the tomb, also died of pneumonia while the man who x-rayed the sarcophagus died from unknown causes at this home in Switzerland. Even Agatha Christie added fuel to the fire with her early Poirot short story "The Adventure of the Egyptian Tomb" (1923) and by the time British newspapers started connecting Egyptian tombs and mummies to strange deaths in Napoleonic France, it was enough simply to say that there were, as Shakespeare has it, "*more things in heaven and earth than are dreamt of in our philosophy*".

John Dickson Carr was doubtless well aware at the time he wrote the play, the tomb of Herihor, the *High Priest of Amun at Thebes* in the reign of *Ramesses XI*, had not been discovered; it remains undiscovered.

"The Curse of the Bronze Lamp" is a revised version of the play with the same title, first broadcast on 7 December 1944 in the fourth series of the BBC program *Appointment with Fear*.

While the radio plays are a concise version of the "Carter Dickson" novel of the same title, published in 1945, the central ploy in the story is essentially a re-presentation of a deception Carr had previously worked in the short story "Strictly Diplomatic" (1939) and also in the radio play "Cabin B-13" (1943). It is of course an inversion of a ploy used most memorably by G.K. Chesterton in the Father Brown short story "The Invisible Man" but it may very well also have been inspired by a throwaway reference in "The Blue Cross", the very first Father Brown story.

Carr is also likely to have had in mind the disappearance of James Phillimore, an untold case of Sherlock Holmes, which was mentioned by Doctor Watson in the "The Problem of Thor Bridge" by Sir Arthur Conan Doyle. Incidentally, in the winter of 1895-1896, Conan Doyle stayed at Cairo's Mena House Hotel where Carr may also have stayed.

Carr would provide a solution to Phillimore's disappearance in "The Adventure of the Highgate Miracle", a pastiche co-authored with Conan Doyle's son Adrian and which was first published in *Collier's* in 1953.

Lair of the Devil-Fish

(*Sound: a ship's whistle*)
(*Sound: theme up*)
ANNOUNCER: *Cabin B-13.* Tonight: "Lair of the Devil-Fish".
(*Sound: theme fades during Fabian's opening narration*)
FABIAN: The giant octopus, with its eight moving tentacles and its huge eyes unwinking in the green depths of the water—guarding the treasure in the sunken wreck—was it a myth, in that Cuban Bay? Down went the diver—and then the terror struck! If you were the young American, Dick Lawrence, would *you* have chosen to retreat—or go down and face the unknown—on the bottom of the Cuban sea? On the southeast coast of Cuba, you will find many bays large bays, deep, secret beyond their channels, where palmetto trees shade dark green water. Into one of them, as dawn is breaking, creeps the big motor-yacht, *Venturer*,—fifteen hundred tons burden.

(*Sound: faint thudding of engines comes in and holds under—*)
FABIAN: (*continuing*) A yacht, dazzling white under her single scarlet funnel. And, as she moves up the channel into the bay, echo-sounder switched on, can you hear the Captain's eternal question from the bridge....
FORBES: (*middle-aged, slight scots accent*) How much water now, Mr. Browning?
BROWNING: Twelve fathoms, sir.
FORBES: Plenty of depth, anyway. That'll do, Mr. Browning. Stop her!
(*Sound: engine-room telegraph rings; thudding dies away.*)
BROWNING: Engines stopped, sir.
FORBES: Let go starboard anchor.
BROWNING: (*calling, away to fo'c'sle head*) Let go starboard anchor!
(*Sound: long rattle of anchor-chain.*)
BROWNING:(*slight pause*) Ugly-looking place, isn't it? Like a jungle with a lake in the middle.
FORBES: That's none of our business, my lad. You might go below—
BROWNING: Yes, sir?
FORBES: And wake up Mr. Stanley. Tell our good owner we've reached Devil-Fish Bay.

FABIAN: Now, in the fiery afternoon, certain preparations are made on the after deck. You see, in that knot of men, the seated figure in the suit of rubber and twill? The lead-soled boots? The helmet of tinned copper, its front glass now open? The air-line from the helmet to the pumps—four men on those pumps—and the breast-rope that carries the telephone wire? That's "Doc" Trencher, Number One diver of the Hoskins Company, New York. In front of him—a big man with an amiable blue eye—Mr. Edmund Stanley, his employer; and Mr. Stanley's son-in-law, Dick Lawrence…

(*Sound: faint murmur of voices, which dies as Stanley speaks*)
STANLEY: Trencher! All right inside that helmet?
TRENCHER: (*Trencher's voice comes with hollow and booming effect from inside the helmet. He is thirty-five or so; American; cheerful; tough*) Absolutely Okay, Mr. Stanley; just as snug as a bug in a rug.
STANLEY: Half a minute, before you get on that ladder and we close this front glass! You're sure you've got the instructions straight?
TRENCHER: (*wearily amused*) Look, Mr. Stanley, we've been over those instructions till I'm cockeyed! I can't miss!
STANLEY: (*hesitating*) You—don't mind the job?
TRENCHER: (*surprised*) Working in sixty feet of water? I've worked a three hundred without much more 'n a headache.
STANLEY: No. I meant this fable about the devil-fish. The giant squid.
TRENCHER: (*earnestly*) Now look, Mr. Stanley—!
STANLEY: And it *is* a fable, I guarantee that!
TRENCHER: It's a hundred to one against findin' squids in open water. If we was workin close in-shore, with rock caves in the rest of it: that's different. But we're not. And these instructions of yours…
DICK: (*interrupts*) Yes. What *are* the instructions?
STANLEY: (*sternly*) You keep out of this, Dick!
DICK: But my dear father-in-law, listen, Sally and I —
STANLEY: There's nothing *dear* about *me!*
DICK: All right, sir. But what's all the mystery? Why won't you tell Sally and me anything? What does Doc Trencher expect to *find* down there, except the wreck of a little boat?
TRENCHER: (*amused*) Don't pay no attention to the kid, Mr. Stanley. He's just sore because you won't let *him* do any diving.
DICK: I certainly hoped you'd let me have a shot at it, sir. It's been my hobby for five years.
TRENCHER: (*grimly*) Diving's no fun, kid.
DICK: It is for me. But maybe I'm wrong.
(*Sound: fade in motor boat, off.*)
TRENCHER: Wait till you lose the shot-rope and can't find your way back to the ship. Wait till you foul your air-pipe. Wait till you come up too quick, and get the bends so bad that…
ROMERO: (*off*) Ola, amigo! Ola, amigo!
STANLEY: What the devil's that?
FORBES: Mr. Stanley!

STANLEY: Yes, Captain Forbes?

FORBES: There's a motor-boat coming up to port. And a little old white-haired chap—brown as coffee—in a white linen suit and a Panama hat, standing up at the wheel and wavin' his arms like a windmill.

STANLEY: (*in explosive despair*) Confound it! Another official!

DICK: Take it easy, Sir!

STANLEY: I've talked to every government official in Cuba. It's taken me four months—four months! to get this permission. If I run into just one more tin-pot magistrate, trying to obstruct me, I'll murder somebody!

FORBES: Better see him, though. You never know.

STANLEY: All right, all right! Where is he?

FORBES: Boat's in, sir. He's comin' up the ladder now.

STANLEY: Red tape! Red tape! Red tape!

DICK: (*not loudly*) Here he is. Try to be polite.

STANLEY: (*with an effort at heartiness*) *Buenas afternoonas, senor*! *Buenas afternoonas*! You spikka da Eenglish, no?

ROMERO: I do indeed speak the English. And, I trust, in no uncultured accent.

DICK: (*under his breath*) That's got you, Sir.

STANLEY: (*under his breath*) Be quiet!

ROMERO: I sweep off my hat—so. I make you the old-fashioned bow—so. I am Leon Romero: your servant.

STANLEY: I make *you* the old-fashioned bow, Mr. Romero. And I want to point out that I've got an order, signed by the Governor-General of Camagüey, authorizing me to conduct diving-operations in these waters. If you want to stop me—

ROMERO: But, my dear sir! I don't wish to stop you. It is merely that I own the bay here...

STANLEY: (*startled*) You own the bay?

ROMERO: Well! I own all the land hereabouts. My hacienda is a mile beyond the trees there. And—I am curious. You are American?

STANLEY: We are!

ROMERO: (*sharply*) May I ask why you have come?

STANLEY: Look here, Mr. Romero. You say you don't want to make trouble.

ROMERO: (*sulkily*) Provided my curiosity is satisfied. No.

STANLEY: If I tell you the whole story—here and now!—will you let us get on with it?

ROMERO: With all my heart. I promise.

STANLEY: Then—what about coming below to the cabin, and having a drink with us?

ROMERO: I shall be honored, senor.

FORBES: Better hurry up, Mr. Stanley! There's a storm comin'!

FABIAN: Below, in the main cabin—white-painted, with its brass-bound port-holes and whirring fans—the heat pressed even more thickly between decks as...

STANLEY: By the way, Mr. Romero, let me introduce my daughter, Sally. She's married to Dick Lawrence here. Sally, Mr. Romero.
SALLY: How do you do?
ROMERO: I am enchanted, Mrs. Lawrence!
DICK: He makes you the old-fashioned bow, Sally. Don't you like it?
SALLY: I love it, Dick! I only wish others could be as gallant. Please sit down, Mr. Romero.
ROMERO: I thank you. Your father, Mrs. Lawrence, has promised to tell me why he comes to explore this bay.
SALLY: (*surprised*) He's promised you that? Then I wish he'd tell us!
DICK: He's been on the track of a murderer.
STANLEY: Not a murderer, Dick. Something more mysterious than a murder, and he's the only one who can see the answer. (*leisurely*) Tell me, Mr. Romero. You're a Cuban, of course?
ROMERO: No. I am a Spaniard, Senor Stanley. I came here only eight, ten years ago.
STANLEY: Then that's why you haven't heard!
ROMERO: Still a mystery, about my own home—
STANLEY: (*ignoring this*) It'll be no news to you, at least, that up to 1898 this island was owned by Spain? And, in 1898, there was war with the United States?
ROMERO: With unhappy results for my country. Well?
STANLEY: Now look out of the porthole, there. At the ruined landing-stage on the other side of the bay.
ROMERO: Yes, I know it well.
STANLEY: In the late nineties all that forest-land, for miles beyond, was a sugar plantation. It was owned by a big man named Gonzales; but nobody called him anything except the Red Devil.
ROMERO: The Red Devil. I enjoy the picturesque.
STANLEY: He was hated—loathed is a better word—by Spaniards and Americans alike. It wasn't a plantation he kept: it was a slave colony. He'd flog men to death when they couldn't work. He'd crucify women to trees if they didn't please him. There were voodoo practices too: that's how the fable of the giant octopus got started.
SALLY: My father doesn't really believe all this nonsense, Mr. Romero. He's just being theatrical.
STANLEY: (*sharply*) *Will* you be quiet, Sally. I'm stating facts.
SALLY: Sorry, Dad.
STANLEY: The Red Devil had one associate. An odd little card named Pedro, who'd knocked all over the world, Pedro had been a sponge-diver in

the Mediterranean. He'd run guns in Morocco. Mad as a hatter, in spite of his smooth manners, and very nearly a match for the Red Devil at torturing people. (*pause*) That sort of thing couldn't go on forever, even with the whole island in a state of civil war. The Red Devil knew that sooner or later he'd have to get out in a hurry. So he and Pedro, with their own hands, built a big cabin-cruiser.

ROMERO: (*doubtful*) One moment, please, I do not quite… a "cabin cruiser"?

DICK: Sort of glorified motor-boat, Mr. Romero. With living-quarters and all.

STANLEY: They moored it to the landing-stage there. And they went on amassing a fortune—in American silver dollars. Ever see a silver dollar?

ROMERO: No, I don't think so.

STANLEY: They haven't been coined for years. But I've got one here.

(*Sound: rattle of large coin on table.*)

STANLEY: Heavy, isn't it? Like a silver cartwheel.

ROMERO: (*worried*) My friend, you are trying to tell me something. Yes, yes, yes! But for the life of me I can't think what!

DICK: That's just the point!

SALLY: Dad's only being mysterious!

DICK: I wonder!

STANLEY: These two, the Red Devil and Pedro, got together a fortune and hid it. Where did they hide it?

ROMERO: Well! Did anyone try to find out?

STANLEY: Many people, in those upset times. A guerilla party even raided the plantation to get it. They searched the house: it wasn't there. They searched the grounds; it wasn't buried anywhere, or the peons would have known. They searched the cabin-cruiser: still no result. Where *had* those two hidden the money?

ROMERO: Do *you* know, my friend?

STANLEY: Yes, I rather think I do.

DICK: (*excitedly*) Look here, Sir! That story about the Red Devil is old stuff. But this new bit, about a hidden fortune…

STANLEY: (*politely*) Shall I go on, Mr. Romero?

ROMERO: (*controlling excitement*) Yes, Senor Stanley.

STANLEY: In the spring of '98, the civil troubles ended in war with the United States, The Red Devil could hear battleship guns from Santiago harbor. Infantry were landing; and there were a number of Americans who'd sworn to get the Red Devil if they didn't do anything else. He decided to make a run for it in that cabin-cruiser…

ROMERO: With his friend Pedro?

STANLEY: No. Alone.

ROMERO: I see.

STANLEY: It was during a tropical thunderstorm, first black as pitch and then white with lightning followed by thunder…

(*Sound: roll of thunder.*)
SALLY: It's going to storm now—as it did then! Look at that sky out there!
ROMERO: Storm? But this—surely?—will interrupt your diving work?
DICK: In a land-locked bay? Not likely!
ROMERO: Go on, please, about the Red Devil.
STANLEY: He hadn't got away any too soon. As he ran for the jetty, people could see the blue shirts of the American riflemen coming through the wood. The two leading ones had a Gatling-gun. Our Red Devil jumped into the boat, started the motor—it was a primitive affair in those days—and started out across the bay. In the next white lightning flash…
ROMERO: Well?
STANLEY: They saw Pedro standing at the end of the pier.
ROMERO: Not to be left behind, eh?
STANLEY: Pedro made a flying leap—God knows how he did it—and landed on the deck. They saw him crawling below, after the Red Devil, with a knife in his teeth. The troops set up their Gatling-gun and sprayed bullets after the boat: apparently they didn't hit it. The boat was half way across the bay when… it happened.
ROMERO: What happened?
STANLEY: An old voodoo-woman later swore she saw a tentacle, a slimy tentacle…
SALLY: This is the part I hate.
STANLEY: A slimy tentacle come up out of the water and fasten round the boat. Whether or not that was true, something happened. The boat didn't merely sink; it was pulled or *dragged* under. They heard the Red Devil scream; they saw a thrashing in the water; the next second—nothing.
ROMERO: And—afterwards?
STANLEY: (*cooly*) Sorry, Mr. Romero. That's all.
ROMERO: *All*?
STANLEY: All until tonight. Until I can send Doc Trencher down and prove my theory. Have I satisfied your curiosity?
ROMERO: Satisfied it? *Madre de Dios*! I am worse than ever!
DICK: Why not stay and see the diving, Mr. Romero?
ROMERO: No, no, no, no! If it is going to rain, I return to my own boat. But—
STANLEY: But what? You're not going to make trouble for us?
ROMERO: No, no, no! I was thinking… both Pedro and the Red Devil died when *something* caught their boat?
STANLEY: Presumably. No trace of them was ever found.
ROMERO: I say no more, my friend. But—I am not easy. What *is* down under that bay?

FABIAN: On deck again, with the sky darkening and the wind-blown palmetto-trees outlined against lightning. Doc Trencher on the iron ladder, ready to go down. The yacht, the dark grey-green water heave in a very gentle swell...

(*Sound: crash of thunder.*)

STANLEY: If my calculations are right, we ought to be just over the wreck of that cabin-cruiser, Dick!

DICK: Yes?

STANLEY: (*indulgently satirical*) As the so-called diving expert, we'll let you take charge now. —All right with you, Trencher?

TRENCHER: (*muffled*) The kid knows his stuff, Mr. Stanley. It suits me.

STANLEY: The job's yours, Dick.

DICK: (*calling*) Stand by the pumps!

BROWNING: (*off*) Ready, sir!

DICK: Fasten on diver's back and breast weights...Easy... Not too tight a hitch. —Okay, Doc?

TRENCHER: Okay, Kid.

DICK: Start the pumps!

(*Sound: the pumps are heard in the background: then taken down so as to be nearly inaudible.*)

DICK: Fasten on diver's face glass. Three turns to the right... slow... That's got it. Down you go, Doc!

(*Sound: thudding footsteps are heard descending an iron ladder.*)

DICK: We can't talk to him now except through the telephone. Will you take the telephone, sir, or shall I?

STANLEY: Let me have it. I want to direct him!

DICK: Here you are.

STANLEY: Hello, Trencher! Hello, Trencher! Can you hear me?

(*Sound: Trencher's voice is now heard against air-noises inside helmet*)

TRENCHER: I can hear you all right, boss. (*formally*) Diver leaving ship!

DICK: Full speed the pumps! Diver leaving ship!

(*Sound: the rush and bubbling as the waters close over Trencher this continues a second or two*)

SALLY: He's well under now. I wouldn't go down there for ten thousand dollars.

STANLEY: Sally! What are *you* doing here?

SALLY: I couldn't stay away! I've *got* to see it! What were those things he was carrying? They looked like...

DICK: A diver's lamp, and an oxy-hydrogen blow-torch.

SALLY: Oxy-hydrogen blow-torch?

DICK: For cutting wood or metal under water. Quiet now!

STANLEY: Hello, Trencher! Hello, Trencher! Can you hear me? (*slight pause*) Trencher!

(*Sound: roll of thunder.*)

STANLEY: Confound that thunder!
SALLY: You don't think anything's...?
STANLEY: *Trencher!*
TRENCHER: (*against helmet-noises*) Keep your shirt on, boss. Everything's under control (*formally*) Diver now on sea-floor!
DICK: (*calling*) What are your pumps making?
BROWNING: Twenty-five per minute, sir.
DICK: That'll do. Keep her steady.
STANLEY: Trencher! How are conditions down there?
TRENCHER: Muddy as hell. Can't see a thing. Wait a second till it settles.
STANLEY: Any tide or swell?
TRENCHER: Practically none.
SALLY: The storm's going to break any minute. I know it can't affect him down there! But I wish it had been a clear day! I wish—
TRENCHER: (*excited*) Mr. Stanley! You were right! It's here!
STANLEY: What is?
TRENCHER: The wreck of the cabin-cruiser! Practically in front of me.
STANLEY: Got your light on?
TRENCHER: Sure, sure! I—(*stops dead*).
STANLEY: What's wrong?
TRENCHER: (*oddly*) Funny looking shadow just went past me.
SALLY: (*bursting out*) Be careful, man!
STANLEY: Careful of what? He's safe as houses. In a few minutes more we're going to learn the whole truth.
DICK: (*exasperated*) Don't you think, sir, it's about time you explained this mystery?
STANLEY: A while ago, Dick, I asked you and Sally and Romero two questions. First what dragged the boat under? Second, what happened to the Red Devil's fortune in silver dollars?
SALLY: (*half guessing*) You don't mean that—?
DICK: Wait a minute! You told us a guerilla party searched that boat without finding the money!
STANLEY: So they did. Because Pedro and the Red Devil had built it with double bulkheads.
SALLY: Double bulkheads?
STANLEY: Double walls, with the money packed inside. And with all that cash in heavy silver dollars would weigh nearly half a ton. And the boat couldn't stand the weight. She was struck below the water-line by Gatling-gun bullets. So she simply cracked up and went down. Now do you understand?
DICK: Yes, I think I do.
STANLEY: There's no devil-fish down there, at least I hope not. But there is three quarters of a million dollars for intelligent people to pick up!
TRENCHER: Mr. Stanley!

STANLEY: Quiet everybody! —Yes, Trencher?
TRENCHER: Somebody's been at this wreck.
STANLEY: How do you mean, at it?
TRENCHER: I mean the bulkheads are broke open. I mean—(*the voice ends in a shrill scream, hollow inside that helmet*)
STANLEY: Trencher! What's wrong?
TRENCHER: (*screaming out*) It's got me. Help me! It's got me! (*the scream begins again, but is choked off as though water had poured into the helmet*)
DICK: Give me that phone, sir!
STANLEY: Well?
DICK: It's dead! The phone's dead!
BROWNING: (*off*) Mr. Lawrence! These pumps aren't working right! Look at the gauge!
DICK: You mean his air-pipe's fouled?
BROWNING: I think—I think his air-pipe's out.
DICK: That's impossible! Haul him up by the breast-rope!
BROWNING: Richards gave it a tug, sir. And it came clean away through the water. The breast-rope's cut too.
STANLEY: (*not loudly*) Air-line cut. Breast-rope cut. What in Satan's name...
SALLY: Yes. What is it?
DICK: Listen, sir! You've got a spare set of diving-gear, haven't you?
STANLEY: Yes, why?
DICK: I'm going down there.
SALLY: You're not! I won't let you!
STANLEY: If his air-line's cut, son, that's the end of it. He's a goner.
DICK: Probably, yes. But in sixty feet of water there's still a chance.
STANLEY: Dick, there's something down there? A thing that cuts air-pipes and breast-ropes as though they were made out of paper?
DICK: I'll take along an oxygen blow-torch, it's hot enough to cut steel. And I'll blast it against anything that comes near me. Doesn't that satisfy you?
FORBES: Mr. Stanley?
STANLEY: Yes, Captain Forbes?
FORBES: There's no telephone attached to the other diving-suit, that's all. If he goes down in that, he'll have to go down with no communication except rope signals.
SALLY: No! I won't allow it!
DICK: I tell you, it's the possible way of saving Doc Trencher's life. What do you say? Yes or no?
STANLEY: All right, son. Get into your gear.

FABIAN: Frantic seconds, frantic minutes. Time for other preparations to be made. Time for another diver to be dressed. Again the churning of the pumps, under a lightning-flecked sky and with the yacht still heaving uneasily. Again the thud of lead-soled boots on the ladder. Again the omi-

nous bubbling rush of water as the big helmet sinks below the surface. Again, on the deck of the yacht *Venturer*, a white faced group waiting, waiting, waiting...
(*Sound: the noise of the pumps rises as the music fades.*)

SALLY: He's been down there for five minutes! Something's happened.
STANLEY: (*fiercely*) Sally! Listen to me!
SALLY: Well, Dad?
STANLEY: He's been down exactly thirty seconds. Look at my watch!
SALLY: I know something's happened!
FORBES: The emergency signal, miss, is four pulls on the air-pipe. And he hasn't given that signal!
STANLEY: The last one we got was one on the breast-rope for "all right".
FORBES: He'll never save Doc Trencher, though.
STANLEY: He'll have a good try, Captain Forbes! He—
SALLY: Dad! Look! The air-pipe's moving!
STANLEY: I see it!
SALLY: One, two, three, f—
FORBES: (*calling*) Emergency signal, Mr. Browning. Haul him up!
BROWNING: (*off*) Aye, aye, sir.
STANLEY: Don't bring him up too fast! You mustn't do that! Doc Trencher says that's what gives divers the bends!
FORBES: He hasn't been down long enough for that, Mr. Stanley! Anyway, we'll have to risk it. Mr. Browning, haul away!
BROWNING: Yes, sir!
FORBES: But not too fast mind you! Easy does it! Easy, easy...
BROWNING: Heavy weight on this rope, sir.
SALLY: You don't mean something's got hold of him?
FORBES: More likely he's carrying Trencher's body. Easy does it. Easy! Easy...!
(*Sound: there is a pause, after which we hear the bubbling rush of a diver surfacing.*)
STANLEY: There's his helmet! He's up safely! And he's got Trencher!
FORBES: Anderson! Young! Stand by to get Trencher aboard. Holmes! Macandrew! Give Mr. Lawrence a hand. Easy does it, now. Easy...!
STANLEY: There's your helmet off, son. Lean back against the bulkhead, now. How do you feel?
DICK: (*slight pause. hard breathing from Dick*) I'm all right, sir. Got a drop of brandy?
FORBES: Get it for you in half a tick, Mr. Lawrence. You're lookin' a bit white.
DICK: Yes. How's Trencher?
FORBES: Can't tell yet. It's—a bad case.
DICK: (*heavily*) Yes. I was afraid of that.
SALLY: (*almost tearful*) Dick, you idiot! You scared us half to death! What

happened?

DICK: I—met the devil-fish.

STANLEY: You...did what?

DICK: I met the devil-fish. And the devil-fish, if you want to call it that, is dead.

STANLEY: (*quietly*) Go on, Dick.

DICK: I was scared stiff when I went down there. I admit that. You can't imagine how lonely it is, slipping down through that water with the light going out over your head.

STANLEY: Go on.

DICK: I had my lamp, but I didn't turn it on till I reached bottom, in case the glass should crack. Then I did turn it on, I found Doc lying in the mud and silt beside the wreck of the boat. And he was right about one thing, too; somebody had been at it.

STANLEY: How do you mean?

DICK: Somebody had cracked open the bulkheads. Somebody, time after time, had been scooping loads of silver dollars out of that boat. And, while I was wondering what in blazes it meant, I saw a shadow.

SALLY: You mean—?

DICK: I glanced up. And, looking at me through the glass of my helmet was...

STANLEY: Was what?

DICK: A human face.

STANLEY: What?

DICK: Nothing supernatural sir. Don't you remember what you told me about Pedro, the little associate of the Red Devil?

STANLEY: Well?

DICK: Pedro has been a sponge-diver. And that means...

STANLEY: It means those fellows who go down, with only a knife and a loincloth, and can stay under water anything up to two minutes...!

DICK: That's right, sir.

SALLY: Then Pedro didn't die when the boat was wrecked?

DICK: Drown a sponge-diver? What do you think?

STANLEY: But Pedro...

DICK: He's been haunting this place for years. Guarding this treasure. Getting money when he needed it. And, when we arrived...

SALLY: Dick! What happened down there?

DICK: He took Trencher from behind, with a razor-edged knife. But this time the fool swam straight in front of me, with his white hair waving and a maniac's face if I ever saw one, I did the only thing I could do: I gave him the blast of the oxy-hydrogen gun straight through the stomach.

SALLY: Oh, Dick!

DICK: I recognized him immediately, of course...

STANLEY: You recognized him? But you've never seen this fellow Pedro!

DICK: Oh yes, I have. So have you.

STANLEY: What's that?

DICK: He must have slipped off his clothes, slid over the side of the motor-boat, and waited for Trencher as he later waited for me. Don't you understand even yet, sir?
STANLEY: (*suddenly realizing*) This "Pedro" was...?
DICK: He was the affable gentleman you just entertained aboard this yacht. (*slight pause*) There's his body floating to the surface now. The late Senor Leon Romero!
(*Sound: theme up to final narration*)

FABIAN: That is the end of the story "Lair of the Devil Fish", a soothing adventure, I trust, for this quiet evening. Next week, I shall tell you of a troublesome, human puzzle—the tale of a man, highly prominent in the last war—later, so closely guarded that no person can possibly kill him. And yet, an enemy found a way which you are challenged to anticipate.
(*Sound: ship's whistles*)
(*Sound: theme fade*)

Notes for the Curious

While "Lair of the Devil-Fish" was inspired by Carr's trip to Cuba in 1930, its setting and substance are called to mind of the short stories of Carr's friend Adrian Conan Doyle. The two men would collaborate on *The Exploits of Sherlock Holmes* (1954), a series of 12 short stories inspired by some of the many tantalizing references to untold cases in the Holmes stories of Conan Doyle's father, Sir Arthur Conan Doyle. It will not have gone unnoticed that the crew of the *Venturer* includes a crewman called Holmes.

"Lair of the Devil-Fish" is a revised version of a play by the same title first broadcast by the BBC on 21 December 1944 in the fourth series of the BBC program *Appointment with Fear.*

The Dead Man's Knock

(*Sound: a ship's whistle*)
(*Sound: theme up*)
   ANNOUNCER: *Cabin B-13*. Tonight, from his notebooks of mystery and murder, ship's surgeon Dr Fabian tells you the story of "The Dead Man's Knock".
(*Sound: theme fades during Fabian's opening narration*)
FABIAN: You know the man was a brilliant scientist—you've read about him—he had important atomic secrets to give to the world. Now, he lay helplessly ill in that cottage, high in the Swiss Alps—with an impregnable guard thrown around him—because his enemies hated him so thoroughly they had sworn to kill him before he revealed those secrets. Mary Hayes, the American writer who told me this story, arrived on the scene, just as those enemies brazenly announced they had discovered a certain way past the guard. Then terror struck suddenly when she found that *she* held the key to murder.

(*Sound: typewriter*)
MARY: (*in despair*) Another sentence crossed out! I can't even seem to *think* straight!
(*Sound: typewriter again*)

FABIAN: But late at night... she'd been drinking black coffee, and writing until all hours... it was far worse. It was dead quiet everywhere; yet the cozy little room seemed horrible: although she felt an evil presence had got in. Once, towards four o'clock in the morning...
(*Sound: typewriter going at speed to end of short sentence: then stop.*)

MARY: (*reading*) "... and it seems incredible that such a murderer could over have existed." Period.
(*Sound: single plop from typewriter; then machine begins under next speech.*)
MARY: "All the same, comma, this murderer..."
(*Sound: typewriter stops.*)
MARY: (*tensely*) Now how do I want to say? "Is of a type so —unusual—so frightening—?"
(*Sound: off, two faint taps suggesting fingers on wood.*)
MARY: (*exclaiming*) What was that?
(*Sound: three taps.*)
MARY: Who's tapping on the wall? Who is it? Which wall? Where are you? (*to herself, muttering: frightened*) I can't stand this room any longer! I can't!

(*Sound: phone receiver off hook: pause: then impatient battering of hook, since no one has answered; at last, receiver off at other end*)

FELIX: (*harassed from lack of sleep: French accent*) (*on filter through*) 'Allo?

MARY: Monsieur Lorac? This is Miss Hayes, room...

FELIX: Ah, M'amselle Hayes! This is Felix, the night porter...you are awake?

MARY: Yes. (*pouring relief*) I just had to call someone.

FELIX: (*curious inflection*) Oh, Mademoiselle Hayes?

MARY: Yes! I know it sounds absurd, at four o'clock in the morning; but... could I speak to the proprietor? Or his wife?

FELIX: The proprietor? Monsieur Lorac? But Monsieur Lorac is on his way to your room!

MARY: (*bewildered*) On his way to my room?

FELIX: Yes, mademoiselle! I was about to call you! Monsieur Lorac is coming with the American gentleman who has arrived in the middle of the night.

MARY: (*still more bewildered*) Felix, did Monsieur Lorac read my mind? I—I'm in room number sixteen. I want to get transferred to some other room!

FELIX: (*gloomily*) Then I suppose you have heard about the dead man.

MARY: (*recoiling*) *What dead man?*

(*Sound: off, two taps.*)

MARY: (*away from 'phone*) There's the tapping again! (*back to 'phone*) Felix listen...!

FELIX: M'amselle Hayes, I don't know what this is about. Monsieur Lorac and the American gentleman, perhaps *they* know!

FABIAN: Voices, loud in the night-stillness, outside the closed door of room number 16! Mary Hayes, her hand on the knob, eased the door a little open to see without being seen. Just outside stood the Swiss hotel-proprietor: a fine figure of a man, his curling black mustachios in contrast to the white nightcap. Opposite stood an equally tall young American...

JEFF: (*urgently sincere*) I hate to ask this, Monsieur Lorac! But I can't help it.

LORAC: (*about 40: deep voice: now a little shocked! French accent*) You wish me, Mr. Randall, to turn the lady out of this room at four a.m.? And put *you* in the room instead?!!

JEFF: (*making excuses in a rush*) She can't like the room anyway! It's built against the side of the hill; it's damp; there are probably still bloodstains where that fellow's throat was cut...

LORAC: (*galvanized*) S-h-h! For the love of heaven!

JEFF: I'm dead serious! I keep telling you...

LORAC: (*drawn up*) And I tell *you*, Mr. Randall: this hotel is fool!

JEFF: (*taken aback*) What do you mean, fool?

LORAC: Fool! *Complet!* No r-room! The winter-sports, they have begun a week ago! (*controlling wrath: dignity*) *You*, perhaps, I could accommodate with

a sofa in the billiard-room. Or in our fine American bowling-alley. But the lady out, Mr. Randall!
JEFF: I'm on a mission for my government. I can't afford to be chivalrous! (*pleading*) Throw the old Gorgon out!
LORAC: (*bewildered*) This English language! What do you say?
JEFF: Gorgon! Medusa! Sour-puss! Didn't you tell me she's Mary Hayes who writes those books about real-life murderers?
LORAC: Yes, Monsieur! But—
JEFF: All right! Let *her* sleep in the bowling-alley!
MARY: (*on: shivering with rage*) Monsieur Lorac!
LORAC: (*startled*) Mademoiselle! Please to forgive my night-attire!
MARY: (*dangerous sweetness*) Of course, Monsieur Lorac But what is this... this *person* doing here?
JEFF: (*contrite*) I'm terribly sorry, miss. My name's Randall, Jeff Randall. I'm looking for—well! Your mother, maybe? An older sister?
MARY: (*drawn up*) *I* am Mary Hayes. The only Mary Hayes in this hotel.
JEFF: (*uncontrollably*) Now, quit clowning! I don't believe it!
MARY: (*white rage: but controlled*) What exquisite manners, Mr. Randall!
JEFF: (*deeply sincere: unheeding*) Big blue eyes.... a face like a Raphael Madonna... You're the loveliest thing I ever saw!
MARY: (*off-balance*) Well! I... I...
JEFF: (*accusingly*) You didn't write that book called *Gentlemen of the Jury*!
MARY: I most certainly did! (*hesitating*) Did you—did you read it?
JEFF: Yes. It was terrible!
MARY: Oh!
JEFF: Now wait! Don't misunderstand!
MARY: (*icy calm*) Tell me, Mr. Randall. What is your *average* number of insults per minute?
JEFF: Look, Miss Hayes. I only meant that some of the technical detail was wrong! I... (*floundering*) May I come in and talk to you? You're wide awake; you'll probably stay up all night anyway. May I come in and talk to you?
LORAC: Miss Hayes, this lunatic wishes to turn you out of your room! You have only to say the word, and I throw him out of the hotel!
MARY: No. That won't be necessary. Let him come in!
LORAC: (*astounded*) Let him ... You *wish* to talk to him?
MARY: Certainly not! I—I'm just taking pity on him, that's all. Good night, Monsieur Lorac!
LORAC: (*with dignity: fading*) Good *morning*, M'amselle!
(Sound: door closes, on.)
MARY: (*on her dignity*) (*pause*) Well, Mr. Randall? (*pause*) *Well?*
JEFF: (*quietly*) You know, Miss Hayes—I'm not as crazy as I sound! (*quickly*) Now wait! Don't make the obvious retort!

MARY: I'm glad you *see* the obvious retort.
JEFF: (*pleading*) Can't we forget this duel for a few minutes? I've fallen for you with just one look; and you know it—
MARY: I don't know any such thing!
JEFF: —so don't take advantage of it! Before I came in here, you were frightened. Badly frightened. Why?
MARY: (*taken aback*) I... how do you know that?
JEFF: I could see it in your face. Why were you frightened?
MARY: Well! Sometimes, in the middle of the night, there'll be a kind of tapping on the wall...
JEFF: Tapping? From where?
MARY: I don't know! (*concentrating*) And yet —it's not *exactly* like a tapping either. You told the proprietor —I heard you! —that a man had cut his throat in this room...
JEFF: He didn't cut his own throat. He was murdered. In that easy chair where you're sitting now. —Sorry! I didn't mean to make you jump up like that!
MARY: *What do you want here? Who are you?*
JEFF: I'm from Washington; let it go at that. My work here is secret. (*quickly*) Now don't look skeptical. I tell you it's secret because—well, I believe I can trust you. In fact, I've got to trust you! (*brooding*) The mystery...
MARY: (*fascinated despite herself*) About this room?
JEFF: No! Not exactly! The real mystery, the problem that's driving me nuts, isn't in this room at all. Will you come here to these French windows?
MARY: Well! If you insist!
JEFF: We'll throw the curtains back...
(*Sound: curtains on rings.*)
JEFF: Like that! We're on the ground floor. Now look down over the valley, a quarter of a mile down, and far to the left of the bobsled-track. Do you see a light shining?
MARY: (*fascinated*) Yes! There's a cottage there; I've seen it in daylight.
JEFF: (*insistently*) It's completely isolated. Nobody could possibly get near it without being seen. Do you agree?
MARY: (*puzzled*) Yes, of course! What about it?
JEFF: In that cottage there's an old man who's got tuberculosis. We don't dare move him out of this climate until he's better; and he'll get better. In the meantime, we have him guarded night and day...
MARY: *Guarded?*
JEFF: Yes! By ten men who know how to do it. The old boy can't be hurt in any way. Poison, small-bomb, long-range rifle, aircraft: we've ruled out everything! He's as safe as though we'd put him in a bank-vault. And yet somebody's going to kill him tomorrow night. *How?*
MARY: (*shaken*) Listen, Mr. Randall! I don't know whether you're making all

this up…
JEFF: Making it up? (*appeal to the ceiling*) Why should I?
MARY: —Or whether you do mean it. I —I think you do! This man you're talking about… is he a scientist of some kind?
JEFF: Yes! Yes, he is!
MARY: Do you trust me enough to tell me anything more about him?
JEFF: I trust you enough to say —he's one of the greatest of modern scientists. In his field, there's no telling what he could give the world— if he lives.
MARY: And who wants to kill him?
JEFF: His own son.
MARY: You're joking!
JEFF: (*quietly*) I'm not joking. The war's over; let's forget it. But the old man got away before the Nazis caught him. His son can't forgive that. His son is Baron Carmer; he took the title when the old man escaped. (*weary*) Mary, what do you think we've been trying to do? He's wanted as a war-criminal! Haven't you noticed the check-up on American and British passports?
MARY: Yes! Come to think of it, I have!
JEFF: Carmer speaks English perfectly. Not just "very well"; but perfectly! He's tall; he's light-haired; he's comparatively young. That's all you can tell from a bad photograph. But we can't find him. Even when we know where he is!
MARY: (*amazed*) You know where he is?
JEFF: Yes. Near here. Possibly staying at this hotel.
MARY: Jeff. That's impossible!
JEFF: (*grimly: unheeding*) Is it? Every day he's been sending a note to his father, by ordinary mail, and saying it's one less day until the old boy dies!
MARY: But… isn't that the poisonous old bluff the Nazis always used? He can't kill a man who's being guarded like that! He isn't a magician, is he?
JEFF: Very nearly. It'll be something completely unexpected! It'll strike from a direction we've never thought of. But *how*?
MARY: (*pause: softer tone*) You —you keep staring out of the window. What are you thinking about?
JEFF: (*weary: bitter*) Oh, I dunno! I was looking at the stars up over the valley.
MARY: You don't find stars like that except in the tropics or the High Alps. They're wonderful!
JEFF: (*suddenly: all in a rush*) *You're wonde*rful! Mary, I've fallen for you so hard that I…! Shut Up! (*fading off*) Let me keep my mind on this problem!
MARY: (*crying out*) You are absolutely the most outrageous man I ever met!
JEFF: (*instantly fading on*) Will you have lunch with me tomorrow?
MARY: (*drawn up*) As it happens, I'm having lunch with Mr. Conyers.
JEFF: *Oh?* Who's Mr. Conyers?
MARY: A very nice American, thank you. Besides! Would you be seen in public

with a Gorgon who ought to live in a bowling-alley?
JEFF: I don't think you're a Gorgon, hang it all!
MARY: Really? You said you did.
JEFF: (*powerfully restrained from outburst*) Look, Mary. It's a fine dining-room in spite of the awful wallpaper. Lorac's got an orchestra there. They always begin with one of those yodeling songs.
MARY: I loathe yodeling.
JEFF: (*hums first snatch of tit-willow song from* The Mikado) That's the tune, Mary! (*pleading*) Have lunch with me!
MARY: Well! I... absolutely not!

FABIAN: A day later. Shortly after noon. Only a few hours now to the time when Baron Carmer has promised to kill his father—the great man lying helpless in the cottage which Jeff Randall once believed to be as safe as a bank vault. (*Sound: "Tit Willow" by Lorac's orchestra as cafe bustle and clatter slowly fade in*) In the dining room of the Inn, Mary Hayes sits at a table... with her luncheon companion...

MARY: (*contrite*) I'm sorry, Jeff. I have been bad-tempered. But now we are at lunch and sitting by a big window, and... (*she lets it trail off*) (*pause: then, forthrightly*) Well, you *could* ask how I like the view... or, at least, make some remark about the hors d'oeuvres.
JEFF: (*intensely*) Mary...!
MARY: That's something. Yes?
JEFF: Mary, when you finish those hors d'oeuvres...
MARY: When I finish them—
JEFF: You're not going to have the rest of your lunch! I'm going to throw you out of here!
(*Sound: knife and fork dropped on plate.*)
JEFF: (*expecting squalls*) Now don't drop your knife and fork. Don't get mad again!
MARY: (*despair*) I'm not mad, Jeff. I'm getting used to you. I—I like it. But you're the craziest, the most impetuous...
JEFF: (*lower voice*) Look around the dining-room, now! What do you see?
MARY: (*hesitation*) The blue-cabbage wall-paper *is* awful.
JEFF: (*quickly*) Yes, what else?
MARY: Well, out through the windows, the long front of the hotel, with two projecting wings...
JEFF: No, no, I mean in here...
MARY: Well, the wallpaper again... but there is a nice grandfather's clock...
JEFF: And the clock says five minutes to two! But I meant the people in the dining-room!
MARY: Well! About a dozen Americans and English. A few French; maybe

Belgians. Oh! There's Mr. Conyers; he'll be furious with me! And Monsieur Lorac with his black mustachios... (*suddenly*) Jeff! Has this got anything to do with the letter?
JEFF: (*guardedly*) What letter?
MARY: The one that porter brought you just as we sat down! Yes; I can see it was the letter! Who was it from?
JEFF: Baron Carmer. Shh, now!
MARY: What did he say?
JEFF: He just said he would *present his compliments* at two o'clock. —Look at the grandfather-clock, Mary! Something, and something unpleasant, is going to happen in less than five minutes. Please get out of here!
MARY: Jeff, I won't do it. I want to stay with you! Besides... never mind the dining-room. Look out of the window here! Down over the valley!
(*Sound: As she speaks, rumble of bobsled is heard, coming closer and going past, with faint cries from occupants, under next speech*)
MARY: There goes another bobsled... and far away —that's the cottage where a German scientist is supposed to get killed by magic. Jeff, *what has my room got to do with it?*
JEFF: (*thinking of other matters*) What's that? Your room?
MARY: Yes! The tapping! And the man who had his throat cut there! How does it fit into the mystery?
JEFF: (*intently*) Your room isn't the mystery, my dear! But —mind, that is only what I think! —it's the key to the mystery.
MARY: Key to the mystery? How?
JEFF: Listen, Mary! It's a small room, oak-paneled in the old style; built against the side of the hill...
LORAC: (*fading on*) Ah, Mees Hayes! (*startled*) *Pardon* if I have make you jump!
MARY: (*recovering*) It's quite all right, Monsieur Lorac!
LORAC: (*beaming*) And Mr. Randall! (*lower voice*) I have good news, monsieur. Mr. Conyers, another American, he is leaving tonight. You can have *his* room, if you wish. (*a loud exclaiming*) *Tiens*, here *comes* Mr. Conyers!
JEFF: (*muttering*) Isn't that your boyfriend, Mary?
MARY: (*muttering: angry*) He's *not* my boy-friend!
JEFF: (*muttering*) He's a big blond so-and-so!
LORAC: (*loudly*) I think Mr. George Conyers, you have met Miss Hayes?
CONYERS: (*about 38, friendly, confident, self-assured voice and breezy manner*) I have indeed met the lady. As a matter of fact, she broke a lunch-engagement with me.
LORAC: (*hastily: fading off*) You will excuse me, please!
MARY: I'm terribly sorry about the lunch, George! But I couldn't help it. This is —my cousin, Mr. Randall.
CONYERS: How do you do, Mr. Randall? (*amused*) But, honestly, my dear Mary, you should learn better tactics! You come into the dining room very late...

it's nearly two o'clock.

JEFF: Yes! By George it is!

CONYERS: —and you hope to find me gone. A little deceit... no! A large deceit —that's easy! (*amused*) Well, I forgive you! As you see by my clothes, I'm going ski-jumping. Won't you both join me?

MARY: Not for me, thanks! Don't you ever break your necks on that ski-jump? Even if there is snow, the hard ground...

CONYERS: The ground isn't hard under thick snow. (*grandiloquently quoting*) "Where the snowflakes fall thickest, there's nothing can freeze!" —By the way, have you solved the mystery?

MARY: (*startled*) *What mystery*?

CONYERS: In your room, of course! The dead man knocking on the wall! — Maybe Mr. Randall hasn't heard the story?

JEFF: I haven't heard about any *ghost*, if that's what you mean! Where did *you* learn about the mystery?

CONYERS: (*surprised*) My dear sir! Gossip! Don't ask how these rumors start.

JEFF: Go on! What do you know?

CONYERS: Well! A German travelling salesman —I don't know his name — came to this hotel about a month ago. He asked for room number 16. He stayed there about two weeks. Then he cut his own throat, or else he was murdered. Afterwards, Mary here was put in the same room...

JEFF: (*as though thinking hard*) Yes. She was! —But what's this about a dead man's knock?

CONYERS: (*amused*) It's only old women's gossip, you know! They're quoting a rhyme from the *Ingoldsby Legends*.

JEFF: (*offering battle*) You seem to enjoy this, Mr. Conyers!

CONYERS: (*accepting battle*) I do, Mr. Randall.

JEFF: What's the rhyme you were talking about?

CONYERS: You really want to know?

JEFF: Yes!

CONYERS: "Fly open, lock, to the dead man's knock,
fly bolt, and bar, and band
— Nor move, or swerve; joint, muscle, or nerve
To the touch of the dead man's hand!"

(*Sound: off, rifle shot: on, heavy crashing of window-glass.*)

MARY: (*screams*)

(*Sounds: commotion in background, dying away*)

JEFF: Sit down, Mary! It's all right.

CONYERS: There's broken window-glass all over this table and that rifle-bullet...

JEFF: That bullet wasn't meant to hit anybody! It's lodged high in the wall! And it smashed the window; it didn't drill a hole. That means it was fired sideways, from the east wing of this hotel!

MARY: (*crying out*) But if it wasn't meant to hit anybody, what *was* it meant for?
(*Sound: grandfather clock strikes two.*)
JEFF: Two o'clock Baron Carmer's compliments!

FABIAN: And so, presently, twilight deepened over that valley, and danger grew nearer. And, in the luxurious basement of the hotel, only three persons remained now in the bowling alley.
(*Sound: fades into sound rolling of bowling-ball down alley, and crash of pins. Music ends.*)

CONYERS: (*calling off*) How's that for bowling, Randall? Strike!
JEFF: (*on, calling: abstracted*) Fine, Conyers! (*back again, fiercely*) Now listen, Mary!
MARY: No, Jeff! You listen to *me*! (*frightened: rushing*) Where did you go after lunch? Where have you been all afternoon?
JEFF: (*suddenly hesitant*) The fact is, Mary, I—(*he stops*)
MARY: You went out of that dining-room like a sleepwalker! You scared me half to death!
JEFF: Anybody might look a little dazed, Mary. When all of a sudden he sees the truth.
MARY: *The truth*? About…?
CONYERS: (*off*) Francois! Where's that attendant? Set up the bowling-pins?
MARY: Go on, Jeff! The truth about…?
JEFF: I know who Carmer is! And how he intends to kill his father.
MARY: (*slight pause*) Jeff, you've got to tell me. I —I've only *written* about murderers! I know you think my books are terrible…
JEFF: (*jumping*) Are you going to start that talk now?
MARY: No! What I mean is; I understand this man's character. He's an egomaniac; he's got to show off; that's why he fired the shot! But *who* is he? *I* only know who he isn't.
JEFF: (*grimly*) That includes a lot of people, Mary!
MARY: He isn't poor George Conyers over there. George was with us at the time of the rifle-shot!
(*Sound: bowling ball down alley.*)
JEFF: Yes. He was. (*slight pause*) And I ought to feel grateful to Conyers, Mary. He handed me the whole answer at lunch.
(*Sound: crash of bowling-pins.*)
CONYERS: (*off*) That's bad! Poor bowling!
MARY: Jeff, aren't you going to *tell* me!?
JEFF: Naturally! But get your instructions first! Now you'll be in no danger—if you —

MARY: Danger? Who said I was in danger?

JEFF: *I* say so! But you're in no danger as long as you keep away from your room!

(*Sound: bowling ball down alley: three pins knocked over.*)

JEFF: In the meantime, I've got to go over to San Moritz for an hour or two...

MARY: What for?

JEFF: To see my chief. And I'm sorry; but I can't take you! He'd have a fit if he suspected I'd told you anything!

MARY: Then don't let him suspect!

JEFF: (*tortured*) I'll try not to... well, I haven't been completely frank with you. And the chief thinks I'm impetuous. And that poor man in the cottage is so terribly important to the world today. And... anyway, you'll be all right as long as you keep away from your room! (*hesitating*) By the way, haven't these noises suggested anything to you?

MARY: What noises?

JEFF: The bobsleds in the daytime! The bowling-alley now! It jumped into my head when Conyers was giving me the clue at lunch. Look, Mary; the whole truth is very simple. Baron Carmer, who is masquerading here as...

FELIX: (*fading in*) Meester Randall! Meester Randall!

JEFF: Who's that light-haired kid in the fancy uniform?

MARY: It's only Felix, the night-porter. He looks and sounds about nineteen; but he's much older. What is it, Felix?

FELIX: I have a telephone message for Meester Randall. From a Meester Rogers at San Moritz.

JEFF: (*quickly*) Oh? What's the message?

FELIX: He say, sir, you are to come *at once*! But in that case you must hurry. There is a snowstorm blowing up and maybe you will not get there!

MARY: (*crying out*) Jeff! Wait.

JEFF: I've *got* to go, Mary!

CONYERS: (*off*) Watch this one! It'll be a real kill!

(*Sound: bowling ball down alley.*)

JEFF: Mary, keep away from your room!

(*Sound: A ball hits bowling-pins for a strike as wind can be heard faintly. A telephone rings.*)

MARY: (*impatiently*) All right! All right!

(*Sound: phone picked up.*)

MARY: Yes? Hello?

FELIX: (*on filter*) Mademoiselle Hayes! You have broke your promise! You are in your own room!

MARY: (*more frightened*) Felix, I had to come here and dress for dinner.

FELIX: Mademoiselle! Meester Randall gave me five thousand francs to keep an eye on you! Come a-way from there at once.

MARY: All right! I'm just going! Good-bye.

(*Sound: phone replaced. wind rises.*)

MARY: (*to herself*) Where's my handbag? I hate this room.

(*Sound: off, noise of key put into lock, rattling, wind rises.*)

MARY: (*calling out*) Who's there? Who's rattling a key in the door? *Who's there*?

(*Sound: door opens and closes.*)

MARY: Oh, it's you—

JEFF: (*fading on, bitterly*) I might have known how far I could trust you.

MARY: But, Jeff! I was only...

JEFF: Don't tell me! You *couldn't possibly have dinner in corduroys and leggings*! You had to change to a dress. *Women*! Has anybody tried to get into this room while you've been here?

MARY: No! Not a soul!

JEFF: Have you *heard* anything?

MARY: No! Nothing except the wind and the storm! Nothing at all.

(*Sound: off, a tap, pause, then another.*)

JEFF: Well, there's the so-called "knocking!" You said yourself, last night, it didn't sound *exactly* like a tapping on wood!

MARY: (*wildly*) Then what is it? What's the secret?

JEFF: This room is built against the side of the hill. You've known that all along?

MARY: Yes, of course!

JEFF: The room's paneled in oak. Not like wallpaper! You could cut out one of those little panels, against the side of the hill, and put it back again without showing any damage!

MARY: Yes, but —what for?

JEFF: The ground doesn't freeze under thick snow. The ground isn't iron hard; that's the key to it! Do you see now what our famous dead man... a fanatical Nazi and a friend of Baron Carmer... was doing here for two weeks?

MARY: No! I don't!

JEFF: He was digging a one-man tunnel. Like an escaping prisoner of war!

MARY: But I keep asking you: *what for*? He couldn't dig a tunnel all the way down to that cottage in the valley.

JEFF: No, of course not! He dug his one-man tunnel, and propped up the sides and top with boards, for maybe a hundred yards along the hillside. In the tunnel he put light charges of high-explosive... each at a distance.

MARY: (*beginning to realize*) And connected with a wire to this room! Is that it?

JEFF: That's it. Throw your switch; set off your high explosive; and you'd get...

MARY: *An avalanche*!

JEFF: Yes, and a sweet one! Ten thousand tons of rock and snow would go roaring down this valley. It would crush the cottage; it would kill Baron Carmer's father—anyone inside or out. —Murder at long distance, my dear! From the direction nobody expected!

MARY: Then this tapping that seems to come from the wall...?

JEFF: The tunnel's not steady, you see. Little loose stones, one or two at a time, fall on a board floor with a sound like...

(*Sound: off, a tap, pause, then another.*)

MARY: (*calling, under her breath*) *Jeff!*

JEFF: What is it?

MARY: The door to the corridor! Behind you! It's opening!

JEFF: (*low*) Never mind! Play up to what I say. (*loudly*) Baron Carmer, Mary, brought his friend here to dig the tunnel and set the explosive. The hotel was empty then. But they had to remove the loose earth and carry in the boards. So Baron Carmer is somebody attached to this place. If you were an escaped Nazi criminal, known to speak English perfectly, what would you do as a disguise?

MARY: I... I wouldn't speak English perfectly. I'd speak it badly.

JEFF: Baron Carmer is known to be light-haired and clean-shaven. What would he do as a disguise?

MARY: He'd dye his hair black! And grow elaborate black mustaches like...

JEFF: Like Monsieur Lorac! The proprietor of the hotel!

LORAC: (*grim: normal voice: fading on*) Don't move, either of you!

MARY: Jeff, he has a gun!

LORAC: Stand back, Mr. Randall!

JEFF: So you've dropped your Swiss accent, Lorac or Carmer?

LORAC: (*hatred: but suave*) I would honor the English tongue by speaking it properly. —Now stand back, both of you!

JEFF: If you're looking for the electric button to the explosive, don't waste your time! The stuff's gone! I found that tunnel this afternoon!

LORAC: That is interesting, Mr. Randall. (*towering*) Did you find the second tunnel?

JEFF: (*taken aback*) Second tunnel?

LORAC: Naturally! My *Fuhrer*, who is not dead, but lives forever, always had two plans. Poor Karl and I —I was forced to kill him in this room —made two tunnels. Over here... (*fading a little off*)... behind a second hinged panel in the wall...

JEFF: Don't touch that panel, you fool! Your father...

LORAC: (*intense hatred*) My father, yes! Here's his passport to the country of the *damned*.

(*Sound: off, muffled, an explosion: pause: two more. rumble of the avalanche begins faintly.*)

LORAC: Two tunnels, Mr. Randall! Each with a board floor, to look at the explosives often and not crawl through dirt!

MARY: Jeff! That noise now...
LORAC: (*exacted*) It will be a spectacle, I tell you!
MARY: It's coming from *up* the valley! In the snow-crags! Won't the avalanche come straight down on this hotel?
LORAC: It may! It may not! Nobody knows! But the traitor down in the cottage...
JEFF: Your father's not in that cottage, you fool!
(*Sound: rumble of avalanche grows louder and closer.*)
LORAC: (*pause*) Not in the cottage? You are lying.
JEFF: No! Do you think we were such fools as to leave him there? A great-hearted scientist who has so much to give mankind. This was a trap to catch *you*! I even lied to Mary about it!
MARY: Can't we run, Jeff? Can't we get away?
LORAC: (*pleased*) No, my dear! If it crashes into this hotel...
MARY: (*screaming*) And you don't care if it kills everybody in the hotel?
LORAC: (*summing up his philosophy*) If *I* die, I prefer that!
JEFF: Here it comes!
(*Sound: roar of avalanche grows to height: on cue, begins to diminish.*)
JEFF: Drop your gun, Carmer! Don't you see anybody outside the French windows? They've been covering you since you came in here.
LORAC: (*now in blind emotional frenzy*) Let the avalanche kill me! I am ready.
JEFF: The avalanche missed us! You'll live to hang!
(*Sound: theme up*)
(*Sound: ship's whistles*)
(*Sound: theme fade*)

Notes for the Curious

The title of this play is taken from the Reverend R.H. Barham's collection of stories and poems *The Ingoldsby Legends* (1840), which Carr also used for the nineteenth Dr, Fell detective novel, published in 1958.

Carr had had a great deal of trouble with the script for this play, which may in part have been because it is a heavily revised version of *"The Room of the Suicides'"* first broadcast on 20 January 1944 in the second series of the BBC program *Appointment with Fear*.

The Man with Two Heads

(*Sound: a ship's whistle*)
(*Sound: theme up*)
ANNOUNCER: *Cabin B-13*. Tonight: "The Man with Two Heads".
(*Sound: theme fades during Fabian's opening narration*)
FABIAN: It is quite probable that you, sometime in your lifetime, have read a story by Leonard Wade. His thrillers are even better known in America than in England. Perhaps, then, when you read of his death last year—only to read, later, that he was very much alive, you were surprised at first—then shocked, then bewildered. I can assure you that this seeming contradiction was no joke on his part. Leonard Wade was the victim of as cruel and horrible a plot as I can conceive—for Wade was one man who actually saw himself lying dead. It was early December, just a year ago, when the *Maurevania* docked at Southampton. With many of the passengers, I came on the boat train to London. Some friends had asked me to their house in the suburbs—and, though it was a night black with frost and raw with fog, I boarded a Number Eight bus and climbed the metal stairs to the top deck…eerie, deserted, its lights blurred by the fog.

(*Sound: fade in rumble of bus, going slowly, as music fades.*)
FABIAN: As the bus rumbled through the muffled cold, every small noise grew sharper in that hollow of loneliness.
(*Sound: bus continues: a beat, then the conductor's footsteps are heard on the metal stairs to the top deck.*)
CONDUCTOR: (*calling off*) Oi! Anybody up there?
FABIAN: (*calling*) I'm here, conductor. Bit difficult to make things out, isn't it?
CONDUCTOR: (*fading on*) Ah. Proper night. Shan't be sorry to see the end of *this* run.
FABIAN: Fourpenny, please.
CONDUCTOR: Fourpenny.
(*Sound: ticket punch pings.*)
FABIAN: I'm sorry you had to climb the steps for just the one fare.
CONDUCTOR: That's all right, sir. There's no one down below neither. The driver and I wouldn't want to make this trip for nothing, now, would we? (*chuckles*) (*fade a bit*) Good thing you brought your newspaper for company.
FABIAN: (*raises voice*) Oh…conductor.
CONDUCTOR: (*halting off*) Yes, sir?
FABIAN: It's been some time since I made this journey, and the fog seems to

be thickening. I know it won't be for a long time yet, but would you be so kind as to give me a shout when we get to Elgin Avenue?
CONDUCTOR: Elgin Avenue. Right you are, sir!
(*Sound: conductor's footsteps clatter down the stairs: the bus rumbles on —*)
WADE: (*pause*) (*early thirties, strong, intelligent, now trying to keep his voice steady and from hysteria*) I beg your pardon.
FABIAN: Good Heavens! Where did you come from?
WADE: Forgive me. I hadn't meant to startle you.
FABIAN: What else could you expect? I believed I was quite alone up here.
WADE: I've been lying down on the seat in front of you.
FABIAN: Lying down? Surely not to make yourself more comfortable.
WADE: I must have seemed a scarecrow, mustn't I, when I thrust my face into yours? But I heard the conductor say you have a newspaper. Is it *The Evening Record*, like this one here?
FABIAN: It is.
WADE: Will you tell me the date of that paper?
FABIAN: (*annoyed*) Really, young man. I...
WADE: (*pleading*) Please! Tell me the date!
FABIAN: (*a beat: then decides to play along*) Very well. December 5th, 1947. This evening's paper.
WADE: Now please humor a man who must seem demented. In the lower right-hand corner of the front page...there, where I'm pointing!... you *may* see a short notice headed... (*quickly*) What is it headed?
FABIAN: "Maida Vale Tragedy: Noted Writer Found Shot."
WADE: Read it aloud, will you?
FABIAN: If you like. "Mr. Leonard Wade, the well-known fiction writer, was found dead early today in the study of his house in Maida Vale, W. 9. He had been shot through the temple, and a .38 calibre automatic pistol was in his right hand. The noise of the shot was heard by Mr. Wade's fiancée, Miss Patricia Bennett, and by his brother, Mr. Stephen Wade, who ran at once to..."
WADE: That's enough. I *didn't* dream it!
FABIAN: Dream...what?
WADE: I stand here clinging to the back of a seat in a familiar London bus, the whole bulk of wood and steel creeping along, creeping along, creeping along as though it would never reach its destination!
FABIAN: The driver daren't go any faster! There's fog!
WADE: (*with feverish courtesy*) Sir, you are a fixed rock of sanity in this nightmare world. (*suddenly*) What's your name? Tell me your name!
FABIAN: My name is Fabian.
WADE: You have a home? And a family? And pleasant dreams at night?
FABIAN: I have no family—my home is a ship. I'm a ship's doctor—and doctors only occasionally have pleasant dreams at night.

WADE: A doctor! Do you by any chance believe in hallucinations? No, don't smile! Or are you thinking of calling the conductor and getting rid of me?
FABIAN: And if I should?
WADE: It won't do you any good to call the conductor.
FABIAN: Why not?
WADE: Because I am Leonard Wade. You have just been reading an account of my death! (*pause, while—*)
(*Sound: bus rumbles up, scraping about a corner: then continues behind —*)
WADE: I killed myself early this morning. I put a bullet through my head. Here!...Here, in my overcoat pocket... here's the gun I did it with!
FABIAN: (*not loudly*) You're mad. You're raving mad.
WADE: Or a ghost. Which am I?
FABIAN: It's difficult to tell, with this dim light and your white face.
WADE: Then how shall *I* know?
FABIAN: Tell me, just what is it you want, Mr. Wade?
WADE: I want company, Doctor Fabian. I want human sympathy. Let me talk to you. May I...may I sit beside you?
FABIAN: (*pause: playing along*) Please sit down. I'll move over.
WADE: Thank you. I didn't want to insist, you know.
FABIAN: It won't help you to threaten me, Mr. Wade. We're coming into the Strand. There'll be people coming up here in a minute.
WADE: True. But if I sit beside you like this...and keep the gun pointing at you, inside my overcoat... I *don't* want to threaten you, Doctor. I only want you to hear me out.
FABIAN: One rarely meets a man who died earlier in the day.
WADE: I *am* Leonard Wade, you see. Is that name familiar to you—outside of that story of my death in your newspaper?
FABIAN: Yes, indeed. I've read many of your stories. You've been highly successful.
WADE: You write a crashing success, and then another. That's where the fear begins.
FABIAN: Fear?
WADE: The fear you can't keep it up; the fear your invention will run out; the fear you're losing your grip. You grind and grind to make it better; you dream of the great things you *could* do; but it only seems to get worse. You overwork. And that means...
FABIAN: You crack up.
WADE: Yes. The two persons I'm fondest of in the world... Patricia Bennett, and my brother Steve... said I had to go away. Far away, to a ranch in Arizona. I left England exactly a year ago tonight. It was a night just like this: bitter cold, with drifting mist, at Southampton. The last time I saw Pat was in a big white-painted lounge, full of milling people, just outside the purser's office aboard the *Maurevania*.
FABIAN: The *Maurevania*?

WADE: Yes. Do you know her?
FABIAN: I've been aboard her. Go on with your story.
 (*Music: sneak in and behind —*)

WADE: I felt lost in that floating hotel. You couldn't hear yourself think for the chatter of crowds. The lounge-doors were open and the fog was blowing up from Southampton Water. Pat was trying to say goodbye.
(*Sound: faint harbor noises, then chatter up and down.*)
PATRICIA: Leonard, darling. I really must be getting back.
WADE: You're not going yet, Pat? We don't sail for another half-hour.
PATRICIA: I hate these drawn-out leave takings. It's like saying goodbye a thousand times. And...I'm not going to see you for another year.
WADE: (*half amused*) Look here, this is all nonsense!
PATRICIA: It's *not* nonsense, darling!
WADE: I never felt healthier in my life. (*hesitating*) At least...
PATRICIA: You will do what you promised, now?
WADE: All right, Pat. If you insist.
PATRICIA: You won't touch a typewriter. You won't go near the publishers in New York. You won't even write a letter to anyone...
WADE: Except you, Pat. I hope I'm not forbidden that much?
PATRICIA: Not even to me! You'd only start worrying about things at home!
WADE: It isn't easy, Pat. You see...
PATRICIA: Yes, dear?
WADE: (*awkwardly*) I've always been a solitary kind of bloke, Pat. Hardly any friends, even, except you and Steve. But this is a bit like going into solitary confinement.
PATRICIA: It's what the doctor told you to do, darling!
WADE: I know. Sorry.
PATRICIA: And I think I'd better go, Leonard, before I begin making a fool of myself. That is, if I can find Steve. (*rattled*) Where *is* Steve? Steve!
STEPHEN: (*off*) Coming, Pat! No hurry!
WADE: (*up*) Is everything arranged, Steve?
STEPHEN: (*fading in*) Your luggage is down in your cabin. Here are your letters of credit; and don't lose 'em. (*faintly envious*) You've made a devil of a lot of money, Leonard. Let that keep you happy.
(*Sound: two blasts on a ship's whistle.*)
PATRICIA: Well...
WADE: Time's getting on, I suppose.
PATRICIA: Yes! Isn't it.
WADE: Goodbye, Steve.
STEPHEN: Goodbye, old man.
WADE: Goodbye, Pat. I...
PATRICIA: (*breaks*) Oh, Leonard—

WADE: Easy, now! Take it easy!
PATRICIA: Hold me! Hold me tighter!
STEPHEN: Hang it all, Pat, it isn't as though you weren't going to see him again. It's only for a year's time. (*slight pause*) Unless, of course, he wants to cancel the whole thing and go ashore with us now.
WADE: (*sharply*) How did you know that?
STEPHEN: Know what?
WADE: What I was thinking. Look over there! That's the window-hatch to the purser's office. If I told them, even at the last minute, to send my luggage ashore…
PATRICIA: Darling, you mustn't! Another of those brain-attacks and… Well, anything might happen. Promise me you won't back out.
WADE: All right, Pat. I promise.
(*Music: in and behind*)
WADE: And so they left me, Doctor Fabian. I went out on deck, among the moving crowd, in that weird light that made faces look like masks. Everything seemed unreal, as though I were no longer a part of myself. Then I wondered if I would write a note to Pat, and send it off before we weighed anchor. So back I went, out of the clinging fog, to the purser's office.

(*Sound: notes of a table-bell struck with the palm of the hand.*)
PURSER: (*very harassed*) Page-boy! Page-boy! Isn't there a page-boy here?
WADE: Excuse me. You're the purser, aren't you? I wonder if…
PURSER: (*trying to be patient*) Yes, Mr. Wade! Yes! I'm doing the best I can. I've *tried* to see to it for you.
WADE: See to it? See to what?
PURSER: (*puzzled*) Getting your luggage ashore, of course. I 'phoned through to your cabin-steward, and…
WADE: (*dumbfounded*) Who told you to send my luggage ashore?
PURSER: But, Mr. Wade…you did.
(*Sound: two blasts of ship's whistle.*)
PURSER: *You* came to me ten or fifteen minutes ago, and said you'd decided not to sail, and could I get your suitcases ashore in a hurry? I said there wasn't much time left.
WADE: But that's impossible! You must be insa—(*suddenly stops, as though with a horrible suspicion*) Yes. Of course. I see.
PURSER: You did tell me that, sir?
WADE: Yes. Of course. I must have. But I…I've changed my mind. Get my luggage back!
PURSER: (*holding hard*) Really, Mr. Wade…!
WADE: Can't you get it back?
PURSER: Stop a bit! There's your cabin-steward now, with the suitcases. (*table-bell rings*) Pearson! Pearson!

STEWARD: Sir?

PURSER: This is Mr. Wade in C-52. He's...er... changed his mind again. He'll be going with us after all.

WADE: Yes! Sorry to give you so much trouble.

STEWARD: (*jovially hearty*) Not a bit of it, sir. Too late to get the stuff ashore anyway, if you ask me. We'll be under way in half a tick. Just you follow me, sir, and I'll take you back to your cabin.

WADE: *Back* to my cabin? But I haven't been to my cabin!

STEWARD: (*calmly*) Just you follow me, sir. Tha-at's it! Round the corner 'ere...along the corridor...Terrible paint-and-rubbery smell these corridors 'ave got, 'aven't they? Stuffy-like. They say that's what makes people seasick, though I never took much stock in it myself. (*pause: then significantly*) Mr. Wade, sir!

WADE: What's wrong? Why are you stopping?

STEWARD: (*guardedly*) It's none of my business, sir. But...

WADE: But what?

STEWARD: (*persuasively*) Now that we're away from other people, hadn't you better let me keep it for you?

WADE: Keep...what?

STEWARD: The automatic pistol. You'd 'a' done yourself in, so help me, if I hadn't grabbed your arm!

WADE: (*after a pause: repressed*) Steward.

STEWARD: Yes, sir?

WADE: Let's pretend I don't understand what you're talking about. (*feverishly*) Let's pretend that, shall we? What happened?

STEWARD: Well, sir! You was in your own cabin...

WADE: When?

STEWARD: Only a few minutes ago. You was standing there holding that gun, like as if you were going to shoot somebody, and you didn't see me when I opened the door. Then all of a sudden you said, "I'll put an end to this!" and you stuck the gun against your own head, and your finger started to tighten on the trigger...

WADE: No!

STEWARD: It's gospel truth, sir. I dived over and grabbed your arm. Then you gave me a funny glassy kind of look... like you're giving me now...and you put the gun in your pocket and ran out of there.

WADE: I don't believe it. You're lying to me!

STEWARD: (*astounded*) Sir!

WADE: I couldn't have done that! I don't remember it! And I've never had an automatic pistol in my life. I...

STEWARD: (*softly insistent*) Sir!

WADE: Well?

STEWARD: Feel in your right-hand overcoat pocket. Tha-at's it: feel in your

right-hand overcoat pocket. Easy, now... Is the gun there?
WADE: Yes. Yes, it's there.
(*Sound: two blasts of ship's whistle.*)
STEWARD: Give *me* the gun, sir. Just to keep for you! Then you can have a nice pleasant crossing.
(*Sound: the bus fades*)

WADE: And that, Doctor Fabian, was what happened on the first night out.
FABIAN: I see. Of course. Most unpleasant, Mr. Wade.
WADE: That was when I first had the feeling of two separate persons, two separate entities, and both of them were myself. One was the self I knew. The other was a kind of horrible soul, that put on human flesh and moved in my image. Mind you, I knew this wasn't real. I knew it was lunacy. And yet...
FABIAN: (*muttering*) Careful! Keep that gun down! People are looking at us!
WADE: (*half waking up*) What's that?
FABIAN: We're in Regent Street, man! The bus is half full.
WADE: (*dully*) Yes. So it is. I...
FABIAN: I'm most interested in your story, having been aboard the *Maurevania*...once. What happened after you found the pistol in your pocket, Mr. Wade?
WADE: I went to that ranch in Arizona. And I cured my brain ... or thought I had.
FABIAN: Thought you had?
WADE: A year of living in the open air. A year without a page to write, a character to think of. Only a sense of immense peacefulness, and sound sleep at night. I could *feel* myself being healed, just as bones knit together after a fracture. I kept the gun with me. Here it is now!...as a kind of challenge. Finally I could laugh at it; do you understand?
FABIAN: Until when?
WADE: Until I got back to England tonight.
FABIAN: Go on.
WADE: I wanted to surprise them, you see. Surprise Pat and Steve. So I didn't tell them I was coming home. All the way across the Atlantic I was in a fever to get back.

(*Sound: fade bus into chug of train engine in hollow space, then footsteps, and crowd murmur of people hurrying along.*)
WADE: Everything was splendid—until I arrived at Waterloo Station tonight, on the boat-train from Southampton. I'd got out of the train, and was walking along the platform behind a man and woman I vaguely remembered seeing aboard ship. I could hear every word they said... clearly
EDITH: Bob!

BOB: Yes, Edith?
EDITH: Isn't it *nice* to be back in England again?
BOB: *I* don't think so. Filthy weather as usual.
EDITH: I haven't had a decent cup of tea for months. Or a decent cigarette. And no English papers!
BOB: Look out, old girl! You're walking straight into a luggage-truck.
EDITH: (*calling to someone off*) So-rr-ry!
BOB: Look where you're going, Edith! Anything in the paper?
EDITH: No. But it's a sign of home. (*remembering*) Oh! There *was* something, rather. You know that man who writes all the best sellers? Leonard Wade?
BOB: Yes? What about him?
EDITH: He's dead.
BOB: Dead, eh?
EDITH: He blew his brains out this morning.
WADE: What did you say? *What did you say*?
EDITH: (*startled*) Bob!
BOB: Well?
EDITH: Did you hear somebody cry out?
BOB: Cry out?
EDITH: A funny, awful kind of cry. It seemed to come from behind us.
BOB: Nonsense, old girl! It was an engine or something. I didn't hear anything. What were you telling me?
EDITH: About Leonard Wade, the writer.
BOB: You needn't walk so fast, Edith! *I'm* carrying the luggage.
EDITH: The paper says his body was found in the study, a ground floor room at the front of the house. It says his fiancée, a girl named Patricia Bennett, is nearly out of her mind. She's a cousin of the family and lives in the house. *She* heard the shot. She ran downstairs, and found him with one side of his head all...Bob!
BOB: What is it *now*?
EDITH: I *did* hear that cry a second ago. I know I did! Like—like —
BOB: It sounded like —
EDITH: Like somebody being tortured.
BOB: What you want, Edith, is a good meal. (*amused*) If you heard anything, it must have been a ghost.

WADE: I vaguely remember getting into a taxi, and giving my address in Maida Vale. I was going home, Doctor Fabian, I was going home. But I hadn't the courage to face what I might find. I told the driver to stop a hundred yards short of the house. I remember walking along the pavement, very slowly, in the drifting mist. And then I realized there were two people walking in front of me. They weren't the same people as those two at the station, of course; but, by one of those horrible tricks of sound in fog, they *seemed* like the same voices…

EDITH: It's along here, you know. We're getting close.
BOB: Close to what?
EDITH: To the house where that writer, Leonard Wade, shot himself this morning.
BOB: Oh. Nasty business, that was. —You're becoming very affectionate all of a sudden, aren't you?
EDITH: Affectionate?
BOB: Grabbing my arm like that!
EDITH: But that's it! Just ahead of us! The grey stone house with the white facings, behind the little wall.
BOB: All right. It won't hurt you to walk past it.
EDITH: But there are lights all over the place! Suppose we —see him?
BOB: See his ghost, you mean?
EDITH: No! But it said in the paper Mr. Wade killed himself in a room on the ground floor front. Suppose they haven't moved the body? Suppose we see— *him*?
BOB: You don't have to look in, do you?
EDITH: No. Of course not. We'll walk straight past it, and never once… (*abruptly*) Darling.
BOB: Well?
EDITH: They haven't closed the shutters.
BOB: Don't stop there! Come on! Don't make a spectacle of yourself! We don't want to look like a pair of morbid sightseers.
EDITH: Darling. I can see him.
BOB: Come on, I tell you! (*wavering*) Not…?
EDITH: Not lying on the floor, no. But there's something on a couch at the back of the room, covered up with a sheet as far as the neck. And it doesn't move. And its face is white. And one side of the head is all…
WADE: (*screaming*) No! No! No!
(*Music: come in strongly, then down*)

WADE: That, Doctor Fabian, was how I saw myself lying dead under a sheet. (*pause*) I screamed out something and ran past those two people. There was a bus on the other side of the road; a big red shape in the mist. It had just stopped, and I jumped aboard it. Since then, Doctor…
(*Sound: bus is now heard under.*)
FABIAN: Since then, Mr. Wade, you've been riding back and forth, back and forth on this bus.
WADE: Yes, wondering if I dreamed it. Wondering if this *is* the fifth of December, and not some pre-vision of the future. I picked up the newspaper, and that confirmed it. Where are we?

FABIAN: Edgware Road, I believe.
WADE: Edgware Road! That means —
FABIAN: It means, young man, that in a very few minutes you'll be back in Maida Vale.
WADE: I won't get off this bus!
FABIAN: On the contrary, Mr. Wade. You must go into your house and have a good look at the thing on the sofa.
WADE: (*amazed*) *You* advise that?
FABIAN: Your experience has been upsetting—very upsetting—but you mustn't let it destroy your common sense. If you can't see any explanation of this...
WADE: Explanation? I've tried to imagine every conceivable explanation.
FABIAN: (*sharply*) If you'll forgive me, that's just the trouble. You have so much imagination, you can't see what really happened!
WADE: (*angrily*) Whereas you can!
FABIAN: I'm not sure, of course, but...
(*Sound: as he says the above, the bus, going faster, swerves sharply, and the horn is sounded...*)
FABIAN: The driver of this bus almost upset us then.
WADE: Never mind the driver! Look here, Doctor Fabian, if you have any kind of a solution, give it to me.
FABIAN: Mr. Wade, all along I've been able to give credence to your story because—I'm ship's surgeon of the *Maurevania*.
WADE: You?
FABIAN: I never saw you aboard her—there are so many passengers on each voyage. But I remember your steward mentioning a man who contemplated suicide on the voyage last year. A man, who, a few moments later, wouldn't believe he'd acted as the steward told him he had. I've been listening to your story closely. Mr. Wade—is there anyone here in England who looks like you?
WADE: (*angrily*) Don't you think I've considered that possibility?
FABIAN: Perhaps you haven't considered it closely enough! *Is* there someone who looks like you?
WADE: Well, it's true there used to be a fellow—an ex-schoolmaster named Rupert Hayes—who looked so much like me that Pat—my own fiancée—couldn't tell us apart.
FABIAN: Then he knew something about you and your affairs!
WADE: Not enough to matter. When I last heard of him, he was down and out. He'd been in prison. And he was going under with T.B. ... And just because he looks like me wouldn't explain...
FABIAN: (*breaking him*) "Been in prison" ... "down and out" ...? You're not mad, Mr. Wade! You never were mad! There's no "other self". This whole game was ...
WADE: Was what? Go on?

FABIAN: It was an attempt to murder you. Carefully planned and arranged by your brother, Stephen!
(*Sound: the bus swerves again, and the horn sounds ...*)
WADE: Do you know what you're saying, Doctor Fabian?
FABIAN: If you died before your marriage, who would be your heir?
WADE: Steve, of course! But...
FABIAN: Suppose he did plan to kill you! He couldn't kill you at home without rousing suspicion. But, with the help of this man who looks like you, this ... this ...
WADE: Hayes, Rupert Hayes ...
FABIAN: Those two were able to commit the perfect crime.
WADE: Go on!
FABIAN: You went aboard ship a year ago tonight. And Hayes followed you with a pistol in his pocket.
WADE: Well?
FABIAN: After your brother and your fiancée had left, Hayes was to shoot you and drop you overboard, in the fog and darkness. Hayes would then go ashore as you.
WADE: (*half realizing*) You mean...?
FABIAN: He would say he had decided not to sail after all. Your brother, Stephen Wade, had already prepared your fiancée's mind for you to make that decision. Remember? As for you, the real you, nobody would inquire after you because no passenger was missing from the ship. As soon as the ship moved out, the knife-blade propellers would catch your body; they would make you only an unidentified corpse picked up at the docks.
WADE: But in the meantime—?
FABIAN: Rupert Hayes, posing as Leonard Wade, had only six months or a year to live. If he made any slips, that could be put down to a brain attack. Then he would die of natural causes. And no policeman, no post-mortem, nothing could ever touch Stephen, because this man really had died a natural death. The perfect crime. Only...
WADE: Only Hayes lost his nerve when it came time to murder me on the ship. Is that it?
FABIAN: I think that's it.
WADE: Hayes tried to get my luggage ashore, but I forestalled him. And that business with the gun in my cabin—the steward saw it...
FABIAN: Hayes, your double, had lost his nerve and couldn't shoot you—so he decided to commit suicide. However, the steward interrupted him and then he changed his mind. Hayes was sick and desperate; he couldn't give up that six months—that year of soft living while he posed as you. He found you on deck—slipped the gun in your pocket and ran ashore. He told your brother he *had* killed you.
WADE: But he must have known I'd come back.
FABIAN: Of course! But he was safe for a while. You'd promised to write nothing—no new stories, not even a letter to your fiancée. But he finally had

to face the reckoning. A year had passed. He was still alive.

WADE: You think he confessed to Steve?

FABIAN: I do—and was killed when Steve found out he'd been tricked—and you were still alive.

WADE: The papers said it was suicide.

FABIAN: Your brother Stephen is a clever and desperate man, Mr. Wade.

WADE: I don't believe it. I can't believe it. Doctor Fabian! What proof have you?

FABIAN: No proof at all. Only a mind that reasons along these lines because of a doctor's experience with human beings.

WADE: Steve—my own brother—wouldn't do a thing like that!

FABIAN: I may be doing him an injustice, of course. But if this *is* true...

WADE: Mind how you stand up. The bus is jolting. You'll fall...!

FABIAN: (*unheeding*) If this *is* true, Mr. Wade, your brother has been living in a fool's paradise! He believes you are dead Now that you're back, what's going to happen when you face him?

(*Sound: bus horn blasts frantically.*)

PATRICIA: (*screams, off—she's across the street*) Look out! Look out! Look out!

CONDUCTOR: (*off, on lower deck of bus*) Be careful, you blasted fool!

(*Sound: screech of brake and gears: a scream of tires as the driver tries to stop the bus within a few feet : a heavy jolting!*)

PATRICIA: (*split second pause: then a horrible scream, off.*)

(*Sound: The bus dies out*)

WADE: Easy, Doctor Fabian. Were you jolted badly?

FABIAN: (*shaken*) You warned me about standing up, Mr. Wade. What happened?

WADE: I can tell you what happened this time! That was Pat's voice we heard! My fiancée's out there! But...

CONDUCTOR: (*shouting off*) We couldn't help it, miss! The perishing fool ran straight in front of the bus! Tryin' to stop us, he was!

PATRICIA: (*off*) Steve! Steve! Steve!

FABIAN: Are your doubts answered, Mr. Wade?

WADE: Steve ran in front of this bus—trying to stop it. Or else—

FABIAN: We shall never know. Rupert Hayes must have left a confession, you know. And if the police found it ...

WADE: I—I suppose we'd better go down and see.

FABIAN: Yes. I suppose we had.

WADE: You'll come along and support me?

FABIAN: If you don't mind, Mr. Wade—

WADE: Yes?

FABIAN: I'm on my way to visit some friends. After all, I'm only a humble ship's surgeon.

(*Sound: theme up*)
(*Sound: ship's whistles*)
(*Sound: theme fade*)

Notes for the Curious

The protagonist of "The Man with Two Heads", surely the worst of Carr's sometimes catch-penny titles, is Leonard Wade, a writer of detective stories and therefore a proxy for Carr himself. Similar Carr-characters appear throughout his work. The earliest is Jeff Marle—who narrates four of the five novels in which Henri Bencolin appears—and Tad Rampole who appears in *Hag's Nook* (1933), *The Mad Hatter Mystery* (1933) and *The Three Coffins* (1935) and, probably, *Death-Watch* (1935).

The area of London where Wade has his home, Maida Vale, was home to Carr and his wife for a matter of weeks before the building was destroyed by a high explosive bomb in the autumn of 1940. In inventing Wade's house, with its study on the ground floor front and-shutters on the windows, it is likely that Carr was thinking of either his home at 118a Maida Vale, near the BBC's emergency studios, or possibly the home of his friend and fellow member of the Detection Club, Christianna Brand, who lived at 88 Maida Vale. Both are near Elgin Avenue, given incorrectly as Elgin Road in the original script.

"The Man with Two Heads" is a revised version of the play of the same title, first broadcast on 6 November 1945 in the sixth series of the BBC program *Appointment with Fear*.

However, the central ploy of a man who returns from a journey overseas to discover that his death has been reported in the newspapers, is borrowed from a plot that Carr had first used over twenty years earlier in the short story "The Legend of the Cane in the Dark", published in his college magazine *The Haverfordian* in December 1927. In the intervening years, Carr had already used the ploy as the basis of two short stories: "The Man Who Was Dead", published in *Dime Mystery* in May 1935; and "New Murders for Old", published in *Holly Leaves*, the Christmas number of the *Illustrated London News* for 1939.

The Bride Vanishes

(*Sound: a ship's whistle*)
(*Sound: theme up*)
ANNOUNCER: *Cabin B-13*. Tonight: "The Bride Vanishes".

(*Sound: theme fades during Fabian's opening narration*)
FABIAN: Terror does not strike only in dark places. There, on the sunlit, fabulously-beautiful Isle of Capri, one woman had already vanished without a trace. They warned Lucy Courtney, the lovely young American bride, that she looked too much like the other woman—that the terror would again strike from nowhere on that balcony of death. Would you have dared to step out upon that balcony alone, as Lucy did?

(*Sound: Santa Lucia-like background, suggesting lightness and gaiety*)
FABIAN: Blue water a-dazzle under the sun. Behind you, the bone-white beaches—and Vesuvius, dull purple in a heat haze. And the island of Capri twenty-miles out, across the Bay of Naples. As I bade goodbye to Tom and Lucy Courtney on the deck of the *Maurevania*, I wished I were going with them to Capri.

(*Sound: small steamer chugging in background: roar of surf*)
FABIAN: I did not hear the story of the horrible events which befell them until we returned to Naples again—a story that began soon after they boarded the small harbor steamer that chugs across the Bay towards Capri.

LUCY: No! I mean—in a funny way! Even your American friend... what's his name...?
TOM: Granger?
LUCY: Mr. Granger. When you introduced him to me at Naples, I thought his eyes were going to pop out.
TOM: (*in a low voice*) Shh... He's standing over by the rail now. He lives at Capri.
LUCY: Why does he persist in wearing that white ten-gallon hat in Italy?
TOM: Before Granger made money in oil-wells, he was a real old-fashioned cowpuncher. And he's proud of it. Good fellow, too.
LUCY: He's too polite to say anything. But *he* keeps looking around at me.
TOM: Well?
LUCY: He looks frightened.
TOM: Frightened? (*worried*) This isn't the time to start imagining things, Lucy.
LUCY: I know. Maybe I'm just so happy I'm afraid it can't last.

Tom: Don't *say* that!
(*Sound: ship comes to stop*)
Lucy: But wouldn't it be pretty awful if something did happen? And we weren't together any longer?
Tom: Wait a minute. Hasn't our ship stopped?
Lucy: Yes. I hadn't noticed.
Tom: Seems a funny place to stop. No sign of a harbor; only rocks and little gray cliffs. (*calling*) Mr. Granger! Mr. Granger!
Granger: Yes, young fellow?
Tom: Do you happen to know why we're stopping here?
Granger: That's an easy one, son. We're stopping so that you and your good lady—and anybody else who's curious can get a look at the Blue Grotto.
Lucy: The Blue Grotto! Where is it, Mr. Granger?
Granger: Shade your eyes with your hand, ma'am. You see that tiny little arch under the cliff?
Lucy: Yes?
Granger: And all the little white row-boats coming out towards us?
Lucy: Yes!
Granger: Now when the first boat comes alongside, you climb down that iron ladder and get in. The boatman'll row you out, and through the arch into the grotto. It's a great big dark cavern. The water in there looks as though it's lit up underneath with blue fire.
Tom: Would you like to go out and see it, Lucy?
Lucy: I'd love to!
Granger: Let me give you a little tip, Mrs. Courtney. The current's pretty fast out there. You'll go shooting under that arch like sixty.
Lucy: Are we likely to upset?
Granger: No. But the arch isn't as high as your head. When you see it coming, lie back flat in the boat. That is, unless you want your head knocked off.
Tom: Thanks, Mr. Granger. We'll remember. (*fade*) See you later.

(*Sound: faint splashings*)
Tom: (*worried*) Easy on the ladder, Lucy! Don't look round yet!
Lucy: (*amused*) I'm all right, darling. And just as good a swimmer as you are.
Tom: I'm in the boat now. Take one more step… steady… now turn around, facing the boatman, and sit down here beside…
(*Sound: heavy splashings*)
Boatman: (*terrified*) *Corpo di bacco!*
Lucy: Tom! What's the matter with the boatman?
Tom: Easy, man! Do you want to upset us? Sit down!
Boatman: You… come… back. Yes?
Lucy: Come back? I've never been here before in my life!
Tom: Push off, man! Start rowing! The other boats are piling up behind you!
Boatman: You… come… back.
Tom: Start rowing, can't you? *Andare subito! Basta!*

(*Sound: after a slight pause, the creak and swish of oar*)
LUCY: (*whispering*) Tom, he can't take his eyes off us.
TOM: I wish he'd watch out where he's rowing.
BOATMAN: (*pouncing*) You come to live at the Villa Borghese, yes?
LUCY: Tom, how does he know that?
BOATMAN: (*panting*) Theesa lady... she eesa-not dead?
TOM: Dead?! Of course she's not dead! What are you talking about?
BOATMAN: She never come to Capri before?
TOM: Never!
BOATMAN: Then I tella you. *She* will disappear, justa like de other one.
LUCY: Disappear?
(*Sound: rowing ceases, but a faint rushing of moving water begins to grow in volume*)
BOATMAN: *Si—si—*I rest on my oars, and I tella you.
LUCY: (*quickly*) Tom, aren't we moving rather fast?
TOM: Yes. That's the entrance to the grotto ahead.
BOATMAN: I tella you. There was a lady. So mucha like you it... *corpo di Bacco!*... it scare me.
TOM: Look, old man. I don't want to teach you your business, but you've got your back to that grotto!
BOATMAN: Take theesa lady back where she come from! Don' take her to the Villa Borghese!
TOM: Down, Lucy! The current's taking us into the grotto! Flat on your back! Down!
(*Sound: loud rushing of water. then the noise of water fades. Sounds now are heard in an enclosed space*)
BOATMAN: (*contritely*) *Signore! Signora!* I am sorry! I almost make you get hurt!
TOM: (*harshly*) Do you know you nearly got your own head knocked off?
BOATMAN: Scusa me, no! I am used to it! Now I weel row you round the Blue Grotto.
(*Sound: rowing begins again*)
LUCY: I don't think I like it much, Tom.
TOM: Neither do I.
LUCY: Dark... except for that blue light under the water. It's transparent. You can see the fishes swimming.
TOM: Just a minute, boatman! This lady who disappeared from the Villa Borghese...
(*Sound: rowing out*)
BOATMAN: Two, three year ago she disappear.
TOM: You say she looked exactly like my wife?
BOATMAN: (*vehemently*) *Si, signore!* She was a-going to be married. She was trying on what you calla her wedding-dress. Her mother and sisters, they were in da room with her. She walk out on a balcony over da sea. You

know what I mean by a balcony over da sea? And nobody ever hear of her again.
LUCY: You mean... she jumped over into the sea?
BOATMAN: (*hurt*) A young girl a-going to be married? Keel herself? No, no, no, no!
TOM: Then what did happen?
BOATMAN: *Corpo di Bacco*, I don't know! But somatimes, they say, you can meet her ghost. Ina here. She float just under the water, where you can see her. And turn over and over. And the wedding-veil is still round her face.
LUCY: Tom. Let's get out of here!
BOATMAN: (*with powerful eagerness*) You want to go? YES?
TOM: (*quietly*) Lucy, if this fellow is stringing us along...
LUCY: He's not stringing us along.
TOM: Then somebody ought to know what this means! If we've inherited a haunted balcony, where people disappear like soap-bubbles, I say it's too much! Let's get back to our steamer and talk to Granger!

(*Sound: small steamer's whistle*)
LUCY: Mr. Granger! Mr. Granger!
GRANGER: Climb aboard, ma'am. And you too, young fellow. This ship's starting in half a second.
TOM: Here give me your hand, Lucy.
LUCY: Yes, dear. Oh, didn't anybody else go to the Blue Grotto?
GRANGER: (*embarrassed*) Well, ma'am—no. (*hesitates*) The other boatman refused to take them after they saw you and Mr. Courtney go.
(*Sound: the ship's engine starts*)
TOM: It's all right. We've just heard the story.
GRANGER: (*bursting out*) I ought to have told you about it myself! All the way out here I've been cussing myself, and thinking what an ornery old badger I am, for not telling you when I first met you in Naples!
TOM: The girl *did* vanish, then?
GRANGER: By a first-rate miracle—yes. In broad daylight, and within twenty feet of her mother and sisters.
TOM: You don't look like a man who'd believe in miracles, Mr. Granger.
GRANGER: I'm not, son. I'm just telling you what happened.
TOM: But why is everybody so excited? Somebody must have thrown her off the balcony!
GRANGER: Josephine Adams was all alone on a balcony forty feet up a cliff smooth as glass. She didn't fall, and she wasn't thrown, because there was no sound of a splash and she didn't come back from the balcony, because her mother and sisters were in front of the only door. Yet within fifteen seconds... *Fifteen seconds*, mind you!... She just vanished.

(*Sound: in the distance, a dog is heard barking faintly*)
TOM: (*incredulously*) You believe that?
GRANGER: Sure I believe it, son. It's a fact?
LUCY: Did you know the girl's family?
GRANGER: Very well. We've got a real English-speaking colony here.
(*Sound: steamer's whistle*)
GRANGER: We're pulling in. In about half a minute, now, I'm going to show you your new home.
LUCY: Can we see it from the deck here?
GRANGER: You sure can, ma'am. It's on the edge of the cliff. Professor Davis's house is on one side of it, and my shack's on the other. (*hesitates*) That's why I want to ask you a question.
LUCY: Of course. Ask anything you like.
GRANGER: (*heavily*) I'm an old stager, ma'am, and not exactly up to the high-toned society around here. But... do you trust me?
LUCY: Yes, I think so.
GRANGER: Then promise me something. Unless you're with somebody you *do* trust, *keep away from that balcony.*
TOM: Do you honestly think there's danger of...?
GRANGER: (*tortured*) I don't know, son! If—I did know, I wouldn't have to talk this way!
(*Sound: close at hand, the dog barks*)
LUCY: (*breaking off*) That sounds like a dog barking! I thought I heard it before.
TOM: It is. A big police-dog. And led by a very handsome woman, if you ask me.
GRANGER: (*under his breath*) Oh, Lord! I didn't know she was aboard!
TOM: Who?
GRANGER: The countess. She lives in our colony.
LUCY: She looks like an American. (*under her breath*) You take your eyes off her, Tom Courtney!
GRANGER: She *is* an American, married a Count Parcheesi, or something like that. Just call her Nellie.
(*Sound: the dog barks*)
NELLIE: (*excitedly*) My dear Harry Granger!
GRANGER: Hello, Nellie,
NELLIE: It's true. Everybody told me so, but I couldn't believe it until I saw her! She *does* look exactly like poor Josephine Adams. Just as small, just as dainty...
LUCY: Please! Is *everybody* trying to give me the jitters?
GRANGER: Nellie, I want you to meet some friends of mine.
NELLIE: You don't need to introduce me! I know who they are! You're the nice young couple who've taken that villa. I'm Nellie Luchesi... And this is my dog, Tiberius.

(*Sound: the dog barks*)

NELLIE: Named after the wicked Roman Emperor, you know, who used to live at Capri. I must confess I'm terribly fascinated by wicked things. Aren't you, Mr. Courtney?

TOM: (*muttering*) Lucy, stop digging me in the ribs! I haven't done anything!

LUCY: (*muttering*) No, and you're not going to.

NELLIE: Tiberius seems to have taken quite a fancy to you, Mrs. Courtney. I've never known him to go up to a stranger before.

LUCY: I only wish I could borrow him. He might be a charm against... oh, I don't know!

NELLIE: We'll be at the harbor in a few minutes. Then you must let me drive you up to the villa. You won't be able to get any servants, I'm afraid, because they won't stay there. But you can camp out... (*breaking off*)... Look! There's your villa! We're passing it now!

LUCY: Where?

NELLIE: On the cliff! Where I'm pointing.

TOM: (*sharply*) Wait a minute. There must be some mistake. That's not the Villa Borghese?

GRANGER: It sure is, son.

TOM: But, that's a palace! Like all the other houses there. And I rented it, furnished, for about twenty-five dollars a month!

GRANGER: Can't you guess why you got it so cheap, son? If you take my advice, you'll turn around and go back to Naples by the next steamer!

NELLIE: Harry Granger, don't be an idiot! Let's have some excitement! (*through her teeth*) Let's have some *excitement*!

LUCY: (*enthralled*) Tom, it *is* beautiful.

TOM: Too infernally beautiful, if you ask me.

NELLIE: There's the balcony.

(*Sound: A murmur, as of a crowd muttering uneasily and rather superstitiously. The dog barks*)

GRANGER: It's all right by daylight... Marble and tapestries. But at night... when you've got to put out the lights... and you start thinking what happened there...

FABIAN: The moon over Capri makes a deathly daylight. You could see to read on that balcony—if anyone went out there. Frosted-glass doors open out on it from a big room on the ground floor. Two calm persons and a dog sit looking at each other...

TOM: (*edgily*) Lucy, stop it!

LUCY: Stop what?

TOM: Stop looking over at that balcony?

LUCY: I'm sorry, darling.

TOM: Why are we sitting *here* anyway? There's another room that's much more comfortable.

LUCY: It's like having a toothache. A very *little* toothache.

TOM: I may be dense, angel, but I don't follow you.

LUCY: You put your tongue against the tooth, to see if it'll hurt. You know it will hurt. But you go on doing it just the same… That's us.

TOM: Maybe you're right.

LUCY: Oh, Tom, did you ever think we'd have a lovely house like this?

TOM: The house is all right, yes. (*bursting out*) Then they have to go and spoil everything—our honeymoon! with this blasted tommy rot about…

LUCY: Please Tom, you're as jittery now as I was this afternoon! (*the dog growls*) Even Tiberius is jittery.

(*Sound: the dog growls, low, again*)

TOM: (*drawing a deep breath*) Yes, I guess I am… Easy, boy! Easy!

LUCY: Well there's whiskey on the table. They call it veeky here. Mix yourself a drink.

TOM: In a minute. Not just now… Lucy, there's *nothing* wrong with that balcony! Suppose you walked out on it this minute…

LUCY: I've had a horrible longing to try it, just because I know I shouldn't.

TOM: Nothing could attack you. All you'd have to do would be yell. That would bring Granger out on *his* balcony like a shot. And the neighbor on the other side of us would… Who is on the other side, by the way?

LUCY: A brain-specialist.

TOM: A what?!

LUCY: A specialist in brain disorders. Professor Davis—he's English —

(*Sound: a door opens and closes way off*)

LUCY: (*sharply*) Listen!

(*Sound: the dog begins to bark furiously. This is followed by a scratching sound as of a dog at a closed door*)

TOM: It's somebody in the outer room. Easy, Tiberius! Easy!

LUCY: Tom, I'm afraid.

TOM: It's all right. You hold Tiberius's collar while I open the door. We don't want him to fly at anybody. We're going into the other room and stay there. Ready?

LUCY: Yes.

(*Sound: door opens. The dog bursts out barking again, but stops abruptly. Door closes*)

DAVIS: Good evening, Mr. Courtney. Good evening, Mrs. Courtney. (*faintly amused*) I am no ghost, though you appear to regard me as one, I am merely your neighbor, Professor Rutherford Davis.

LUCY: (*relieved*) Oh! Yes. Yes, of course. Mr. Granger mentioned you.

DAVIS: I trust you will pardon this intrusion? No one answered my knock, so I ventured to come in.

TOM: It's no intrusion, Professor Davis. We're—a little disorganized here, that's all.

DAVIS: Naturally. Mr. Courtney. I wish I could say, "Welcome to Capri". But I have a very different message.
TOM: Well?
DAVIS: (*quietly, but great intensity*) If you value Mrs. Courtney's life, you'll go back to Naples immediately.
TOM: Not you too!
DAVIS: I do not say that as a ghost-hunter, sir. I say it as a specialist. May I sit down?
LUCY: Of course! Please do!
DAVIS: Thank you.
TOM: (*unsteadily*) We seem to be forgetting our manners, Professor Davis. Will you have a drink?
DAVIS: Thank you. Perhaps a small whiskey?
LUCY: (*with decision*) *I'll* get it, darling. You sit down and talk to Professor Davis.
TOM: You're not going back into that room alone!
LUCY: (*soothing*) I'm only going to get the drinks, Tom! I promise to be good. And Tiberius can come with me. Can't you, Tiberius?
(*Sound: the dog barks*)
DAVIS: Oh, I see. You've borrowed Tiberius from the Countess Luchesi.
LUCY: Yes. She was kind enough to offer him. Excuse me. I'll be back in a minute. Come on, Tiberius!
(*Sound: dog barks. Door opens and closes*)
TOM: I hope this is all right, Professor.
DAVIS: No, sir, it is *not* all right. Your wife is in very great danger.
TOM: (*desperately*) But why? Because of that balcony?
DAVIS: No. Because she looks exactly like the late Josephine Adams.
TOM: (*bewildered*) I don't get it!
DAVIS: Mr. Courtney, did you ever hear of paranoia?
TOM: It's some kind of mental disease, isn't it?
DAVIS: Yes. The paranoiac begins by imagining that he—or she—is being persecuted by someone. Persecuted by the most unlikely and harmless kind of person, as a rule. First he hears things. A voice in his brain whispers, "You'll be killed, you'll be killed, you'll be killed." He hears it in the tick of a clock, in the rattle of a train, in the footsteps on a street. There are holes in the walls, through which his enemy is always watching. Invisible speaking-tubes bring him messages. There are pains in his joints, and nightmares of attempts to poison him. His brain bursts, and he kills—he kills—he kills! (*checking himself*) Excuse me for speaking so—strongly.
TOM: But how does this affect us?
DAVIS: Mr. Courtney, will you examine this sheet of paper?
TOM: What is it?
DAVIS: The fragment of a typewritten diary. I found it on the cliffs months

ago. Don't ask me who wrote it, but I know that a criminal lunatic on this island imagined that poor, inoffensive Josephine Adams was his enemy. So he killed her.

TOM: Killed her? *How?*

DAVIS: (*flatly*) I don't know.

TOM: And what happened to the girl's body?

DAVIS: I am not a detective, sir. The body was carried out to sea, perhaps. Or washed along the cliffs and into the Blue Grotto to be lost. But don't you understand the danger to your wife?

TOM: You're not suggesting...?

DAVIS: To somebody's cracked brain, your wife is Josephine Adams created all over again.

TOM: Kill Lucy? It couldn't be done!

DAVIS: It *was* done, my friend.

(*Sound: thinly, we hear the howling of a dog*)

DAVIS: Listen—!

TOM: That sounded... like a dog howling.

DAVIS: (*quietly*) Mrs. Courtney is rather a long time in getting that whiskey.

TOM: She wouldn't go near the balcony! She promised not to go out on the balcony!

DAVIS: People do very perverse things, my friend, when they know they shouldn't.

TOM: (*crying out*) Lucy!

(*Sound: the dog howls. the door is banged open*)

TOM: *Lucy!*

DAVIS: That seems to be Tiberius, out on the balcony. I can't see anything else from here.

TOM: (*fading*) She's gone. She's gone. She's... *gone!*

(*Sound: the dog howls*)

FABIAN : An empty balcony. A howling dog. And a sea turned clear silver under the moon...(*Sound: bring in motorboat engine behind*) That was how it was pictured to me with such intolerable vividness that I seem to have lived through it. Then, after the tumult and shouting, there are other pictures. Don't you hear the noise of that motor-launch, with a half-demented young man at the wheel? Three other familiar figures are gathered round it. Don't you recognize the white ten-gallon hat of Harry Granger? And the neat pointed beard of Professor Davis? And the brunette prettiness of Nellie Luchesi...?

NELLIE: But what on earth is he going to *do?*

GRANGER: I'd like to know that one myself.

TOM: (*hoarsely*) Listen! Please! All of you!

GRANGER: Take it easy, son. We're with you.

TOM: What time is it?
GRANGER: (*blankly*) Time?
TOM: Yes! What time is it?
NELLIE: It's half-past two in the morning. Going on for three.
TOM: Twelve hours! Then the tide ought to be just where it was this afternoon.
GRANGER: What's the tide got to do with it?
TOM: A whole lot. Somebody set a trap, and made Lucy fall off that balcony. I know it.
NELLIE: (*crowing*) That's absurd!
TOM: If Lucy's been carried out to sea, there's nothing we can do about it. But if she's been carried along with the current, and into the Blue Grotto...
NELLIE: The Blue Grotto?
DAVIS: (*acidly*) One moment, sir. You are not proposing to run this big launch under that arch after dark?
TOM: Yes, Professor. That's just exactly it.
NELLIE: (*fiercely*) Go on! Do it! I'll back you up! Let's have some excitement!
DAVIS: It will be exciting enough, I assure you; Mr. Courtney have you got some wild hope of recovering your wife's body?
TOM: I've even got a wild hope she may be alive. Lucy's a very strong swimmer.
GRANGER: You're acting like a nut, son!
TOM: Get set, everybody. I'm going to swing around.
(*Sound: the engine-sound grows faster and mingles with the rushing noise of water, then cut motor*)
NELLIE: We're in the current now. Better hold tight.
TOM: I've got to duck my own head when we go through. Everybody else—flop down!
(*Sound: the rushing grows louder*)
DAVIS: I still protest against this! Don't you understand, Mr. Courtney, that...
TOM: Get ready. Here we go!
(*Sound: a loud roaring, a heavy bump and then a short pause. the voices sound hollow now*)
NELLIE: (*breathing it*) What on earth is wrong! There's no Blue Grotto. It's as black as pitch!
(*Sound: water splashes faintly*)
DAVIS: My dear Nellie, I kept trying to tell all of you. The "Blue Grotto" effect is caused by the sun's rays. There never is one except when the sun is out. Just how does our friend propose to find anything in here?
TOM: Listen!
(*Sound: splashings*)
NELLIE: Something's got hold of the side of the boat! I felt it move!

TOM: There's a hand there... a wet hand... *Lucy!*
NELLIE: She's not... *alive?*
TOM: Mr. Granger, help me lift her up over the side. Easy! Don't tip the boat! Lucy! Are you all right?
LUCY: (*a thin and breathless thread of sound which gradually grows stronger*) To-om. To-om! (*coughs*)
TOM: Are you all right, Lucy? Can you hear me?
LUCY: (*panting*) All ri'. Jus' exhausted. I got in here. Couldn't...swim out. 'Gainst current.
TOM: Don't try to talk.
LUCY: (*desperately*) Got to talk. Going to faint. Tom! Who's... with you?
TOM: Only our friends!
LUCY: (*still gasping*) Who's with you? Is... the murderer with you?
DAVIS: A pleasant prospect—to be shut up in the dark, at three o'clock in the morning, with a criminal lunatic...
LUCY: (*terrified*) Who spoke then?
TOM: Lucy, don't hold me so tight! Let go, dear! I'll get the boat started and have you out of here in a second!
LUCY: Who spoke then?
TOM: Only Professor Davis.
LUCY: Tom. (*coughs*) Got to tell you... Know how that girl...Josephine Adams... died... Almost killed... *me.*
TOM: Has anybody here got some brandy? Or a flashlight?
DAVIS: *I* have a flashlight, my friend. Will you allow me, as a medical man, to examine Mrs. Courtney?
TOM: Better keep back for just a second, Professor. She's hysterical. Give me the flashlight.
LUCY: (*voice growing stronger*) I walked into—other room. Nobody with me. All alone. Except Tiberius.
TOM: Yes, Lucy?
LUCY: Somebody—called my name. From the balcony, I thought... Very soft. "Mrs. Courtney." It said. "Mrs. Court-ney".
TOM: Did you recognize the voice?
LUCY: Yes. That's why I went.
NELLIE: (*In a whisper*) Hadn't you better start up this boat and get out of here?
LUCY: (*terrified*) Who spoke *then?*
TOM: Don't pay any attention to them, Lucy. Nobody can hurt you now.
LUCY: I went out on balcony. Bright moonlight; bright as day! But there was... nobody there.
TOM: Nobody on the balcony?
LUCY: No. I looked out over the sea. And something came at me. Something flew out of the air and came at me.
DAVIS: Just one moment, before Mrs. Courtney goes on! Is anybody in this boat carrying a revolver?

Tom: Not that I know of.
Davis: Excuse my mentioning it, but I felt something metal, brush past my hand.
Nellie: (*in a whisper*) It was only the flashlight, probably.
Tom: Will you please let Lucy go on and finish? Lucy! You were on the balcony, and something came at you...
Lucy: Yes! Like a snake! Sideways. Out of the air. It went over my head, and fastened round my neck. It was a rope... with a noose in it.
Tom: A rope?
Lucy: That's it! A rope. It was thrown...from another balcony. I'm small and light. Like Josephine Adams. It pulled me sideways, and over the rail. I fell.
Tom: Take it easy, now! You're perfectly safe!
Davis: *Is* she perfectly safe?
Lucy: The murderer...let her fall on the rope. But the rope was jerked tight long before she struck the water. That broke her neck! Then the murderer lowered her, softly.
Tom: So there wasn't any splash! And the current took her away, rope and all.
Lucy: (*fiercely eager*) That's it! It would have happened to me...only....rope slipped through the murderer's fingers.
Tom: Through *whose* fingers.
(*Sound: a pistol shot, hollow-sounding in an enclosed space, and a heavy splash*)
Davis: Somebody in this boat *has* got a revolver!
Tom: Who's overboard? Somebody went!
Davis: Switch on that light, my friend, and shine it on the water!
Tom: All right, Professor. There's your light. (*slight pause then a gasp*) Look at it! Turning over and over! The water in the Blue Grotto is red now.
Lucy: Tom! Come back to me!
Tom: It's all right, Lucy. I swear you're safe now.
Lucy: Did he...shoot himself?
Tom: Yes.
Nellie: (*screaming*) Did *who* shoot himself?
Tom: Who had a balcony, exactly like ours, on the house next door? Who began life as a cow-puncher, and would have known how to use a lasso?
Davis: Who knew Josephine Adams well, and got it into his maniac head that Mrs. Courtney was Josephine Adams all over again?
Tom: Harry Granger! Look, there's his ten-gallon hat floating away!
(*Sound: theme up*)
(*Sound: ship's whistles*)
(*Sound: theme fade*)

Notes for the Curious

With Carr's health failing, the final three *Cabin B-13* scripts were all adapted from earlier scripts. The first, "The Bride Vanishes", had been broadcast in CBS's long-running *Suspense* on December 1, 1942 and—in a slightly revised form and under the title "Into Thin Air"—on the BBC's *Appointment with Fear* on September 21, 1943 and September 11, 1945. The *Suspense* script was printed in *Ellery Queen's Mystery Magazine*, September 1950 and it was first collected in *The Door to Doom and other Detections* (1980).

While the story of "The Bride Vanishes" is original, a crucial aspect of the plot is strongly reminiscent of "The Miracle of Moon Crescent", a Father Brown short story by John Dickson Carr's great literary hero, G.K. Chesterton.

Till Death Do Us Part

(*Sound: a ship's whistle*)
(*Sound: theme up*)
ANNOUNCER: *Cabin B-13*. Tonight: "Til Death Do Us Part".
(*Sound: theme fades during Fabian's opening narration*)
FABIAN: Late one night in December of 1941, a man and his wife sit by the fire in their country cottage. This man… look at him!… He is an Austrian refugee and a professor of mathematics. Stout, middle-aged, and guileless as a child. In the remote corner of England where he lives with his pretty English wife, they say of him…

MAN'S VOICE: Jolly decent fellow, you know, for a foreigner.
WOMAN'S VOICE: (*warmly*) Isn't he! Always with a smile for everybody, and so *polite!* (*lowering her voice*) That's why it's such a shame about his wife and that young American.
MAN: (*fiercely*) Sh-h!
WOMAN: (*confidentially*) There hasn't been anything between them *yet*, I'm almost sure. But if the American stays here much longer…
MAN: Sh-h, I tell you! (*fading*) All gossip—idle gossip!

FABIAN: A happy man, this Professor Krafft. His cottage in the country is rather isolated: three miles from the nearest house. No electricity, or central heating, or telephone. And on December nights like this, a great wind comes rushing off the Sussex Downs…
(*Sound: wind rises strongly.*)
FABIAN: … to rattle at the windows, and growl in the chimney, and make unsteady the oil-lamps. Professor Erwin Krafft sits before the fire in a snug book-lined room. And across from him, sewing, sits his young wife Cynthia. A domestic scene. A *very* domestic scene.

(*Erwin Krafft has a plump and throaty voice, with hardly a trace of accent*).
ERWIN: (*lyrically*) Ah, my pet, how I enjoy my home! It's a real pleasure to be indoors on a night like this.
CYNTHIA: (*Cynthia is twenty-eight. Just now her voice is casual and rather colorless; but it can become very different*) Yes. I do hope those water-pipes won't freeze.
ERWIN: I've wrapped flannel round them, my love. They'll be all right. (*indulgently*) Did my little pet have a good day?
CYNTHIA: Just about as usual.
ERWIN: (*jocosely*) No adventures? No?
CYNTHIA: Not exactly. I walked in to the village.

ERWIN: (*gloomily*) I blame myself for—for burying you out here! I ought to get you a car!
CYNTHIA: (*rather sharply*) That's not necessary, thanks.
ERWIN: (*hurt*) Come, now! Did something happen to upset my little pet today?
CYNTHIA: (*nerves showing*) No! No! No!
ERWIN: (*tenderly*) I look at you, Cynthia, and I marvel.
CYNTHIA: You marvel at what?
ERWIN: At a wife who can actually blush! Yes! (*admiringly*) With a skin so fair, and a conscience so transparent, that she can actually blush! You restore my faith in human nature.
CYNTHIA: (*quickly*) I wasn't blushing about...
ERWIN: About what?
CYNTHIA: About anything you might be thinking.
ERWIN: (*laughs*)
CYNTHIA: It's your horrible habit of putting everybody else in the wrong.
ERWIN: (*hurt*) The neighbors do not think that about old Papa Krafft, my love.
CYNTHIA: The neighbors don't have to live with you. *I* do.
ERWIN: And she must not scratch, either! Not when we are so snug here, all alone together. And the kettle on the fire nearby boiling, and the rum and the lemon-juice and sugar ready for her medicine...
(*Sound: the kettle is heard simmering through the next, growing faintly louder*)
CYNTHIA: Erwin, *must* I drink that stuff? I don't *like* rum!
ERWIN: (*mildly*) You have a cold, my love.
CYNTHIA: I haven't got a cold! Really I haven't!
ERWIN: Twice today, my pet, I heard you cough. (*cajolingly*) You are going to take your medicine, Cynthia—take it here and now—and not offend your clumsy old husband by refusing.
CYNTHIA: (*despairingly*) When you keep on treating me like a girl of sixteen, I still don't know how to answer you!
ERWIN: I love to treat you like that, Cynthia.
CYNTHIA: Evidently.
ERWIN: (*quietly*) Because I cannot fathom your thoughts. You lock up your thoughts; and that is a dangerous English habit. Thoughts accumulate, and won't be stifled. And sooner or later, when you least expect it...
(*Sound: the simmering kettle boils over.*)
CYNTHIA: Look out! The kettle's boiling over!
ERWIN: (*flatly*) So it is.
CYNTHIA: Erwin, please! Lift it down from there!
ERWIN: (*affectionate again*) Of course! I apologize to my little pet. There!
CYNTHIA: For a second, you know, you almost frightened me.
ERWIN: (*astonished*) *I*? Frightened you?
(*Sound: the kettle ceases to sputter and sizzle.*)
CYNTHIA: I suppose it's foolish.

ERWIN: You have war-nerves, my dear.—I put two tumblers on the coffee-table, so. A spoon in each, so that the heat doesn't crack them...
(*Sound: rattle of spoons*)
ERWIN: Then a small rum for me...
(*Sound: liquid poured*)
ERWIN: And a large rum for you...
(*Sound: liquid poured*)
CYNTHIA: (*protesting*) My dear, *must* you give me so much?
ERWIN: We're going to cure that cold of yours, Cynthia. —Then lemon-juice... hot water to the top...
(*Sound: liquid poured*)
ERWIN: And two lumps of sugar for each of us. Drink up, my pet!
CYNTHIA: Erwin, listen!
(*Sound: wind rises. we hear, however, another sound. There is the faint sound of something musical; it is muffled yet distinct. it suggests someone dumping or knocking against an accordion: a short squeak*)
ERWIN: I didn't hear anything.
CYNTHIA: *I* did. It came... it came from that cupboard over there. It sounded like your old accordion!
ERWIN: Nonsense, my pet!
(*Sound: the accordion creaks*)
CYNTHIA: There it is again!
ERWIN: (*indulgently*) It's only the wind, Cynthia. Or perhaps a rat that's got into the cupboard.
CYNTHIA: Erwin, I'm terrified of rats! Go and kill it. Would you mind?
ERWIN: (*wryly*) You set heavy labors, sweet, for one of my weight. Still, if you insist! (*as though rising; deep breath*) A good heavy poker from the fire-place... (*moving off microphone*)... a little trip to the cupboard...
CYNTHIA: (*crying out*) Erwin, wait!
ERWIN: You haven't changed your mind, again, my dear?
CYNTHIA: It would probably run out across the floor! Come back!
ERWIN: It would not run far, I think. Still, again if you insist! (*returns*)
CYNTHIA: I can't think what's the matter with me tonight!
ERWIN: (*easily*) No, my pet?
CYNTHIA: No!
ERWIN: You're *sure* nothing upset you in the village today? Some trifle, perhaps?
CYNTHIA: Certainly not!
ERWIN: But come, my sweet! This young American... the fledgling doctor... what's his name...?
CYNTHIA: (*casually*) Do you mean Dr. Craig, by any chance?
ERWIN: (*pleased*) That's it! Dr. Craig. (*reflecting*) Didn't someone say he was leaving today? For London, and then back to the States?

CYNTHIA: I believe so. That's what Lady Randolph told me.
ERWIN: (*surprised*) And you didn't say goodbye to him?
CYNTHIA: Certainly not!
ERWIN: (*reproachful*) But that was not kind of you, my pet! That was not friendly! Er... don't you like the rum and lemon?
CYNTHIA: (*as though gagging*) No. But you'll give me no peace till I do drink it!
ERWIN: That's right, my dear. Take it down like a good girl. I'm keeping you company.—How pretty she looks, with her yellow hair in the fire-light!
CYNTHIA: Thank you.
ERWIN: And her red mouth, and the light little hands! —There is just one other thing, Cynthia. I gave you a letter to post this afternoon. Did you post it?
CYNTHIA: Yes.
ERWIN: And register it?
CYNTHIA: Yes!
ERWIN: And did you notice, Cynthia, to whom the letter was addressed?
CYNTHIA: (*half laughing*) Everybody notices the address on an envelope. It was to some Mr. Hatherby, at Market Sheppard. But I don't know who he is, if that's what you mean.
ERWIN: Mr. Hatherby, Cynthia, is the coroner of this district.
CYNTHIA: (*startled*) The coroner?
ERWIN: That's right, my love.
CYNTHIA: But is there any reason why you should be writing letters to the coroner?
ERWIN: (*agreeably*) There will be, tomorrow morning. We have just been drinking poison, my pet.
(*Sound: crash of breaking glass, and wind rises*)
ERWIN: Don't drop your glass on the hearth, Cynthia. It's much too late now.
CYNTHIA: I don't believe it! You're teasing me!
ERWIN: Just as always, eh? Good old Papa Krafft!
CYNTHIA: You couldn't do a thing like that!
ERWIN: This will interest you, Cynthia. You were a trained nurse, I believe, before I—picked you up. The poison was aconite. Monk's hood. Home-grown in our own garden. One sixteenth of a grain, you know, has been a fatal dose.
CYNTHIA: There's no telephone here! No car! No neighbors!
ERWIN: Exactly, angel.
CYNTHIA: (*breathlessly*) Take your hands off me! Let me get up!
ERWIN: (*gently*) No, my pet. In about five minutes, now, the first symptoms will come on.
CYNTHIA: Symptoms?
ERWIN: Our throats will grow dry. Our eyesight will turn dim. Presently we'll lose the use of our limbs. There are convulsions before the end, I

believe; but we'll not feel them.

CYNTHIA: Let me *up*!

ERWIN: If you try to hit at me, angel, you'll upset that lamp. And, if you upset the lamp, this cottage would go up like tinder. We don't want to burn to death. Now do we?

CYNTHIA: (*wildly*) Erwin, why are you doing this? Why are you *doing* it?

ERWIN: (*softly*) Do you think old Papa Krafft is blind, my pet? (*through his teeth*) If *I* can't have you, Cynthia, nobody else is going to have you!

CYNTHIA: You mean… Jim Craig?

ERWIN: Ah! So it's "Jim" Craig now?

CYNTHIA: That was nothing! My… my tongue slipped!

ERWIN: A cynic would say, my dear, that your foot slipped. Do you think I don't know what happened the other night? At the schoolhouse?

CYNTHIA: Schoolhouse?

ERWIN: Yes. The Market Shepherd schoolhouse. At Lady Randolph's little concert in aid of the War Relief.

CYNTHIA: Nothing happened! I swear it didn't!

ERWIN: No, my pet?

CYNTHIA: No!

ERWIN: It was a coincidence, I suppose, that you and good Dr. Craig didn't arrive until the concert was nearly over.

CYNTHIA: Yes, it was! We—we didn't go there together! (*fading*) We met in the little hall outside the auditorium, and…

(*Music: in and behind.*)

FABIAN: A country schoolhouse. Two or three classrooms, and a little auditorium at the back. Don't you notice the familiar smell of chalk and washed blackboards? Don't you see the glass doors to the auditorium? Inside those doors, on a platform draped with Union Jacks, Lady Randolph sits above the orchestra. But outside the doors, in a dimly lighted hall, two persons are approaching…

(*Sound: Craig's steps fade in —*)

CRAIG: (*In his thirties: he is grave, and intensely reserved. Both he and Cynthia are a little confused, and certainly constrained and awkward*) I *beg* your pardon! It's so dark here I almost bumped into you. (*sharply*) Isn't that Mrs. Krafft?

CYNTHIA: Yes. Good evening, Dr. Craig.

CRAIG: We seem—we seem to be late.

CYNTHIA: Very late, I'm afraid.

CRAIG: I was—detained on a case.

CYNTHIA: And I—didn't feel like coming here at all.

CRAIG: Just one moment, before I open that door for you! Won't it look a little funny? Our arriving here together?

CYNTHIA: (*sharply*) Funny? Why should it?

CRAIG: No reason at all! Only... Cynthia, listen to me!

CYNTHIA: (*quietly*) Do you know, Dr. Craig, that's the first time you've ever called me by my first name?

CRAIG: One doesn't take liberties in England.

CYNTHIA: (*flatly*) Have you ever tired to take liberties? No.

CRAIG: What I meant was this. I did want to have a word with you, somehow. Of course you've heard the news?

CYNTHIA: What news?

CRAIG: On the radio. For the past couple of days.

CYNTHIA: We're too far out to get much news. And my husband isn't interested.

CRAIG: (*slowly*) He isn't interested. England welcomed him, and fed him, and clothed him, and sheltered him from the enemy. But he isn't interested.

CYNTHIA: I'd rather you didn't talk like that about my husband.

CRAIG: I'm sorry.

CYNTHIA: And can't you at least push the doors open a little? Lady Randolph is saying something!

CRAIG: Oh, very well—but the door's sure to creak if I open it.

(*Sound: a creak. We hear, rather loudly, the murmur and mutter and shuffling of a crowd which never quite ceases through the following*)

LADY RANDOLPH: (*In her forties, with a firm and carrying voice. She is jocular, but not offensively so*)...and in conclusion, ladies and gentlemen! I'm sure we have all enjoyed our friend Professor Krafft's musical numbers on the accordion...

(*Sound: loud applause, held off*)

LADY RANDOLPH: ... and the vicar's conjuring-tricks...

(*Sound: laughter and applause, held off*)

LADY RANDOLPH: ... and little Miss Linshaw's spirited recitations. It only remains for me to tell you that the collection for this little entertainment will amount to... (*breaking off*)... Yes, Colonel Thompson? What is it?

CYNTHIA: Colonel Thompson is going across that platform in rather a hurry. It looks like an announcement of some kind, Dr. Craig.

LADY RANDOLPH: Ladies and gentlemen, your attention! We have just received some late news by the nine o'clock bulletin.

CRAIG: I think I can guess what it is, Cynthia.

LADY RANDOLPH: Following yesterday's declaration against Japan, the Congress of the United States today declared war against Germany and Italy.

(*Sound: the murmur abruptly stops in dead silence.*)

LADY RANDOLPH: No applause, please. I think I can say that these things go too deep for applause. *We* entered a war lightly; and we have learned. But, before the vicar ends this meeting, I shall ask the orchestra to play us the song numbered eighty-three in the book. You all know what it is.

CRAIG: Close the door, Cynthia.
(*Sound: door closes with a soft creak*)
CYNTHIA: Jim! Jim Craig! This doesn't affect *you*?
CRAIG: Naturally it does.
CYNTHIA: You won't be—leaving England?
CRAIG: Probably in a very short time. They'll be needing doctors.
CYNTHIA: But does a formal declaration of war make any difference? What does it mean to you? What does it *mean*?
(*Sound: the orchestra is heard through the doors*)
CRAIG: I can't explain much, Cynthia. It's just that my country is in the war now—
CYNTHIA: But can't you do just as much good here? In England?
CRAIG: I don't know. That depends on what the Army says.
CYNTHIA: And doesn't anything depend on what *I* say?
CRAIG: We haven't got much time, Cynthia. That crowd will be out in a minute.
CYNTHIA: Yes.
CRAIG: And we won't admit it, will we?
CYNTHIA: Admit what?
CRAIG: Admit how we feel about each other?
CYNTHIA: (*crying out*) I haven't said...!
CRAIG: Nor I. I was only talking about what we were thinking.
CYNTHIA: No. We won't admit it. You say you can't explain about the war. And I can't explain about this.
CRAIG: Don't try. It's better this way. They'll be coming in a minute.
CYNTHIA: Erwin's been very good to me. And he's such a *childlike* person!
CRAIG: (*seriously*) Yes. Everybody likes him.
CYNTHIA: He has his tempers. And he's not easy to live with sometimes, in spite of what they think. But I can't do anything to hurt him, because he's never done anything to hurt me. Never! Never! Never in the world.

FABIAN: Never, Mrs. Krafft? When the great wind howls round the cottage, and the oil-lamps flare, and the poison is already taken, and a smiling husband stands over you as you crouch on that sofa...

(*Sound: wind outside*)
CYNTHIA: And that's what I told Dr. Craig about you, Erwin. (*with intense disgust*) That's what I *said* about you!
ERWIN: A very fair estimate of my character, too, Cynthia. So you *are* in love with the young Doctor?
CYNTHIA: I wouldn't admit it before. But I admit it now. Yes!
ERWIN: (*tenderly*) My poor Cynthia—Do you feel anything yet?
CYNTHIA: Feel anything?
ERWIN: Dryness, and muscular contraction of the throat?

CYNTHIA: Yes!
ERWIN: Ah, I thought so! Your leg-muscles will presently go, and then I'll not be compelled to stand over you.
CYNTHIA: (*crying out*) I won't die! I won't!
ERWIN: And how do you propose to stop yourself?
CYNTHIA: If I could get to the kitchen... mustard and water!...
ERWIN: (*amused*) Mustard and water, my pet? Against aconite?
CYNTHIA: Why not?
ERWIN: It's the strongest poison in the register. Your only chance would be to reach the village infirmary. And I propose to see that you don't get there.
CYNTHIA: What if the poison takes you before it takes me? And you can't stop me?
ERWIN: It won't, my pet.
CYNTHIA: You seem terribly sure of that.
(*Sound: jangle from an accordion*)
CYNTHIA: (*terrified*) What was that?
ERWIN: Only the rat, my dear.
CYNTHIA: What rat?
ERWIN: The rat over there in that cupboard. Scuttling and squeaking 'round my accordion. Have you forgotten, my pet? You wanted me to kill it, and then changed your mind. But as I was saying...
CYNTHIA: Yea! About the poison!
ERWIN: We've both taken much more than a fatal dose, you see.
CYNTHIA: I won't die! I won't!
ERWIN: But the amount I gave you... as you perhaps noticed?... was more than I gave myself. I am going to follow my little pet out into the dark, where there are no Dr. Jim Craigs. But not too quickly. I shall still have most of my faculties, Cynthia, when your convulsions are just beginning.
CYNTHIA: (*sharply*) I—wonder if you will!
(*Music: accordion jangles*)
ERWIN: Why do you say that?
CYNTHIA: You're turning an awfully queer color, Erwin.
ERWIN: Am I, pet?
CYNTHIA: And your legs don't seem any too steady.
ERWIN: I... (*uncertainly*)... the heat of the fire, perhaps... the heat of the room....
CYNTHIA: (*softly*) If I got up from this sofa now, I don't believe you could stop me. Try!
ERWIN: (*heavily*) You'd better not attempt to get out of here, my sweetest angel.
CYNTHIA: (*still softly*) Try to stop me! Try!
ERWIN: (*more heavily*) Cynthia, my pet. Listen to me.
CYNTHIA: Yes, Erwin?
ERWIN: There's a copy of *Taylor's Medical Jurisprudence* on the shelf over

there. Get it for me!
CYNTHIA: I'm afraid you'll have to get it for yourself, my dear. That is, if you can.
ERWIN: (*through his teeth*) I'll get it, my love. I'll...
CYNTHIA: Mind the lamp Erwin! We don't want the house afire. Just as you said yourself.
ERWIN: I'll mind the lamp. I'll... Listen to me. Some people's systems aren't tolerant to poisons. They experience in minutes what ought to take— hours.
CYNTHIA: Does it hurt, Erwin? (*with intensity*) Does it hurt?
ERWIN: You'll find out soon enough, my pet. Because you'll never make three miles to the village on a night like this.
CYNTHIA: You think not?
ERWIN: I know it, sweet. And just remember this. If anything *has* happened to me, I shall be waiting. (*gasps*)
CYNTHIA: Waiting?
ERWIN: Out in the dark and cold, where there is neither marriage nor giving in marriage. Waiting for my little pet to come and join me. I shall be...
(*Sound: two steps.*)
ERWIN: *a choking noise.*
(*Sound: a heavy thud*)
CYNTHIA: Erwin!
(*Sound: the wind whistles*)
CYNTHIA: (*pause*) Erwin!
(*Sound: another pause. Two steps*)
CYNTHIA: You're too heavy to turn over on your back! (*breathlessly*) Can't you take hold of my wrist? I hate you, I loathe you. I'm afraid of you. But I don't want you to die because of me. And yet you are dead, Erwin. Because there's no pulse-beat. (*pause, fearfully*) (*in a monotone*) I'm not going to join you, Erwin. I've never prayed much, but I'm praying now. Whatever comes over my wits and makes my senses weak, give me strength enough to get to that village. Just give me strength enough to get to that village!
(*Sound: running footsteps, and the bang of a door.*)

FABIAN: An empty room, now, except for the motionless figure by the fire. The great wind enters through an open front door, and makes the lamps shake—dangerously!—on the tables. The whole house creaks. Otherwise it is very quiet. And the apparent corpse... sits up. Professor Krafft looks pleased, doesn't he? Very pleased, very alert, as he moves over to a certain cupboard door...

ERWIN: (*agreeably*) And now, I think, we can begin the real business of the evening.

(*Sound: accordion jangles*)
ERWIN: (*up*) Patience, my friend, while I unbolt the cupboard door!
(*Sound: bolt rattles: door opens*)
ERWIN: There we are. I hope you haven't been too uncomfortable, Dr. James Craig.
CRAIG: (*slight pause*) (*evenly*) I'm all right, thanks.
ERWIN: So you managed to get the gag out of your mouth? Eh?
CRAIG: I managed it, yes. Just now. And too late.
ERWIN: But you're still securely tied up, I'm glad to say. Roped, sealed, and delivered. You gave me several unpleasant moments, young man, when you got your foot on that accordion.
CRAIG: Did I?
ERWIN: Cynthia thought you were a rat, and wanted me to kill you. She shows very good sense sometimes.
CRAIG: (*holding himself in*) I could hear both of you talking, thanks very much.
ERWIN: (*crowing*) Of course! Excuse me! I forgot that.
CRAIG: And I could see you, too. Through a crack in the door.
ERWIN: (*chuckles*) Of course. You were intended to see us. First of all, I'll just drag you out of there...
(*Sound: jangle of accordion then the rattle as of objects piled in a cupboard and finally the sound of a body being dragged*)
ERWIN: ... and prop you up in a chair here.
CRAIG: Answer me just one question. How much aconite did you give Cynthia?
ERWIN: Cynthia? About—two grains.
CRAIG: (*thunderstruck*) Two grains!?
ERWIN: Rather more, if anything.
CRAIG: I see. Then she can't possibly...?
ERWIN: No, Dr. Craig. She can't possible live until morning. But she can live long enough to testify that she saw *me* die.
CRAIG: And how much poison did you take yourself?
ERWIN: None at all.
CRAIG: None... at... all?
ERWIN: (*pityingly*) Come, now! Is old Papa Krafft such a fool as to hurt himself, when there are others to be hurt for him?
CRAIG: But you mixed those drinks out of the same materials! I saw you do it!
ERWIN: There was no poison in the rum, young man. Two lumps of sugar, steeped in aconite, were dropped into Cynthia's glass. I marked them, and I didn't make a mistake. Can't you see the beginnings of Papa Krafft's plan?
CRAIG: I see the beginning. I can't see the ending.
ERWIN: Cynthia left the door open, my friend. And there's a *very* strong

wind blowing tonight.

CRAIG: Well?

ERWIN: Observe how it lifts the table-covers, and flutters the magazines, and makes the lamps tremble. I should not be surprised, you know, if one of those lamps blew over. A fine crash, and a sheet of flame... eh?

CRAIG: (*satirically*) The lamp goes over by accident, of course?

ERWIN: Of course!

CRAIG: Go on.

ERWIN: But *I* am supposed to be dead. When they come here tomorrow morning, after Cynthia's testimony and my letter to the coroner, they will expect to find at least a few charred bones among the ruins. And, of course, they must *find* some remains.

CRAIG: Whose remains?

ERWIN: Yours.

CRAIG: You've got me tied up pretty well, haven't you?

ERWIN: Yes. You were last seen going towards the railway station, to London and then to America. Nobody will inquire after you.

CRAIG: Except Cynthia.

ERWIN: Except Cynthia, who will be dead. That I waylaid you and brought you here, while Cynthia was in the village, will not be known to our good coroner. And I shall disappear.— What do you think of it, young man? *I* think it's rather good.

CRAIG: You're going to let me burn to death?

ERWIN: I shall enjoy the necessity. Did you admire *my* performance as a dead man?

CRAIG: I don't see how it fooled Cynthia. She was a trained nurse! She'd have known if there was any funny business!

ERWIN: Let me assure you, young man, there was none of what you call funny business.

CRAIG: Not even when she said you were dead?

ERWIN: Not even then.

CRAIG: But your heart had stopped!

ERWIN: I beg your pardon. My *pulse* had stopped!

CRAIG: What's the difference?

ERWIN: A very great difference. Take a very small hard-rubber ball. You can buy one in a toy-shop. Simply put it up under your arm, beneath the shirt, and press the arm against your side. That stops the flow of blood for as long as you like. It's a good trick. I learned it from the vicar.

CRAIG: From the *vicar*?

ERWIN: He's a parlor magician. Too bad you missed his performance at Lady Randolph's concert. But then, I think, you were otherwise occupied?

CRAIG: You could call it that.

ERWIN: Occupied, I think, in making love to my wife. You hurt my vanity, young man. And you're going to suffer for it.

CRAIG: I never made love to your wife!
ERWIN: No, young man!
CRAIG: No. But I don't suppose you could possibly believe that.
ERWIN: Are you begging for mercy? (*eagerly*) Come, now! Are you begging for mercy?
CRAIG: No, I think not.
ERWIN: (*sharply*) Young man, I don't like the way you're taking this.
CRAIG: Don't you?
ERWIN: You ought to be afraid. All decent men should be afraid, and no man is heroic when he sees death coming. You're as white as a plate. But you can't take your eyes off me, and you seem to be expecting something.
CRAIG: Maybe I *am* expecting something.
ERWIN: Expecting what?
CRAIG: (*thru his teeth*) Wouldn't you like to know!?

FABIAN: Does Professor Krafft look a little less pleased, now? Certainly not. He is a mathematician. He has calculated his murders with infinite care and precision. The mental torture of his wife and of the young American, helplessly bound in the cupboard, have been neatly, beautifully devised.
(*Sound: car fading in from off, from 'way off!*)
FABIAN: The good Professor feels so mathematically-secure, he has not even worried about the door, swinging wide on its hinges, or the possible effect that the sight of a man, bound tightly, might have upon a chance passerby. No, this part of England is too remote, too forgotten...

ERWIN: Listen! What was that?
CRAIG: It sounds like an automobile. Coming along the high road.
ERWIN: It won't stop here. No cars ever stop here!
CRAIG: Maybe this one will.
ERWIN: Were you expecting it?
CRAIG: No.
ERWIN: (*softly*) I think I can persuade you to tell what's on your mind, my friend, if I use the poker out of the fire. I am not like you Americans. I am a mathematician. I leave *nothing* to chance. Where I spent most of my life, at Dresden...
CRAIG: Dresden? But that's in Germany! I thought you came from Austria!
ERWIN: So did a certain other man, who has achieved some fame in this world. But he's a very good German for all that.
(*Sound: the car roars up outside and stops*)
CRAIG: (*fiercely*) Don't you hear anything now, Professor Krafft? The car *has* stopped.
ERWIN: They won't come in here!
CRAIG: Of course they will, you fool. Anybody will. You've left the front door tending wide open in a blacked-out night!

ERWIN: Do you think to upset me with that?
CRAIG: *Something's* upset you. Take a look at yourself in a mirror.
ERWIN: Everything is ready. My clothes and money are in the stable. This place, my pretty little cottage, will be a furnace. I have only to go over and pick up a lamp... like this....
CRAIG: Can you reach the lamp, Professor Krafft?
ERWIN: I... I... (*crying out*)... Something is wrong with me!
CRAIG: You're not acting this time, are you? You're not pretending this time? But can you move your legs?
ERWIN: You young swine, what have you done to me?
CRAIG: Nothing.
ERWIN: You *have* done something to me! I feel it! There is sweat all over me; and my throat is choking; and...
CYNTHIA: (*calling, from a distance*) This way, Lady Randolph! Through the gate, and up the path!
ERWIN: (*gasping*) That sounded... like Cynthia's voice!
CRAIG: It *was* Cynthia's voice.
LADY RANDOLPH: (*off*) I can't understand what's wrong with you young people nowadays! Anybody would think you were drunk.
CYNTHIA: I'm sorry, Lady Randolph!
LADY RANDOLPH: Stopping me in the road, and asking to be taken to the infirmary at eighty miles an hour, and then finding there was nothing wrong with you!
ERWIN: (*heavily*) I am... hearing things. This is not possible. *Nothing wrong with Cynthia*?
CRAIG: Listen, my murdering friend. Did your plans include the fact that Cynthia doesn't like rum?
ERWIN: Not... like... rum?
CRAIG: You poured a very large drink for her, and a small one for yourself. Then you filled both glasses with hot water. And, when she got you to go over towards that cupboard... remember...?
ERWIN: I remember!
CRAIG: Cynthia changed the glasses. You've drunk two grains of aconite, and nothing on earth could save you now!
ERWIN: (*appealing*) Help me, my friend! Help me!
CRAIG: I can't help you.
ERWIN: (*babbling*) I implore you in the name of pity, help me! My plans... do not *include* this!
CRAIG: Look at you! You think you're trying to reach a lamp. But actually... can't you feel it?... you're staggering straight into the cupboard! Into the cupboard! Into the...
(*Sound: footsteps, a choking cry. and a thud accompanied by a long screech from the accordion*)
CYNTHIA: (*close at hand*) Jim Craig! What are *you* doing here?

CRAIG: Come in, Cynthia! Come in! And take a look at the man who died twice!

(*Music: theme up to Fabian's closing narration*)

FABIAN: So ends my story which I call "Til Death Do Us Part" and which, I trust, has been attended especially by those mothers who want their daughters to marry men who are smiling and polite. Next week, I shall tell you of another young American who left the *Maurevania* to meet adventure of a kind he least expected. This young man knew Paris was full of adventure—but when he found the pretty girl of his dreams, he also found witchcraft—and a room which no one had ever left alive. And so when next week I tell you the tale I call "The Devil's Saint", will you join me, Doctor Fabian, in my cabin, *B-13*?

(*Sound: ship's whistles*)

(*Sound: theme fade*)

Notes for the Curious

"Till Death Do Us Part" is a revised version of the play of the same title, first broadcast on 15 December 1942 in the CBS program *Suspense*. Neither is connected with Carr's novel of that title, published in 1944. However the trick by which Professor Krafft stops his heart will be familiar from the Colonel March short story, "Error at Daybreak", published in *The Strand Magazine* in July 1938.

The Sleep of Death

(*Sound: a ship's whistle*)
(*Sound: theme up*)
ANNOUNCER: *Cabin B-13*. Tonight: "The Sleep of Death".
(*Sound: theme fades during Fabian's opening narration*)

FABIAN: A circular bedroom, high in a castle tower—hung with rare tapestries—filled with the haunting atmosphere of witchcraft and death. The young American, Ned Whiteford, knew that for two hundred years no person who had slept in that room had lived through the night. Whatever it was that killed left no trace. Would you, like Whiteford, have dared to rest your head there because you were in love? Ned Whiteford crossed with us to France aboard the *Maurevania*, back in '38. He was looking forward to his new position at the American Embassy. He was young—and even war-jittery Paris was a magic land to him. It was on St. Catherine's Day that Ned unknowingly made a decision that brought him to the threshold of unspeakable terror and death—and he made it in the midst of the gayest celebration Paris knew—the President's Costume Ball at the Opera...Look at Ned now...wearing the uniform of one of Lafayette's officers. Look closely at the dark-haired young girl in the costume of a nymph, sitting across from him at the little table, half-screened by the palms...

(*Sound: crowd murmur up then fades out after scene is established*)
ILEANA: (*not very convincingly*) Ned, don't! Please! You mustn't.
WHITEFORD: Why not? You don't really mind, do you?
ILEANA: No, of course I don't mind! Only you mustn't.
WHITEFORD: (*quietly*) Look here, Ileana. We've got to settle this thing. You have enjoyed being here tonight, haven't you?
ILEANA: Ned, I've loved it! After being hemmed in at my uncle's place in the country, it's like heaven!
WHITEFORD: All right! When I take you back to the hotel tonight I'm going to face this dragon uncle of yours.
ILEANA: *No!* You mustn't.
WHITEFORD: I'm going to say that you and I intend to get married! and that's that.
ILEANA: (*quietly*) I can't marry you, Ned. I've told you that.
WHITEFORD: (*desperately*) But why not? Give me just one good reason!
ILEANA: Because...I can't. My uncle would never allow it.
WHITEFORD: And that seems to you a good enough reason.
ILEANA: Yes.

(*Sound: music ends followed by applause*)
WHITEFORD: This uncle of yours...What's his name?
ILEANA: Count Stephen Kohary.
WHITEFORD: He's a Hungarian, I think you said?
ILEANA: Yes. So am I. My mother was an American.
WHITEFORD: What's he like, actually?
ILEANA: (*hesitating*) He's—a little eccentric. Please don't misunderstand! He's a scholar and a wit and a historian. Only—he's a little eccentric. He... (*breaking off*) Ned!
WHITEFORD: What is it?
ILEANA: There he is now!
WHITEFORD: Your uncle?
ILEANA: (*agitated*) Yes!! The elegant man in plain evening clothes, with the Order of the Golden Fleece across his chest.
WHITEFORD: I see him. He looks as black as a thunder-cloud.
ILEANA: He's throwing those two devils aside as though they didn't exist! Give me my mask! Quick! Before he sees us!
WHITEFORD: No, Ileana.
ILEANA: Why not?
WHITEFORD: We'd better face this out now. Sit still.
KOHARY: (*slight pause. Kohary has a heavy slow-speaking, slightly accented voice.*) (*levelly*) Good evening, Ileana.
ILEANA: (*confused*) Good evening, Uncle Stephen. Uncle...may I present Ned Whiteford?
WHITEFORD: *How* do you do, sir?
KOHARY: (*flatly*) How do you do. —Ileana, do you think that costume is quite the thing to wear in public?
ILEANA: (*quickly*) Why not?
KOHARY: An older generation might call it immodest. It looks like...
ILEANA: Like what?
KOHARY: Nothing! Will you go and get your cloak, or your domino, or whatever you wore here?
ILEANA: Uncle, *please* don't make me go home so soon! It's hardly eleven o'clock.
KOHARY: (*suavely*) I was not asking you to go home, my dear. Doubtless this young man will see that you return to the Hotel Maurice as quietly as you left it. I was merely asking you to put on a wrap.
ILEANA: All right. I'll get it. You stay and talk to Ned.
KOHARY: (*grimly*) I shall be delighted.
WHITEFORD: Will you sit down, sir?
KOHARY: Thank you. You seem to have had quite a gathering at this table.
WHITEFORD: Yes. Some friends of mine from the Embassy. They're upstairs dancing now.

KOHARY: (*agreeably*) Glasses, glasses, and still more glasses! I was quite an adept, once, at musical-glasses. Have you ever tried it, young man? You take a spoon, like this, and....

(*Sound: several tingling bell-notes from glass, suggesting scale.*)

WHITEFORD: (*awkwardly*) Forgive me sir. There's something I'd like to ask you.

KOHARY: Yes, young man?

(*Sound: more glass notes*)

WHITEFORD: I don't exactly know how to say this, so I'd better say it in the shortest way. I want to marry your niece.

(*Sound: short, sharp crash of breaking glass.*)

WHITEFORD: Look out, sir! You've smashed one of the glasses.

KOHARY: (*repressed*) Doubtless a few francs will pay for it. There are other things with a higher value. At least for me.

WHITEFORD: (*embarrassed*) Maybe I ought to mention that I'm attached to the American Embassy here. That I have some money of my own—enough to support Ileana well.

(*Sound: more musical glass-notes.*)

KOHARY: Indeed.

WHITEFORD: I only mention that to show—well, that Ileana will be well provided for. The Ambassador will vouch for me, if you'd like to ring him up.

KOHARY: I ought to mention—I have always kept Ileana carefully guarded from the world.

WHITEFORD: Almost too carefully guarded, don't you think?

KOHARY: That, young man, depends on my reason.

WHITEFORD: (*despairing*) Sorry again!

KOHARY: You have known Ileana... (*pause*) how long?

WHITEFORD: Four days—

KOHARY: (*dryly*) Four days! You would not choose a business partner in four days. Yet you want to marry Ileana four days after you meet her!

WHITEFORD: We know our own minds, sir.

KOHARY: Then you know more than the wisest men of the world. However! As one whose dearest wish is Ileana's happiness...

WHITEFORD: (*intently*) I hope it is, Count Kohary.

KOHARY: (*sharply*) You doubt what I say?

WHITEFORD: No, sir. Go on.

KOHARY: Let me make you a counter-proposition. I own an estate in Touraine, not far from Paris.

WHITEFORD: I know. Ileana told me.

KOHARY: Then here is my suggestion. Why not come down and visit us for a week or two?

WHITEFORD: (*surprised*) That's very decent of you, sir!

(*Sound: the spoon begins to play a tune on the glasses. this tune, ringing slowly,*

can be discerned as Handel's dead march from Saul.)
KOHARY: Not at all. If, at the end of that time, you are not cured of this infatuation...
WHITEFORD: (*fiercely*) It's not an infatuation! I swear it's not!
KOHARY: If, at the end of that time, you are not cured... *permanently*... of this feeling, you may take Ileana with my blessing. Is that fair?
WHITEFORD: It's more than fair, Count Kohary! I don't know how to thank you!
KOHARY: Don't try. (*softly*) There is just one thing, however.
WHITEFORD: Yes, sir?
KOHARY: At the Château d'Azay there is a certain bedroom. We call it the Tapestry Room.
WHITEFORD: Well?
KOHARY: I assure you it will be very interesting to sleep in that room.
WHITEFORD: (*puzzled*)—Why? Is it haunted, or anything like that?
KOHARY: Not exactly.... haunted. —And now, if you don't mind, I shall say good-night. I think I can trust you to bring Ileana safely to the hotel.
(*Sound: a quick murmur of voices is heard in the background*)
KOHARY: (*sharply*) In the meantime, look there!
WHITEFORD: What is it *now*?
KOHARY: Those streams of our fellow-guests, pouring down the main staircase. Shapes of nightmare. Shapes of delirium. Insane dead masks where only the eyes move. Mightn't you be terrified, perhaps, if you could look behind those masks, gargoyle ffaces.
WHITEFORD: No, I don't think so. They're only ordinary people like ourselves.
KOHARY: (*amused*) That, sir, is where you make *your* mistake. I shall expect you for the weekend. (*fade*) Good-night.
ILEANA: (*pause, calling softly*) Ned! Ned!
WHITEFORD: (*indulgently*) It's all right, Ileana! You can come out from behind the palms!
ILEANA:(*nervously*) What was my uncle saying? I couldn't hear.
WHITEFORD: Ileana, it couldn't be better. He's a very decent old boy, actually. And he's invited me to the Chateau d'Azay.
ILEANA: Did he say anything about... the Tapestry Room?
WHITEFORD: Yes. He asked me if I'd mind sleeping there.
ILEANA: And you said?
WHITEFORD: (*surprised*) I said I would. Naturally.
ILEANA: (*fiercely*) You mustn't *do* it, Ned! I won't *let* you do it!
WHITEFORD: But why the devil not?
ILEANA: Because everybody who sleeps in that room... dies.
(*Sound: glass on glasses*)
WHITEFORD: Are you serious?

ILEANA: Oh, Ned, please don't do it.
WHITEFORD: Nonsense! There are a lot of superstitions about every old house!
ILEANA: This isn't a superstition, Ned. It happened once when *I* was a little girl. A man insisted on sleeping there. They found him dead in the morning.
WHITEFORD: (*a little shaken*) So? How did he die?
ILEANA: They don't know. There wasn't a mark on his body. He wasn't shot, or stabbed, or strangled, or poisoned, or hurt in any way. He was just... dead.

FABIAN: Two nights later, in the Department of France now known as Indre-et-Loire, but once called Touraine. The wind moans down the valleys, and rain flickers across the apple-trees and thunder stirs in those haunted hills...

(*Sound: rain and thunder*)
FABIAN: It brings little comfort to a young man driven in an ancient carriage from the railway station along snakelike roads. (*sneak sound of carriage*)... to *what* destination? (*hold for carriage*) Ahead a flash of lightning shows the gray walls and conical slate-roofed towers of a chateau set some distance back from the road. Lights shine from its narrow windows, dimly seen through the rain.

(*Sound: carriage behind—*)
WHITEFORD: Driver! Coachman!
DRIVER: (*dully*) Yes, monsieur?
WHITEFORD: Is that the Château d'Azay? Up ahead?
DRIVER: Yes, monsieur. I will take you to the very door, if...
WHITEFORD: If what? Why do you cross yourself?...
DRIVER: ... if I am permitted.
WHITEFORD: What should stop you?
DRIVER: Only fear, monsieur. And I am not—*much*—afraid.
(*Sound: carriage stop— pause then dogs howl in distance*)
WHITEFORD: Listen! What was that?
DRIVER: Only the dogs, monsieur. They keep many dogs, large dogs, at the Château d'Azay.
WHITEFORD: Are those dogs dangerous? Are they apt to fly at anybody who goes to the front door?
DRIVER: I can't say, monsieur. But I should advise you to make haste.
(*Sound: carriage door opens*)
WHITEFORD: Here's your money.
DRIVER: Thank you. And good night, monsieur. And if one so humble as my-

self may be permitted a word of advice...
(*Sound: dogs howl louder*)
WHITEFORD: Well?
DRIVER: Beware of the Tapestry Room.
(*Sound: door closes. The carriage drives away. A burst of thunder and rain then knocking. A door is opened.*)
MADAME FLEY: (*elderly; not unpleasant*) *Et alors, monsieur? Vous chechez...?*
WHITEFORD: *Je cherche le Château d'Azay et je.... je...*
FLEY: (*grimly amused*) Perhaps it would be better if monsieur spoke English. You are Edward Whiteford?
WHITEFORD: *Yes!*
FLEY: Monsieur is expected. Please to enter.
(*Sound: door closes: noise of rain ceases.*)
FLEY: Monsieur's hat and coat?
WHITEFORD: Thank you.
ILEANA: Ned!
WHITEFORD: Hello, Ileana.
FLEY: (*warningly*) *N'embrasses pas, ma petite! Garde a ton oncle!*
ILEANA: You'd better not kiss me, Ned. Madame Fley says to look out for my uncle. (*under her breath*) Madame Fley is our housekeeper.
WHITEFORD: Where is your uncle now?
ILEANA: In the drawing-room. Come along.
WHITEFORD: Ileana, is anything wrong?
ILEANA: Everything's wrong! Two of my dogs were in horrible pain this afternoon. Doctor Saulomon had to put them out with chloroform.
WHITEFORD: You don't think...?
ILEANA: I hope nobody's—practicing, that's all. Here we are.
(*Sound: doors open and close behind.*)
WHITEFORD: Nice tiger-skins on the floor. (*lower*) I say! Who's the little old man with the gray beard, sitting over by the fire?
ILEANA: That's Doctor Saulomon.
WHITEFORD: He's got funny-looking eyes.
ILEANA: He watches, and watches, and watches. But he's an old friend of the family. Shh...Come on, let's get this over with.
KOHARY: (*fade in*) Ah, my young friend. So my niece has anticipated me. Welcome to the Château d'Azay!
WHITEFORD: Thank you, Count Kohary.
KOHARY: You must be very wet, after your long drive. Go up to the fire and warm yourself. Madame Fley!
FLEY: Yes, Monsieur?
ILEANA: (*under her breath*) Don't do it, Ned! I won't be responsible if they made you do it!
WHITEFORD: But look here, Count Kohary. What *did* happen to the last fel-

low who slept in the Tapestry Room?

KOHARY: You must not call him a "fellow," young man, He was a very saintly gentlemen, the Bishop of Tours. That was some time ago: and Ileana was only fifteen years old. But surely she must remember it?

ILEANA: (*shivering*) I remember it.

KOHARY: The church, said our Bishop, has no use for superstition. He insisted on sleeping there. I—made him as comfortable as possible. But he was found dead next morning, with the crucifix still in his hand.

(*Sound: roll of thunder.*)

WHITEFORD: Was it....poison?

SAULOMON: (*vehemently*) There was no poison, monsieur!

KOHARY: Hear Doctor Saulomon!

ILEANA: (*under her breath*) It's true, Ned!

KOHARY: There were just two curious things in connection with the death, Mr. Whitehead. On the mantel piece was found burning a stick of incense. Ordinary incense. Nothing wrong with it!

WHITEFORD: Yes, sir?

KOHARY: And under the dressing-table—the police found it was an empty jar of ointment. Now, come, use your detective wits! A dead man, some burning incense, and an empty jar of ointment. What do you make of that?

WHITEFORD: (*bewildered*) I don't make anything of it.

KOHARY: (*through his teeth*) Please do not speak like that.

WHITEFORD: I'm sorry!

SAULOMON: It is *still* the wrong season of the moon.

WHITEFORD: (*doggedly*) But what I really meant, sir, was this. Is there any *reason* for this story of death?

KOHARY: Reason?

WHITEFORD: Any legend attached to the room, or something like that?

KOHARY: Yes. There is.

WHITEFORD: Well, sir?

KOHARY: (*musingly*) We are a very old family, my friend. Old, and perhaps accursed. When certain of my ancestors moved from Hungary to France in the seventeenth century, they brought certain beliefs with them. The Old Religion.

WHITEFORD: (*puzzled*) The Old Religion?

KOHARY: Yes. The cult of Diana. (*sharply*) The witch-cult, if you prefer.

WHITEFORD: Now look here, sir—!

ILEANA: (*crying out*) *Must* we talk about this?

KOHARY: (*agreeably*) Ah, you smile! When I say the word "witch", Mr, Whiteford, you think of some humorous picture on a Hallowe'en card. It was very different in the Middle Ages, believe me. There were many to worship unashamed at the Grand Sabbat; to receive all favors from Satan, their master; and to dance forever, joyously, in the red quadrilles of the

nether world!
(*Sound: dog howls*)
KOHARY: Some two hundred years ago an ancestress of mine, Catherine Kohary, was tortured to death in the Tapestry Room for professing the Old Religion. Many persons have not thought it safe to sleep there since. Are you answered?
WHITEFORD: Come, sir. This is some kind of elaborate joke.
KOHARY: (*stung*) Joke? The Bishop of Tours did not find it a joke!
SAULOMON: Not a mark on his body. I assure you as a physician, not a mark on his body!
KOHARY: You hear Doctor Saulomon?
WHITEFORD: I hear him.
KOHARY: (*kindly*) Understand me, my boy! There's no compulsion in this. If you have not the nerve to sleep in that room...
WHITEFORD: (*not loudly*) Who says I haven't got the nerve?
KOHARY: You're weakening, I think. I can see it in your face.
WHITEFORD: Would you like to make a little bet on that?
KOHARY: What sort of bet?
WHITEFORD: If I spend the night in this famous room, and come out of it alive...
KOHARY: Go on.
WHITEFORD: ... will you give your consent to the marriage *immediately*? Tomorrow morning?
KOHARY: Why tomorrow morning?
WHITEFORD: Because I don't think the atmosphere of this house is good for Ileana. What do you say? Will you do it?
KOHARY: Very well, my boy. I accept the terms of your wager.
ILEANA: (*wildly*) Don't do it, Ned! For the love of heaven don't *do* it!
(*Sound: crash of thunder—rolling off into distance.*)

FABIAN: High up in the north tower of the Château d'Azay, under the conical slate roof, is the circular room hung with faded tapestries. These tapestries move slightly, with uneasy mimic life, to the clamor of the storm outside. Candles burn along the mantelpiece, and beside the great four-poster bed. The flames of these candles waver, too, as the door opens.

(*Sound: door opens*)
FLEY: This is the Tapestry Room, monsieur.
WHITEFORD: Thank you, Madame Fley.
FLEY: *That* is the mantelpiece where the incense burned. *That* is the bed where Monseigneur the Bishop died.
WHITEFORD: Very inviting, isn't it?
FLEY: Will there be anything else that monsieur requires? Some sandwiches? A decanter of whisky?

WHITEFORD: No, thanks. I had a drink with Count Kohary before I came upstairs.
FLEY: *Bien, monsieur.* Monsieur's shaving-water will be brought up in the morning—if he requires it. Good night.
(*Sound: door closes.*)
WHITEFORD: (*muttering, with the rack of nervousness*) Infernal old harpy! Trying to scare a fellow out of his wits just because... well, they've built a good fire, anyway. I didn't realize how cold it was. Temperature must have dropped. (*distant dog howl*)
(*Sound: soft knock on door*)
WHITEFORD: (*crying out*) What's that?
(*Sound: door opens*)
ILEANA: (*calling softly*) It's me. Ileana. May I come in?
WHITEFORD: No, Ileana! Get out of here!
ILEANA: That's not very gallant of you.
WHITEFORD: I don't want you exposed to whatever-it-is.
(*Sound: shut door.*)
ILEANA: Ned, listen! Are you going to bed, or are you going to sit up all night?
WHITEFORD: I'm going to sit up all night. Naturally.
ILEANA: Then let me sit up with you.
WHITEFORD: No!
ILEANA: Why not?
WHITEFORD: First, because it may be dangerous. Second, because I promised your uncle I'd go through this alone.
ILEANA: (*worried*) I wish you hadn't had that drink with him.
WHITEFORD: He couldn't have done anything to it! *You* poured it.
ILEANA: Yes. That's true. Only... listen! (*dog howl and the sound of slow, heavy footsteps*)
WHITEFORD: It was only one of the dogs—
ILEANA: No, It sounded like somebody walking *inside* the wall of this room! Don't you hear it?
(*Sound:* (*more steps and out*)
WHITEFORD: By George, it *is* somebody walking inside the wall! Get behind that tapestry, Ileana! Quick! Hurry!
(*Sound: a very long peal of thunder.*)
WHITEFORD: Count Kohary! Where did *you* come from?
KOHARY: Forgive me, my boy, for seeming to appear out of the wall, and between the tapestries like Mephisto appearing to Faust. This red dressing-gown perhaps adds to the affect.
WHITEFORD: How did you get here? A passage between the walls?
KOHARY: Exactly. A little device of my ancestors for visiting this room when its occupant was so unmannerly as to bolt the door.
WHITEFORD: The door's not bolted. You could have walked straight in.

KOHARY: But I could not have done it... unobserved.
WHITEFORD: No. Maybe not.
KOHARY: Have you had any other visitors, my boy?
WHITEFORD: (*slight pause*) no.
KOHARY: You're sure of that?
WHITEFORD: Quite sure.
KOHARY: Then, since nobody saw me come here, I'll just sit down by the fire. Please sit opposite me.
WHITEFORD: Is this the showdown, sir?
KOHARY: I don't understand you.
WHITEFORD: There's got to be a showdown between us. Is that why you're here?
KOHARY: I am here, young man, to explain certain things to you. —Will you have a cigarette?
WHITEFORD: I...
KOHARY: (*amused*) They're not doped that's what you're afraid of.
WHITEFORD: I'll have one, yes.
KOHARY: Good! A light?
WHITEFORD: Thank you.
(*Sound: scratch of match*)
KOHARY: (*leisurely*) When I was discussing the witch-cult a while ago, you did not appear to think I meant what I said.
WHITEFORD: Do you want a perfectly frank answer to that?
KOHARY: Yes.
WHITEFORD: I think you're mad enough to mean anything.
KOHARY: (*quietly*) What you say, in a sense, is quite true. In an old and ill-bred family like ours, the mind can crack and the fantasies of witchcraft become as real... more real!... than the living world. Let me give you an example.
WHITEFORD: Go on.
KOHARY: The saucer on the table beside you is Ming porcelain. It was once owned by Catherine Kohary, a martyr of the Old Religion. Yet you are using it as an ashtray.
(*Sound: a dog howling*)
WHITEFORD: I beg the witch-lady's pardon. I'll blow off the ash.
KOHARY: A dangerous remark, sir! Don't you understand that the worship of evil can be as strong as compelling as the worship of good? That... to a sick brain which *knows* but can't help itself... you have profaned this room merely by entering it. Therefore you deserve to die.
WHITEFORD: Like the Bishop of Tours?
KOHARY: Exactly.
WHITEFORD: You're not going to tell me the devil killed *him*?
KOHARY: The devil's agent may be flesh and blood.

WHITEFORD: (*pouncing*) Then it *was* murder?
KOHARY: Of course, it was murder. Murder so cunningly contrived that no one ever saw through it.
WHITEFORD: Go on.
KOHARY: I asked you before to use your detective wits on this problem. —Incense was burned in this room. Why?
WHITEFORD: Suppose *you* tell *me*.
KOHARY: Obviously, I think, to conceal something else which would be too easily noticed.
WHITEFORD: To conceal what?
KOHARY: The smell of chloroform.
WHITEFORD: Chloroform?
KOHARY: Yes, a drug not well understood by laymen. Doctor Saulomon was using chloroform this afternoon, to dispose of some dogs.
WHITEFORD: So I've heard.
KOHARY: Doctor Saulomon is old. And—forgetful.
WHITEFORD: (*a little unsteadily*) You mean... chloroform could be stolen?
KOHARY: It *could* be, easily. Now suppose... just suppose!... I take a pad saturated with chloroform. I place it over the mouth and nostrils of a man already sleeping or drugged, so that he gets no other air.
WHITEFORD: (*unsteadily*) Wait a minute! That... won't do!
KOHARY: Why not?
WHITEFORD: (*with an effort*) Chloroform burns and blisters when it touches the skin! You'd leave marks!
KOHARY: Not at all, my friend. Not at all!... if I first covered the mouth and nostrils with some substance like...
WHITEFORD: (*crying out*) Ointment!
KOHARY: (*agreeably*) Ah, we're waking up!
WHITEFORD: (*dizzily*) I.... I....
KOHARY: Now observe what follows. In a few seconds, unconsciousness. In two minutes, three minutes—death.
WHITEFORD: Certain death. Yes.
KOHARY: But chloroform! It evaporates. Delay your post-mortem for twenty-four hours—a very easy matter, in these country districts—and no trace remains in the blood. Murder without a mark, my friend. Murder without a mark.
WHITEFORD: (*heavily*) There's just one thing you're forgetting, Count Kohary.
KOHARY: What's that?
WHITEFORD: *I'm* not sleeping. And I'm not drugged.
KOHARY: Oh, yes you are.
(*Music: sting chord.*)
WHITEFORD: (*slowly comprehending*) In... the cigarette?
KOHARY: No. In the drink you had with me.

WHITEFORD: What... was it?
KOHARY: Morphine, You've had enough to put three men to sleep. —That's it! Try to get up!
WHITEFORD: I'll try! And I'll do it!
(*Sound: crash and clang of metal.*)
KOHARY: You see? You've knocked over the fire-irons. You'd have been in the fire yourself if I hadn't caught you.
WHITEFORD: Take your hands off me!
KOHARY: Just as you please.
WHITEFORD: (*desperately*) If I could reach that bell-pull...
KOHARY: You can't. Better sit down again.
WHITEFORD: You murdering lunatic! So that's how you killed the Bishop of Tours! And that's how you're going to kill me!
KOHARY: (*amazed*) *I*?—You don't think *I* killed the Bishop of Tours?
WHITEFORD: Didn't you?
KOHARY: (*bitterly*) You young fool! I'm not trying to kill you! I'm trying to *save* you! —Doctor Saulomon!
SAULOMON: Yes, *monsieur le Comte*?
KOHARY: Come out from behind the secret door! Come out, and be my witness!
SAULOMON: Yes, monsieur. I shall always guard the family honor, even when I guess how men die.
KOHARY: This young man evidently thinks I've been talking about *myself*. —Am I, in the popular parlance, mad?
SAULOMON: Heaven forbid, monsieur! I have never known a saner man.
KOHARY: Have you any notion, Mr. Whiteford, why I brought you to this house? You would not have believed me if I had merely told you. So I had to bring you here and *show* you.
WHITEFORD: Show me...*what*?
ILEANA: (*hysterical laughter, off*)
KOHARY: Come out from there, please! (*fiercely*) Come out!
ILEANA: (*laughter.*)
WHITEFORD: Ileana!
KOHARY: Why have I kept Ileana so well guarded from the world? Why, at a fancy-dress ball did I object to the costume of a medieval witch? Whose dogs were poisoned so that chloroform should be bought? *Who poured you the drink drugged with morphine*?
WHITEFORD: (*screaming*) In the devil's name, what are you trying to tell me?
KOHARY: Ileana! She has been hopelessly insane for more than ten years!
ILEANA: (*laughter, up— then fades, echoing down halls—*)

(*Sound: theme up to final narration*)
FABIAN: And so ends my story, "The Sleep of Death"—a tale which may give

uneasy moments to those who fall in love at first sight. Next week I shall tell you a story many of you have asked me to tell again. It is the adventure of an easygoing, straight-forward New York detective, who followed a beautiful murder suspect to Port Said, the crossroads of crime and who learned that duels are still fought with swords as well as with thirty-eights. And so, next week, when I tell you this tale I call "The Dancer from Stamboul"... will you join me, Doctor Fabian, here in my *Cabin B-13*?
(*Sound: ship's whistles*)
(*Sound: theme fade*)

Notes for the Curious

"The Sleep of Death" is very reminiscent of the gothic horror of the American writer Edgar Allan Poe whose influence on John Dickson Carr is most apparent in his juvenilia, the Bencolin novels and the early Merrivale mysteries.

The man whom Carr revered as "*the father of the detective story*" is referenced most obviously in two short stories: "William Wilson's Racket" (1941), which features Colonel March; and the audacious historical detective mystery "The Gentleman from Paris" (1950). In addition, the unpublished manuscript of a completely unknown story by Poe features in *The Mad Hatter Mystery* (1933).

Carr also adapted two of Poe's horror stories, "The Pit and the Pendulum" and "The Tell-Tale Heart" for *Suspense* and *Appointment with Fear*, and he presented a biblio-biographical profile of the writer for BBC radio in 1944, based on Hervey Allen's biography *Israfel* (1926).

In CBS's original press release "The Sleep of Death" was given the title "The Devil's Saint" and it is in fact a revised version of the play of that title, first broadcast on 19 January 1943 in the CBS program *Suspense*.

Cabin B-13

Columbia Broadcasting System: July 5, 1948 to January 2, 1949

Director	John Dietz
Editor	Charles S Monroe
Supervisor	Robert Heller
Music Series 1 -	Merle Kendrick
Series 2 -	Alfredo Antonini
Dr John Fabian	Arnold Moss (All episodes except those listed below)
	Alan Hewitt ("Below Suspicion", "The Power of Darkness", "The Footprint in the Sky" and "The Man with the Iron Chest")

NB John Dickson Carr regarded the primary purpose of a title as simply being to entice the reader —or listener, and he was not remotely concerned if it was not directly relevant. In this way a *Cabin B-13* play with a familiar title may have little, if anything, in common with any novel, short story or radio play with the same title.

Series 1

"A Razor in Fleet Street"	8.30-9.00pm, Monday, 5 July 1948
"The Man Who Couldn't Be Photographed"	8.30-9.00pm, Monday, 12 July 1948
"Death Has Four Faces"	8.30-9.00pm, Monday, 19 July 1948
"The Blind-Folded Knife Thrower"	8.30-9.00pm, Monday, 26 July 1948
"No Useless Coffin"	8.30-9.00pm, Monday, Aug. 2, 1948
"The Nine Black Reasons"	8.30-9.00pm, Monday, Aug. 9, 1948
"The Count of Monte Carlo"	8.30-9.00pm, Monday, Aug. 16, 1948
"Below Suspicion"	8.30-9.00pm, Monday, 23 Aug. 1948
"The Power of Darkness"	10.00-10.30pm, Tuesday, 31 Aug. 1948
"The Footprint in the Sky"	10.00-10.30pm, Tuesday, 7 Sept. 1948
"The Man with the Iron Chest"	10.00-10.30pm, Tuesday, 14 Sept. 1948

Series 2

"The Street of the Seven Daggers"	8.30-9.00pm, Tuesday, 3 Oct. 1948
"The Dancer from Stamboul"	8.30-9.00pm, Tuesday, 10 Oct. 1948
"Death in the Desert"	8.30-9.00pm, Tuesday, 17 Oct. 1948
"The Island of Coffins"	8.30-9.00pm, Tuesday, 24 Oct. 1948
"The Man Who Couldn't Be Photographed"	10.00-10.30pm, Tuesday, 31 Oct. 1948
"The Most Respectable Murder"	10.00-10.30pm, Tuesday, 7 Nov. 1948
"The Curse of the Bronze Lamp"	10.00-10.30pm, Tuesday, 14 Nov. 1948
"Lair of the Devil-Fish"	10.00-10.30pm, Tuesday, 21 Nov. 1948
"The Dead Man's Knock"	10.00-10.30pm, Tuesday, 28 Nov. 1948
"The Man with Two Heads"	10.00-10.30pm, Tuesday, 5 Dec. 1948
"The Bride Vanishes"	10.00-10.30pm, Tuesday, 12 Dec 1948
"Till Death Do Us Part"	10.00-10.30pm, Tuesday, 19 Dec. 1948
"The Sleep of Death"	10.00-10.30pm, Tuesday, 26 Dec. 1948
"The Dancer from Stamboul"	10.00-10.30pm, Tuesday, 2 Jan. 1949

THE ISLAND OF COFFINS

The Island of Coffins and Other Mysteries from the Casebook of Cabin B-13 is printed on 60-pound paper, and is designed by Jeffrey Marks using InDesign. The type is Cambria, a transitional serif font, commissioned by Microsoft and released with Microsoft Vista. The cover is by Gail Cross. The first edition was published in a perfect-bound softcover edition and a clothbound edition accompanied by a separate pamphlet of John Dickson Carr's *Secret Radio. The Island of Coffins and Other Mysteries from the Casebook of Cabin B-13* was printed by Southern Ohio Printers and bound by Cincinnati Bindery. The book was published in December 2020 by Crippen & Landru Publishers.

Milton Keynes UK
Ingram Content Group UK Ltd.
UKHW020805231024
450026UK00001B/179